Maya Blake's hopes of beco[...] when she picked up her first [...] Little did she know her dream would come true. Does she still pinch herself every now and then to make sure it's not a dream? Yes, she does! Feel free to pinch her, too, via Twitter, Facebook or Goodreads! Happy reading!

Millie Adams has always loved books. She considers herself a mix of Anne Shirley—loquacious, but charming, and willing to break a slate over a boy's head if need be—and Charlotte Doyle—a lady at heart, but with the spirit to become a mutineer should the occasion arise. Millie lives in a small house on the edge of the woods, which she finds allows her to escape in the way she loves best: in the pages of a book. She loves intense alpha heroes and the women who dare to go toe-to-toe with them. Or break a slate over their heads…

Also by Maya Blake

The Greek's Forgotten Marriage
Pregnant and Stolen by the Tycoon
Snowbound with the Irresistible Sicilian

Diamonds of the Rich and Famous collection

Accidentally Wearing the Argentinian's Ring

Also by Millie Adams

A Vow to Set the Virgin Free
The Forbidden Bride He Stole

From Destitute to Diamonds miniseries

The Billionaire's Accidental Legacy
The Christmas the Greek Claimed Her

The Diamond Club collection

Greek's Forbidden Temptation

Discover more at millsandboon.co.uk.

PREGNANT AND CLAIMED

MAYA BLAKE

MILLIE ADAMS

MILLS & BOON

First published in Great Britain 2024
by Mills & Boon, an imprint of HarperCollins*Publishers* Ltd,
1 London Bridge Street, London, SE1 9GF

www.harpercollins.co.uk

HarperCollins*Publishers*, Macken House, 39/40 Mayor Street Upper, Dublin 1, D01 C9W8, Ireland

Pregnant and Claimed © 2024 Harlequin Enterprises ULC.

Greek Pregnancy Clause © 2024 Maya Blake

Her Impossible Boss's Baby © 2024 Millie Adams

ISBN: 978-0-263-32018-3

08/24

This book contains FSC™ certified paper
and other controlled sources to ensure responsible forest management.

For more information visit www.harpercollins.co.uk/green.

Printed and Bound in the UK using 100% Renewable Electricity
at CPI Group (UK) Ltd, Croydon, CR0 4YY

GREEK
PREGNANCY
CLAUSE

MAYA BLAKE

MILLS & BOON

CHAPTER ONE

IT WAS A spectacularly beautiful day to become an orphan.

Despite the profoundly sacrilegious thought, Odessa Santella breathed in deep, letting the salt-tinged sea breeze fill her lungs, tilting her head to the sunrays in the hope it would reach her cold, frozen insides. She dug her bare toes into the rough pebbles beneath her feet, willing the discomfort to ground her.

Opening eyes she'd squeezed shut, the better to experience this monumental day, she watched dappling light bouncing off the water, ignoring the craggy cliff face, the sheer drop and the jagged, deadly rocks ten feet beyond where she stood.

It was indeed a beautiful day to—

A rough throat was cleared behind her, shattering her peace—such as it was.

'*Signorina.*'

The prompt held warning, as most of her interactions with anyone connected to her father had for as long as she could remember.

It didn't matter that her father was dead. That she was minutes away from witnessing the final rituals following his death. She would never be free of him. He'd seen to that in the meticulous, cruel way he'd ruled her life.

Odessa took one resigned step back, then another, her pitch-black dress growing heavier on her body as the breeze dropped away and the weight of fate pressed down on her. Taking another moment, she slid her black pumps back onto her feet.

She'd thought she'd be free once Elio Santella had succumbed to his cancer.

How foolish she'd been!

A hundred yards away, two dozen pairs of eyes watched her approach, each set evaluating her, wondering whether she would become a problem they'd have to deal with or whether she would, like all the other women in the family, *know her place. Stay in her place.*

One set in particular made her skin crawl. Dark as soot. Deadly as a viper.

Vincenzo Bartorelli had revealed his intentions the second Odessa had turned twenty-one. It had only been through a series of mishaps keeping him out of her father's good grace that she'd been saved from his unwanted advances for the last seven years.

Now, with her father out of the picture, this man who was over twice her age all but salivated every time he clapped eyes on her. And he'd made sure those occasions were frequent since Elio's death a week ago.

Hell, he would've all but moved into the twenty-bedroom mansion her father had called his castle but Odessa termed her prison, if Uncle Flávio hadn't called first dibs on the property he'd not so secretly coveted since his brother had built it thirty years ago.

Her gaze slid over to her uncle, hoping for some sign that the nightmare hurtling towards her was all in her fevered imagination. The harsh look reprimanding her for keeping everyone waiting and warning her not to make a scene eviscerated any such hope.

His eyes trained on her, he tapped his hand against his leg in silent summons—a demeaning cue he'd picked up from her father. She wanted to yell that she wasn't a dog to be called to heel. Pursing her lips, she slowed her feet and lifted her chin, her heart thumping as his eyes narrowed.

No doubt her rebellion would earn her punishment before

sundown, but she'd grown accustomed to verbal lashes and the occasional backhander.

At some point she'd decided that not behaving herself was worth it.

It kept her soul from shrivelling and dying.

She slotted herself into the too-narrow gap between her two living tormenters and stared down at the casket containing her dead one.

Her father had grown more bitter and vicious in the months before his death. The news that his illness was terminal had warped him into a crueller version of the previously tyrannical mob boss everyone feared. Faced with his dwindling mortality, Elio hadn't sought to go peacefully. He'd railed against fate and everyone who came within ten feet of him, blaming everyone and everything but the expensive cigars he'd inhaled every day for five decades.

Odessa listened to the priest intone words of peace and salvation. Her lips twisted. Her heart was unable to wish this man who'd tormented her for so long rest. She hoped her mother gave him hell in the afterlife, the way she hadn't dared when she was alive. She hoped—

Her thoughts stalled, then scattered as the muttering around the graveside rose.

'What are they doing here?'

'Is that really him?'

'I never thought I'd see him here ever again.'

'Have you heard how powerful he is now?'

That last statement jerked Uncle Flávio's attention away from the priest, power and influence being the twin drugs he rabidly fed on. When he wasn't boasting about how he'd acquired them, he was greedily plotting nefarious ways to gain more.

Odessa, knowing she would inevitably be trapped in whatever web his plans created, redirected her attention from her father's casket too, her heart squeezing in dread at whatever calamity was approaching. Because she'd learned to her cost that there was always, without fail, a worst-case scenario with the Santella family.

Following the gazes of the mourners, realising even the priest's words had trailed off, she blinked away tears she didn't remember shedding.

Then her heart stopped altogether.

What *was* he doing here?

Because this was truly the last place she'd expected to see him.

Aristotle Zanelis.

Ares.

The name exploded in her head like the earth-shaking feats of his Greek namesake.

In the years since she'd last seen him he'd conquered the world, moulded it to his will and made himself a formidable force to boot.

He wielded the kind of power Flávio and Vincenzo would give their limbs for. And he was here, at her father's funeral?

Belatedly she saw the smaller man striding at his side.

Sergios Zanelis—his father. The man who'd chauffeured her father for the better part of twenty years until crippling arthritis—and her father's unscrupulous behaviour—had forced the gentle Greek to retire.

'Who invited *him*?' Flávio barked, but already she could hear the thirsty speculation in his voice, the fervid scramble to work this angle to his advantage. She felt more than saw his hard eyes drill into her temple. 'Did you—'

'No,' she interjected strongly, still unable to take her eyes off the towering, broad-shouldered man who bore down on them as if he owned the very land he walked on.

Odessa would've speculated that he probably did—considering his international real estate mogul status these days—if she hadn't known for a fact that the mansion she'd been born in now belonged to her uncle.

Besides, considering how they'd parted ten years ago, she wouldn't have dared to reach out to Ares for anything—never mind condolences for her father, who'd treated him as deplorably as Elio had.

What about what you did?

Vines of shame and righteous indignation twisted around her heart, strangling her as he drew closer. Or was it the sheer magnificence of the man who'd lived up to every promise of the drop-dead gorgeousness his younger self had predicted?

Because...*angeli sopra*... Ares Zanelis was carved from the very best of celestial moulds.

'Who is this?' Vincenzo snapped.

Flávio stepped away without answering, crossing the grass towards their unexpected guests. Completely ignoring the senior Zanelis, her uncle held out his hand to Ares, his initial vexation totally eradicated by his covetous smile.

Odessa's heart leapt with alarm when Ares's hand remained at his side, his face formidably imperial. But she watched his lips move and a tense second later Flávio was transferring his greeting to Ares's father, who shook his hand and nodded solemnly.

Only after the older man had been greeted did Ares shake Flávio's hand. The whole spectacle lasted less than twenty seconds, but it was shockingly clear who'd gained the upper hand in the little exchange.

Odessa gasped as her wrist was trapped in a crushing grip.

'Answer me when I talk to you, girl,' Vincenzo growled beside her, sensing the balance of power shifting and petulantly resenting it.

'Let go of me.'

Her demand was low and hoarse. His cruel grip and the knowledge that later she would be sporting a bruise hollowed her stomach in an unmistakable portent of what was to come.

She tried to snatch her hand away, but he merely tightened

his hold. About to protest further, she froze when Ares Zanelis arrived next to her, his imposing body blocking out the sun.

'Release her.'

The rough and viciously animalistic growled command raised the hairs on her nape. As did the gaze he concentrated upon the man holding her captive. Its savagery caused Vincenzo's eyes to widen in swift alarm as he quickly heeded the order.

His will imposed, Ares redirected his gaze to her.

Odessa rubbed her stinging wrist, tilted her head up and up—had he always been this tall?—and met the cold liquid hazel gaze of the man who had dominated her thoughts once upon a time. But while she'd been able to read his expression back then, he was now a dark, impenetrable tower, content simply to stare at her without uttering a word.

In her teens, she'd likened his heart-stopping demeanour to one of the mythical Greek creatures of old. Even back then his dominance had been unquestionable.

That aura was a hundred-fold more potent now, and the ferocity of it snatched the air out of her lungs and accelerated her heartbeat.

Her alarm that he was here, in the place he'd left without so much as a goodbye, mingled with her nerves as she cleared her throat. 'I… Ares… Thank you for coming.'

Odessa was painfully aware that her statement lacked warmth and held a definite query.

'It isn't me you should be thanking,' he replied, in a voice that had definitely deepened with time, and once again warning tingles danced over her neck and shivered down her spine.

Before she could ask what he meant, his father was stepping up to her, the older Zanelis' trademark smile dimmed only by the solemnity of the occasion.

'Odessa, it is good to see you,' Sergios Zanelis said, reaching out to grasp her hands in a much gentler hold. 'I hope you don't mind that we're here, but I insisted we pay our respects.

Your father was generous enough to keep me in his employ for over twenty years. I will never forget that.'

Ares's jaw clenched at his father's words, and an absurd hollow opened inside her. It couldn't have been clearer that this was the last place he'd have come if his father hadn't insisted on it. Or that his father's positive outlook didn't match Ares's own view of past events.

Telling herself that she might easily have gone another few decades without clapping eyes on Ares Zanelis would've been a lie. For one thing, he dominated the news these days, his power and influence a source of breathless material for both mainstream and social media.

That was how she knew he was unmarried. How she knew his relationships barely lasted a handful of months, with the princesses, actresses and supermodels of this world who apparently lined up round the block for a chance to be his latest flame getting the revolving door treatment with eye-watering frequency.

That was how she knew his father was the only constant in his life.

When she'd read about the car crash that had almost taken both their lives four years ago it had sent her to the tiny Santella family chapel every sunrise for the three weeks Ares had remained in a coma in California. And in that chapel she'd made fervent promises she hadn't been sure she'd be able to keep.

Aware of the thick silence, and especially of Ares's laser gaze boring into her, Odessa cleared her throat and summoned a whisper of a smile. 'It's very good of you to come, Mr Zanelis. I really appreciate it.'

And she did, because in this sea of men with nefarious intentions and a willingness to mow everyone down including her—*especially* her—in their bid to become the next head of the Santella organised crime family, seeing this man who'd gone about his work with an incredibly sunny disposition was a balm she couldn't help but greedily latch on to.

She grew even more conscious of Ares's stare as she spoke, his scrutiny sharpening over her face as if gauging the veracity of her words.

The priest clearing his throat pointedly gave her the excuse to turn away. To face her father's casket once more. She kept her gaze fixed on it even while her senses whirled in frantic alarm as Ares took Vincenzo's place at her left side, with his father displacing Uncle Flávio on her right.

And it was in the thirty minutes as the service resumed— as her uncle's dark eyes moved speculatively over her and Vincenzo's gaze promised hell—that the seed of her desperate idea was born.

Because, while she'd been unable to read Flávio's expression fully, she'd seen it enough before—deciphered that look after she'd spotted it countless times on her father's face, and on those of most members of her family and his so-called business partners.

Resentment. Judgement. The promise of retribution.

In Ares's eyes she'd spotted something else. The ghost of an emotion she'd thought long dead.

Lust.

Awareness of the feeling she'd thought had been left behind when he'd walked away from her that fateful night drew from her fresh tingles of danger and partly shame. But, while this occasion was the last place she should be thinking of such things, his proximity, his aura... Dear God, even the way he smelled—like thunder-tossed rainstorms and smoked wood— was undeniable and erotic in its invasiveness.

And if she wasn't wrong about what she'd seen in his eyes maybe she could...

God, could she?

She drew in a shaky breath as the priest ended the ceremony. As she tossed the white rose she'd plucked from the offered vase onto her father's lowered casket and mourned the parent not for his death, but for what he'd never been able to give her in his life, she knew, deep in her bones, that she needed something to change.

Remaining under Flávio and Vincenzo's already strangling hold would be the end of her. But, just as she knew that, she also knew that merely running wouldn't work.

Her move needed to be bold. Drastic. Terminal in a way that burned bridges neither Flávio nor Vincenzo could repair. Because if she didn't…if she was somehow half-hearted in this…

A tremor shook through her and Ares's sharp gaze swung to her.

Pushing the frightening thought aside, she glanced around her and noticed the mourners were slowly dispersing, while casting furtive glances at the two men stationed on either side of her.

Feeling another presence behind her, Odessa glanced over her shoulder. Flávio stood there, but his beady gaze was fixed squarely on Ares.

'Zanelis, there's a reception back at the house. We would be obliged if you would attend,' he offered, disingenuous charm oozing from him.

Again, Ares's face tightened at this deliberate snub of his father, even though the older man seemed unconcerned.

After an age of his gaze never leaving hers, he answered tightly, 'If that is what Odessa wants.'

The sound of her name on his lips, with that slight evocative Greek accent which had remained despite his spending most of his formative years in Italy, made her pelvis tighten.

Regardless of his words, though, his eyes told her to refuse. That it wasn't what *he* wanted. Righteous indignation rose again. He had a nerve to hold a grudge. What she'd done back then had been to protect him. While he…

He was her last hope, no matter how bleak and spurious her idea might turn out to be. No matter how aloof and hostile he

seemed now, she would cling to the memory of the less intimidating man she'd known back then. The man who'd whispered
promises to her beneath the stars...

Because she couldn't let Ares leave. Not yet.

'I would like that very much.' She ignored her uncle's smug
expression and turned to Sergios. 'If you have the time, Sergios?'

She was playing a risky game, exploiting the past affection the older Zanelis had had for her. She prayed she would
be forgiven her transgression. Ares's narrowed eyes when
she glanced at him from the corner of her eye said he'd seen
through her ploy. Still, she kept her eyes fixed squarely on
his father.

'Of course, my dear,' Sergios responded, immediately offering his arm.

Relieved, she clung to him all the way up the hill, back to
the house that had been a prison for as long as she could remember.

Nearing it, she examined the imposing facade closely.

Had the vines creeping around the windows always been
this dense, almost suffocating the structure as the house did
her? Had the drapes framing the thick bulletproof windows
always been this gloomy? Every door, stone and blade of grass
was in pristine shape, of course. The staff were trained to fear,
and knew that flaws wouldn't be tolerated under any circumstances and that they would sometimes be severely punished
for infractions.

Case in point, the sweet man walking beside her, who'd
been summarily sacked the moment his arthritic fingers had
become an imperfection her father hadn't been able to tolerate.

Odessa had moped for months after Sergios had left the
Santella household, even as a part of her had been soothed by
the thought that he was reuniting with Ares.

Ares, the man whose contempt pulsed from him as he strode
in tense silence beside her.

Ares, the man she intended to use to grasp her freedom.

Thoughts of the perilous road ahead made her shudder, and her step faltered momentarily before Sergios's surprisingly strong grip held her up.

'The loss may seem insurmountable right now, but it will lessen,' he said, mistaking her stumble for grief. 'It will never go away, but you'll learn to live with it.'

She felt like a fraud, accepting comfort when she didn't miss her tyrannical father one little bit. When she knew that once she escaped—*if* she escaped—she would never set foot on this cursed soil ever again.

Far too soon they were inside the largest *salone*, the place where Elio had held court and lorded his superiority over his subordinates.

It was in this very room that he'd told Sergios his services were no longer required because he was old and useless.

It was in this very room that he'd told her never to speak to Ares Zanelis again, *or else…*

It was here, only a few short months ago, that he'd told her he would be marrying her off to Vincenzo Bartorelli, a man older than he himself, to consolidate his power.

Odessa avoided this room unless strictly necessary. The dark green furniture was stiff and uncomfortable, the thick residue of cigar smoke hanging in the air too cloying. It was a room where men made plans about women and expected them to bend or break to accommodate them.

No, she would not miss this room one little bit.

She thanked one of the maids offering her a tray of drinks and chose a mineral water, needing to keep every wit about her. She rarely drank anyway, and when she did it was at functions where refusing would draw her father's disapproving glances.

In fact, the last time she'd been anywhere near tipsy it had been with…

Her gaze flicked to Ares as she wondered if he remembered that night on her seventeenth birthday, when they'd sneaked out at midnight and sat on the cliff-edge with a stolen bottle of her father's Dom Perignon. How they'd lain on the grass, the backs of their hands touching under the canopy of stars with the raging waters beneath their feet. How they'd whispered their hopes and dreams to one another.

Did he think of her at all? Had he spent a single moment on *what if*?

'Does it hurt?'

She started, then followed his gaze to her reddened wrist, where imprints of Vincenzo's cruel hold were already proclaiming her fate if she didn't find a way out of this nightmare.

'Um…not really.'

His face darkened, hazel eyes turning molten bronze. 'Either it does or it doesn't. Which is it?' he grated, not bothering to keep his voice down.

'Okay, it's a little sore,' she muttered, hyper-aware that they were the centre of very speculative attention—especially from Vincenzo Bartorelli.

She tensed when, after a moment of dark observation, the older man started across the room, his destination unmistakable.

Panic rising, she turned to Ares. 'Can I talk to you?'

One jet-black eyebrow lifted. 'What makes you think we have anything worth saying to each other? I'm only here because of—'

'Your father. I know. But…' She swallowed, wondering if she shouldn't find another way between the rock barrelling towards her and this man who'd disappeared from her life once already. But the sands of time were fast slipping through her fingers. Ares might be a devil, but at this point he was the lesser of two evils.

'Please,' she whispered. 'It's important.'

A mix of curiosity, censure and suspicion darted across his face. Her heart squeezed, threatening to mourn, because there'd once been a time when only curiosity and amused interest dashed with the intoxicating and forbidden had existed there.

'Important to you, perhaps. Not to me.'

His gaze flickered past her to where his father was speaking to the butler, another man who'd been in the Santella household since long before Odessa was born.

'I don't intend to be here long enough for whatever—'

'Odessa. A moment of your time?' Vincenzo interrupted, a hard edge in his tone.

Her heart plummeted. She knew what was about to happen. She'd heard whispers of it, and seen enough of Flávio and Vincenzo's clandestine meetings in the past week to know.

She darted an imploring gaze at Ares, uncaring if he read the naked plea in her eyes. He didn't say a word…not for a long stretch of time that shredded every nerve in her body.

Then, when she thought she'd have no choice but to seal her fate by publicly refusing Vincenzo, Ares bit out tightly, 'It'll have to wait. Odessa's wrist is sore. It needs immediate attention. So if you'll excuse us…'

It wasn't a request for permission. It was a pointed barb that struck true from the look on Vincenzo's reddened face as his gaze dropped to where he'd gripped her so mercilessly.

He opened his mouth, no doubt either to excuse himself or to belittle Ares's comment. Either way, he wasn't given the chance.

'Shall we?'

At her nod, Ares's firm fingers wrapped around her elbow and he led her towards the closest door.

Relief lightened her feet—until reality set in. She had the opening she sought, but she was nowhere near home free. There was still a mountain to climb.

But as she walked beside the man she'd once thought would be hers for ever, she knew there was no going back. There was no way she would marry Vincenzo Bartorelli.

If she didn't succeed, she'd simply have to find another way. She would rather die than live beneath another man's thumb.

With uncanny accuracy, considering he hadn't stepped foot inside this house for over a decade, and even back then he'd rarely been permitted indoors, Ares led her down two long corridors, bypassing her father's study to enter the small library.

Unlike most rooms in the Santella mansion it was nondescript, almost bordering on simplistically pleasant. It had been her mother's favourite room only because her father had hated it and spent the least money on it in his grand villa plans.

Odessa had dreaded her father turning it into another gaudy showpiece after her mother had died, but for whatever reason Elio Santella had left it intact. It had become Odessa's favourite room in the house…the place she felt closest to her mother.

Was that why Ares had brought her here? Did he remember?

The way he turned his back on the bookshelves and view, facing her with narrowed eyes and arms folded, said that he probably didn't.

'Thank you for your time.' She paused, cleared her throat. Would he agree to her outrageous proposal? 'I…'

'Spit it out, Odessa. I don't have all day.'

Irritation bit into her, sending her chin up before she could stop herself. 'I need your help,' she blurted.

For the longest time he eyed her, his focus unblinking. 'Let's bypass your assumption that you have the right to ask anything of me and skip to the part where you believe I would *want* to help you in any way.'

Her heart juddered at his acid tone. The last remaining ounce of her pride screamed at her to walk away, hold her head high and fight the fate barrelling down on her another way.

But the way he'd dealt with Vincenzo just now shoved aside her pride and bolstered her hope. 'Look, I wouldn't ask if I didn't need… Besides, you…' *Owe me*, she'd been about to say. But she bit her tongue against revisiting that part of her past, and what she'd done to ensure his safety.

'I what?' he demanded, eyebrows raised and with no ounce of give in his features.

She shook her head, dismissing the unsavoury consequences she'd had to bear for simply associating with her father's chauffeur's son. 'It doesn't matter.'

She couldn't think about the past now. Not when her future was so bleak—

'You have thirty seconds. Then I walk out,' he warned in a soft, dangerous murmur.

She believed him. After all, hadn't he done that once before, this man who was a world removed from the younger version she'd known.

Or was he…?

Hadn't he possessed this overwhelming presence even back then, only caged it better?

Now the full force of it was bearing down on her, Odessa was at once wary of and drawn to it—like a hapless moth dancing towards a destroying flame.

She watched, mesmerised despite herself, as his folded arms slowly dropped. His large, masculine hands drew attention to his lean hips, the dangerously evocative image he made simply by…*being*.

Silence ticked away, and she watched that eyebrow slowly arch, as if he was surprised by her audacity in letting her chance whittle away.

Go big or go home.

Except this home was one she was desperate to escape.

At what felt like the last second, Odessa took a deep breath and took the boldest leap. 'Before my father's funeral is over Vincenzo Bartorelli will announce our engagement.' Acid flooded her mouth at the very thought. 'I would rather dive naked into Mount Etna than marry him. So I'd… I'd like you to say that I'm marrying you instead. And in return…'

Dio, was she really doing this?

'And in return I'll give you whatever you want.'

CHAPTER TWO

IT WAS ONLY because he kept such a rigid control over his emotions that Ares didn't burst out laughing. Even then, an abstract part of him barked raucous laughter in his head, while another part grew intensely furious. Not with her. Or perhaps a little with her... Because, *Thee mou*, hadn't she dragged confounding emotions out of him from the very first time he'd laid eyes on her?

'I'd rather dive naked into Mount Etna...'

That snatched glimpse of melodrama was one of many reminders he'd tried to forget about her. That it had triggered a different sort of amusement made him stiffen.

He wasn't here to traipse down memory lane. Or be reminded of everything he'd hoped for during those foolish years of his youth.

He'd once dreamed he'd be the one offering a life-changing proposal. All these years later, and with the benefit of hindsight, he knew he'd had a lucky escape. Yet his chest continued to tighten as he looked at her now, this insanely beautiful woman who had only grown maddeningly more alluring in the years since he'd last seen her.

He should dismiss this nonsense, march back into that room he hadn't been permitted to enter as the son of the boss's chauffeur, insist to his father that they were leaving. That this was indeed the absurd idea he'd suspected it was when Sergios had suggested it.

The look in her eyes—appeal battling with the pride she
so very staunchly hung on to—stayed him. Was that all that
was stopping him leaving? Or was it that taunting, delectable
little addendum she'd thrown in?

'In return, I will give you whatever you want.'

He hated himself further for the memory those words
evoked...for the time when he'd craved just that from her.

To have her. To walk away. Never look back.

Wouldn't that make him as bad as the very people he despised with every fibre of his being? Men like her father? Her
uncle? That cretin Bartorelli, with his too-harsh thuggish hands
and slimy lust in his eyes?

'I know you heard me,' she muttered, then pursed her lips,
drawing his attention to her mouth.

The full mouth that he'd only had the opportunity to taste
once before it had been wrenched away from him. The mouth
she'd used to betray him, casting him aside as if he was nothing.

'Say something,' she pushed at his prolonged silence.

'Are you sure?'

Her beautiful eyes blinked. 'What do you mean, am I sure?'

'Do you really want me to say something? Because there's a
high probability that you won't get the answer you wish if I do.'

She swallowed, and again his gaze was compelled to that
part of her body, noticing how smooth her neck was, how
creamy and so very inviting.

He clenched his gut, unwilling to be led by desire down
another disastrous road littered with betrayal.

Her chin lifted another notch, and perhaps that was the cat-
alyst that stopped him from walking away. Because the urge
to master that pride and defiance, watch her crumble completely, slowly shattered his resolve. The need to win, just for
once, in this insane situation with Odessa Santella trumped
any other need.

That she would dare to flaunt her pride in the face of apparent abject hopelessness was a challenge he couldn't resist.

'Yes, I want to know your answer,' she replied, her voice firm, her eyes boldly locked on his. Daring him to tell her no.

Again, he felt that urge to laugh—an absurdity in this situation that should never even have occurred. But then didn't his father continue to stump him with his own unique outlook on life? And hadn't he vowed a long time ago never to be like his father?

As much as he loved him—and he did, with an unfettered well of affection that had surmounted their many challenges—he still couldn't accept or forgive how his father had allowed himself to be treated by the Santellas. What his misguided devotion had cost his own family before he'd been chewed up, then spat out, disposed of with barely the clothes on his back when he'd outlived his usefulness. Yes, the ultimate betrayal lay with his mother, but Ares couldn't help the sliver of bitterness for what his father's own actions had prompted.

'Very well then,' he said, taking perverse pleasure in the statement. 'My answer is...no.'

Pride and defiance deflated like a pricked balloon, her shoulders sagging. She went pale, her bottom lip trembling for a second before she firmed it. Her most unique trademark, the Santella silver eyes that had haunted his dreams for far longer than he wanted to admit, darted around the room, then returned to his face, searching, as if unsure whether to believe him or not. He held her gaze, infused his own with ruthless purpose until her eyes dimmed in acceptance.

'I see.'

Silence reigned, and he found himself holding his breath, gut clenched tight. In anticipation of what? He realised that he was waiting for something more from her. For her to fight harder for him?

Yes.

When he registered that she wasn't going to speak, a disarming confusion bubbled inside him, which triggered more volatile emotions.

She wasn't going to fight now, just as she hadn't fought back then. Was it because, despite seeing him as a last resort, she still deemed him inferior? Or, he amended cynically, was it because she'd chosen to make herself clear back then in a very different way by betraying him with another?

'If you don't wish to marry that idiot with his too-eager hands, why don't you simply tell him that?'

Sparks lit her silver eyes, her mouth twisting. 'Surely you haven't forgotten how things work around here?' she threw at him.

His mouth soured. No, he hadn't forgotten. But wasn't she the princess of the castle? Or, better yet, the queen now? 'Your father's gone. Surely you're free to do as you wish now?'

Bitterness pinched her mouth, drawing his eyes back again to the sensual curve of it, the soft, velvety plumpness that made heat flow with eager abandon through his pelvis. It was an unwelcome indication that in some ways things hadn't changed. This woman still drew effortless sensations from him.

'You would think so, but apparently he's made sure he rules my life even from the grave.'

His jaw clenched. The recollection of the ruthless, power-hungry brute Elio had been—a man who put his interests ahead of everything and everyone, including his own daughter—was a bile-inducing one. Ares had batted off the threats and taunts from the crime boss, but the betrayal from Odessa still dredged up fury and bitterness that lingered.

It especially chafed that he hadn't managed to make the old man pay for the way he'd treated his father. He'd thought he had time—had been stunned when his father had informed him that Elio had succumbed to cancer mere months before his sixtieth birthday.

Coming here today, it had crossed his mind briefly to make

the daughter pay for her father's transgressions, but he'd discarded the idea.

Odessa had enough of her own sins to account for.

'Anything you want...'

The idea tantalised him far too much. Made his shaft thicken as he fantasised ways to enact his own sweet brand of retribution.

Footsteps echoed outside the door.

Odessa's gaze darted to it and he watched her face grow haunted.

Rage mounted—both at the thought of Bartorelli being responsible for that look, and at the fact that he utterly loathed the thought of that man touching her.

Hell, the idea of *any* man touching her drew an uncustomary red glaze across his eyes. He told himself that it was because he despised bullies, and every male member of her family deserved that label. But when it came down to it Ares suspected it was that tempting little addendum that made him reach out to stop her jerky step towards the door, one arm wrapping around her waist and the other cupping her chin to redirect her focus to him.

And just like when he'd led her out of the *salone*, that sensation of her skin beneath his fingers made his breath catch. He accepted in that moment that he'd forgotten a few things about Odessa. Dear God, she was as soft and yet firm as he remembered. And that little sound she made in her throat as she faced him was equally intoxicating, twice as dangerous.

'"I see"?' he echoed sardonically. 'That's all you're going to say?'

The sparks flared in her eyes, turning them molten and mercurial, in shades he'd found far too fascinating back when he'd known no better.

'You want me to beg?' she goaded. 'Is that what you're waiting for?'

Oh, yes.

'That would be a good start.'

Her nostrils quivered—a delicate sight that sent yet another shock of heat through him.

'I didn't imagine you'd become a sadist.'

'Looks like we're learning new things about each other.'

And obsessing far too much about old things. Like what would've happened if you hadn't betrayed me.

She opened her mouth, perhaps to berate him. He never found out, because in that moment, knuckles rapped hard on the door.

She flinched. His teeth gritted. *Ne*, he hated that reaction in her. Just as he hated everything about this day.

Then his mood darkened even further, as the door started to open without his express permission.

Acting solely on instinct, he dropped his hand from her chin. Then, wrapping his fingers over her nape, he tilted her face up to his.

'We will discuss this further in a while. But for now...'

Sealing his mouth on hers, Ares gave in to the deep, dark temptation that had stalked him ever since he had spotted her at her father's graveside.

He swallowed her soft grunt of surprise and swept his tongue through her parted lips, tasting her with a hunger he partly despised and partly welcomed, because perhaps he might need this further down the line, when he exacted due retribution.

He hadn't altogether decided which way he was going to go, but *this* was a good start.

Dragging her closer to his ravenous body, he gloried in the soft curves that seemed sculpted to his, that flashed reminders he didn't want, but couldn't resist.

She gave a throaty moan and opened her lips, her hands coming up to wrap around his waist. He couldn't help the rumble of satisfaction that erupted from his chest. So many things he'd been denied with this woman were finally achieving reparation.

He didn't need to assure himself that he could have had her any other way, but it helped that she was as helpless to this strain of insanity as he was.

In the years he'd been gone from this place he'd had a glut of liaisons—enough to satisfy him that he didn't need any one person...especially a forbidden princess named Odessa Santella.

Yet here he was, devouring her as if she was the sole reason he drew breath.

Ares ignored the pointed throat-clearing from across the room and tangled her tongue with his, unable to resist one last taste.

It came again—louder, insistent.

Odessa pulled back sharply, her hands pushing at him as she tried to put distance between them.

Deliberately or reluctantly—he couldn't be sure—he took his time in releasing her, lifting his head to lock his eyes on their unwanted intruder.

'Flávio.'

If Ares had despised Elio, his younger brother came a close second simply because he'd been more than happy to ride his brother's thuggish coattails and carry out his orders without compunction. Flávio had been the messenger who had gleefully delivered Elio's poisoned edict, which had triggered the events that had sent Ares away from this place.

He watched the other man take in their embrace, watched his calculating eyes working out how to turn it to his advantage. Ares's mouth soured, but still he didn't release her.

'I don't remember giving you permission to enter.'

Flávio's eyes blazed momentarily with malice. Ares knew that ten years ago Flávio would've reacted differently. And, yes, he knew there was definite satisfaction in watching the other man mind his tongue. Just as he knew that by challenging him he'd made Odessa's situation ten times worse.

So did she, by the way she stiffened and then tried to push away from him.

'Stay.' He rasped the warning in her ear.

For a microsecond she heeded him, and then the innate rebel smothered by years of oppression fought back, tossing another log onto the fire blazing within him. Her body brushed his, bringing an unwanted reminder that he was fully aroused at being this close to her, and he felt her soft breath against his jaw, smelled her spicy scent in his nostrils.

He hissed as her movement brought her wrist over his engorged flesh. Ignoring Flávio, Ares slid his finger beneath her chin, bypassing her swollen lips to snag her gaze.

'If you want my help you'll do as I say.'

She stilled after another second, her eyes narrowing on his. He wanted to remind her that he never said anything he didn't mean. But what use was that reassurance when he knew the same didn't apply to her? She'd heeded his command when it mattered. That was a good start. Her rebellion would be enjoyable in the right setting.

Registering that he was making plans as if this was a forgone conclusion disconcerted him, but he hadn't achieved success beyond his wildest dreams by not being able to think on his feet.

'You're still here, Flávio. Can we help you?'

Odessa made a tiny, protesting noise, her eyes flashing wildly at him. He slid a soothing hand down her back before he could help himself.

'My niece's presence has been missed. It's her father's funeral, after all. We don't want to raise questions.'

Ares laughed. 'You don't? Because you care about impropriety?'

Flávio's gaze dropped to his hand on her waist and his face

tightened. 'Odessa is a good woman. It won't do to have her honour questioned.'

'We both know her honour isn't why you're here. Run along. We'll be out shortly.'

'You shouldn't have done that,' she murmured once Flávio had departed, the hard click of the door signalling his displeasure.

His gaze dropped to her mouth, savage hunger tearing through him. 'Which part? The part where I reacquainted myself with how surprisingly sublime you taste? Or getting rid of your uncle?'

Colour surged into her face and he itched to trace it with his fingers. Then his mouth.

'Both! You may enjoy baiting a viper, but I don't.'

He drifted his fingers down her arms, delighted in the shivers that raced after his touch. 'Hmm…let's go and find out how effective we've been, shall we?'

Catching her fingers in his, he tugged her after him.

'Ares, what are you doing?' she hissed.

Something hard and hot and decadent punched through him at hearing his name on her lips after all this time. The sexy Italian huskiness of her voice had first turned him on as a callow youth—the chauffeur's son enchanted by the princess in the dark castle. It partially grated that its erotic effect hadn't entirely waned.

Perhaps it was a good thing, he mused. A heightened libido wasn't altogether bad.

He continued until he'd reached the door of the *soggiorno* and then, pausing in full view of the guests, he cupped her delicate jaw. 'Anything I want. Those are still your terms, correct?'

Her silver eyes grew saucer-wide, her pupils dilating as her tongue emerged to dart nervously over her bottom lip. 'Ares—'

'Yes or no?' he pressed. A rabid need was pounding through him, filling his ears with an unstoppable roar.

She sucked in a breath, the awareness that she was caught

between a rock and one immovable Greek visible in her mercury eyes. The longest three seconds of his life dragged past. Then...

'Yes,' she answered, and that punch of bold almost-dare kicked like a narcotic in his blood. As if inviting him to do his worst.

Just wait, s'agapo. *You'll see.*

Triumph equal to or perhaps even surpassing what he'd felt after his last multi-billion-dollar real estate deal surged through him. But he wouldn't celebrate just yet. He knew better where this woman was concerned.

'You'd better hope that your oaths mean more to you now than they did all those years ago, *agapita.* Because trust me when I say you'll regret it otherwise.'

Warning delivered, he dropped one hand but left the other in the small of her back, using it to draw her close as they faced the now hushed room.

Slowly he took in people's expressions, cataloguing which men would pose a problem and need handling, noting the ones eager to get into his good graces. His gaze lingered longest on Bartorelli, saw the moment the other man recognised he'd been bested.

Then Ares's gaze shifted to his father.

Up until that moment he hadn't been entirely sure he'd go through with this madness...whether he would only go far enough to ensure Odessa was removed from the threats that dogged her—for a yet to be determined price but no more. Because she was and should remain where she belonged.

In his past.

But the flash of hope that arrived and then lingered on his father's face as it darted between him and Odessa sealed his decision.

Ares kept his gaze on Sergios for another second, then glanced down at the woman who'd held a compulsive fascination for him once upon a time. Who, he admitted, continued to have an absurd grip on him that he needed to rid himself of once and for all.

Ne, perhaps she'd handed him the very tools to do so...

'Our apologies for our absence,' he started, without taking his eyes off her. 'Odessa and I were getting...reacquainted.'

His tone dripped with deliberate innuendo and he didn't regret it one bit. Tugging her even closer, he captured her hand in his and raised it to his lips. Catching her shocked inhalation, he allowed his lips to curve, his eyes to grow hooded as they raked her flushed face.

Then he levelled his gaze once more on the mourners. 'While this isn't the venue I would've chosen, we're too impatient and eager to keep the news to ourselves.'

'What news?' Flávio demanded, his eyes flaming with a mix of speculation, anger and greed.

Ares let the suspense linger for a few seconds, then he gripped her hands tighter. 'That your lovely niece has just accepted my proposal. Odessa and I are to be married. As soon as possible.'

Oh, God. Oh, God. *Oh, God.*

Light-headedness assaulted Odessa as Ares's announcement dropped like flaming hailstones on her.

He'd just...just announced—

She'd done it!

She tucked her free hand behind her back and dug her fingers into her palm to test if she was still awake. The sting registered firmly enough to reassure her that, yes, she was indeed conscious.

Somehow, by some miracle, her bold and wild gamble had paid off.

But at what cost?

Because his firm grip on her waist and that silkily drawled warning about keeping her word, that hard look in his eyes and the tension in his body despite the charming smile he was displaying...

Everything indicated strongly that Ares Zanelis wasn't coming to her aid out of the goodness of his heart. Hell, his initial cold *no* still resonated like distant thunder in her ears.

A formidable reckoning was headed her way—one she didn't fool herself into thinking wouldn't exact a crushing toll.

She knew it in her bones.

And as hushed whispers swelled into rushed speculation she was left in no doubt at all that she'd truly set the cat among the pigeons.

But at least she'd evaded Vincenzo and her uncle's clutches.

As frying pans and fires compared, she'd take that outcome. For now.

She pushed the harrowing thoughts away as Ares leaned in close, his lips almost brushing her earlobe, and another cascade of shivers crashed through her body, reminding her in vivid colour of how she'd reacted to that kiss.

Dear God, she'd allowed him to kiss her—heck, she'd all but fallen into his decadent kiss—*at her father's funeral.*

'I know you're in mourning, but try for a small smile at least, *agapita*. This was your idea, after all, and you've just been granted your heart's desire. Act like it.'

She couldn't refute that. So Odessa forced lips that still tingled and stung from his voracious kiss to curve. Forced herself to focus as the crowd surged towards her, morbid curiosity driving them forward.

She was almost thankful when Ares raised his hand, halting the advancing guests.

'Please respect that my fiancée is mourning her father. If you wish us well, we accept gratefully, but I'm sure you'll understand that she'd like to conclude this occasion as originally scheduled before discussing any new matters.'

Her heart thudded wildly when he lifted her hand and brushed his lips across it once more.

Then he was urging her across the room—not towards her uncle, but to where his father stood, a pleased smile on his face.

Sergios grasped her free hand the moment she was within touching distance, a joyful light glinting in his eyes. 'My dear, let me be the first to welcome you to our family. You have no idea how happy you've made an old man.'

Her startled gaze flew to Ares. The clear caution in his eyes stilled her tongue, but inside a shrill voice screamed. She blinked in surprise and alarm when she saw the film of tears in the old man's laughing eyes. And as he turned to address his son in rapid-fire Greek cold waves of consternation washed over her.

What had she done?

She hadn't considered the old man's feelings when she'd hatched her desperate plot. The thought of upsetting him settled over her like a suffocating cloak making it hard to breathe. Was it too late to—

'No room for regret now, *eros mou*,' Ares rasped in her ear, eerily and accurately dissecting her thoughts.

His ominous words reverberated through her head in the hour it took for the funeral to conclude. They grew even louder when they were finally alone with Flávio, Vincenzo and a handful of distant relatives.

Sergios had gone to see the butler's much talked about newborn grandson—a move she suspected had been orchestrated by Ares. And now her heart stuttered for a different reason as Vincenzo strode towards him, fury blazing in his eyes as they shifted from her and settled on Ares.

'I don't know who you think you are—'

'Were we not introduced properly?' Ares interrupted coolly, pivoting to face Vincenzo, who was at least a foot shorter and was made to feel every millimetre of it when Ares peered down from his great height. 'Let me correct the oversight. I'm Ares Zanelis, Odessa's betrothed. And you are…?' he drawled, his tone sounding bored in the extreme.

The older man spluttered in outrage before spinning towards her uncle. 'Flávio, inform this little upstart who I am, will you?'

'This is Vincenzo Bartorelli. A…a business acquaintance,' her uncle stated.

Odessa, breath held, waited to hear her what else her uncle would add. To her shock, Flávio's gaze caught Ares's. A pointed look passed between the men, clearly fully deciphered by Vincenzo. His beady eyes narrowed and his fingers tightened around his glass until she feared it would shatter.

'You will all regret this,' Vincenzo snarled, encompassing Flávio, Ares and her in his look.

A cold shiver danced down her spine, but Ares shrugged off the threat. 'I doubt it sincerely.'

Vincenzo's livid stare switched to Flávio, who pretended interest in the contents of his glass. With a thick curse loaded with venom, Vincenzo turned on his heel and stormed out.

The ensuing silence was broken by Flávio's throat-clearing. 'Now that's settled, it would be remiss of me not to express my own concerns. At the very least I would've hoped to be asked for my niece's hand before you made the announcement.'

Ares's jaw clenched. 'Pretending to be old-fashioned when it suits your purposes isn't a great look on you. You have a price. We'll discuss it while my fiancée packs her bags.'

Alarm and rebellion ignited in her belly. 'What? I'm not leaving—'

'You wish to stay here?' Ares breathed, his eyes glinting cynicism.

No, she admitted reluctantly. She didn't. But she hadn't anticipated a cataclysmic move so soon. And while a part of her swelled with relief, a disconcerted part couldn't help but wonder what came next for her.

Because they hadn't even discussed what he expected in return for helping her. Considering the circumstances of their parting ten years ago, would it be as intolerable as her current situation?

Her stomach churned with something that skated past terror and into charged excitement. And then apprehension. What if she couldn't fulfil her part?

'Odessa?'

'I… I do need a little time to pack.'

Ares raised a cold eyebrow at her uncle.

Flávio shrugged. 'Certain wheels are already set in motion and will take considerable effort to halt,' he said. But with a quick glance at Ares's set face he hurriedly added, 'But I anticipate it all going smoothly since we both only have your best interests at heart.'

She barely stopped herself from snorting. Just this morning he'd intended to follow her father's wishes and barter her to a man over twice her age without so much as a by-your-leave. A man he knew to be cruel and violent.

Her sore wrist tingled. She rubbed at it absently, then tensed when Ares's gaze dropped to follow the action, his face tightening.

'Let's get this over with,' he grated at Flávio.

To his credit, her uncle obviously sensed the capriciousness of Ares's mood and nodded immediately. She watched them stride to the door, her breath shortening as she took in Ares's imposing form.

Every ounce of the playfulness of the man she'd known a decade ago had disappeared, leaving behind a breathtakingly formidable man whose presence made her breath catch.

He turned without warning at the door, catching her staring. A layer of tightness evaporated, and whatever he saw on her face drew a ghost of a smile.

'You have one hour. No more.'

One hour to leave her old life behind.

Odessa walked through her bedroom, wasting time she didn't have in trailing her fingers over possessions she'd never grown attached to. As a crime boss, her father had insisted on his daughter keeping up appearances, which had meant wearing the right in-season clothes and jewellery, and hanging out with the daughters of other influential and powerful men on the rare occasions he'd allowed her out.

But the very idea of being on display all the time—an undertaking she remembered her mother hating—had long ago become a chore she'd taken no pleasure in.

So she picked up and set down objects she wouldn't miss, her open suitcase on the bed still mostly empty a long while later.

'You're not packed?'

She whirled around at the drawl from her open doorway. Had the hour passed already? She glanced down at her watch, a diamond and platinum Cartier gifted to her by her father in a lavish display of ostentation at her birthday party two years ago. As usual it had come with a price—this one a dinner date with the son of a burgeoning rival her father had wanted mollified.

She'd failed, her fierce rebellion against being used as a pawn fuelling her defiance. He hadn't been happy.

She saw Ares catch her shudder at the memory, and preempted an interrogation by replying, 'Not quite yet.'

He glanced around the room, disdain staining his face. 'That's good. Because you will bring nothing with you. Including that.' He nodded at the watch.

Surprise stiffened her spine, despite her having had the same thought a minute ago. 'What?'

'Tell me there's anything here that you're remotely attached to?' he challenged coolly.

She wanted to protest, but secretly she was relieved to leave it all behind. Everything here signified oppression under her father's ruthless thumb.

But aren't you exchanging one version of hell for another? This man shattered your dreams...left you behind.

No, this path was of her own choosing. And while Ares had gained a ruthless reputation, he hadn't turned cruel, had he?

'What is it?'

She started, and realised she'd been examining him with rabid intent. Was it to see if he wore his cruelty as proudly as her father had worn his?

'Odessa?'

'I'm wondering if you'll be as cruel to me as my father was,' she confessed brazenly.

She was done with walking innocently into situations, trusting as blindly as she'd trusted him years ago. It was the only way she could guard her emotions. After all, if she wasn't pinning any foolish hopes on him she couldn't be disappointed, could she?

He stiffened, his expression growing remote. Within a heartbeat he was sliding his fingers into her hair, tilting her face up so he could spear her with outraged eyes. 'You dare compare me to that monster?' he seethed.

Her heart squeezed. 'I thought I knew you...back then. But it turned out I was wrong, so who knows?'

'*You* do. You just choose to misremember. To make yourself feel better by pretending what's happening to you right now is entirely everyone else's fault when you must bear some responsibility.'

'That's not true. I've just learned that nothing stays the same. People change. The evidence is standing right before me.'

His eyes gleamed, as if he found her amusing and infuriating all at once. Then, just as quickly, his expression hardened. 'No, people don't change. Sometimes they just hide who they are until it suits them to reveal themselves. Other times the people in their lives just choose not to notice.'

He meant her, of course.

Odessa bit her lip, felt the urge to explain herself, to explain Paolo and *that kiss* stalking through her. But before she could fabricate the words he swung away, impatience bristling in his towering frame. Just as he'd turned away that night. Only he hadn't just turned away. He'd seized the role of judge, jury and executioner, and then abandoned her without a backward glance.

Remember that!

'It's time to go, Odessa.'

Not without some assurances.

'My uncle—'

'Is not going to be a problem,' he said, jaw tight.

A spike of anguish lanced her. 'Should I ask how many silver shekels I was sold for?'

'No. It's not important,' he rasped.

She wanted to scream that it was to her. But she knew she'd just be furthering her heartache. She'd been a pawn for every power-hungry member of her family her entire life.

But no more.

She raised her chin and caught a flash of something in his eyes almost like surprise...admiration. But then he was slanting an impatient glance at his watch.

She went to her bedside drawer. Opening it, she took out her most treasured item. Her mother's locket. It held the only picture she had of Renata Santella. Her father had disposed of everything else in a fit of drunken pique soon after her mother had died. Odessa had been conveniently out of the house. It was one of the many things she'd never forgiven him for.

She sensed Ares wandering close. 'You still have that?' he enquired gruffly.

She cradled the delicate locket in her hand. 'Some things are worth hanging on to. No matter what.'

Unsure why she'd said that, she caught her breath as she glanced up, saw the ghost of a prickling gentleness—because this man would never be *completely* soft—before his expression hardened once more.

They stayed like that for charged seconds before he pivoted away, leaving her to breathe freely again, to pick up the credit card holding the five thousand euros her mother had been able to secrete away and pass to Odessa to keep for a desperate rainy day.

It was definitely torrential today. And petrifying. Because she was still in the dark about the price to be paid for Ares freeing her.

'Are you done?'

The query was gruff, but not impatient. Why, she couldn't tell, because his face was back to being coolly distant.

A pair of jeans, a few tops, shoes and two changes of underwear packed, she snapped the case shut.

She wasn't surprised when Ares took hold of it with one hand, his other circling her elbow as he guided her out.

Her heart lurched, then thumped, when she saw Flávio waiting in the grand hall, a false smile playing at his lips even as his eyes continued to assess her keenly, searching to see if she'd done anything to ruin whatever he'd extracted from Ares.

She knew the moment he realised he'd succeeded in whatever deal he'd struck.

He came towards her, arms wide open.

Under the pretext of kissing his niece goodbye, he whispered in Italian. 'You've surprised me, niece. I didn't think you'd manage to pull a stunt like this. *Brava.* You're a true Santella after all. But don't forget where you came from. And remember... I'll be watching.'

'What did he say to you?' Ares asked after they'd stepped out into the late-autumn sunshine.

She shook her head, eager to forget Flávio's threat. 'It doesn't matter.'

Now it was happening, she wanted to get away from here immediately. More importantly, she wanted to ask Ares where he was taking her, what he wanted from her.

But he was ushering her down the steps to where a gleaming limousine waited, with a sharply dressed driver holding the back door open. Ares grasped her hand lightly and helped her in, then he followed.

Odessa looked around in surprise as the driver shut the door and hurried to settle behind the wheel. 'Isn't your father coming with us?'

A hard smile twitched his lips as the engine started. 'He is.'

When he didn't expand, she glanced out of the window, then realised they were driving away from the main house, heading towards the servants' quarters. Where he and his father used to live. Where the other staff members including the butler still lived.

The vehicle rounded a curve and stopped in front of the garages.

Odessa had avoided this part of the estate in recent years, mostly due to the man who now sat next to her.

It was in the orange grove beyond the servants' quarters that Ares had kissed her for the first time. Where he'd touched her, whispered sultry Greek words in her ear she hadn't understood, and made her dream the impossible.

After his departure she'd been unable to return here, the memories too painful. Plus, her father had threatened all the servants against entertaining her near their quarters, mistakenly believing that they'd colluded in her secret liaison with the chauffeur's son. It had been better for everyone that she stayed away.

Now the memories rushed at her, so fast and furious she clenched her fingers in her lap.

'Haunted by your demons, *agapita*?' he rasped.

She tightened her grip on her composure. 'My demons? What about yours? Or does the great Ares Zanelis not have any?'

'Hmm, you've got better at deflecting...but it still doesn't answer me.'

About to snap back with a sharp retort, she stopped as Sergios emerged, the butler following behind with his grandson cradled lovingly in his arms. Beside her, Ares tensed, his focus fixed on his father.

Inscrutable expressions twitched across his face. Odessa didn't know why they sent trepidation dancing down her spine.

She pushed it away as a clutch of staff approached the limo. Ares watched with narrow-eyed intent when she stepped out and was immediately engulfed in hugs and whispers of farewell, well wishes that made her chest squeeze in shame. But looking into their faces she saw understanding, and—surprisingly—encouragement.

Odessa sucked in a breath when she sensed Ares behind her. He muttered in Greek to his father. The older man nodded impatiently then, turning to the newborn, brushed stiff fingers over the child's cheek, a wistful yearning crossing his face before his trademark smile returned.

As they returned to the car she caught the look of deep introspection on Ares's face as his gaze lingered on his father.

And once again a heavy tingling took hold of her nape.

CHAPTER THREE

'WHERE ARE WE GOING?' Odessa kept her gaze fixed ahead, her poise admirable as they drove through the absurdly ostentatious gilded gates that guarded the entrance to the Santella estate.

It was a reasonable question, and Ares was surprised she hadn't asked before now, but now that she had it irritated him a little. He wanted to ask why she cared. Surely anywhere else on earth was better than what she'd just left behind.

He wondered if she would've lobbied any other man for opportunistic deliverance if he hadn't been present.

The very idea shot icy repugnance through his gut.

From the corner of his eye he watched her nurse her sore wrist, anger and that spurt of disquieting protectiveness unsettling him all over again. He tightened his fist, stamping out the urge to take her hand in his, to soothe the bruise. For one thing, his father's speculative glance was growing heavier by the minute.

While he mostly confided heavily in his father, he was curiously reluctant to divulge his innermost thoughts to his parent just now.

Perhaps because he still wasn't sure just what his intention was? Or because the very idea of it unnerved him in the extreme and yet he couldn't rid himself of it?

He shifted in his seat, eager to dislodge the knot that had anchored itself to his chest, resisting the urge to grit his teeth when it refused to budge.

'We're flying to Rome,' he answered eventually. 'I have business to take care of there tomorrow. Then we're heading home to Athens. After that…we'll see.'

Eyes widening a touch, she nodded serenely, her posture almost regal. 'Okay, but…' She paused, her gaze darting to Sergios.

Ares knew why she'd hesitated, and was glad of his father's presence. It bought him time to deliberate over this rash decision. To decide whether the prime piece of real estate in Porto Novo he'd handed over to Flávio Santella—warehouses worth two million euros—was worth the headache he'd just landed himself with. Quite apart from that, and more concerningly, the absurd, unconscionable notion that had rocked him just now was one he needed distance from as quickly as possible.

'We'll discuss the details later…when we're all rested.'

Irritation sparked across her face, curiously making him want to laugh. True, he wasn't usually one to crave rest with deals waiting to be made—especially when it was barely mid-afternoon. He'd closed more deals in the hours between when most people clocked off for the day and midnight than he could count. But he wasn't about to dissect his decision now.

He watched her glance out of the window, then shift her whole body until she was looking through the rear-view mirror at the gaudy, oppressive mansion where she'd grown up.

Before he could stop himself, he cupped her chin, redirected her focus to his. 'No looking back,' he said. 'You will look forward from now on.'

He'd meant it as an order, yet it emerged gruff and low, as if infusing her with a strength he didn't owe her. And, like in the bedroom, her wide silver eyes darted to his and held. The punch those eerily beautiful eyes packed sent an alarming jolt through him.

He removed his touch before he did something insane… like caress her smooth skin one more time.

He'd done enough of that today.

His father's smug look once she'd faced forward sent tingles through Ares's body. Tingles he ignored, thankful that Sergios, for whatever reason, was choosing discretion over his usual exuberance. But he couldn't forget the vehemence with which Sergios had demanded to come to Elio's funeral, his eagerness to search out his ex-boss's daughter.

The journey to the private airport was thankfully short, but the breath of fresh air when he stepped out did nothing to uncoil his tension or remove Odessa's alluring fragrance from his senses.

He stalked away towards his plane, leaving his father chatting to her as he boarded. Choosing a solo armchair, he drew out his phone and busied himself with business as they took off and winged their way towards the Italian capital.

Ares knew his tension wasn't making things better, but he couldn't help himself.

Thee mou, it grated to remember that he'd never been able to help himself all those years ago, when infatuation had led him down a dangerous path. But he was his own man now.

And this time she would dance to *his* tune.

Two hours later, he stopped out of the shower in the penthouse suite at the Bella Regenciana on Via Labicana. The iconic building that overlooked the Colosseum held a particular significance to him. It'd been the first substantial deal he'd lost to a more ruthless competitor when he'd first tried to acquire it. Five years later he'd bought it for cents on the euro, when the greedy, severely over-extended mogul had lost everything.

These days he was used to having the last laugh.

He didn't feel like laughing when he entered his bedroom and saw his father lounging on the plush sofa opposite the bed.

Ares stifled a groan. 'What are you doing here? You should be resting.'

'Ah, this "resting" thing seems to be going around a lot today.'

He cringed at his father's air quotes.

'Is there something on your mind, Baba?'

'I'm more concerned about what's on yours,' Sergios replied.

He could pretend he didn't know what his father was talking about, but they'd long passed that stage of their relationship. They'd needed to stop hiding behind walls and façades a long time ago, when rejection, cruelty and grief had bound them together in an unbreakable bond.

Decades later, Ares still couldn't stem the searing pain when he thought of his two-year-old sister Sofia and the mother who'd selfishly broken their family apart. Her last resort—claiming Sofia wasn't his father's—had been particularly cruel, a vicious retaliation for her husband's supposed neglect.

It hadn't mattered to her that Sergios had been bending over backwards to give her the life she craved. Or that Elio Santella was a devilish taskmaster who'd demanded unreasonable loyalty. His mother's unhappiness had unfolded in the worst possible way, starting with her desertion and ending in tragedy.

Her death a mere six months later in a fiery car crash, along with Sofia and her new lover, had almost destroyed Sergios, and Ares knew he'd never forgiven himself for the mistakes he'd made.

Ares had grown up knowing his father wanted more than one child. And Sergios had been overcome with grief at losing the daughter he'd barely had a chance to know. But he'd buried it for Ares's sake.

Ares had never forgotten that.

But, as much as he was still to decide on the final outcome of his actions, he didn't want his father disillusioned. The old man had suffered enough at his mother's hands.

'I know it seems sudden, but I know what I'm doing,' he said.

Sergios's brows rose. 'Do you?'

Ares strode towards his dressing room, avoiding his father's stare. 'If you're concerned about how things have turned out today, don't be.'

'Oh, I'm not. On the contrary, I think she's perfect for you,' his father mused.

Ares stiffened, and a punch of something closely resembling panic slammed into his gut as that tingling from earlier returned. 'Was that why you insisted on attending the funeral? Because you'd hoped for this outcome?'

'What outcome?' Sergios returned, his eyes probing deeper. 'Are you referring to the unfinished business between you two? The thing that's been holding you back from true happiness?'

Hot and cold chills danced over him as the weight of those words pressed down on him.

'True happiness is a myth,' he growled. 'And no one's perfect, Baba. You know that.'

He kicked himself for the flash of pain that flitted across Sergios's face at the despised reminder that they'd both been deserted in the cruellest way possible, and then visited with unspeakable tragedy while they'd still been licking their wounds.

Ares's fingers gripped the cotton shirt he'd plucked from a hanger, his thoughts rearing back in time, even though he didn't need any mental gymnastics to work out that his sister would've been turning thirty this year if she'd lived.

Silence thickened behind him as he dressed, then pressed more heavily when he returned to the bedroom, his cufflinks in his palm. 'I know what I'm doing, Baba. And please don't get your hopes up, okay?' he implored.

His father stared at him through unusually pensive eyes. Then he rose. He stopped long enough to tap Ares lightly on his hard cheek, then headed for the door.

'You're a strong powerful man, but even you can't stop me from hoping, *yios*. For both our sakes, don't make the same mistakes I did.'

Ares's tension remained long after the door had shut behind

his father…long after he'd secured the cufflinks and shrugged on his jacket.

He was straining to switch himself into business mode when he stepped into the living room and saw her on the terrace. She'd changed into a pair of jeans that did infuriatingly delicious things to her backside and her long, shapely legs. From this angle he couldn't ignore the way her top moulded firm, high breasts and a flat stomach, or the fact that her hair was down, skimming her lower back and almost touching those firm globes.

He'd felt that heavy mass of lustrous curls more than once… knew the very real temptation it held for a man to bury his fists in it. To draw those curls to his nose and luxuriate in her scent. To picture those tresses spread across his pillow.

Ares cursed under his breath when his body rudely awakened. He took an involuntary step towards her before he caught himself.

No, his misguided moments of dancing to this princess's tune were in his past.

Reversing direction with another pithy curse, he exited the penthouse, his father's words ringing in his ears.

The first morning of her freedom.

Odessa stood on the balcony; her face raised to the sun.

Like yesterday evening, the air smelled fresh and crisp, with a tang of lemons that drew a smile. The distinct absence of a sea breeze pressed home the fact that she was no longer in Alghero. That her bold strike had succeeded in removing her from under her uncle's thumb. That, despite the unanswered questions hanging over her head, she'd slept more soundly than she could ever remember sleeping.

'Enjoying your liberation?'

She tensed, then turned around to find Ares lounging against the door.

Despite it being barely seven o'clock, he was dressed in formal business attire, his clean-shaven jaw and the slight sheen to his hair drawing attention to his chiselled face.

The espresso cup in his hand next drew her gaze to his long, elegant fingers. Her breath shortened, her traitorous body rousing in appreciation of the virile, sophisticated picture he made.

Odessa gripped the railing tighter to ground herself. 'Enjoying the morning air, *si.*'

His gaze lingered. The thundercloud of displeasure he'd exhibited during their plane ride from Alghero to Rome had seemingly dissipated sometime between their arrival at the hotel and now. Her next breath came easier, because while squaring off with him was strangely invigorating, she welcomed the respite.

'Have you ever been to Rome?' he asked, almost conversationally, stepping onto the terrace.

She shook her head. 'Capri for the summer still remains the extent of my travels. Until now, at least.'

Capri was where her father had decreed that the family would vacation. He hadn't liked going where he wasn't known, or where he couldn't effectively lord his status over everyone else. During her late teens she'd been constrained, when most women her age, with the kind of means she'd grown up with, would have been exploring the world. His grip had only tightened in the years after Ares left, with her heartbroken defiance sealing her fate.

She swallowed down the rising bitterness.

As if Ares sensed her thoughts, his lips firmed. A second later he threw back his beverage and set the cup and saucer down on a nearby table.

'The day is yours. Feel free to explore. We'll go out to dinner tonight. Rome at night is not as special as Athens, but it's still quite spectacular.'

Her grip tightened. She knew she couldn't succumb to the awed sensation attempting to sweep her away. There was a catch. There was *always* a catch.

'You didn't bring me here to play tourist. Are you going to tell me what you want in return for helping me or is it going to hang over my head like the sword of Damocles?'

He strolled closer, his hands sliding into his pockets. The movement threw the breadth of his shoulders into relief, inviting attention to the muscle play beneath his shirt.

'I thought we already settled that, *agapita*? We're getting married.'

Her jaw dropped, and then, after the tiniest wild agitation, her heart along with it. 'But that's... *No*. You just said that yesterday to throw Uncle Flávio and Vincenzo off. It was never meant to be real. I was thinking more along the lines of a fake engagement for a while, maybe a few months, then calling it off...' Her words trailed off when his expression grew sardonic.

'Were you?' he drawled.

Heat filled her face. 'Don't mock me, Ares.'

His amusement evaporated. 'And don't presume you have any power to dictate how things proceed. You handed that over, remember?'

'Actually, no. I didn't.' She swallowed the knot in her throat. 'I said anything you want. Not everything,' she ventured, even while that *'we're getting married'* continued to ping wild desires through her blood.

Santo cielo, what she wouldn't have given to hear that years ago. *But it was a pipe dream. Remember that...*

He stared at her for a short stretch before glancing down at his watch. 'I'm going to be late for my meeting. You'll have the day to yourself, but be ready to go out when I return at seven.' He started to turn, then paused. 'Make no mistake, *agapita*. You will marry me, as per your request. And you will also give me that *anything I want*.'

She watched him leave, her insides a sickening mess of wild agitation and shock.

Ares wanted to marry her?

Why?

It sure as hell wasn't because he wanted her. He'd stated plainly yesterday that he wasn't there for her. And hadn't he responded with a cold hard *no* when she'd first made the ludicrously hopeful suggestion?

What on earth could've changed between then and now to make him want this? Surely not the *kiss*?

Questions dogged her, sending her pacing through her suite after breakfast with Sergios. He tried to coax her into going for a walk with him afterwards, but she was too riled up about his son's announcement to be tempted to stretch the boundaries of her freedom for the first time.

Her rollercoaster of agitation only intensified when the concierge rang at four p.m. to say there was a couturier heading up to the penthouse. The elegantly dressed middle-aged woman swept in with two assistants, one tugging a gold porter's trolley bearing three sleek garments bags and boxes of matching accessories, and the other carrying a large case that turned out to contain the very best in luxury make-up.

The folded note bearing her name attached to one garment bag was short and succinct.

Choose a gown. I prefer the red. A

On the heels of spending hours in the grip of confusion, Odessa's first knee-jerk reaction was rebellion. And that spurt of rebellion hardened when the garment turned out to be a sleeveless floor-length blood-red satin sheath with a plunging neckline and no back at all.

Heat flared in her cheeks as she imagined herself in it with no underwear—because there was no way she could pull off wearing panties, never mind a bra, in this dress.

'Diavolo, no!' she snapped under breath, ignoring the looks that passed between the other women.

Thrusting it aside, she reached for the next bag, somewhat mollified when she saw an off-white dress. It was better, but still a little too risqué, with its thigh-high slit and geometric gaps beneath the bust and at the hipline. She wasn't in the mood to show so much of her midriff and hipbones, thank you very much.

The last garment made her exhale in relief.

Ice-blue, with a waterfall skirt in soft chiffon, the halter neck design would leave her arms free in the cool early autumn air, and while a slit in the back negated wearing a bra, it was still tasteful enough that she reached eagerly for it.

'This one.'

The couturier snapped her fingers. Within minutes, matching accessories had been laid out. A quick shower later, and she was in front of the mirror in her dressing room, the experts barely intruding as her hair was blow-dried, curled and styled in an up-do with tendrils framing her face. The make-up accentuating her eyes in dark and silver shadow was understated, and yet dramatic enough to make Odessa's mouth gape in astonishment.

All three women gushed compliments, and once her dress, shoes and clutch bag were in place, they were spirited away as dramatically as they'd arrived.

It wasn't the first time she'd dressed up to meet a man. Her father had paired her up and dangled her in front of friends' sons and acquaintances more times than she could count. But this was the first time she'd dressed for Ares Zanelis. And as much as she despised the nerves chewing her up, she couldn't stem them.

She rose from the sofa when he entered, and watched him grind to a halt, his eyes wide with something heavy and profound that restarted the rollercoaster all over again. She withstood his intense scrutiny, feeling every second of the thorough, almost obsessive head-to-toe inspection, and his utter fascination with looking into her eyes.

She knew the make-up made her eyes look saucer-wide and almost haunting, but…

'If you're going to make a big deal about me not wearing

the red dress, save your breath. I'd rather wear nothing at all than wear that *thing*.'

She only realised what she'd blurted a moment later and groaned under her breath.

Ares prowled closer, his fingers undoing his suit jacket before he shrugged it off. Odessa hated it that she had to fight to drag her gaze away from the chiselled perfection he revealed.

'Is that so? Well, far be it for me to subject the public to the scandalous spectacle of your nakedness.'

The smile teasing his lips sparked a suspicion that drew a gasp. 'The red wasn't your real choice at all, was it?'

His amusement deepened and she knew she'd been played. 'I suspected you would want to show your claws. You always were your fiercest when given an order.'

The recollection of him saying something similar years ago landed sharp and raw between them, making her pulse race. But his amusement evaporated a second later, indicating that he hadn't meant to bring that up. Hadn't meant to share that memory with her.

'I'll be ready in fifteen minutes,' he clipped out, then strode off, leaving her stomach churning once again.

She'd barely got her runaway pulse and scattering senses to calm when he returned. His business suit had been swapped for a black dinner jacket and matching trousers with a thin strip of black satin down the side seam that accentuated his lean athleticism. The first few buttons of his midnight-blue silk shirt were undone, baring his strong throat and the faintest wisps of chest hair.

Odessa was immediately thrown back to a younger Ares, rising out of the sea after an illicit midnight swim. Even back then she'd been in complete girlish awe over his chiselled form. Now every womanly cell in her body heated at the erotic sight of all that raw male perfection, barely restrained by the trappings of sophistication.

'Shall we?' he rasped.

Blinking to drive away the lascivious thoughts, she glanced past him. 'Is Sergios not coming with us?'

He shook his head. 'No. He needs to rest. Besides, this evening is just for you and me.'

She wasn't going to apply any deeper meaning to that. He'd all but said outright this morning that he'd be finally stating his demands.

Her insides continued to twist into knots as he ushered her into the lift. Strained silence ticked between them, with Odessa grasping and discarding subjects she'd once been able to freely discuss with this man who was a complete stranger to her now.

She stepped out in relief when the doors opened—relief which was immediately shattered when he caught her hand in a light hold.

She glanced up and saw the pointed look in his eyes.

Right. To the outside world, they were getting married. Because she'd asked him and, for soon-to-be-disclosed reasons, he'd obliged.

And now what? They must pretend to be happily about to be engaged?

She swallowed a snort before it could escape, eager to get outside, where hopefully a dose of fresh air would clear her head. But awaiting them were eager staff who jumped when they saw him coming, hotel guests who eyed them with wide-eyed speculation, and the latest model Ferrari supercar idling kerbside. She knew it was worth over a million, because Flávio had greedily and openly coveted it for the last six months.

Sliding in, she felt her senses immediately latch on to Ares's unique scent, seemingly imprinted in the space. It only intensified when he dropped into the bucket seat beside her, his large frame shrinking the interior until it felt as if he was all she could see, all she could breathe.

In a wild bid to dissipate the charged atmosphere she revisited the subject they'd skimmed minutes ago, as Ares gunned the engine and accelerated into the Rome night.

'What you said about Sergios… Is he all right? Did the accident—'

'How do you know about that?' he demanded sharply, his body stiffening.

'We have TVs in Alghero, you know. Besides, I could hardly miss it. You seem to be a big deal these days.'

He eased the car into the road, the clench-unclench of his thighs playing in the strobe of passing streetlights. 'Am I?'

'Self-effacing doesn't become you.'

A layer of tension released and the corner of his lips quirked. 'You'll be hard pressed to find anything that *becomes* me, *agapita*,' he murmured evenly, but she heard a slight bite behind the statement.

She wondered again what had been involved in his meteoric rise to the top in just a short decade. Before she could ask, he was continuing.

'My father likes to pretend he'll live for ever. And as much as I'd like that…'

His lips pursed and she saw a flash of bleakness that was stark and stomach-hollowing under the next passing streetlight. 'They discovered a heart condition during his recovery.'

Her heart squeezed. 'I'm… I'm sorry. Is it serious?'

He remained silent for a tight stretch. 'Most heart conditions are—especially at his age.'

It was said in a finite way that didn't invite more speculation or questions. But she was reluctant to return to the charged silence…reluctant to probe her own feelings too closely.

'And you? You were in a coma for a while.'

She felt his probing gaze when he pulled up at a traffic light.

'You were paying attention that much, *agapita*?'

That edge was present in his tone, but there was something else. Surprise? Curiosity? The tiniest softening? Or was it wishful thinking?

'No matter what happened between us, I never wished you ill, Ares.'

His chest moved and her heart lifted with…hope? But his lips had tightened again.

'That's good, because in the telling of our brief story you would've been hard pressed to come out the victim at any point.'

Her insides twisted hard, but she pushed the anguish away. 'I don't think of myself as a victim. But neither am I a villain. Our past is—'

'In the past,' he interrupted. 'Tonight is about what comes next for you and me.'

Before she could respond, Ares was pulling up in front of one of the many centuries-old buildings the city was known for. It looked nondescript from the outside, but even its act of attempting to look plain hinted at hidden delights.

She wasn't mistaken.

The moment Ares alighted, a smartly dressed young man approached, took his car keys, and waved them through the ordinary-looking doors.

After a dozen steps on a black carpet they came to dramatic red double doors and a stone-paved corridor lit with large medieval fire lamps thrust into the walls high above their heads. It was so evocative of a bygone era that she stared around her, her mouth agape.

'Where are we?'

'Teatro Romana di Caracalla. A private exclusive theatre owned by a friend. It was a rundown apartment building when I sold it to him two years ago. He's turned it around admirably. At any other time I would've preferred for us to have the place to ourselves, but tonight calls for a curated audience.'

Her breath snagged in her chest. 'What's special about tonight?'

One eyebrow arched in a satirical mockery. 'You do want the message reinforced, don't you? Or would you rather leave Bartorelli with the impression that he still has a chance?'

A cold shudder went through her. 'No, I wouldn't.'

'Good.'

He tugged her hand onto his sleeve and escorted her to the end of the corridor, which opened up into a wide balcony. Below the balcony a semi-circular theatre was set out not with rows of seats but with twelve semi-circular dining tables with chairs facing the stage. The whole theatre rose three storeys high, with more fire torches fixed along the walls up to the ceiling.

It was spectacular, and she would've loved to explore, had Ares's intentions not been uppermost in her thoughts.

He led her to a table clearly set out centre stage, briefly acknowledging the occupants of the other tables. Odessa was keenly aware that they were the cynosure of every pair of eyes, and murmurs of interest were flaring.

Vintage champagne set in a silver bucket was poured into crystal flutes as the lights went down. Then the first haunting strings of a familiar opera drew fresh tingles down her spine.

Her gaze darted to Ares. *'Tristan and Isolde?'*

A ghost of a smile drifted over his lips as he clinked his glass against hers. 'Your favourite story, *ne*?'

Her breath caught. 'You remember?'

'The curse of having a steel trap memory,' he said with a throwaway shrug, his face shuttered in a way that made her heart drop.

The first act of the twisted, heart-tugging love story was accompanied by a superb lobster salad and then sublime gnocchi, salmon and truffle cheese served by unobtrusive attendants trained in the art of melting into the background.

By the time the lights came up on first intermission, Odessa's emotions were threatening to strangle her. The reasons behind Ares choosing an opera that celebrated a fierce forbidden love that ended in tragedy had triggered higher emotions and put her on fierce alert.

Was it a metaphor for them? A warning against reading anything into his actions?

Her gaze dropped to the table, to the expensive-looking square velvet box he was sliding across the table, and a loud gasp erupted through her jagged emotions. 'This is... You can't—'

'Open it,' he commanded, and there was a hoarse roughness to his voice despite his carefully neutral expression.

Her brain shrieked at her not to, but that foolish sliver of a doe-eyed girl lurking deep within her compelled her to reach out a trembling hand.

The blush-pink diamond was surrounded with two rows of tiny, flawless cushion-cut white diamonds mounted on a platinum base and narrow band, each one glinting and sparkling beneath the candlelight.

A gasp echoed somewhere to her right, and within a minute wild applause broke out, their audience cunningly pulled into this seemingly euphoric moment.

On cue, Ares rose, closed the gap between them, lifted the ring from its plush velvet cushion and slipped it onto her finger. All the while Odessa's mouth gaped in what might be construed as romantic shock but was in reality astonishment at how expertly she'd been played.

Under the pretext of brushing her lips with his—an act which left her mouth tingling and heat arrowing sharply between her legs—Ares took her chin in his hand, his eyes gleaming as he murmured, 'I would get down on one knee, but since we've been forced to put the cart before the horse I feel that moment has passed, no?'

Words failed her—both at the sheer magnificence of the ring and the image of Ares on one knee, playing out the secret impossible fantasy she'd harboured for far too long during her teenage years.

'When did you do this?' she asked, pushing away the more pressing questions she wanted to blurt out. Like *why* he was pushing this ruse. Why was he going to such great lengths for something neither of them truly wanted?

Are you sure?

'Does it matter?' he drawled dismissively, as if a proposal that would've made an enormous swathe of women swoon was merely an item he'd ticked off his list tonight.

'You're right. It doesn't matter,' she forced out.

Theirs wasn't a reunion filled with breathless proclamations and the obsessive need to tabulate every single moment of their for ever pledge. She'd made a desperate request and he'd grudgingly obliged, with conditions of his own he'd yet to make fully known to her.

'Are we going to get the suspense over with now?' she rasped, aware that they were under even more intense scrutiny.

Hell, that diamond on her finger commanded an audience all its own.

He took his seat, and she noticed he'd moved much closer to her. With their table distanced from the other tables, they were out of eavesdropping range. The enforced proximity ramped up her tension, her stomach churning as he watched her for an age before he spoke the words she suspected would turn her life as she knew it inside out.

'In return for keeping you out of the clutches of your uncle and that bastard,' he started, his eyes glinting hard as his gaze dropped to the faint yellow marks on her wrist, 'you'll stay married to me for five years, or however long it takes for you to give me two children—minimum. If we're blessed with more in those five years, then they will be well received. After that, you'll be free to live your life however you want.'

CHAPTER FOUR

IN THE DUMBFOUNDING seconds that followed his words—words that should have arrived with cymbals and trumpets and exploding fireworks, considering the impossible utter insanity they evoked—Odessa fully grasped why Ares had chosen to do this in public.

Just like with the proposal, he'd sought to contain her response. And, oh, was he clever in doing so…

Because she only managed to keep the predictable screech of disbelief and outrage trapped in her throat by the most valiant fight with her willpower.

The hooded look in his eyes said he knew it.

He watched with avid interest as her heart raced madly and her hands bunched on the table, shaking with the force of suppressed emotion and causing the ring to sparkle in its mocking presence even brighter.

She felt the blood drain from her head and take her belly along with it to her toes.

Her lips parted but no words emerged.

Was it even worth reacting to this absurdity? *Yes*, her frantic senses screeched. Because the steely determination in his face screamed that he was serious.

Dio mio.

'Before you express anything other than complete ecstasy at my request, remember our audience,' he warned under his breath.

'This is why you brought me here? To corner me so I couldn't tell you how utterly crazy you are?' she hissed.

Despite the twitch of his lips, his eyes remained deadly serious, without a trace of insanity. 'My reasons are exactly as I stated. You get to enjoy your favourite opera, be offered the requisite diamond ring, and more importantly get your unwanted suitor off your back. In return, I've stated my demands. That you find it insane doesn't change the fact that those are my wishes. If you want to continue this conversation elsewhere, I'll be happy to oblige.' He looked around, his eyes gleaming with triumph. 'I think we've satisfied our objectives.'

He finished speaking just as a rotund man with a booming voice who introduced himself simply as 'Armand' approached. He expressed congratulations in Italian, to which Ares responded, speaking in a perfect accent that reminded her he spoke her mother tongue fluently.

Somehow Odessa managed to smile and respond, to hold out her hand when his wife arrived to gush over the ring. In minutes, they were inundated with other well-wishers.

Ten minutes after that Ares was firmly but good-humouredly announcing that they were leaving to celebrate in private. Odessa was still reeling as he escorted her out to their waiting car.

'That should take care of the publicity side of things. Armand's wife alone will ensure our news spreads across the continent before morning.'

She turned on him, her heartbeat still roaring in her ears. 'You... Tell me you were joking back there!'

'No. I was not.'

'Ares...'

She saw him tense at the whisper of his name, his fingers tightening briefly around the steering wheel before he relaxed them.

'We will be married long enough for the two children I require to be born or for five years—whichever comes first,' he reiterated, his voice like rumbling boulders that dropped onto her shoulders. 'And they will be born in Greece,' he tossed in, as if geography mattered one iota when she was grappling with his ludicrous demand.

'If all you need is a womb for hire, why do you need marriage at all? Surrogates are a dime a dozen these days.'

A muscle rippled in his jaw for a moment before he rasped, 'Because I wish to do things properly. For my father's sake. I'm sure you remember he's old-school in most ways?'

It was the last thing she'd expected him to say and it robbed her of speech, right along with the shock of the moment before. Because in some baffling way it made sense.

'Right. I see.'

And she truly did. In father and son she'd witnessed an unbending devotion that had sparked both yearning and envy. It had been the model she'd based all the foundations of her relationship goals on. Still...

'Why go through this...subterfuge? Isn't he going to be upset when he finds out?'

Tension clearly still riding him, he zipped them through traffic for a full minute before he replied.

'He'll never find out. As far as he's concerned every aspect of this marriage will be real. If I remember correctly your acting skills are impressive. You'll do everything in your power to convince him that our reunion is real. And if...' He paused, a flash of something resembling bleakness darting across his face before he neutralised his expression. 'And when the time comes for us to separate, I'll break the news to him in a way that minimises the damage. Hopefully by then he will be too preoccupied with his grandchildren to care.'

'You don't need to count on any imaginary acting skills you think I possess. I'm not participating in this...sham. Not for one year. Never mind five...or...' She waved that absurd thought away, the layers of shocked pain settling over her shoulders like an unwanted cloak as her brain struggled to grasp the unthinkable scenario he was drawing up. 'Are you really okay with pulling the wool over his eyes like this?'

'The eventual benefits will far outweigh the means of achieving my goals. It's salutary advice you'll do well to apply to your own circumstances.'

She swallowed a bark of hysterical laughter before it leapt free. He was really serious about this.

'Why five years?'

'Because it's the right age for a child to relinquish dependence on an absent parent. Any later and the damage could be irreparable.'

'How do you know this?' she asked, and then stinging recollection made her inhale sharply. 'Your own mother left when you were seven,' she murmured, almost afraid of voicing the reason he was pushing for this. 'Is this about…? Do you wish your mother had left earlier?'

His expression morphed into granite. 'This isn't about me.'

Of course it was. His whole being screamed it. But Odessa wisely didn't belabour the point.

'So I give you a child…children…and we divorce in five years?' Why did the words sear a path of pain in her throat?

Fully expecting him to agree, she was stunned when he shook his head. 'No. We will stay married for a minimum of five years. But if…when you decide to leave, you will relinquish full custody of our children to me. We won't divorce until my father is…' He stopped, expelling his breath in a rush.

Again absurdly, considering the utter lunacy of this conversation, Odessa's heart cracked for him, sympathy filling spaces long left wanting and hollow. She didn't need him to spell it out. Her mother's passing might have happened long ago enough for her only to recall hazy moments with the woman forced to stay in her husband's shadow, but deep in her heart the pain of losing her parent lingered.

She pushed back the memories to find Ares watching her.

'Five years is also a good age to ensure a child's memories fade sooner rather than later,' he tossed in.

The pang was sharper this time, lancing hard enough to make her gasp. 'Ares, this is insane!'

'And yet these are my terms. Take it or leave it.'

It didn't even register that they'd returned to the hotel's underground car park until the silence pressed in on her. The finality of his statement battered at any hope of getting him to rethink this streak of insanity, but she wasn't about to be cowed into submission.

'You don't really expect me to bear your children and then simply walk away when this sham marriage you fully expect to fail falls apart, do you?' she demanded, firming every sinew in her shocked body.

The faintest hint of something almost resembling compassion flashed across his face. Then it was gone so swiftly she wondered if she'd imagined it.

'Don't pretend it will be a hardship for you,' he said.

Anger at the cavalier way he dismissed her feelings bunched her fists. 'How can you say that? Of course it'll be a hardship for me! It'll be impossible. How dare you imply this is a decision to be taken lightly?'

His nostrils flared. 'We both know how flighty you can be. You say one thing and mean another. Do I need to remind you that I have first-hand knowledge of that? That you went straight from my arms into another man's with barely a pause in between? After you assured me that Paolo Romani meant nothing to you?'

The accusation stung, even though she knew the full truth behind it. The very real threats from her father…the vicious examples he'd made her witness. Her fear that he'd make true on them.

'Am I to bear punishment for one mistake for the rest of my life?'

The smile that curved his sensual lips was all cynicism, no mirth.

'But it wasn't just the one mistake, was it, *agape mou*? You knew I was there, listening, when you denigrated me to your father,' he accused, citing the awful night when they hadn't covered their tracks as well as they should have.

In her eagerness to meet with Ares in their secret spot, a few nights before her eighteenth birthday, she'd failed to ensure her father was otherwise occupied. Elio had found her in the orange grove. Her quick actions had thankfully ensured she seemed to be alone, but she'd been aware that Ares remained nearby, a protective presence but privy to every caustic put-down her father had unleashed upon her.

She'd remained silently defiant…until her father had whispered a vicious threat against Ares and Sergios. One so low and deadly she'd been certain Ares hadn't heard it.

Terror and panic had pushed her into responding regrettably, in the only way her young mind had offered.

She'd hotly denied her attraction to his chauffeur's son, and then gone one better and sworn he wasn't her type, that she'd never be attracted to him.

Even from his hidden spot, she'd felt the force of Ares's affront, the blow to his pride. And his cold rejection of her next day—the day she'd planned to go several steps further than the light kisses they'd so far shared—had hurt. Nevertheless, she'd understood.

She had hoped to explain that she'd said what she had to prevent the serious bodily harm her father had threatened Ares and his father with. She'd seen first-hand how Elio treated his enemies. The last thing she'd wanted was for him to act on his threats.

Until she'd discovered Ares's own plans.

Ares Zanelis had always planned to leave her behind. To shatter the foolish, girlish dreams she'd woven around him.

Having secured a string of near-dilapidated buildings with

the nest egg his father had given him, he'd made plans to leave Alghero—information she'd discovered through the servants' gossip the day before he'd left.

Thankfully, he'd never witnessed the extent of her devastation. How she'd cried herself to sleep for months afterwards, with her father's cruel jabs at her clear unhappiness driving the knives in even deeper.

Tell him now. Set the record straight.

'I knew you were still in the orange grove that night, Ares. I said all those things to take my father's interest off you. I was protecting you. He threatened to have you beaten. Or worse.'

His mouth twisted, scoffing at the idea that a man like him would need someone to save him, even back then.

'Considerate of you. But I've never needed anyone to fight my battles for me. Bravo for trying—and you were shockingly convincing. Enough to make me wonder if it was your subconscious speaking the truth on your behalf.'

'No, it wasn't,' she protested hotly. 'I never thought you were beneath me.'

'You moved on very quickly after that. Or were you also protecting me when you kissed your father's lieutenant's son the very next night, in the same spot where you'd let me touch you?' he seethed.

Regret and shock ripped a gasp from her throat. 'You saw?'

Censure etched into his face. 'Oh, yes. But then I always saw you, didn't I? You made sure of that.'

'What do you mean by that?'

'It means we lived at opposite ends of your father's estate and had no business crossing paths—and yet there you always were.'

'You pursued me too!' she protested hotly, her face flaming.

He shrugged. 'You were as beautiful then as you are now. Perhaps as irresistible to me as you pretended I was to you. But you also proved to be fickle, didn't you? Maybe for once I shouldn't have ignored your father when he said you were meant for another. That I was a dress rehearsal for the real thing.'

She inhaled sharply. 'He said that to you?'

His sardonic smile widened. 'That and much more—including those threats you believed you were protecting me from. He never missed an opportunity to warn me away from the precious daughter he intended to marry off to Paolo Romani. The same bastard I saw you kissing, *agapita*,' he accused icily.

Odessa shook her head, choosing to remain silent. How could she tell him that it had been a misguided effort to forget him without sounding pathetic? That he'd been imprinted so deeply on her that she'd feared she would remain lonely for ever in the face of her father's determination to keep them apart? The formidable man beside her now would deem any excuse a weak protest, his judge-and-jury conviction of her character one she suspected he'd cemented a long time ago.

And more than his damning indictment it was the mocking endearment that threatened to flatten her. Because where it was all cynical now, he'd meant it once upon a time. Or had he? Had he, even back then, been skilfully adept at this level of hypnotic charm? Had she been so starved of care and affection that she'd seen only what he'd wanted her to see?

That cold wave of possibility made her stare harder, desperate to find the truth, or at the very least an inkling that she was wrong in her fears. She refused to be drawn back to the past. Not when this remarkable present demanded every atom of her concentration.

'I'll take your silence as an admission of guilt, shall I?' he asked.

She shook her head. 'No, it's not. I made a mistake. But whatever you think about me, I never misled you.'

Surprise flashed in his eyes, but again it was gone a nanosecond later.

This man's ability to master his emotions was almost fascinating to watch. *Almost.* Because Odessa would have given

her eye teeth for a glimpse of lasting emotion. For some hope
that the future he painted for her wasn't as terrifyingly bleak as
it sounded. Not having his children. Oh, no. That had formed
a big chunk of her teenage daydreams—the deep yearning to
lovingly craft the antithesis of the family she'd been born into,
always with Ares as the husband and father figure.

Hell, she'd foolishly confessed those dreams to him once,
as they'd lazed under a lemon tree in one of those stolen summer nights when she'd sneaked out to meet him. That was why
she wasn't surprised he wanted more than one child. He'd confessed that back then too, and they'd shared their antipathy to
the loneliness of growing up without siblings. It was something
they didn't wish on their children—especially Ares, who'd
known what it was like to have a sibling only to be robbed of
her in the cruellest way possible.

God, had she supplied him with the very weapons to destroy her?

Sucking in a shaky breath, she opened her mouth to demand
an answer to that horrifying possibility.

But he was exiting the car, his towering frame blotting out
the light and throwing him into shadow as he came around,
opened her door.

'Delving into our innermost feelings isn't why we're here.
The clock is ticking, Odessa. What's it going to be?'

One night.

She'd insisted on one night to grapple with the most profound decision of her life, and already the hours were slipping
through her fingers like wispy clouds burning in the sunlight.

Ares hadn't been happy with her unwavering demand. But
she'd stood her ground, the stubborn defiance that had got
her into trouble with her father more often than she cared to
count asserting itself.

And holding firm had been bolstering. Perhaps even ex-
hilarating.

Now, as she tossed and turned, the sheets twisting around her legs almost as tangled as her thoughts, her mind wasn't firm at all. Her thoughts veered from an outright *no* to his insane proposal to skirting the very edge of Ares's demands.

Could she…?

Her instinct shrieked a resounding *no*.

But the alternative…

She shivered at the thought of Ares throwing her back to the wolves. One wolf in particular—Vincenzo—who wouldn't hesitate to make her pay for the trick she'd pulled.

She could run. Get up, grab her small case and just…run.

And prove Ares correct in his denigration of her character? He already thought the worst of her. For unfathomable reasons, proving him right made her chest tighten unbearably.

She'd given her word.

And, yes, she'd landed herself in this situation with that *'I'll do anything'* she'd stupidly blurted out.

Because she'd never thought he'd ask her for *this*!

But the alternative…

The shiver that gripped her now was colder, more ominous in a way that she couldn't overlook. Going back to Alghero would be akin to a death sentence, with her uncle choosing to look the other way despite being fully aware of Vincenzo's intended treatment of her. The alternative—walking away from Ares and striking out on her own—would mean her looking over her shoulder for the rest of her life. Maybe even worse. Because no amount of defiance would keep her safe from Uncle Flávio or Vincenzo. And once she was caught, Vincenzo, like all men of his ilk, would force her to breed, just to prove his manhood.

Wouldn't she be better off staying here? Bearing Ares's children?

The very idea that she was even considering it made her squeeze her eyes shut, smashing her face into the pillow until the scream trapped in her throat ripped free.

The picture that formed in the aftermath of that tiny catharsis didn't repulse her, like thoughts of Vincenzo did. Hell, it was the opposite. She'd dreamed of bearing Ares's children once upon a time.

But that had been the daydream of a forcibly sheltered girl on the cusp of womanhood, whose only true exposure to the opposite sex had been the tall, dark Greek with brooding, hungry eyes. Hadn't it?

She exhaled, her eyes flying open, in a wild bid to dispel the thoughts weaving so seductively in her head. The whispered *what ifs* that pressed so heavily on her, demanding attention. Ares's terms said five years, after which they would separate...*if* she wanted to leave. That meant the option to stay was hers. Wasn't it?

What if she agreed to his terms—for now—with a view to altering them later?

Odessa gulped down a rising bolt of unease. But it wouldn't diminish.

She'd requested his help on a wild whim that had saved her from a fate worse than death. Dared she risk gambling again, on making this work too?

Her thoughts were still spinning when she finally fell into a restless sleep.

Alarmingly she felt stronger when she woke, showered and dressed a few short hours later, and then went to find the man who'd put his ring on her finger last night, and tossed her world into pure chaos.

The sun was barely peeking through the ancient Roman buildings, but Ares was already up and dressed, sipping an espresso on the same terrace Odessa had used yesterday.

He rose from the pristinely set table the moment she stepped out, dressed once more in her jeans and another simple top, and she couldn't fail to see the contrast between them.

But for all his suave exterior and iron composure, his neatly combed hair and polished shoes, there was a coiled tension within him, an intensity in his eyes, that said her answer mattered to him. That perhaps he'd donned this bespoke armour because there was a chink he was determined to guard.

Delusional, perhaps, but Odessa ruthlessly clung to that, the same way she'd excavated pockets of defiance to fight her oppression over the years. She'd lost more than she'd won, but fighting had kept her spirits alive. And as long as she had breath in her body she'd keep fighting.

Especially if she was fighting for her children.

Because somewhere in the early hours she'd reasoned that if Ares truly was doing this for his father, and he wasn't completely heartless in his endeavour, then perhaps at some point down the road she might sway him into accepting a different, better role than full custody.

And if he didn't?

She shrugged inwardly. Then she'd just fight harder.

She'd persuaded him into granting her a lifeline out of the hell she'd faced in her father's house, hadn't she?

'Odessa.'

Her name was a command. And, really, wasn't she just torturing herself by withholding the answer she'd decided to give?

Slicking her tongue over dry lips, she stepped forward. The vital need to look into his eyes and see something…anything that would give her hope…was too compelling to deny.

'It's a yes, Ares. My answer is yes.'

She saw it then. The quiet exhalation. The release of tension. The flash of relief in his eyes.

She held up her hand when he opened his mouth to speak.

'But before you celebrate, you should know this. I won't abandon my children. *Ever.* No matter what.'

His eyes glinted fiercely with layers of triumph, then surprise, before settling on heavy scepticism. 'We'll just have to wait and see, won't we?'

He might deny them, but she intended to remind herself of those vital tells. Frequently.

Ares wasn't inhuman.

She *would* change his mind down the road.

Anything else was unthinkable.

She raised her chin, met his gaze. 'Hold your breath if you want. Or don't. I won't even bother with *I told you so* when the time comes.'

They landed in Athens later that afternoon to frenzied tabloid interest.

One of their own—powerful and influential, the shining epitome of rags to riches—had snagged himself a beautiful bride. A woman he'd apparently grown up with, they breathlessly reported. Perhaps even a childhood sweetheart?

Ares held her hand, kissed her knuckles and brushed his lips over her temple. His eyes locked hungrily on hers. And he ignored the shouted questions.

Beside them, Sergios beamed, his approval clear despite the sometimes circumspect looks he levelled at Odessa.

For her part, she kept her mouth shut, for fear she'd blurt something untoward or reveal that, contrary to the paparazzi's view, it wasn't a fairy tale marriage. Hell, they hadn't even discussed when or where they'd be getting married.

'First things first,' Ares drawled when they were ensconced in another sleek limo, his fingers flying over his phone screen.

'What?'

'You need a new wardrobe. Would you prefer to go shopping or shall I have a selection brought to you?'

She frowned. 'I don't need new clothes.'

'You intend to wear those jeans on every occasion until they fall off you?'

She opened her mouth to argue, then pursed them again when she accepted that he had a point. 'Fine, but I can buy my own clothes.'

As Ares Zanelis' wife, and soon-to-be mother of his children, she clearly had an image to project. The full scope of his existence had only just come into focus for her in the last day.

There would be no enforced seclusion on a cliff-front estate the way her father had hidden her away. The thought was at once freeing and mildly panic-inducing.

The hand that reached for hers and patted it gently was surprisingly not Ares's. She glanced up at Sergios's benign smile.

'My son can be overbearing at times. He can't help himself. But you deserve to be spoilt, *mikros*. And besides, all women enjoy shopping, *ne*?' Leaning forward, he stage-whispered, 'Or you can get your own back by dragging him along with you while you spend his money. I'm told it's a fate worse than death.'

Aware of Ares's sharp gaze—and with the reminder that they were pretending at the very least to be wildly attracted to each other with a view to starting a family—she summoned a smile in return. Then her gaze caught on the landscape whizzing by, in the very first country she'd ever visited outside Italy.

'I'll choose my clothes, thanks,' she answered.

'*Kalos*. I've cleared my calendar for the afternoon,' Ares said.

Surprise widened her eyes. 'You have?'

'*Ne*. And while we're out we can discuss wedding plans.'

That combination of panic and excitement fizzled harder. 'Already?'

His eyes gleamed, sweeping over her face in a blatant appraisal that made heat pummel her. 'I don't see any point in waiting. I want us to start our lives together. Don't you?'

The pointed question was a veiled reminder of their agreement.

Exhaling for composure, she replied, 'Yes, I do.'

Satisfaction darkened the gleam.

Across from her, Sergios's smile widened.

Her heart thumping wildly in her chest, Odessa gazed out of the window, where the vibrant streets of Athens impressed upon her the fact that her life was well on course to change irreparably.

Ares finished the next call on his list, tuning out the sales assistants' excited chattering as they flitted around Odessa. He sat in the waiting room of a luxury boutique, an untouched glass of Dom Perignon ignored at his elbow, as he continued to make plans as if the devil himself were snapping at his heels.

His father had been right. This was torture. But not in the way Sergios had meant. It was torture because Ares couldn't seem to find the willpower to get up and walk out. Leave Odessa to her own devices.

He'd thought he'd be satisfied once she'd agreed to his demands. Instead, that peculiar sense of urgency had only escalated. He wasn't sure whether it was a good or a bad trait he possessed that meant once he set his mind to a thing he tended not to rest until his goal was achieved.

Pausing on his next phone call, he examined his true feelings for a minute, in the wild hope that it would clear his mind of this idiotic urgency.

Even now he could hear the assistants cooing over the engagement ring he'd procured yesterday with that same driving agitation.

Was it the five years already ticking down? Was he so eager for this project to be underway? So he could see if he was dealing with the same kind of situation his mother had put him through? Or was it more that since Odessa's vehement protests in the car last night he'd yearned for a crystal ball, to see whether she would stay true to her word? If she would deliver on some of the foolish, forgotten promises she'd eagerly made all those years ago.

And wasn't that a hell of a thing to crave? Especially when he knew better...

And…*mummy issues*? Really?

He wanted to scoff at the thought, but he couldn't deny that it was there, a glaring black hole in his life he'd never been able to distance himself from.

While he was sure some therapists would lay the blame of his reluctance to marry on his tragic situation, Ares knew it was a series of events, ending with the woman currently hidden behind heavy curtains, trying on the clothes he intended to grace her stunning body with, who'd cemented his decision never to encumber himself with a wife.

Or at least he'd believed that until her impassioned protest that she'd been attempting to *save* him. To place herself between him and her vicious father.

Ares shifted in his seat, the recollection dragging an unfamiliar uncertainty from him. But even if she'd meant that, he couldn't ignore her other actions. How swiftly she'd turned away from him and into another man's arms.

His mother's desertion and cruelty had taught him that he didn't need a wife or a so-called life partner to enhance his life. Hell, the lack of one would remove any threat of rejection altogether for his future offspring. Better to start off with zero expectations than harbour foolish notions, right?

Ne.

Control reasserted, he straightened as Odessa stepped out. 'Leave us, please.'

The assistants scurried away immediately, but it took him another handful of seconds to drag his gaze from her stunning body and the control-wrecking things the black lace dress did to her figure.

He pulled up the images on his phone and turned the screen to her, watching closely as she swiped through the pictures, her breath catching as she glanced up.

'It's breathtaking. Where is that?'

'Ismene—my private island. We'll get married there a week from today. Does that work for you?'

He expected her to protest, or the very least make a show of unhappiness. To his surprise, she handed his phone back and shrugged.

'Sure, why not. It's not like I have any pressing engagements. It looks like a perfect place for a wedding.' She looked over her shoulder. 'Is there something else you want to discuss, or shall I get the assistants back?'

His fingers drummed restlessly on his thighs. 'No, that's all.'

She turned immediately, dismissing his presence. He bit back a growl.

'Odessa?'

She paused, silver eyes flicking to his. *'Si?'*

He nudged his chin at the black lace dress. 'Keep that dress. I like it.'

Satisfaction at her blush was short-lived. And for the life of him Ares couldn't understand why his grouchy mood persisted as the hours passed.

Perhaps it was because, unlike women he'd known in the past, she didn't gush with joy at being lavished with hundreds of thousands of euros' worth of clothes and jewels. Or because she mostly ignored him, chatting happily to Sergios during dinner and at breakfast the next morning.

He'd saved her, damn it—in a twisted knight in shining armour situation he was almost convinced had been orchestrated by his father.

Where was her gratitude? Her hero-worship?

Hell, she'd been insultingly eager when she'd excused herself to meet with the wedding co-ordinator he'd lined up to visit before they left for Ismene. And she was equally perky on the way back home now, her interest in the local landmarks reminding him of how cloistered she'd been in Alghero.

Ares stopped himself from playing the tour guide—from postponing their imminent departure to Ismene so he could take her on an extended tour of his beloved Athens.

She wasn't here on a sightseeing trip.

She was here to take his name, to bear his children, and then to be monitored with eagle eyes if she so much as hinted at taking a leaf out of his mother's book.

'Hold your breath if you want to. Or don't...'

Challenging words. But she didn't know him well if she thought he wouldn't accept that gauntlet.

He would be right there when she failed. And this time if she betrayed him he'd dispatch Odessa Santella and there would be no going back.

Goals reaffirmed, he grabbed his tablet, ignoring the woman whose head was now whipping back and forth, who gasped delightfully at her first sight of the Acropolis, her neck craned with almost endearing eagerness until the iconic landmark was out of view.

CHAPTER FIVE

CONTRARY TO HER belief that the week would speed towards the moment she married Ares, Odessa thought it crawled by treacle-slowly. So slowly so that she came within a whisper of suggesting they bring the date forward.

She only held her tongue because, despite her bravado, nerves were killing her.

Also because her feigned flippancy seemed to get under Ares's skin, and for some insane reason she preferred his brooding watchfulness and rasped interrogation about every aspect of her wedding planning to his icy aloofness.

It had started when he'd shown her the breathtaking private island where they were to wed. The punch of pure joy on seeing the setting, plucked straight from every daydream she'd ever harboured about her wedding day, had disturbed her enough to scramble to hide it, inadvertently sparking a restive reaction in him. Almost as if he needed regular evidence that she meant to keep her word.

She'd made a game of providing it, having no qualms about interrupting his work day to ask his opinion about linen colour themes or primary flower choices.

It was a situation Sergios had found hilarious, egging her on with winks and approving nods.

Their one serious clash had come when she'd protested that she didn't want anything from him when their marriage ended. That had drawn a sceptical glare that had sent his lawyers scrambling away to give them privacy. And in the ensuing twenty minutes she'd discovered just how cynical this new, mega-successful Ares had become.

No, he *didn't* believe her pious claim not to want anything from him.

No, he *wasn't* about to accept that she wouldn't sue him for a stake of his fortune further down the line.

Yes, her protests were useless.

To shut him up, Odessa had signed the prenup that granted her twenty million euros should they divorce. A fortune most people would give their eye-teeth for, but to her would mean she was leaving something vital behind.

They'd carried on like that until now, the morning before the wedding, when a less formally dressed but still furnace-hot Ares entered the living room where she was watching TV with Sergios after breakfast—although the old man had already dozed off in his favourite chair.

'Are you ready?' he drawled, his gaze shifting over her in that mildly possessive way he'd taken to using when looking at her, then returning to her face and her puzzled frown. 'Did you check your phone?'

She grabbed the sleek new phone he'd handed her the morning after their arrival. There, tucked away in a text box, was his prompt about a ten a.m. appointment.

'Where are we going? Do I need to change?'

His gaze slid down her floral wraparound dress to the matching wedge heels. 'You're fine as you are. We're going to see my private doctor.'

'I'm to be checked over to see if I fit my brood mare status, am I?' she blurted before she could stop herself.

The time she'd had to dwell on what was happening was taking its toll on her nerves.

He slanted her an enigmatic look. 'The examination isn't for just you. It's for both of us.'

Surprise snatched her breath away. 'You're getting checked too?'

'Indeed. If only to make sure my robust stallion status is at premium level.'

It took her a startling moment to realise he was cracking a joke. Her lips curved in response, her heart leaping. For a second while Ares had forgotten himself she'd caught a glimmer of the younger man she remembered.

Even after his amusement waned, she let that memory sustain her. Let it shore her up to withstand this older version's more dynamic battering of her senses.

That glimmer made another fleeting appearance when they were both pronounced rudely healthy two hours later, and a layer of tension left his shoulders.

In contrast, her own heartbeat escalated when she noticed that his gaze had grown even more brooding, the hand he placed on her back as they left his doctor's office that much more possessive. Even in the car and heading home he kept her close, his eyes pinned on her in a way that made her hackles rise.

'You're acting strangely. Is something wrong?'

He cupped her jaw in his strong hand, his hold making her feel far too delicate, its gentleness opening those vulnerable spaces within her she needed to keep shut.

'Not at all. I'm appreciating the fact that nothing stands in our way now. You're mine. There's no getting away from me now, *glykia mou.*'

The raw, primitive throb of possessiveness should have alarmed her. And yet, unlike every dark omen visited upon her in the past, Ares's words made her heart race with fevered yearning.

No matter the circumstances that had triggered this, the end result would be special and life-changing. A secret yearning brought to life.

If the trend of her cycle went according to plan, she could be pregnant by this time next month.

'There's one thing we need to discuss.' She cursed the heat rushing into her face, but the subject was too important to ignore. 'How I'm going to get pregnant. I'm assuming it'll be through IVF—'

The wicked and humourless laugh dried her words. 'No, *agapita*. You assume wrong. When I said everything about this marriage would be real, I meant it. And *everything* includes your presence in my bed every night until we are absolutely certain my seed is growing in your womb. Even then, I reserve the right to perform my marital duties.'

She gaped at him, askance, while the feverish cyclone inside her swirled higher. 'But…why? You don't even want me that way.'

His eyes narrowed. 'And how did you come to that conclusion?'

'Come off it, Ares. At this point I'm fairly sure you don't even like me!'

A muscle ticked at his temple. 'Do I need to like you to put a baby in your belly?' he asked.

But the query wasn't as clinical as the words suggested. And beneath the steady, almost mocking regard, she sensed he wasn't quite as calm as he projected.

It was almost admirable—to a point.

'How did I not see this crafty version of you back then?' she murmured.

His mouth twisted and his thumb drifted almost absentmindedly over her cheek. 'Perhaps you preferred to see your own version of the truth. I have always been like this.'

Her fists bunched. She refused to accept that she'd been so hoodwinked. 'I don't believe that I could've been so blind.'

'Then that's on you, Odessa.'

They stared each other down for an age, then she sucked in a breath. 'Then maybe I should be thankful things turned out the way they did.'

His face shuttered completely, and he withdrew his touch a moment later. 'Indeed. But it doesn't change the fact that you'll come to me on our wedding night and I will possess you completely.'

* * *

Ismene was halfway between Athens and Crete, east of Santorini. The four-square-kilometre jewel in the South Aegean
was the stuff of fairy tales and endless opulence, with its reality far surpassing what the pictures had promised.

As they circled the island in preparation to land, Odessa
spotted the beginnings of a marquee and a flower-festooned
arched trellis on one pristine lawn a short distance from a
white sandy beach, and that punch of illicit excitement returned.

'If I had my way we'd be married before sundown tonight,'
Ares murmured beside her, making her jolt as his breath
washed over her ear. 'But my father insists I must not be a
complete brute about the entire thing, so you'll get to find
your bearings, rest and enjoy your last night as a free woman.'

He caught her hand in his and raised it to his lips.

Her stomach dipped with the altitude of the landing plane,
and a thrill lanced her, despite knowing he was putting on a
show for Sergios, who watched them with another indulgent
smile.

The villa was a single-storey sprawling gem, with more
inviting outdoor terraces than she could count, all of them
showcasing a breath-catching view and an open invitation to
bask in the gorgeous Greek sun.

The staff of six, headed by a buxom grey-haired matriarch
in her sixties, greeted her with halting Italian and Ares and
Sergios with lyrical Greek, their beckoning leading them to
a large table laid out with refreshments.

Whether intended or not, the table overlooked the part of
the garden being decorated for the wedding.

'Interested in seeing all your hard work up close?' Ares
asked, his gaze intent on her face as he handed her a sparkling drink.

The force with which she wanted to say *yes* almost sucked
the breath from her. It was that rabid yearning that made her

hesitate. She couldn't afford for her feelings to become embroiled in this.

'It's your wedding. Some would say it's your absolute right to interfere,' he said.

'The organiser has been very accommodating, but I think I'm this close to earning myself a Bridezilla label,' she murmured.

Sergios slid her a plate of sugar-coated snacks. 'Nonsense. You have a kind heart, *mikros*. That is what I've always liked about you. But Ares is right. You have a right to see to it that your special day is exactly as you want, *ne*?'

She smiled at him, his words warming her as always. 'Okay,' she replied, and then her heart thudded harder as they both rose with her.

Together they approached the lawn where the stunning wedding arch had been constructed, the white and purple flowers she'd settled on expertly woven into the trellis. She'd known the end result would be any bride's dream. And even if she wasn't *the* dreamy bride, she couldn't stop her heart fluttering at the knowledge that she was about to marry Ares Zanelis, the man of her deepest fantasies.

After which she'd be just a brood mare, forced to accept the trappings of marriage so Ares could ensure his bloodline and please his father.

'It all looks perfect,' she said, despite the vice tightening in her chest. She tagged on a smile for Sergios's sake. Ares, she ignored, not risking a glance his way in case he caught her anguish.

Forcing herself to eat a few bites of the refreshments, she allowed the conversation between the two men to wash over her.

The reappearance of the housekeeper brought a hidden sigh of relief.

'Demeter will show you to our suite,' Ares told her. 'We'll have dinner early tonight.'

Her eyes widened at the *'our'*, but she couldn't ask the question bubbling on her tongue. His pointed look answered her anyway. They would be sharing sleeping space for the foreseeable future. At the very least until he'd planted his seed in her womb.

She turned away, hoping he didn't see her flush at the thought.

It turned out she needn't have been so disturbed by the prospect of sharing a bed with Ares. The suite was vast, and as she followed Demeter into the sprawling space she realised there were *two* bedrooms, linked by a sumptuous private living area, a wraparound terrace and even a plunge pool that could easily accommodate a dozen people.

It was easy enough to identify Ares's domain from the bold slate-grey and white colour scheme. And as Demeter showed her to where her things had been unpacked and neatly placed in the white and soft lilac themed dressing room that matched the second bedroom, she told herself that the hollow feeling in her belly had nothing to with the anti-climax of realising she wouldn't be sharing a bed with Ares immediately.

That it was merely relief…

Starting as she meant to carry on, Odessa latched on to one excuse after another for the next twelve hours.

When Ares didn't show up for dinner, a twinkly-eyed Sergios eagerly cited the fact that his son had decided to honour the tradition of not seeing his bride the night before the wedding.

Then, in the morning, she excused the butterflies in her belly as indigestion rather than pre-wedding jitters.

Even the tears that filled her eyes when the wedding couturier inserted the last diamond hairpin into the elaborate up-do, set the stylish veil on her head and finally allowed Odessa to catch the first glimpse of herself in her bridal gown, she excused as over-tiredness and the fraught situation.

Not the fact that the dress was plucked straight out of her dreams and had made her heart leap the first time she'd spotted it, its halter-neck silk overlaid with delicate lace that cinched in at the waist, moulded her hips and flared slightly at the knees to end in a short train.

Not the fact that underneath it she wore her mother's locket and couldn't help but yearn for her presence today.

And most definitely *not* the fact that the man whose name she would be taking an hour from now continued to be the only man her conscious and subconscious continued to conjure up every time she dared to dwell on who her ideal husband and the father of her children would be.

All that denial threatened to bubble over and explode when, finally ready, she stepped out of the suite and found Sergios waiting, looking nervous and hopeful and so endearing in his tuxedo, with a rosette of the same tiny flowers that were woven into her bouquet and hair inserted into his lapel.

His gaze swept over her, and Odessa was almost certain he blinked back tears.

Before she could speak, he grasped her hands. 'I know this isn't tradition, but it would be my honour to escort you down the aisle—if you'll let me?'

Odessa swallowed a lump in her throat. 'Are…are you sure?'

He squeezed her fingers, his voice gruff as he said, '*Ne, mikros.* Very much.'

Pressing her lips together to stop emotion bubbling free, and wishing her own father had taken a single leaf out of this man's book when he'd been alive, she smiled shakily. 'Thank you.'

That shakiness continued as they went down the stairs to the hall, to be flanked by smiling household staff, organisers and wait-staff, who murmured genial wishes, and then outside to join the small but impressive gathering of people she didn't know, invited by Ares to witness his marriage.

Then every scrap of her attention was captured by the man who stood beneath the immaculate arch, his complete focus riveted on her, with not a single sign of the nerves eating her alive on his face.

He wore a bespoke slate grey suit, its lines falling on his form with mouth-watering perfection.

His gaze flicked to his father for a nanosecond, a potent look passing between them before those eyes returned to her. Locked.

It was almost as if she was all he could see. All he wanted to see.

Under other fantastical circumstances Odessa might have allowed herself to be swept away into sheer bliss by that look. But she knew what it meant. It was a look of pure conquest. She'd handed herself over on a platter and he intended to devour every last piece of her.

When they finally reached the top of the aisle, father and son exchanged another long, speaking look, which was topped off with an approving nod from Sergios.

Then Ares was facing her, grasping the hands his father had just released, raising the one bearing his dazzling engagement ring to his lips.

The resulting electricity only added to the fireworks occurring within her, and again Odessa had to caution herself that it was all for show—the same as when he raked her with a heated gaze and murmured throatily, 'You look exquisite, *eros mou*,' in a way that made the priest smile and nod, thoroughly ignorant and approving the compliment.

She tried not to let those fanciful fireworks consume her as they repeated the vows that would bind them together. She scrambled for pragmatism when afterwards they walked back down the white-carpeted aisle and into the marquee overlooking the ocean where their reception was to be held. It was decorated with lavish ice sculptures, and priceless caviar and vintage champagne flowed.

And she clawed that pragmatism especially close when Ares took her in his arms, possessiveness blazing in his eyes and running through the body that he pulled dizzyingly tight against her as they swayed in their first dance.

'Once again I find myself wishing time and everyone away,' he murmured in her ear, and the twist of his mouth in an attempt at humour was immediately eroded by the heated purpose in his eyes.

'Because you want this to be over as quickly as possible?' she ventured, even while the see-sawing in her belly made a mockery of that flippant response.

The heat intensified. 'On the contrary... When we're finally alone I'll wish for time to stand still, so I can savour the moment.'

The thick layers of anticipation and exultation were hard to dismiss when they ruffled her own unsettled emotions so expertly.

'Gloating is a sin,' she told him. 'You know that, right?'

His flawless teeth flashed in unabashed elation as he pressed her closer still, his breath brushing her cheek as he said, 'I welcome the punishment. Because nothing and no one will stop me from savouring every inch of you, *matia mou*. As much as I have wished to deny it, I can't help but accept that I've waited a long time for this moment. And make no mistake: I mean to take it.'

There was nothing to say to that, even if she'd managed to speak above the traitorous currents rushing through her while she battled for her heart to remain above this erotic and emotional fray.

The battle continued as Ares handed her over to his father for the next dance, and as they were toasted and showered with gifts from well-wishers. And then, once Ares had draped a flawless diamond bracelet on her wrist, and drawn the requisite gasps from their guests, he was swinging her into his arms and striding off with her to raucous applause.

He didn't stop until he'd crossed the threshold into his... *their*...suite.

When she glanced longingly at her side of the room, he intercepted the look and shook his head. 'Oh, no. You won't be returning there for quite some time,' he rasped in her ear.

Her foundations had grown shaky, but she still fought on. 'Can we talk about this?'

'No. The time for talking is over. Accept it. Unless you mean to go back on your word?' he dared, his eyes blazing into hers.

Hating him a little, for knowing the exact buttons to push, she raised her chin. 'Never.'

The slightest tinge of relief in his eyes was wiped away by triumph as he strode up to the bed, then slid her down to her feet. She couldn't fail to notice the hard, screamingly male angles of his body, or easily dismiss their effect on her.

Nor could she fail to take in how imposing his king-sized bed was up close. She'd only looked at it briefly when Demeter had escorted her to her room yesterday. Now, the waist-high mattress festooned with pillows and sleek sheets evoked images that sent pulses of fire though her veins, burning her from the inside out.

But while she was dying with nerves at the thought of the unknown—because she'd only done this once before, in a furtive, shamefully unremarkable three-minute fumble that had left her mourning the gift she'd so carelessly thrown away—Ares was simply…watching her.

As if now he had her he wanted to stretch out the inevitable.

Well, she didn't.

In a blind need to stop the rollercoaster, she reached for the diamond bracelet he'd gifted her just an hour ago.

His hand flashed out, stopped her. 'No. Leave that on. In fact…'

He caught her wrist and tugged her after him towards a painting she suspected would more than hold its own at the Uffizi.

'What are you doing?' she asked, when he pressed a hidden button and the painting sprang a couple of inches away from the wall.

Behind it she saw a state-of-the-art safe, inserted into the wall. With a thumbprint and a swiftly entered code, the thick door popped open. Ares released her long enough to pull out two pouches and a large oblong box that screamed more priceless jewellery.

She was proved right when, after sliding his hand around her waist and nudging her to the bed, he upended the contents of all three, leaving her wide eyed, mouth agape.

'Indulging another fantasy. What else?' he answered her belatedly.

'A fantasy?' she echoed, part of her not wanting to know what that might have been because it would make what was happening so much more unbearable.

His gaze turned a touch heavy, almost contemplative. 'I left Alghero with little above a pittance in my pocket, but with big ambitions and perhaps foolish dreams.' He shrugged. 'One of those was to drape you in diamonds at the very first opportunity,' he rasped.

Pain stung her heart. 'But you left without telling me—'

He pressed his fingers to her lips and his jaw clenched a touch before he released it.

'I don't wish to start this with disharmony. Turn around,' he instructed.

She complied—partly because she wanted a reprieve from the intensity in his eyes. But the touch of his fingers at her nape, brushing her bare skin as he freed the silk-covered buttons one by one, was torture in itself.

The dress pooled at her feet, leaving her clad in only a pair of white lace panties that barely covered the lower half of her butt cheeks.

Ares inhaled sharply and she felt the agitated rise and fall of his chest, felt her skin burning with the ferocity of his regard.

'*Thee mou.* You are Aphrodite herself,' he breathed, a moment before firm hands gripped her waist and tugged her back against the hot pillar of his body.

It was her turn to lose her breath. The sensation of being plastered against him was so searing, and so divine, a moan escaped before she could stop herself.

He caressed her waist for several seconds, then leaned past her and plucked the first gem set off the bed. The cold touch of a platinum chain puckered her nipples and beaded her skin. She glanced down, her eyes widening at the sight of a diamond-studded body chain, at the centre of which hung a shorter pendant chain that ended in a thumb-sized teardrop diamond.

She was so busy being awestruck at this very personal, very erotic piece of jewellery, she didn't notice her panties were halfway down her thighs until Ares lifted her free of them.

Blushing, she drew her hands up to shield herself.

He caught her wrists and firmly drew them away, then turned her around. 'No, *yineka mou*. Your breathtaking body was made to wear priceless diamonds,' he muttered thickly, and then his gaze roved her body, his breathing turning harsher as he took in her naked diamond-ornamented form. 'You are even better than I dreamt you'd be.'

Before she could even begin to grasp the fact that he'd dreamed of this, he was continuing, almost to himself.

'Perhaps I should commission more of these…'

'Please don't.'

His head reared up, eyebrows rising. 'Why not? Most women would—'

She snatched her hands from his, blind and hot jealousy punching her in the chest. 'I'm not "most women". I think the earlier we establish that, the better it will be for both of us.'

He leaned forward, brushed the tip of her nose with his, then inhaled deeply. For whatever reason, the move immediately calmed her roiling emotions.

'*Ne*, you're right. You're my wife. And as such you hold a special place.'

Somewhat mollified, she bit her tongue against further protests. She'd learned a long time ago that an intransigent Ares was as immovable as Vesuvius.

'I will have one made for here...' He trailed the fingers of both hands over her clavicle, then down between her breasts to the upper curve of her waist. 'And then another to pay homage to this glorious piece of heaven.'

His arms circled under her waist to her bottom, grabbing both globes in his hands before he let loose a deep, throaty groan.

'Ares...'

'I'm in two minds about how to decorate these, though...'

He dipped his head, flicked his tongue over one nipple, then sealed his hot mouth over it. Heated arrows shot between her legs, stinging and dampening her core with such sweet pleasure she cried out, her hands darting up to grab his shoulders before her weakened knees gave way.

'*Dio*...please.' A full-body tremor shook through her.

'Please what, *matia mou*?' he muttered, his tongue still shamelessly lapping at her painfully aroused buds.

She convulsed, her nails digging into him. 'You...you don't need to torture me. You already have what you want.'

'And what's that?' he asked, with a hint of tightness in his tone.

'Me. You have me. Can't that be enough?'

He straightened, replaced his mouth with his hands, and moulded her breasts as he took his time to consider that.

'No. Not until my seed is fully implanted and growing in your womb. Then I may consider this thing halfway to being successful.'

With that, he nudged her firmly backwards, watched her tumble onto the bed with triumph blazing in his eyes. Then he was prowling over her, dragging her up until she lay there, displayed like the sacrifice he fully meant her to be, in the middle of his bed.

He reared back then, settling on his knees and tugging off his jacket. He watched her with fixated intensity. Tossing it away, he undid several shirt buttons, then ditched his undressing and grabbed the next piece of jewellery.

An anklet.

Shamefully aroused, Odessa watched him tug one of her legs up. One large hand circled her ankle, brought her leg up to rest her foot against his bare chest, while the other trailed the delicate anklet which bore the same yellow teardrop diamond as its centrepiece up her inner thigh.

Shivers racked her body, drawing a wicked smile to his arousal-etched face. 'You're so intoxicatingly responsive…' he rasped thickly.

After securing the piece, he raised her foot, dropped a kiss on her instep, then slowly widened her legs until her core was bare to his rabid gaze.

Until he couldn't miss how wet, how thoroughly turned on she was.

'I've waited a long time for this,' he breathed. There was a heavy vein of satisfaction in his voice, but also a sliver of bittersweetness to his confession.

'You don't sound happy about it.'

'As much as the end result is satisfactory, if I'd had my way it would've happened much sooner.'

Her heart lurched. She opened her mouth—to say what, exactly, she wasn't sure. It wasn't to apologise again. At this point Odessa deemed she'd served whatever penance she deserved for her actions on her eighteenth birthday.

As much as it hurt, the ball was in Ares's court.

His thumb slid a little roughly, insistent, over her mouth from top to bottom, then along her lower lip. His breathing intensified as she parted her lips, her body surging into stinging life as he explored her with the avidity of pirates exploring their loot.

For the longest time they simply existed in that thickened

bubble of sensate touch, their breaths mingling as arousal mounted.

'Suck,' he ordered gruffly, sliding his thumb tightly between her lips.

She closed her lips immediately, her nipples peaking and a soft moan floating up from her throat at the dirty, sublime sensation.

'*Theos...*' he cursed, voice hoarse, eyes so dark they were almost black.

Odessa's face flamed as triumph blazed in his eyes, unable to look away as he undid his belt and tugged down his zipper. Then—again as if he couldn't help himself—he abandoned his undressing and trailed his fingers down her body from throat to midriff, to circle her belly button before slowing his caress to pause where the diamond lay against her mound. His eyes rising to lock on hers, he slipped his fingers lower, lower, until his hand completely covered her femininity.

'Mine.'

Primal. Raw. *Absolute.*

Her every nerve-ending shuddered at this visceral possessiveness.

'Say it,' he insisted.

'Y-yours,' she whispered, drowning in sensation.

Sliding his thumb out of her mouth, he dropped forward and then onto one elbow, hazel eyes still locked on hers, his fingers between her thighs.

He caressed her while slowly plucking the pins out of her hair. The diamond fasteners scattered onto the bed, each one glinting and sparkling as her restless body moved under his expert ministrations. And even as he took his time to spread her hair all over his pillow, whispering sensual Greek words in her ear, the fingers between her thighs moved faster, strumming that nerve-filled nub and driving her to the pinnacle of insanity.

Odessa's cries grew louder as sensation built and built and

built. As the tension gripping her body reached fever-pitch and she had no choice but to dig her fingers into his thick biceps, to hold on as heady and terrifying bliss rushed at her.

'Ne...' he encouraged, his fingers spearing into her hair to hold her still, to direct her gaze to his, before he commanded huskily, 'Give it up, Odessa. Come for me. *Now.*'

Pleasure annihilated her, and it was made more electrifying by his rapt absorption in her every reaction, the way he hungrily devoured her surrender, then fused his lips to hers as her climax abated.

Her breathing was still worryingly agitated when she felt him rise, his fingers leaving her. It made her want to protest. But she knew he wasn't done with her. And that mortifying need for more turned her head, let her watch him as he finally shook off his remaining clothes.

Ares in his early twenties had been breathtaking. A decade later, with time and intelligence and maturity thrown into the mix, his raw masculinity was utterly enthralling.

'You like what you see?' he asked, his hands braced on his hips, positively entrenched in his confidence and unabashed about his impressive erection.

Heat suffused her face, drawing low, deep laughter from him as she dragged her gaze away.

'It's okay...you don't need to answer. I can tell for myself.'

Her eyes flew to his and he held them for a moment before staring blatantly at her peaked nipples and her twisting thighs. As much as she wanted to deny her body's reaction, it was no use. He knew how overwhelmingly he affected her. What was the point in hiding it?

She forced herself to relax her limbs, felt her own confidence growing when she saw her effect on him. It was a good time to be reminded that back then he'd seemed captivated by her. Not as much as she'd been by him, but enough for her to accept that perhaps, all these years later, this thing wasn't one-sided.

After all, would he still be so incensed about that kiss on her eighteenth birthday if he didn't care?

Buoyed by the reminder, she raised her hands and raked her fingers through her hair, pushing it away from her sweat-sheened skin.

Fierce dark eyes followed the movement, and then she watched him swallow. Watched him jerk forward onto the bed, as if compelled by a power beyond him, to resume his position between her thighs.

Her confidence threatened to falter then. Because he was big. Overwhelming. Once again she was so focused on him that he was all she could see. All she could *feel*.

And when he took her mouth in a bold kiss, he was all she could taste.

The kiss was decadent. Control-wrecking.

The slide of his hand down the same path it had taken a handful of minutes ago reignited barely banked flames. Higher. More ferocious.

His hair-roughened thighs parted her smooth ones...

And there, among the priceless diamonds, the greedy grasping and sliding of flesh, the devilishly sublime feasting and quickly snatched breaths, Ares Zanelis finally possessed the forbidden princess he'd coveted for far too long and against all logical reasoning.

He basked in her smooth, silkiness. Exulted in her hitched breath as he entered her for the first time and her sublime, warm, *tight* sheath momentarily addled his brain before a deep breath restored a fraction of his mental prowess.

It was enough for him to luxuriate in her hungry cries, her broken demands for *more* and then for mercy. To watch her glorious mane ripple on his sheets in the way he'd yearned to see for so long. To watch his diamonds glitter on her skin the way he'd vowed they would an aeon ago, battling for supremacy against her sublime beauty and failing to outshine Odessa Santella...

No, Odessa Zanelis.

And even in this, Ares smugly concluded, his name sounded better alongside hers.

Wherever you are in hell, old man, I hope this makes you burn faster.

He drove harder into her, roared when she screamed his name and clung to him as if he were the last raft in a world-ending tempest. Then he held on, by a very thin thread, as she tumbled once again into a shattering climax around him.

He let go too, then, allowing utter mindlessness to consume him completely, knowing that while the reprieve was welcome—greedily embraced, even—the gnawing, obscene hunger that continued to grow within him would still be waiting once this victory was absorbed.

That perhaps it would even be worse.

Because he was beginning to accept that things between him and Odessa might not be as cut and dried as he'd intended...

CHAPTER SIX

'KALIMERA.'

The voice was close. Low and husky enough to draw from her a shiver, then rain down on every scintillating memory from last night and the early hours of this morning.

'You can pretend to be asleep, but your body betrays you,' Ares rasped.

A very unladylike curse spilled from Odessa's lips before she could stop it, drawing mocking laughter from the man whose arm circled her waist, pinning her in place.

'Good morning,' she said, cringing a little when her voice emerged far too husky.

Feeling heat rising into her cheeks, she pressed her face deeper into the pillow.

'Do you plan on ignoring me for ever?' he asked, just before his lips trailed down the shell of her ear.

Her shrug was a vain attempt at pretending she was unaffected, when deep inside her body was already rousing, melting for him.

'You'll have to excuse me. I'm not used to the morning-after thing.'

She wasn't sure what she expected when she chanced a furtive glance at him. It certainly wasn't for his humour to vanish...for his nostrils to flare in blatant displeasure.

She opened her mouth to do something stupid, like ask him what was wrong, but Ares was already moving. She hated it that she immediately grew cold, craving his warmth.

Dragging the sheet up to her neck, she sat up.

He stood at the side of the bed, his narrow-eyed stare fixed on her.

'What have I done now?' she blurted.

He seemed reluctant to voice his thoughts, the rise and fall of his chest quickening as he stared at her. 'Tell me that idiot wasn't your first,' he grated out, hot Greek temper leaping wildly in his hazel eyes.

'You'll have to be specific. You seem to believe any man I interact with who isn't you or your father is an idiot or a bastard.'

'I only go on the evidence I'm presented with,' he said haughtily.

A shadow of amusement lightened his eyes. Then they hardened again into condemnation almost immediately, at whatever he was thinking.

'I mean Paolo Romani—that fool I saw you kissing on your eighteenth birthday. The man your father had been taunting me with for months.'

The reminder chilled her further. 'You saw everything?'

Her first mistake had been to throw herself at Paolo Romani in desperation. Little had she known that it had all been cleverly orchestrated by her father—that Paolo had been a willing participant in setting her up so that Ares would witness it. By the time she'd come to her senses, Ares was gone.

His features hardened further, his eyes no longer amused. 'I saw enough,' he breathed. 'You should thank your lucky stars that my father counselled restraint. I would've ripped you from his arms, then throttled you both.'

It explained a few things—although she suspected Ares hadn't seen the last part when, horrified with herself, she'd pushed Paolo away, then fought even harder when he'd pinned her against the wall. Labelled her a tease. It had necessitated her knee to his groin before she'd been able to make her escape.

More than discovering that Ares had seen that error of

judgement, born solely out of desperate loneliness, confusion and defiance, it was knowing that his father had witnessed her behaviour too that made her cringe. 'Ares—'

'Did you enjoy it? Did he make you feel the way I do? The way I did back then?'

His words were like shards of glass, slashing at her to dig out secrets. Exposing truths she couldn't hide.

'No.'

His eyes narrowed, his body tight with tension. 'Don't lie to me.'

She laughed, the grating sound searing her throat raw. 'Trust me, I wish I could say differently. That it was the best kiss of my life. Then I wouldn't have hated you—and myself—so much.'

His gaze dropped to her mouth, then dashed back up to her eyes. 'He didn't hurt you, did he?'

Not at first.

'He was tepid. Boring.'

He wasn't you.

She didn't add that because, *Dio mio*, she'd exposed far too much of herself already.

'Well, one thing you're not when you're with me is bored, *ne*?'

His tone reeked of masculine arrogance. She hated the fact that it was well-earned. That he made every cell in her body shriek with excitement, breathless anticipation, and the feeling of living on the edge that adrenaline junkies craved.

It was almost addictive…in a way that made her fear for her emotions. Because it turned out neither time nor distance had shifted the gravity of how he made her feel. How eagerly she anticipated their interactions. How he drove her so effortlessly to the limits of emotion, then kept her poised there, in that heady space between despair and elation.

Odessa wished she could hate him for it, but the naked truth was that Ares Zanelis made her feel like nothing and nobody else had in her entire life.

'Can we be done with this? You have your answers. The kiss was boring. Romani wasn't my first. My first time, when it happened, was uneventful. I'm here now, with you. As you want. You should be happy.'

He wasn't happy.

Ares despised the unsettled sensations coursing through him two weeks after that far too exposing morning-after conversation. He'd let inconsequential demons get the better of him, and the enlightening recounting of her eighteenth birthday had taunted him with what he'd been denied.

Denied then, but fully enjoyed now, he tried reminding himself.

Why couldn't he be satisfied that the useless usurper Paolo Romani—the man Elio Santella had taunted him with—hadn't succeeded either. That, if anything, he—Ares—was the victor now? Why was he still disgruntled?

Because it felt hollow?

He'd put a ring on her. He'd strapped her down for the next five years, at least. So...*why*?

Because, as always with this woman, he craved *more*.

They'd settled into a routine in the fortnight since their wedding. He could run his empire from anywhere in the world, except on the rare occasion a face-to-face meeting was necessary. Leaving Odessa and his father on Ismene suited him just fine when he had to go away. And, yes, it helped that his new wife had taken an obvious liking to his island.

Also optimal was her eager welcome for him when they went to bed. He was nowhere near sating his hunger for her—which, again, was a good thing, since there was an end goal to all that sex.

What didn't satisfy him at all was that he'd been gone only

forty-eight hours and his very skin jumped with need, like an addict denied a vital narcotic.

He rose from the seat on his plane, his restless gaze returning to his watch once more—as if he hadn't been checking every few minutes since he'd left London. He stopped pacing when an attendant approached.

'Can I get you anything, Kyrios Zanelis?'

'No, but you can find out how long before we land?'

'Of course, sir.' She returned in a minute. 'We'll land in fifty minutes.'

Fifty minutes. Then he could wrap her in his arms once more. Ensure the process of getting her pregnant was progressing smoothly.

Is that all?

Yes!

Nothing else mattered but that goal.

Except fifty-five minutes later his arms were empty and a clutch of dread lurked far too close to his heart.

'They've what?' he snapped at his housekeeper.

Demeter eyed him steadily, looking irritated, with her hands propped on her wide hips, her head tilted as if questioning his hearing.

'They took the car out half an hour ago. Kyrios Sergios said they were exploring the island.'

'The car. Not the buggy? Are you sure? Who was driving?' he snapped, dreading the answer.

Sergios had grudgingly given up driving because of his arthritis, but Ares knew he missed it dearly. If his father had talked his wife into taking out his sports car on unfamiliar roads...

'Was it Odessa?'

He was sure Demeter mentally rolled her eyes.

'Ne,' she confirmed.

'But she doesn't drive,' he replied, and even before a response was out of her mouth he was reversing his direction towards the front door and going to the garage where the sports car he rarely used should be.

It was a ridiculous idea to have a car on the island, but he'd given in to his father's passion for engines. And on the rare occasions when they transferred the car to his yacht and went to Mykonos or Santorini he enjoyed driving the streets with Sergios.

But there were strict rules to those arrangements.

He cursed under his breath as he stood staring at the empty space. Plucking his phone out of his pocket, he started to dial— just as the sound of a powerful engine reached him.

He whirled in time to see the yellow Spyder cresting the hill half a mile away, then zipping forward.

Thee mou, she was driving too fast.

Ares's legs propelled him down the driveway, so he could get a better view. So he could be driven out of his mind as he watched it jerk, then stall, before shooting forward once again.

His grip tightened around the phone, his heart in his throat. If anything happened to her…to them…

The urge to call out and tell her to stop the car immediately hurtled through him. But what if that distracted her? A cold shiver scrambled over his nape and for the next four minutes he stood stock still, watching the yellow speck grow larger until it appeared at the bottom of the driveway.

Then it stalled again, and he winced, feeling his teeth on edge as he heard the grinding gears. The car jerked once more, then sped up again, before coming to a screeching halt a dozen feet from where he stood.

Both occupants were grinning—but their expressions altered when they saw him.

Kalos.

He stalked towards her before the engine was turned off. 'What the hell do you think you're doing?'

'Hello to you, too,' she snapped back.

Ares refused to admit how good she looked behind the

wheel. How good she looked, full stop. The Greek sun clearly agreed with her, and her tanned skin set off her startlingly beautiful eyes.

'I asked you a question,' he grated, residual terror unwilling to release its stranglehold on him just yet, even as other parts of his body reacted to the sight and heavenly smell of her.

'We went for a drive.' Her tone suggested she was stating the obvious.

He glanced at his father, his eyes narrowing when he saw amusement in his eyes. 'It's not funny,' he snapped at the old man in Greek.

Sergios raised both hands in mock surrender, then dropped a quick kiss on Odessa's temple before stepping out of the vehicle and making himself scarce.

'Is that scowl supposed to scare me?' she demanded.

He flicked at the button that elevated the gull wing door and held out his hand. 'Keys.'

She tossed them over with a glare.

'Get out. We'll talk about this inside.'

Her lips pursed, but she didn't respond when he caught her arm and led her indoors. His study was the closest room and he made a beeline for it, slamming the door behind him despite his attempts to control his temper.

He watched her take a seat on the sofa before the tall fireplace, crossing her long legs and watching him with a composure he faintly resented as his senses leapt with the pounding reality of how much he'd missed her. How much even the thought of her being a little bit hurt had sent terror hurtling through him.

And he accepted that this situation was far from ideal.

Odessa watched him pace for a full minute. Then stop dead before her.

'Do you even have a licence?' he demanded. 'If I recall,

your father forbade you from going near the garage. Women aren't supposed to drive, according to him, no?'

She flushed, the scorching reminder tightening her chest.

It was one of the many ways her father had limited her and kept her firmly under his thumb, before suddenly allowing her—in a rare display of magnanimity—to take lessons. Although he'd scoffed at the idea several times before her determination had finally worn him down.

'I do, actually,' she said, secretly pleased when she saw Ares's surprised look.

'And how many times have you driven yourself?' he tossed back.

She shrugged, self-consciousness dragging embarrassment through her. 'A few...'

'A *few*?' he echoed derisively. 'And how many of those "few" times included a vehicle with an actual engine and not the electric buggy you used to get around your father's estate?'

Irritation made her exhale sharply. 'Antonio let me drive his car to the shops once in a while.'

When her father hadn't been around.

'You mean Antonio the gardener, in his jalopy that barely went over twenty miles an hour before it threatens to shake itself into extinction?'

'What's your point, Ares? You don't want me to touch your precious sports car? Trust me, I've got that message. Or is it something else?'

'Something else?' he echoed coldly.

'You don't want me getting close to your father?'

Her heart squeezed as she said it. In a very short time she'd been reminded of Sergios Zanelis' inherent goodness and kindness, and in the last two weeks she'd found herself seeking his company, her yearning for the kind of father she'd never had alternately intensifying and being sated by the old man.

The thought that Ares might resent that sent a shaft of pain through her.

He sucked in deep, pent-up breath and she got the feeling he was trying to hold himself together. Why that both riled and excited her, she didn't want to delve into.

'Odessa, that car has more horsepower than a small plane. One mistake and you could've been...' He paused again, his eyes darkening as whatever thought he'd been about to express turned inward. 'Things could've gone very badly.'

A small gasp left her throat as she grasped his meaning. Shame engulfed her. 'I'm sorry, Ares. It didn't occur to me... I didn't think about your accident... Sergios was talking about how much he missed driving and I offered to take him. I should've—'

He jerked forward. 'I'm not talking about my father!'

This close, she saw his ashen pallor. Her heart leapt in wild giddiness. 'You were worried about *me*?' she whispered, stunned.

His irritation vanished with an exhalation. 'Does that surprise you so much?'

'Well...a little bit, yes.'

Something flashed in his eyes. Something like...hurt. It was gone in a second, of course, but she'd seen it and her heart lurched.

'Ares...'

'Your health and safety aren't to be compromised under any circumstances. That's non-negotiable.'

Non-negotiable. Like their agreement.

Of course. His concern wasn't over *her*, but the possible child she might be carrying. The whole reason she was here in the first place.

'I didn't mean to jeopardise my position as your brood mare,' she threw out, anguish tinging her voice with acid. 'But I won't be wrapped in cotton wool, so you're going to have to accept that.'

He stiffened, but that flare of emotion in his eyes lingered, making her wonder if she'd read him wrong.

'Strike a balance between those two extremes and we won't need to have this conversation again,' he said. 'That includes taking out a supercar you can barely drive around an island with sharp bends and dangerous cliffs. Is that clear?'

It was maddeningly reasonable. She didn't agree immediately, because she wanted to keep fighting. She was still looking for a sign that he saw her as more than just the incubator contracted to carry his children.

'Odessa…?'

'Yes, Ares. We're clear.' She rushed to her feet. 'Can I go for a swim now? Or is that too dangerous, too?'

His expression relaxed, his hard edges easing a touch. 'Not at all. I'll join you. You taking risks on the road wasn't exactly the welcome home I was hoping for. We can both do with cooling off.'

Half thinking he would insist on his baby-making rights once they were upstairs, Odessa was oddly disappointed when he strode off to his side of their suite without looking back.

They arrived at the pool to find they weren't the only ones with cooling off in mind. Sergios was reclining on one of the loungers, peering over his bifocals at a car magazine. He set it aside when they approached, a smile breaking out when his gaze rested on her.

He said something to his son in Greek.

Ares glanced at her, amusement teasing at the corners of his mouth as he responded. Sergios laughed, then replied with something that made Ares's gaze probe deeper.

Odessa headed for the lounger next to Sergios, trying not to watch Ares from the corner of her eye as he tugged off the white torso-hugging T-shirt he'd changed into.

'You do know it's rude to speak a language someone in your company doesn't understand, right?'

Ares's smile stretched in genuine humour. It was beautiful and devastating to witness, robbing her of breath.

'That should be an incentive for you to learn my language quickly.'

She attempted a frown, to conceal the whirlpool of high emotions eddying through her. 'What did you two say?'

'My father said that the Greek sun agrees with you. I concurred and said you looked beautiful.' He paused, his eyes raking her face as her colour rose. 'And you grow even more enchanting when you blush,' he added, his humour lessening as heat and another emotion she couldn't quite fathom replaced it.

She reached for her sunscreen, just for something to do instead of gaping at him, and wondered at this dichotomy of hot and cold that set her senses spinning.

But was it hot and *cold*? Or hot and raw? Hot and savage? Hot and cynical? Hot and protective of his father and the baby she might be carrying? Was he staging a clever game, with the ultimate aim of ensuring he got the best of both worlds?

The uncertainty that had dogged her since she'd arrived, and was building with each day, threatened to smother her. She wasn't even aware that the bottle was slipping from her hand until Ares jack-knifed up, catching it before it fell to the floor.

Eyeing her with frowning concern, he swung his legs to the ground, poured a glass of refreshing juice and held it out to her. 'Hydrate,' he said.

She took the glass and drank—again just for something to do while her brain spun like a leaf in a tornado. When she couldn't settle her roiling emotions she stood, then threw off the thigh-length beach kimono that matched her caramel and gold bikini.

Stingingly aware of Ares's eyes raking over her every curve, she strolled to the edge of the pool and dived in, hating herself a little for enjoying how much she liked his eyes on her. How much she'd missed his presence in the two long days he'd been away. How eagerly she anticipated—with arousal pounding within her—the thought of sharing his bed again tonight.

She had no idea whether she was pregnant or not. Her period wasn't due for another few days. A simple pregnancy test while he was away might have solved the unknown, but she'd been reluctant to set the ball rolling.

Because she feared a positive result would mean the end of her presence in his bed?

Her heart lurched as the answer screamed in her head. Surfacing, she gasped in air—then jumped when firm hands closed on her waist.

'I was concerned you would stay under for ever. Or you had turned into a mermaid,' Ares drawled.

She turned, then lost her breath all over again when the very sight of him, with drops of water glinting off his bronzed perfection, destroyed her breathing.

'So you came to rescue me?'

His teeth flashed. 'I came to demand the welcome I didn't get when I arrived home. Did you miss me?'

'Not at all,' she replied airily, ignoring the ache in her breasts and between her legs. Ignoring how utterly delicious and close his sensual lips looked. 'Your father and I kept ourselves entertained.'

His eyes darkened for a moment, then dropped to settle on her lips. 'Perhaps a reminder is necessary, hmm?'

She sucked in a breath, which made her breasts brush his chest, drawing a low groan from him.

'Ares, your father—' she started to protest weakly.

'Has dozed off.'

His legs tangled around hers, his hands pulling her closer until she was plastered against him. He lowered his head until his lips hovered tantalisingly, excruciatingly close.

'Kiss your husband, *agapitos*.'

With a helpless moan she surged forward that last fraction, pressed her lips to his, then shuddered in carnal delight when he immediately took over, sweeping his tongue over her eager lips before driving inside, tasting her with an erotic boldness

bordering on aggression. An aggression she welcomed because—sweet heaven—Ares knew how to kiss her and drive
her right out of her mind.

For long moments they kissed, deeper and deeper, with
her arms clinging to his broad shoulders so she'd stay afloat.
Against her belly his erection was imprinted urgently against
her, a solid reminder of how he felt inside her.

Just when she thought she would be reduced to shamelessly
begging for him to take her, right there in the pool, he eased
back and broke the kiss.

Burnished eyes raked her face, satisfaction darkening his
eyes at whatever he saw on hers.

'That's more like it,' he rasped. He dropped another hard,
brief kiss on her lips. 'Unless we want to risk scandalising Sergios and the staff we'll have to pick this up again later. *Ne?*'

Still caught up in a whirlpool of sensation, Odessa simply
nodded.

After a moment he released her, then swam a few laps before getting out. She knew he was watching from the lounger,
despite his fingers flying over his phone. She tried to ignore
him, swimming laps of her own in a wild bid to calm her
senses, belatedly considering that she should have stipulated
that these hot little *extras* were not part of their deal.

She hadn't. Now she was bearing the consequences.

Glancing over at him, finding his heated gaze still fixed
on her, she knew deep down that she couldn't renegotiate. He
would demand to know why. And she could hardly say she
feared for her heart, could she?

She stayed in the pool until she risked turning into a prune.
Until she breathed the tiniest sigh of relief when Ares's phone
rang. Watching him pace away, keeping his voice low in consideration of his father, made her foolish heart trip again.

She insisted she was even more relieved when he sauntered
back into the house. But she knew she was lying to herself.
She craved the sight of him far more than she could comfort-

ably admit. Knew she was nowhere near mastering how to stay aloof from Ares when she stepped out of the pool minutes later.

As she neared the lounger, she realised Sergios was awake.

He looked up, and although he attempted his customary smile, she saw a shaft of pain dart across his face. Saw the hand he was trying to flex.

'Are you okay?'

He exhaled a vexed sigh. 'My body is reminding me that I'm an old man with old hands.'

Odessa glanced at the tube of cream Ares usually used on his father. 'Have you used your lotion yet?'

He shook his head. 'My son is caught up on one of his interminable phone calls.' He eyed her, then nudged the tube towards her. 'Would you mind?'

She reached for it, then paused. 'Are you sure you don't want Ares to do it for you?'

'He's not here. You are. And yours are softer hands than his,' he teased with a smile, then laughed when she blushed. 'You're my daughter now, *mikros*.'

Her heart squeezed, both with the deep yearning that assailed her and with the ache of wishing this wasn't a carefully orchestrated marriage with an end date hanging over her head.

Unless she proved Ares wrong.

Uncapping the tube, she squeezed lotion into her palm and then, reaching for his hands, slowly massaged it into his stiff fingers. His sigh of relief made her heart melt.

'I knew you would be perfect,' he said, then tossed her a cheeky wink.

Odessa burst into laughter just as heavy footfalls approached.

Ares froze when he saw them. His fierce expression made her fingers tremble. Sergios glanced up too, either oblivious to or totally ignoring the tension as he smiled.

'You're too late. I have a new apprentice. And, *ne*, before you ask, she's doing a much better job than you.'

Ares snorted at his father, but the look he pierced her with a second later was intense. Protective and probing far too deep. Odessa wasn't surprised at all when he pulled up a chair, sat down and proceeded to scrutinise every second of her ministrations.

If it wouldn't have risked upsetting the old man, she would have asked Ares to explain that look that seemed to say he possibly approved but was deeply wary too. She would have assured him that he had nothing to fear. That she wouldn't let him down.

'*Efkharisto, mikros,*' Sergios said, startling her.

'*Parakalo*, Sergios,' she responded automatically, her thoughts still consumed by Ares.

Ares drew in a sharp breath, covered by his father's pleased laughter.

'See? She's learning our language. Very soon she will be fluent.'

'So I see,' Ares responded a little gruffly. 'We should go and get changed. Dinner will be served soon.'

Again, he didn't coerce her towards his side of the suite when they returned upstairs, and throughout dinner he remained introspective, casting her heavy-lidded looks that slowly wound up her nerves until it was a relief to be done with coffee and dessert. To escape, despite knowing she'd still be dwelling on why Ares had seemed so eager to kiss her at the pool but didn't want to insist on his conjugal rights.

Had he changed his mind in the short time he'd been gone?

Unable to bear the tension any longer, she rose. 'I'm heading upstairs. Goodnight, Sergios. I'll see you in the morning.'

Ares's gaze bored harder into her, compelling her to look at him. When she did, his eyes raked her face, his hunger blatant.

'I'll be up in an hour.'

Her heart stumbled in her chest at the thick promise in his voice. Maybe he hadn't changed his mind…

She was berating herself for how eager she was, how she

couldn't quite catch her breath because of the excitement fizzing in her veins, when he walked in.

His first words hacked that foolish excitement to pieces.

'My father is important to me, Odessa. Hurt him and you'll never know peace in this lifetime.'

Now her heart lurched for another reason, shrinking in her chest as she watched him prowl towards her. As much as it hurt to know he could think that of her, a part of her understood. She would have given her left arm to possess the kind of connection Ares and Sergios had with either of her parents. Would have protected it zealously with everything she had, the way he did with his father.

'I won't. I promise.'

Surprise flared in his eyes. His hands went to his shirt and he started to unbutton it with his gaze still fixed on her. 'You made another promise once. You broke it,' he drawled, almost reluctantly, his usual sharpness muffled. As if he wanted to wish it away but couldn't.

Maybe she could help?

She licked dry lips. 'Shall we talk about that?'

His gaze stayed on hers for a moment, before drifting down her body. 'Maybe later. Right now I'm in need of something else. Something that will guarantee our deal stays on track.'

Her nipples tightened at the raw hunger in his voice, even as her heart squeezed at his refusal to hear her out. To let her attempt to state her case for her actions all those years ago.

But he was tossing his shirt away, closing the gap between them with savage intent in his every step. And she could only draw a long, deep breath, hoping to replenish her lungs before he snatched it away. Because his hands on her body would do just that—drive her out of her mind until she didn't know whether she was coming or going.

He grasped her waist after discarding his loafers and trousers and picked her up as if she weighed nothing. A second later she was pinned against the bedroom wall, their faces a mere inch from one another as he speared her with his gleaming eyes.

'How eagerly your legs wrap around me… It's gratifying to see that in this we're on the same page.'

She hadn't even been aware she'd done it. That already her fingers were exploring his bare skin, her nails raking the hair at the back of his head, her core furnace hot and ready in anticipation of his possession.

The ease with which he derailed her thoughts and emotions fired up her spirit and her temper. She gripped a luxuriant handful of hair, tightened her hand until he gave an animalistic hiss and pressed forward, imprinting his thick erection deeper against her centre until her panties and his boxers might as well have been non-existent.

'If you don't want to hear me out, then maybe you need to stop talking and start acting.'

Her challenge fired him up, as she'd known it would.

His fingers dug into her buttocks, his eyes growing hooded as they devoured her mouth. 'Is that so? You're confident you're ready for me?'

'I know I am. In every way,' she stated bravely—even as her heart quaked and her instinct warned that there might not be much of her left by the time she came through this tempest.

That belief was scarily cemented when he thrust into her, powerful, hard and delicious, and had her screaming his name in under thirty seconds.

Then when it was all over, it had her clinging to him like a limpet, unable to let go as they tumbled into bed. And she fell asleep with her head on his chest, her heart singing, because this was *exactly* where she wanted to be.

CHAPTER SEVEN

OVER THE NEXT few days the unsettling possibility that whatever feelings she'd had for Ares in her teenage years hadn't diminished but had possibly intensified drove Odessa on restless, long walks around Ismene.

She was quietly awed by the extent of Ares's wealth, and the fact that, unlike her, he'd striven to fulfil his dreams, attaining impressive power and influence to boot.

As for his island—she accepted that she'd totally fallen in love with Ismene.

Where Alghero had been all vicious waves crashing onto craggy, dangerous black rocks and sheer cliff faces, Ismene had a few perilous bluffs and hairpin roads on the northernmost point, but was mostly white sandy beaches and a sea so calm and blue she suspected this was what heaven looked like.

She was sitting on one such bluff, enjoying the peaceful breeze in her hair, when her senses tingled. A moment later her husband's shadow fell over her.

'Odessa.'

Her head-to-toe shiver was so predictable, so damn Pavlovian, that she laughed quietly under her breath.

'Something funny?'

His low, deep voice rumbled through her. She delayed looking up into his face, into those mesmerising eyes, for several seconds, although the compulsion soon grew unbearable.

'Until a few seconds ago I was comparing this to heaven.'

Most likely tired of her not looking at him, Ares crouched down to her level and, like clockwork, her focus swung to him.

His eyes probed. As always.

'And my arrival changed that view?' he asked.

She shrugged, watched his eyes flit to her bare legs before returning to her face. 'Well, Lucifer was once an angel, if I recall correctly.'

His mouth twitched. 'Which am I? Devil or angel?'

'Both? I think if any man can achieve the impossible, it'd be you.'

His head tilted the smallest fraction. 'Explain.'

Odessa couldn't quite account for the words that flew out of her mouth next. 'I begged you to save me. You did. Then you turned the situation back on me.'

His eyes darkened, and then a moment later his nostrils flared. 'You continue to give the impression that it will be a hardship for you, *agapita.*'

Her heart shrivelled. 'At what point in our past did I give you the impression that I'd be okay with abandoning any child I gave birth to?'

A muscle throbbed at his temple. 'So you still mean to prove me wrong?' he rasped, but the probing intensified, as if her answer mattered.

'Absolutely,' she hissed fervently.

After an eternity with his eyes locked on hers, his gaze snapped to the horizon. She followed it, her heart thumping hard in her chest. Part of her wanted to push away this important but sensitive subject, but a larger part of her loathed the thought of letting it remain unconfronted, like a festering wound. And, considering the news she needed to divulge about her possible pregnancy, she needed a moment. Because it felt larger than life…soul-shaking in a way she couldn't wrap her mind around.

If she was pregnant, then her life was about to change.

And if she wasn't…

How could she be bracing herself to mourn something she

hadn't even contemplated this time last month? How could her heart be aching over the possibility that their activities hadn't reaped the desired results?

'What are you doing?'

She started, then refocused on where his gaze was locked on the sketchbook she'd brought on her walk. Heat flooded her face as his focus sharpened on her drawings.

'Nothing much. Just some doodling.'

'It looks like more than just doodling.' He held out his hand. 'May I?'

She shook her head, echoes of her father's ridicule rising in her head. 'I don't think so...'

'You think I'll mock you because others did? I'm guessing your father?'

Her chest tightened at this insight, but she didn't answer.

Nor did Ares put his hand down.

After a minute of silent battling, she reluctantly handed it over. Then drowned in mortified silence as he took his time to leaf through the two dozen pages. Just when she thought she'd die of embarrassment he raised his gaze. His expression—surprised, mildly shocked, *impressed*—choked her breath.

'You did all of this?' he asked.

'Yes,' she whispered, still not sure she wanted to hear what he'd say next. 'I know they're—'

'Seriously impressive?' he interrupted. 'Indeed.'

Her eyes widened. 'What?'

'I remember interior design was your passion.' His jaw gritted. 'Did he let you attend the college you wanted?'

He? Her father. *As if.*

'Of course he didn't,' she scoffed, and then felt a twinge for speaking ill of the dead. 'But I took some online courses on my own a few years ago.'

He nodded, his eyes still gleaming with surprise and warming respect. 'Good for you, going after what you want.'

Her heart lifted, prancing pathetically in her chest. Because she'd impressed Ares Zanelis, a multi-billionaire who owned some of the most impressive real estate in the world.

His gaze returned to the sketchbook. 'Speaking of what we want…' He handed the sketchbook back, but his gaze sharpened, drifting over to linger on her belly.

Odessa's heart lurched for a different reason, then squeezed at the thought of what she needed to divulge.

She sucked in a long, sustaining breath, her fingers tightening around the sketchbook now pressed to her chest, as if it might save or steady her.

'I don't know if I'm pregnant or not. My period didn't arrive yesterday…but I'm spotting a little today.'

The excruciatingly sluggish hours before she'd known she'd definitively missed her period had prompted a dizzying exhilaration—only to slide into horror when she'd spotted the blood. Even now, with the possibility that she might not be pregnant, Odessa clung to faint hope as she looked up at Ares.

To see hard, mercurial emotions flitting out of his face.

Bewilderment. Pride? Shock. *Fear?*

She shook her head. Perhaps she was deluding herself and it was all in her imagination.

'You're spotting, and you didn't think to mention it?'

His words emerged from a throat that was threatening to freeze up with the surfeit of emotions coursing through him. They moved too fast for any one of them to establish supremacy.

He'd delayed asking her despite his every sense clamouring to know. He knew enough about the path to conception to know the odds of it happening so soon were improbable. And yet…

The unsettled feeling he'd carried since the morning after their wedding had gone, making way for other, equally alarming sensations. Disappointment. Desolation. *Panic.*

She pulled her lips between her teeth, her silver eyes shadowing before she answered. 'It happens sometimes with my period.'

'I see.' The words emerged clipped. Controlled. A direct opposite to what was going on inside him. 'What does that mean, exactly? That it didn't happen?'

The anguish darting across her face arrowed straight into him, making him realise the depths of his own expectations. And that she was equally affected. But then her chin rose in a way that would have amused him and made him proud had he not been stewing in peculiar sensations.

'I hope I don't need to remind you that it takes two to tango. Maybe we got the timing of things wrong.'

'Easy, *agapita*. As much as I wish to vaunt my virility, I know instant pregnancy isn't guaranteed, no matter how many times we have sex.'

Her shoulders relaxed a little, but her fight remained. 'Well… I…'

'Yes? You are expecting me to jump down your throat?'

She shot another fire-tinged gaze at him and his body responded. It was a call it apparently couldn't resist, no matter the circumstances. Ares was beginning to accept—resignedly—that it was a power he might have to concede to her. *Secretly.* It wouldn't do at all to make her aware of it…

'It wouldn't be unexpected,' she said.

Her meaning was clear. Stung more than he cared for.

'It seems you need reminding once more that I'm not one of those Neanderthals who blame their shortcomings on their women.' He shook his head, dragged his fingers through his hair, trying to gain some composure. 'Or am I wasting my time with that?'

She didn't answer immediately, and something shrivelled inside him.

Did she really think him a monster? *No.* He wouldn't lower himself into comparing what he was doing with what her father had done to her. He'd given her an option for freedom, for heaven's sake! And he continued to live with the unnerving, chest-searing sensations that recollection brought. The oddly stomach-churning possibility that she might exercise that choice in a few short years, despite her insistence to the contrary.

Elio, on the other hand, had treated his own daughter like a second-class citizen. A chess-piece he could move around his power-hungry board in ways that benefited him.

He crouched down to her level once more, wrapped his hand over her nape and tipped her gaze up to meet his. 'Tell me that's not what you think of me,' he demanded, and there was sensation that felt jarringly like desperation stirring in his gut as he searched her expression.

Her lips firmed and her eyes dug into his. Searching just as hard. 'Do you care what I think of you?' she whispered.

Ne. More than he suspected was wise.

'I can wait for that verdict.' He stood, held out his hand while digging out his phone. 'Come.'

She frowned. 'Where are we going?'

'You're spotting. That doesn't mean you're not pregnant. Let's go and make sure one way or another, shall we?'

She glanced down at his hand. Then, in another impressive flare of mutiny, she shook her head. 'Not until we discuss a few things.'

Harsh laughter seared his throat. 'I'm impressed, *agapita*. You have timed it perfectly to pull a stunt like this.'

'It's not a stunt,' she flashed back, her voice husky. 'I'm fighting for what I want. Even you must respect that.'

A part of him did. If he was being truthful with himself, the fact that she'd been born into an organised crime family and yet had managed to remain morally untainted had been one of his initial draws to her. Which had made her actions back then all the harder to swallow. And in light of Elio's clear manipulation of the situation, Ares had been teetering towards absolving her.

Now, his chest tightening anew, he curled his rejected hand

into a ball and dropped it to his side. With his other, he dialled the number to summon his helicopter pilot, told him to ready the chopper for a trip to Athens.

The moment he hung up, she blurted, 'I'm not happy with granting you full custody of my child.'

An equally visceral need propelled a forceful answer from him. 'The original terms of the agreement stay. I can't risk my children going through what I did.'

She rose to her feet and brushed the sand from her dress with a grace so ingrained it was mesmerising to watch. Then she faced him, bold and unflinching.

'Ares, what your mother did to you and to Sergios was horrible. You have my word that I would never—'

'No,' he interrupted, the reminder of his lost sister and the parent responsible for everything he'd lost filling him with fury and bitterness. That Odessa would choose to bring it up…

He swallowed a growl. 'She swore too. I've seen videos of my parents together when they first married. They were ecstatic. She had stars in her eyes when she married my father and she vowed he was the love of her life.'

'Surely she didn't just change overnight?' she queried, bewildered. 'Something must have happened?'

He pursed his lips. 'My father thought she deserved the world and he wanted to give it to her.'

Odessa's eyes softened in that way they always did over his father. He was mildly jealous of it, truth be told.

'But she wasn't prepared for the long hours or his dedication to his job,' he went on. 'Nor, eventually, was she satisfied with being a chauffeur's wife, living in the shadow of all that Santella wealth.'

Recollection of the betrayal and pain he and especially his father had suffered dredged through him like spiked anchors, threatening to uproot his very soul.

'It took some time, yes, but their vows turned to ash. I watched my father bend over backwards and turn himself inside out to hang on to her. When he couldn't, he begged her to leave my sister behind. She refused. She took a helpless child she didn't really want because she knew how much it would hurt him. I can't… I will never permit that to happen to my own children.'

Mutiny etched deeper into her face and in the haunting eyes that threatened to condemn him. 'They're…they will be my children too! Doesn't that count for something?'

Hot on the heels of that unwanted trip down memory lane, the answer was dragged from his shattered soul. 'We've only just begun this journey, *agapita*. So the jury is still out.'

She reared back with a sharp exhalation, her eyes filled with anguish and fury. 'We may have just begun this journey, but you're quickly running out of road for goodwill, Ares. Keep that in mind.'

On top of the knots twisting in his stomach, he didn't appreciate the lance of guilt that impaled him.

And yet there it was, drilling deeper as she sailed past him, pale, defiant.

Condemning.

'The jury is still out.'

Odessa had no qualms about proving him wrong. And she would be damned if she'd wait five years to do so. Because as much as she'd endured in her life up till now, the reality of handing over custody of her child would completely annihilate her.

That urge to act sooner grew stronger the closer they got to Athens.

Beside her, Ares sat in brooding silence. With any other man she'd have attributed it to nerves, maybe even worry about what lay ahead of them. But he'd been steadily working on his tablet—although he'd rejected every call that had blared on his phone as the helicopter raced them towards the Greek capital.

Within an hour of landing they were in his doctor's office.

Odessa tried not to read anything into the inscrutable looks that passed between him and the doctor as she was thoroughly examined, blood samples taken. Nor did she let in hope when the doctor's seriousness lightened a fraction and Ares finally stopped pacing in the small but luxurious private room.

But by the time the doctor returned, after an excruciating half-hour, she was ready to jump out of her skin. So she didn't mind her manners when she heard the doctor address Ares in Greek.

'Tell me what's going on!'

Although she addressed the doctor, she couldn't drag her gaze off Ares, and the fact that he'd gone stock-still.

When she managed to look, she found the doctor beaming at her.

'As I suspected, the spotting is nothing to worry about. I wanted to double-check, of course, but everything is all right. Congratulations, Kyria Zanelis. You're healthily pregnant.'

She would've snapped that he could've told her that earlier, to save her going out of her mind, but the weight of his words snatched her breath and deadened her vocal cords.

She was pregnant. With Ares's child.

The child he intended to gain full control of the moment she stumbled.

Joy, panic and determination swirled like a vicious cyclone inside her as her gaze shifted to find Ares watching her with a ferocity that made every nerve in her body scream in confused, absurd exhilaration.

If she'd thought him possessive before, it was nothing compared to his expression now. It was almost as if he wanted to consume her.

She barely heard the doctor excuse himself. Her entire focus remained on Ares as he slowly prowled towards her, then stood examining her face for a moment before he slowly, inexorably, speared his fingers into her hair.

One hand cupped her jaw, angled her face up to his, while

the other drifted down between her breasts, past her midriff to settle low on her belly, over the womb now cradling his seed.

'Mine,' he breathed.

She wanted to tell him he'd said that before, but it sounded flippant in the face of the seismic, life-altering reality unfolding between them.

'Ours,' she insisted, feeling that feral need to stake an equal claim on her child.

His nostrils flared and the possessive blaze in his eyes intensified. Odessa didn't back down. This was the most important battle of her life. And even as the warmth from his hand seeped into her belly, triggering a wild need to lean into his hold, their gazes continued to clash.

When he drew away she bit back a whimper, the loss of warmth so acute she shivered.

He saw the reaction, his eyes speculative.

Before he could probe that telling weakness, she turned away and snatched up the bag. 'Are we going back to Ismene?'

'Didn't you hear the doctor? He'd like us to stick around for a day or two, to make sure the spotting doesn't return. I also have some business to take care of in Athens.'

She shrugged. 'I was too busy watching your Neanderthal instincts attempting to consume you.'

For whatever reason, that produced a glimmer of amusement. 'And? Did they succeed?'

'That remains to be seen.' She glanced outside, to the sun-dazzled vista of Athens in the autumn sunshine. 'Are you going to growl at me if I say I want to take a walk out in the sunshine? Enjoy some of this hard-won freedom I've earned for myself?' she challenged.

Something stirred in his eyes. Want? A quiet clamour?

'I was going to suggest lunch. With me.'

The need to say yes was shockingly visceral. As was the caution not to give in to the insane urge to inhabit his orbit.

'I don't think I could eat anything just yet.'

Not until she'd digested the news that she was carrying a child.

Dio mio, she was going to be a mother.

She gasped when his hand's warmth returned to her belly, and he didn't try to hide the peculiar expression moving over his face.

'I don't want you getting heatstroke, so just one hour outside. Then the driver will take you home, and you will eat something, then rest. *Ne?*' he offered gruffly.

Odessa swallowed the emotions clogging her throat. *'Ne.'*

His eyes darkened dramatically, his gaze dropping to the mouth she'd used to answer in his own language. But perhaps she imagined the rough sound he made under his breath, because in the next moment he was grasping her hand, leading her out of the private clinic and into the back of the luxury SUV. Crisp instructions were issued to the driver, who nodded.

Fifteen minutes later they pulled to a stop outside a sleek six-storey building with a discreet Cyrillic 'Z' sign in silver at the top.

Ares's headquarters.

His gaze rested on her for an age before he said, 'Enjoy your walk. I'll see you at dinner.'

The moment he stepped out, Odessa wanted to call him back, to say she'd changed her mind about lunch with him. She pressed her lips together to stop exposing herself so completely, watching as his tall, imposing stride carried him away, several heads turning as his magnetism drew lesser beings to marvel at the god walking among them.

The vehicle pulled away and she found her own hand replacing Ares's on her stomach, awe tunnelling through a kaleidoscope of emotions. In less than nine short months she would be responsible for a baby. Would need to nurture it in a way she hadn't been nurtured. A way her mother hadn't been allowed to care for her because of her father's unreasonable archaic notion that a daughter was useless to him.

Odessa felt calmer knowing that, whatever its gender, Ares would do right by their child. His relationship with his father set her own heart at ease in that respect.

But not the fact that he prejudged her ability to be a good mother.

Was he right?

She pushed the idea away, desperately quashing the pain that pushed into her chest. She would move mountains to ensure her baby's happiness.

'Where do you wish to go, Kyria Zanelis?'

The driver's question cut through the raucous jumble of her emotions. Taking a deep breath, she glanced out of the window. One god currently dominated her life. If she didn't stand to lose so damn much Odessa suspected she would give in a fraction. Okay, maybe more than a fraction. She was woman enough to admit to herself that she enjoyed Ares's earthy brand of domination.

But not with the stakes this high.

Noticing that the driver was still awaiting her response, she forced a smile. 'I want to play tourist for a while. Then maybe find a park?'

He nodded. 'Of course.'

Traffic slowed their journey, but it was worth it when they reached the Temple of Athena Nike. Even more jaw-dropping was finding Ares there, leaning against a powerful, gleaming black motorbike, his suit swapped for hip-hugging jeans, T-shirt and black leather jacket.

Every feminine nerve sprang to attention. 'I only just left you…what are you doing here?' she asked as she stepped out.

He shrugged. 'I've decided I'm a much better tour guide.'

She rolled her eyes at his sheer arrogance, while her insides strummed with unfettered delight. 'I thought you had work to do?'

He waved it away. 'My meetings can wait.'

He handed the driver the bike's keys in exchange for the

SUV's and for the next hour proved his claim, offering titbits of history and salacious gossip she knew she'd never read in any history book. And because he was Ares Zanelis, he naturally had exclusive access at every monument, heightening an already unforgettable experience. And through it all he held her hand, drifted his fingers down her arm to direct her attention to where he wanted, pulled her close when other tourists invaded their space.

He called a halt exactly one hour later.

Stepping out of the SUV to admire the spectacular view from Lycabettus Hill, she ignored the tingling in her nape as she breathed in deep, smiling when her stomach started to growl at the tantalising scent of cooking.

'What's that smell?'

Ares smiled. '*Souvlakis*. Hungry?'

She nodded. 'Can we get some, please?'

'Of course.'

They'd stopped near a small park, with walkways interspersed with busts of gods set on pedestals.

Ares stepped out too. 'The vendor's just across the street. I'll be right back.'

Odessa had wandered over to the first pedestal when that tingling from before returned. Before she could turn to verify the source of her uneasiness her arm was grasped in a crushing hold, her captor frogmarching her towards the car park.

'Did you really think you could get away from me for ever?'

She shuddered at the cruel, too-familiar voice. And if the bruising grip hadn't been enough to tell her, she looked up into the livid eyes of Vincenzo Bartorelli.

'No, you can't be here—'

'Yes, I can. I have every right to retrieve my property.'

It was useless to ask how he'd found her. Men like him always found a way. What she needed to do was get away from him as quickly as possible—especially when the open back door of an SUV parked a dozen feet away revealed his intention.

Odessa didn't think twice about struggling, and then screaming as he yanked her towards the vehicle. She clawed at the hand imprisoning her, swallowing her mounting fear when he only dragged harder.

Dear God, she was being kidnapped in broad daylight.

If he succeeded…

If Vincenzo discovered she was pregnant with Ares's child…

The terrifying thought made her kick harder, her heart lurching as the open door loomed closer and the heavyset man standing guard advanced towards them.

Knowing that once he'd helped Vincenzo bundle her into the vehicle it would all be over, Odessa loosened her knees. She risked hurting herself, but he wasn't expecting a dead weight, and she momentarily slipped from his hold onto the baking pavement.

She'd bought herself mere seconds, but—

A vicious roar ripped through her thoughts. The scuffle, like everything else that had happened, took only seconds. Odessa didn't even have time to scream again before Vincenzo and his bodyguard were laid out cold.

She was struggling upright when strong arms closed around her, engulfing her with warmth and safety.

'Odessa! Are you all right?' Ares demanded, concern hoarsening his voice.

She nodded, her throat closing as she burrowed into him. 'Y-yes… I'm fine. I…'

'Shh, it's okay…'

Murmuring words in Greek, he moved his hands over her, stroking and soothing as approaching sirens rippled through the air. Minutes later, the authorities were carting away an incandescent Vincenzo.

Ares, visibly shaken, barely holding back his fury towards her attacker and his concern for her, watched as paramedics examined her.

From her struggle-tossed hair to her grazed knees and the soles of her bare feet, he seemed to devour every inch of her in minute detail, his nostrils flaring as his gaze dwelled on the large rip in her dress.

With a single shake of his head, he gathered her in his arms. '*Thee mou*, Odessa…'

Her name was a command, a question, a declaration.

A shaken plea.

She shamelessly clung to the lapels of his jacket, her breath emerging in sob-tinged gulps. 'I'm f-fine…'

'I will be the judge of that,' he rumbled, in a voice so rough, so dangerous, a few passers-by exchanged nervous looks.

He ignored them all, his stride unwavering as he marched towards the SUV.

'But…the police—'

'They can wait until I'm good and ready.'

He buckled her in, his gaze once again roving feverishly over her before he shut the door with quiet, suppressed movements.

Settling behind the wheel, he gunned the engine and accelerated away, his jaw set in rigid steel.

He was clearly operating on a razor-thin edge. She wasn't going to be the one to tip him over. Hell, she was still shocked by Vincenzo's appearance.

'I can't believe Vincenzo is here…'

Realising she'd blurted her thoughts aloud, she cringed.

Ares's fingers tightened around the steering wheel and a growl rumbled from him. 'It was foolish of me to underestimate how much he wanted you.'

The words were laced with regret and thick fury as he roared into the driveway of his Athens home.

Before she could think about exiting the car he was there, scooping her into his arms once again.

'Ares, I can walk,' she protested.

'I'm aware,' was all he said as he stormed through the front door, held open by his subdued, patently concerned house-keeper. A few other household staff lingered, but Ares ignored them, mounting the stairs two at a time and heading straight for his suite.

There he set her on the edge of his bed, then strode off towards his bathroom.

With a minute he was back, minus his jacket and shoes.

The sight of Ares crouched before her, his face set in rigidly bleak lines as he slowly pulled off his T-shirt, snatched at her already fractured breath.

He tossed it away, then without a word spoken grasped the hem of her dress and started to draw it up.

Her hands flew to cover his. 'What are you doing?'

A flash of distress crossed his granite features. 'I need to see for myself that you're unharmed. And I'd really like to wash that bastard's touch off you. Are you going to fight me on this, Odessa?'

The intensity in his gravel-rough tone juddered through her. And, since the second part was what she wanted too—what she would've done had she been alone—she shook her head.

Mere seconds later the dress was off, and he was tossing it away. Her bra and panties followed, and then she was caught in the sizzling net of his thorough scrutiny as his hands and eyes raked every inch of her body. When he reached the grazed skin on her knees, a garbled sound left his throat. His eyes were near-feral before he sucked in a calming breath. Still he muttered words under his breath she was sure weren't meant for polite company.

Rising, he scooped her up again, tucking her high against his chest, his eyes locked on hers.

'This is the second time he's put his hands on you. There won't be a third,' he vowed, with a dark rumble forged in fire, brimstone and retribution.

CHAPTER EIGHT

ODESSA WAS TOO consumed by the sensation of his near-naked body against hers to form words. And, really, what could she say that wouldn't tip this man still hovering on a dangerous precipice over the edge?

Was it only a few hours ago she'd teased him about his Neanderthal tendencies? She was witnessing them in full effect now. And, since they both needed time to come to terms with a day filled with glorious highs and disturbing lows, she let him work his way through his emotions.

He did that by first cleaning her grazes and then, leaving his boxers on, urging her beneath the warm shower. He washed her with a gentleness that brought another lump to her throat, quickly washing himself thereafter. Then he towelled her hair dry and wrapped her in a soft, thick cotton robe.

Once again taking her in his arms, he returned to the bedroom.

A tray had been delivered while they were in the shower.

Ares placed her in the middle of the bed and tugged the covers over her just as his phone began to ring. He glanced at the screen, and grimaced. She followed his gaze, saw it was his father.

His reluctance to leave her evoked a melting sensation she couldn't for the life of her harden. But perhaps it was okay, just this once, not to fight it so much. To bask in his care and attention to ease her ordeal.

'It's okay. Answer him. I don't want him to worry.'

A layer of his tension visibly evaporating, he nodded.

Their conversation was mostly in Greek, but Odessa didn't mind. It gave her time to collect herself, to permit the hovering relief that she was safe. That her baby was safe.

A soft sound left her throat as she collapsed against the pillows, unable to quite shut out the worst-case scenarios whizzing through her brain. Her hand sliding over her belly, she sent up a fervent prayer of gratitude that none of them had come to pass.

It took a moment for her to realise that Ares was silent. That his gaze was fixed on her, and the same emotions she'd felt were reflected in his face.

She struggled upright, her heart thumping at the force of his reaction. An emotion she absolutely didn't want to read into for her own peace of mind.

'Is he okay?' she asked instead, deflecting the heightened atmosphere between them.

A rough, bewildered sound left his throat. 'You're asking after him when you should be concerned for yourself?'

She shrugged. 'He's a worrier. And I suspect it's not fun when the people you care about are in trouble, but out of your reach. Besides, I can multitask quite well.'

Her attempt at humour fell flat, but she was beyond caring. What absorbed her attention was Ares, ambling closer, that gaze never straying from her for a second.

'No, it's not fun,' came Sergios's disembodied voice.

Her jaw dropped when she realised the call hadn't been concluded. Ares's mouth twitched as he held out the phone.

'He wouldn't hang up until he'd seen you.'

She took the phone, her smile wobbling a little when Sergios's worried face filled the screen.

'Mikros?'

'I'm fine. I promise.'

He nodded, but the reminder of what he'd been through was

reflected in his sombre eyes. 'It's my turn to say a prayer for you, like you did for me five years ago.'

She inhaled sharply. 'How do you know about that?' she whispered.

'Know about what?' Ares enquired.

She pressed her lips together, shaking her head at Sergios.

His was warm, benign, his smile all-encompassing. 'Tell him, *mikros.*'

She raised her gaze to Ares. 'When I found out about the accident I said a prayer for your father,' she confessed, and then, after a moment, she added, 'And for you.'

Myriad emotions flashed across his face, too quick to read but all heavily weighted.

'She did more than that. She lit a candle every morning and every night. And she petitioned the staff to do the same.'

Mortification and panic at this exposure of her emotions weakened her. 'Sergios…'

The old man shook his head at her protest. 'No, my dear. I won't be quiet about it. You defied your father to spend hours in the chapel, praying for me and my son. He deserves to know it.'

Her face heated and emotion clogged her throat, sending prickles to her eyes.

Ares's eyes flared, searched harder, then blazed with whatever emotions were moving through him. 'Is that true?'

'Do you want it to be?'

He looked poleaxed for a second, then fiercely intent. 'Answer the question, Odessa.'

'Yes. It's true,' she confessed in a whisper, dragging her gaze away, because the reminder of those three awful weeks when his life had hung in the balance was still viscerally heart-wrenching and something she didn't like to revisit often.

He took the phone from her, said a few words to his father, then ended the call. 'Look at me, Odessa,' he commanded, his voice gruff and uneven.

She raised her head, boldly met his eyes even though she wanted to run. Shield herself from further exposure.

But that wasn't what she witnessed. He looked…nonplussed. Unsettled. And, probably for the first time in his life…uncertain.

As if she… Odessa…had shaken his foundations.

'Why?' he rasped after several heartbeats.

Several unguarded reasons rushed to the tip of her tongue. She barely managed to bite them back. She'd revealed too much already.

She pursed her lips, debating not answering, then… 'Because, whatever you think of me, I'm not a monster.'

For an eternity, he simply stared at her. Then he rose, strode away to the other side of the room. She should have been relieved he was dropping the subject, but all she felt was deflated. Then that charge he carried with him, that sheer vitality, infused her again when he reversed his course. Kept coming until he reached her.

Crouching beside the bed, his eyes teeming with the indecipherable emotions he seemed to be grappling with, he reached out, brushed his fingers down her hot cheek. 'You're many things, *agapita*. Some I'm yet to fully discover, because it seems you can throw a wrench in my beliefs, but one thing you're most definitely not is a monster.'

He stared at her for another age before, leaning forward, he dropped a kiss on the corner of her mouth.

'Efkharisto.'

'Parakalo,' she answered, the response natural and automatic now.

But inside she was a mess, and the feeling that they'd turned a corner was unwilling to leave her frantic brain.

'I can't believe Sergios got the butler to tell him about that,' she blurted, eager for a distraction.

'He cares for you,' Ares said, his tone gruff.

That melting feeling grew warmer. Comforting. But it lacked something vital. Something she was fearful to hope for.

'I know.'

'He wants to return to Athens. I told him not to.'

She nodded. 'It's not necessary if we're going back to Ismene soon.'

A look crossed his features, too quick for her to decipher. Then he was placing the tray on her lap.

'You never got around to eating,' he drawled.

But she caught the trace of wicked humour in his tone. He, too, was attempting levity.

A small chuckle broke free before she could stop it. Then she curbed it when she heard the tinge of hysteria tingeing it.

Her eyes widened when she saw what was on the plate.

Souvlakis.

She wasn't going to question how this had been whipped up so quickly. Maybe it was relief, residual adrenaline, or knowing she was eating for two now, but her stomach growled again as the aromas hit her.

Folding warm bread around the slices of meat and gooey sauce, she bit into it.

At her soft moan of appreciation, Ares's eyes darkened.

He watched her eat two, then nudged a third towards her when she hesitated. She took it, eating more slowly this time.

When she was done, he removed the tray and tucked the covers over her. He watched her for another second, then brushed a kiss on her temple. 'Rest now.'

The combination of life-changing news and the awful event that had followed had sapped her energy, and although it was barely evening, Odessa sagged against the pillows, her eyes already drooping by the time Ares's broad form disappeared through the bedroom door.

She slept fitfully, her rest disturbed by choppy dreams. Twice she felt hands soothing her, running through her hair, calming her as she fell back into sleep. When she woke a few hours later it was to find Ares pacing the terrace outside his suite, the phone plastered to his ear as he conducted a low, heated conversation.

Sensing her regard, he ended the call and entered.

'Is everything all right?' she asked.

He glanced down at the phone with a frown, then slotted it into his pocket. 'Not entirely, but I'm working on it.'

'Was that the police?'

He hesitated for a second, then nodded. 'The police chief is a friend. He's assured me that the idiots Bartorelli hired to assist him have ratted on his intention to kidnap you. He also made the mistake of committing the crime in Greece, not Italy. He has significantly less sway in my country, and I've ensured that his assets are not available to him. Your uncle, too, has been put on notice that if he lifts a finger to help Bartorelli he stands to lose substantially. Not that he needed much persuasion... Bartorelli out of the way suits him just as much as it does me.'

The speed of his retribution while she'd been asleep made her grip tighten on the covers. Was it the same swiftness with which he would remove her from their child's life?

'So, in essence, you threw your weight around?'

His arrogant nod was unapologetic. Determination blazed high and formidable in his eyes. 'Indeed. And I won't hesitate to throw even more around to get what I want.'

For her or for his child?

While she knew the feminist in her should rail against it, for the sake of keeping her child safe Odessa fully embraced that ruthless fortitude. But she vowed to herself that if—when— he attempted to use it against her, she would fight with everything she had. For now...

'For what it's worth, thank you,' she said.

For some reason her words drew a dark frown, which he visibly shook off as he perched on the side of her bed. Her breath caught as he reached out to brush back her hair and caress her cheek.

'How do you feel?' he rasped.

Odessa swallowed before she could speak. 'I'm fine. I'm glad it's behind me.'

Again, shadows chased across his face. Then he stood. 'Is there anything you need before we leave?'

Reminded that they were only supposed to be in Athens for her appointment, she shook her head.

'*Kalos.* We'll leave within the hour,' Ares said, and then, with another prolonged look, he returned to the terrace.

She got up and, ignoring the discomfort in her knees and arm, went to her own side of the suite.

Her ruined dress had disappeared—thankfully. Going to the closet, she selected a pair of wide palazzo pants and a white batwing top made of cotton so soft and luxurious Odessa was certain it had cost the earth.

But it covered her bruises, and with her deepened tan the colour looked good on her, and she greedily took the boost it provided, sliding her feet into heeled gold mules before adding gold hoops to her ears. A quick brush of her now dried hair before containing it in a loose bun, a spritz of her favourite perfume, and she was ready.

Returning to Ares's suite, she momentarily panicked—until she saw her bag and the sketchbook tucked into it.

Ares was waiting in the foyer when she came downstairs, his gaze latching on to her as if he needed to read her every expression. Odessa's face reddened and, forcing her gaze away, she smiled reassuringly at the hovering housekeeper.

Outside, the sight of an additional SUV full of mean-looking bodyguards made her grimace.

'Is that really necessary?' she asked Ares.

A grasp of her hand, which he settled on his thigh, then a solid, implacable 'yes' was all she got.

Until, after staring out of the window as the SUV bypassed

the helipad and headed for the private side of the airport, she turned to Ares as the vehicle stopped in front of a large, sleek-looking jet.

'Why the jet? Are we not taking the chopper to Ismene?'

He shook his head. 'No. Change of plan,' he stated grimly.

'Are you going to tell me what that plan is?' she demanded when he didn't explain.

His face was shuttered for longer this time. 'Did you like it on Ismene?'

Unable to deny it, she nodded. 'Yes.'

'Then be assured you'll like where we're going just as much. Maybe more.' He held out his hand and beckoned her. 'Come.'

Intrigued despite herself, Odessa took a deep breath and went.

Several hours later, she turned a full one hundred and eighty degrees on a lush green lawn, unable to catch her breath at the beauty that surrounded her.

They'd flown south, to the island of Zanzibar. A slice of heaven just off the coast of Tanzania, to her it had been a paradise destination only ever longingly explored on a map. Until now.

The long journey from the airport, with the windows down in their Jeep, had given her a breathtaking glimpse of the exotic island that offered an intriguing blend of African, Arabian and European cultures.

Like on Ismene, Ares's sprawling villa was poised on a glorious beach. But, unlike on Ismene, the swaying palm trees that bordered the Zanelis estate, the powdery white sand beneath her feet, the turquoise beauty of the Indian Ocean, the promise of exploration of coral reefs and the knowledge that there were now a few thousand miles between her and Vincenzo washed away her worries.

Well…most of them.

Ares had grown more brooding, insisting she rest, and absenting himself when she refused. And, unlike on Ismene, they didn't share adjoining suites. A sombre part of her turned downright despondent when she discovered that his suite was in the opposite wing from hers.

Deliberate or unintentional?

Odessa wanted to berate herself for reading too much into it, but since nothing was settled between them, and her instincts were clamouring more strongly than ever, she couldn't very well dismiss it.

And yet, over the next few days, every time she tried to broach the subject Ares knocked the wind out of her sails by snapping out of his mood and displaying the same disarming gentleness he'd provided the evening of her attack.

It toyed with her heart and emotions, making her doubt her own inclinations.

Thoroughly fed up, it drove her into his study a week after their arrival.

He'd left to make some work calls after their light lunch overlooking the ocean. But lying in bed, her senses refusing to settle as she stared up at the heavy saffron silk canopy surrounded by dreamy white muslin curtains that made up her gorgeous four-poster queen-sized bed, she'd suddenly snorted her impatience at herself and searched him out.

Botticino marble floors cooled her feet, but her palms were clammy when she lifted her hand to knock, her heart thumping hard in her chest when his deep, roughly husky voice answered.

He sat behind a desk, building plans and files strewn all over the massive surface.

'Odessa.' Her name was tinged in surprise as he rose and met her halfway. 'I thought were going to take a nap.'

'So did I. Turns out I can't sleep when I have things on my mind.'

His brows pleated. Taking her hand, he led her to an armchair. Thinking he wanted to see her seated, Odessa was once again disarmed by his sitting down and settling her in his lap.

'What things?' he asked.

Up until then, she hadn't even known how to broach the subject, or what to bring up first. Turned out her psyche was fully prepped.

'Would you have sent me back to Vincenzo and Flávio if I hadn't agreed to have your baby?'

He tensed beneath her, but she refused to take back the question.

'That doesn't matter now,' he said.

'But it's not a no. Or a yes. Would you really have sat back and watched Vincenzo force me into marriage?'

Face set, his fingers absently brushed the almost faded grazes on her knee. If he sensed that it toyed with her breathing, he didn't give any sign of it.

'No, I wouldn't have sent you back,' he admitted after a tight stretch of silence. 'Does that satisfy you?'

She tried to stop her heart from singing. She failed. 'Yes, it does.'

He caught her wrist and tugged her close, until she tumbled against his chest. Then his fingers spiked into her hair, training her attention on him.

'Don't think that gives you any upper hand,' he rumbled in warning.

'I wouldn't dare.'

His eyes narrowed. 'Why do I suspect you don't mean that? That you're simply saying what you think I want to hear?'

It took monumental effort to curb the smile fighting to slip free. Just as it did to remain still within the magnetic force-field of his arms.

'Because you have a very suspicious mind?'

'Stop wriggling,' he growled, his eyes dark and smouldering with so much heat she wondered why she wasn't engulfed in flames.

'Then let me go,' she countered.

He didn't.

Instead, those eyes dropped to her mouth, and a groan slowly rumbled from deep within his chest. His lips parted and his warm, minty breath washed over her.

Everything tightened within her in howling anticipation. But just when she thought he'd claim a kiss, devour her in the way they both so blatantly wanted, Ares released her.

Her limbs were too leaden for her to scramble off his lap as fast as she'd fallen into his hold. Or perhaps it was the sting of rejection, despite her visceral awareness of his arousal pressing hot and heavy against her hip?

'Do you not want me any more?' she blurted, before she could stop herself.

He stiffened, his eyes darkening dramatically. 'What gives you that idea?'

'Besides the very obvious altered sleeping arrangements?' she scoffed, although her voice emerged a little shaky.

For a long time he remained silent, his eyes hooded, his jaw set. Then he exhaled harshly.

'You were attacked, *agapita*. Right under my nose. On the day I found out you are carrying my child. The day I discovered you prayed for me when I was…incapacitated. I feel that does indeed alter things a little between us.'

Her heart lurched. Did that mean he'd changed his mind about her?

'In what way?' she asked, hope making her breathless.

His hands returned to her hips, tightened on her flesh momentarily before, almost reluctantly he released her again.

'At the very least I don't want to visit my…needs on you. Unless you expressly wish me to.'

'So you're saying the bedroom ball is in my court?' she ventured, at once touched and disappointed.

It was a hard thing for the domineering man she knew him to be to admit to, thus explaining his recent brooding. But Ares, after several moments, gave a grudging nod.

'*Ne.*'

It wasn't entirely what she'd hoped for…but it was progress. She could build on it. And, while she wanted to throw caution to the wind and jump his bones immediately, she managed to rise, stay steady on her legs as she walked to the door, keenly aware of the need pulsing between her thighs.

But, more than that, she was entirely too conscious of the warmth burrowing deep into her heart. Those two profound sensations should have kept her moving, and yet her feet slowed at the door, her hand braced on the frame as her body pivoted to face him.

'Ares?'

His eyes darted up from where he'd been staring at her bottom. *'Ne?'* he responded gruffly, the faintest flare of heat colouring his cheekbones.

'For what it's worth, I appreciate you coming to my rescue then, too. Thank you.'

For the longest time he simply stared at her. Then he nodded abruptly, jerking forward and reaching for his tablet. 'Close the door on your way out,' he rasped.

She left with her heart only just a touch more at ease. And, yes, she did realise how easily he'd regained the upper hand.

There were more subjects to discuss, of course. But they'd resolved one. She had over eight months before the baby came. The remaining obstacles would be tackled in time.

The tiny voice that taunted her, saying that she was burying her head in the sand, she strongly ignored, heading for the kitchen.

Most of the French doors and windows were thrown open during the day, letting the light, salty breeze weave its magic through the room. Odessa breathed in deeply and entered the kitchen, a strong yearning filling her heart.

The resident chef looked up, his friendly smile turning a touch wary, then almost comical as she relayed her request.

She was elbow-deep in her preparations when her skin began to tingle. She didn't need to look up to know who was striding towards her. His scent alone easily gained superiority over the aroma of rich bechamel sauce and ragu.

For a long moment Ares leaned against the marble counter, only raising an eyebrow to address her when her compulsion to look at him won.

'What are you doing?' he asked.

'What does it look like? I'm making lasagne.'

'I have a house full of staff, including a Michelin star cook. Whom I'm told you have sent away?' He looked around, his brow twitching at the mild chaos around him.

'Yes, I did. He's French. He doesn't make lasagne like my mother did.'

'Your mother?' he echoed, with a slight softening in his eyes.

She nodded. 'It's one of the few memories I have of us,' she whispered, then shook off the shaky emotion. 'Anyway, she used a secret recipe I intend to pass on to my son or daughter. I can't have your chef around.'

She passed her hand over her stomach and his expression changed again. He looked disarmed. Shocked. *Affected.*

But a moment later his feelings were back under tight control, his gaze sliding to the melting, mouth-watering bechamel and the meat sauce bubbling gently on top of the stove. His tongue slid to the tip of his lower lip and Odessa was sure he didn't realise he was doing that.

She curbed a smile and didn't revel too long in the satisfaction welling inside her. Picking up a spoon, she scooped up a taste of sauce, blew on it, then held it up. 'Try it.'

He tasted it, and cursed under his breath.

She bit her tongue to keep from smiling openly. 'Is it that bad?'

His mouth twitched. 'It's adequate.'

'Hmm… Well, I'm guessing that's why you're licking your lips?'

He harrumphed. And Odessa knew she was at high risk

of being lost when she realised that she thought it the sexiest sound in the world.

He remained silent as she finished layering the pasta and sauces and slipped it into the oven. Then... 'Is this to be a regular occurrence?'

'Why? Let me guess... You're going to object to me lifting a finger?'

He shrugged. 'Lifting a finger, no. Exerting yourself too much, yes.'

She sighed. 'I'm not going to be lounging about drinking fruit punch and demanding pedicures for the next nine months, so kill that idea immediately.'

Deeper amusement flitted over his lips before he shook his head. 'I didn't think you would be. But I have an idea.'

She paused in tossing the salad, setting the tongs down almost warily. This was the first time they were having a conversation that wasn't either fraught with past recrimination or thick with sexual tension. It was almost...congenial. So much so Odessa was concerned the slightest wrong move would shatter it.

She followed his gaze to the timer on the oven clock, then he held out his hand.

'We have time. Come.'

Her wariness morphed into a different sort of apprehension. They hadn't touched properly recently, besides the occasional brushing of fingers when he helped her up or down the stairs. Deliberately holding his hand felt...far too intimate.

He started to frown.

Not wanting to lose this lightness between them—because it was new and, yes, because she wanted it to remain a little too desperately—she slid her hand into his.

The almost pained glance he sent their clasped hands a moment later swelled a sensation far too close to her heart.

She was still grappling with it when he walked her into his study and over to the mini-conference table set beneath the window across from his desk. As she neared it, she saw several miniature replicas of Zanelis buildings.

As impressive as they were, it was seeing her sketchbook on the table that rattled her.

'I had it brought down,' he said as he intercepted her expression.

'Why?'

'Because I could use your drawings—if you're willing to share your talent?'

Her heart jumped into her throat, along with surprise and shock. 'Really?' she echoed, her voice husky with overflowing feelings.

His nod was brisk, and yet he studied her with his usual intensity that said he was invested in her response. 'They're too good to sit around collecting dust.'

The fervent yearning and joy gripping her was almost overwhelming. She tried to tamp them both down. Her life had so far been a series of wrenching transactions sucking at her soul and her emotions.

'Behave and you'll not be punished.'

'Atone for not being born male and you'll be spared my wrath.'

'Make friends with this family so we can benefit.'

'Marry me and I'll save you if you have my children...'

Sure, the first part of the deal with Ares had been at her instigation. Was this offering now out of the goodness of his heart? Or was there a hidden agenda?

'You're overthinking it,' he said when the silence lengthened.

'Am I?' She saw his eyes darken. She waved a dismissive hand, hoping her torn feelings weren't plastered on her face. 'Okay, tell me what you mean.'

He stared at her for several seconds before nodding at the tallest structure. 'My latest project in Abu Dhabi will be completed in six months. The top forty floors are residential, including five penthouses. The remaining floors are retail and business. My team is in the process of head-hunting interior designers. I can tell them to stop searching if you're willing to take on the job and work from here.'

Her jaw gaped, and then she shook her head. 'I couldn't— You—' She bit her tongue as heat rose in her face.

'Speak your mind, Odessa.'

'You don't need to throw me a bone just because I'm carrying your child.'

His lips twisted, half amused, half sardonic. 'I didn't get where I am today by making decisions based on sentimental whims.'

Why didn't that surprise her?

'So you're not worried about being called out on possible nepotism?'

A conceited shrug moved his muscled shoulders. 'I'm in the prime position of being rich and powerful enough not to care what people think of me. And you being this worried means you'll provide a premium service. The job is yours if you want it.'

She almost swallowed her tongue. 'Just like that?'

'Ne.'

The confirmation was simple. Immovable.

Several seconds passed, and then, registering he was serious, she stared down at the perfectly crafted miniatures. Luxury skyscrapers. Warehouses. A sports complex or three. Whole streets of residential properties with cute little parks.

They all had names—seemingly with a theme she couldn't quite fully grasp yet—except for the building he'd just been talking about.

'What's this one called?' she asked, more to give herself time to digest his offer and feel how much her heart yearned to embrace it than anything else.

When he didn't respond immediately, she looked up to find

a quizzical expression. As if she'd caught him in an uneasy, vulnerable moment.

A moment later, his jet lashes swept down. 'I haven't decided yet.'

Odessa suspected that wasn't the complete truth, but since she didn't want to add to the tumult now occurring inside her, she let it go.

'So?' he pressed a minute later.

She gulped down the knot building in her throat. 'I... I'll put together some samples and we'll take it from there.'

He nodded. 'Good. But that means allowing the chef back into his kitchen to do his job, yes? I suspect he'll throw a tantrum if he's kept away much longer.'

Odessa couldn't stop the smile that tugged at her lips, or the buoyant feeling that built and built inside her as she returned to the kitchen, Ares prowling lazily behind her. Or the simple contentment that gripped her when he devoured a helping of her lasagne and immediately demanded seconds.

She couldn't escape the pressing confirmation that her feelings for her husband were far from platonic. Hell, had they ever been?

With the no echoing in her head, she admitted, too, that his offer just now had touched her more than she'd expected it to. For the first time in her life she was embracing a true sense of accomplishment that was reawakening the fire in her soul.

The career and the family she'd only ever dreamed of was creeping tantalisingly closer...

There was still the problem of Ares's deep mistrust and full custody plans hanging over her head, but she decided with a firm promise to herself that she would tackle that too. Or at the very least put contingencies in place in case she needed them later.

Because the subject of her child—her *children*—was too precious to leave to chance.

CHAPTER NINE

Six months later

ODESSA ACCEPTED THAT she shouldn't have left things to fester for this long.

Because unlike her pregnancy, which had sailed along smoothly after a few weeks of morning sickness, the atmosphere between her and Ares had stagnated into tepid politeness—with the occasional bout of wild lovemaking when her need built and built and then drove her into his bedroom late at night. There they slaked their lust with a wild fervour that mocked their daytime interactions, that mocked the emotional barricades she'd fought so hard to put up. Because Ares, for all his consideration, remained immovable over their agreement. Had coolly shut her down the handful of times she'd tried to broach the subject.

Sergios had lightened the atmosphere when he'd joined them on the island. Or maybe they'd just stepped up their pretence of a happy marriage…

But she suspected Sergios wasn't fooled…his shrewd looks missed very little.

And now Odessa's increasingly anguished heart had finally cracked, and she was unwilling to let sleeping dogs lie any longer.

Starting with an hour-long confidential consultation with a lawyer who reassured her that she'd have a good case to petition for shared custody of her children, should it come to that.

Any flashes of guilt she felt at proceeding with that meeting, she pushed away. If anything, she was simply taking a leaf out of Ares's book. He'd gone to great lengths to draw up an agreement to distance her from her children. She had every right to seek her own counsel.

And, yes, she also acknowledged that she was praying it never came to that.

That hope burned in her heart as she made an appointment to see the lawyer when she returned to Athens. Since Ares had written into their agreement that his child was to be born in his country of birth, she anticipated they would be returning soon.

Now, as she lay back in preparation for the last scan before the baby came, her hand travelled over the hard bump of her growing baby, seeking comfort from her baby as she'd been doing increasingly over the last couple of months, once her figure had changed and the reality of motherhood had become irrefutable.

Ares entered the guest suite, and she braced herself for what the sight of him did to her. He ruined her in the best possible way every time she grew weak with need and sought his arms. So much so that she feared she was past the point of effectively guarding her heart any longer. Especially when his gaze raked over her, lingered on her belly and his nostrils flared with open, unfettered possessiveness.

'Are you ready?' the female doctor asked, smiling. 'Maybe today we might be lucky and get to discover the sex, yes?'

Ares settled himself beside her, as he'd done both times before, his piercing gaze fixed on her. 'You still want to know?' he rasped.

'Yes.'

He nodded.

The doctor went to work, passing the wand over her swollen belly.

The moments before their baby's heartbeat echoed in the room were heart-stopping. The second it did, and the 3D image appeared, Ares slid his fingers between hers. That was a first. The electric sensation of their palms touching, an act only usually replayed in bed, made her breath catch, made her wonder if their peculiar stalemate was fracturing. Whether this was the opportunity she needed to take.

'I'm happy to report your baby boy looks completely healthy,' the doctor announced.

Ares inhaled sharply, his eyes growing fever-bright as they latched on to the screen, then swung to her a moment later.

She blinked, her own eyes prickling as he leaned over and brushed a kiss over her temple. 'He's beautiful. As are you,' he murmured.

Her fingers tightened within his, her racing heart screaming everything she wanted to say and was terrified to.

The doctor's following words barely registered, but Sergios's entrance into the suite broke her momentarily out of the urgency biting at her.

'A healthy grandchild is all I have prayed for,' he said. 'But I am looking forward to teaching my grandson a thing or two about classic engines,' he added with his customary eye twinkle. Then his expression grew serious. 'Along with a few life lessons about not repeating your mistakes. You know?'

His stare bored into his son's, then drifted to her. It was the most pointed he'd ever been, and that urgency dug into her harder.

Which made it all the more disconcerting when she tracked Ares down two short hours later and saw the open suitcase.

'You're leaving?'

She hated how much her voice shook. How hollow her chest felt already. It was a testament to how she'd grown to long for his scraps of occasional affection that she'd mourn his absence.

He looked up, his fingers tightening momentarily on one of the ultrasound photos they'd been given. 'Yes.' His lips tightened. 'I'll be back in a few days.'

She lifted her hand to brush back her hair, and the tanzanite bracelet and marching necklace she'd crafted at a local jewellery workshop should have reminded her how much she felt at home here. Today it only reminded her of how long she'd been in this gilded paradise. That its beauty couldn't take the place of what her heart truly craved.

'Okay, this has gone on long enough,' she told him. 'How long do I have to stay here?'

He tossed another shirt into the case. 'Until your safety is guaranteed.'

'And until then, what? We're going to keep playing this hot and cold but mostly cold game?'

She almost wanted to laugh at how bewildered he looked. Then she wanted to grieve. Because this level of ignorance meant she didn't mean as much to him as her heart yearned to.

'What are you talking about?'

Dio, she hated how steady, how utterly commanding he was, while she floundered so desperately. The only time Ares seemed to be moved by anything was when it pertained to her pregnancy. Or when her needs got the better of her and she sought his touch.

Well, she was sick of it. And also sickened that this conversation needed to happen.

'You can barely look me in the face. When I enter a room, you leave within minutes.' Her voice choked. 'You're showing the traits of my father, Ares. And, yes, you might find it offensive to be compared to him, but that's my only yardstick. And guess what? It's just as deplorable when you do it.'

His face lost several shades, and even his eyes snapped in affront. 'Odessa—'

'No. I won't live like this any more. Tell me what I've done or I'm leaving—even if I have to swim a hundred miles to get to land.'

He dragged his fingers through his hair. 'I gave you a choice. You made it clear you would use it—use *me*—only sparingly. I'm guessing I have your pregnancy hormones to thank for that consideration?'

Her jaw dropped. 'Wait... Are you accusing me of using you for s-sex? I didn't see you complaining when—' She stopped, her face flaming.

His hands raked through his hair, then he shrugged. 'Something is better than nothing, I guess.'

Her mortification grew. 'Ares...'

His face tightened at whatever it was he heard in her voice. 'I don't require your pity or—'

'That's good, because I wasn't about to offer it,' she snapped, and then the greater need to settle this once and for all drove her closer to him. She almost reached for him, but a lifetime of rejection loomed large, so she kept her hands balled at her sides. 'Look, can we agree that sex isn't really our problem?'

He stiffened, his eyes narrowing, but she caught something on the edges of his expression. Anticipation? Hope?

'Then what is our problem?' he asked.

She pressed her lips together, then made the plea. 'Have faith. In me.'

In us.

The unspoken words dislodged a tightness in her chest. Her hand found its way to her belly again, reminding herself what she was fighting for.

'That history won't repeat itself.'

His eyes blazed as they dropped to her stomach. For a blind moment she was sure he would say something. But then he turned away, his movements jerky as he finished packing.

'I need to go to Abu Dhabi to see to the final arrangements for the tower. Vincenzo's sentencing is also this week. I need to be in Athens.'

She'd forgotten about that. After months of delay and attempts to weasel his way out of jail, Vincenzo had finally pleaded guilty, eliminating the need for Odessa's presence at his trial—an outcome she suspected Ares had made happen.

But, while her heart attempted to melt, because he'd saved her that ordeal, too, she still needed to fight her corner.

'Once he's officially behind bars we can discuss you coming back home.'

Her temper ignited at that. 'You're talking as if I need your permission to leave. I don't remember agreeing to being carted off around the world at your whim.'

He went rigid, but the fingers clutching his case betrayed him, his knuckles turning white at her response. 'This isn't a whim, Odessa. And you're wrong. Our agreement says differently.'

She inhaled sharply. 'Excuse me?'

His lips twisted. 'You need to read the small print. I have the right to take you with me wherever I go in the world. My business is global. How else would I get you pregnant if I didn't have you with me at all times?'

'I'm already pregnant,' she said, stating the *very* obvious.

He shrugged. 'Doesn't change the wording of the agreement.'

Cold invaded her chest, shrivelling her heart. 'Why are you doing this? Surely you can't still believe that I'm an emotional threat to this child?'

He opened his mouth, but she beat him to it.

'Nothing! I have done nothing wrong in the first place. You're judging me by impossible standards. I'm human. I'm bound to make mistakes.'

'Not with my children you won't,' he seethed.

'Enough, Ares! I kissed a boy who wasn't you when I was eighteen! And I said some things I didn't mean to my father about you. Are you going to punish me for ever for those two things?'

'No,' he growled, stepping up to her and blotting the sunlight, so all she could see and all she could feel was him. 'But—'

He gritted his teeth.

'But what?'

'You made me yearn for things I couldn't have.'

Her mouth gaped open. 'Things like what?'

His own lips parted, but he said nothing. They breathed the same roiling air for a minute, before he slashed his hand through the air.

'It doesn't matter now.'

'Of course it does. I'm being judged for something I didn't even know you wanted from me. At the very least I have a right to know, don't I?'

His gaze dropped to the ultrasound photo, which was at risk of being crushed between his fingers. When he locked eyes with her once more, the flash of bleakness she saw strangled her breath.

'Fine. You made me *hope*. Until I saw you in another man's arms, I thought that the words and promises we'd made to one another meant something.'

'They did.'

His eyes narrowed, his judgement scorching her where she stood. 'Tell me, then, *matia mou*... How would you have felt if our positions had been reversed and my tongue had been down another woman's throat, her hands touching parts of my body the way you wanted to touch me? Would you have brushed it off as a simple mistake?'

Her throat clogged, blocking any answer she'd hoped to give. It would've killed her. And, God, she didn't know whether she would've forgiven him. But...

'I'd like to think I wouldn't have condemned you for the rest of your life,' she whispered, the part of her that insisted he was better than this stubbornly clinging on to hope.

That hope grew when he lifted his hand, traced a thoughtful path down her cheek, then was shattered conclusively with, 'Ah, but then I'm Greek, *agapita*. The fires of retribution burn brighter and hotter within me. Now, enough of this. Whatever rows unfold between us, you remain the vessel carrying my child. I won't have your health harmed.'

That was as definitive as it could get. No matter the highs and the lows, Ares would see her first and foremost as a brood mare.

Waves of pain at his words crashed through her, leaving her unable to catch a full breath.

'Do you even hear yourself? Who refers to the mother of their child as a "vessel"? You know what I think? You don't hate me for kissing someone else under some misguided notion of self-preservation. I think you're afraid to reach for what you truly want. You want to guard yourself against all future pain. That's fine. But do you have to be cruel to me to achieve that?'

For the first time in her life she saw Ares Zanelis totally nonplussed. His mouth gaped slightly and extreme bewilderment filled his expression.

After a handful of seconds, he shook his head. 'I didn't mean—'

'Yes, you did. And the sad thing is you don't even realise how hurtful you're being. Or that you don't need that stupid wall you've erected around yourself. Why don't you do us both a favour? If you can't be the kind and considerate man I know lives in there somewhere, maybe you shouldn't come back at all.'

The words seared her very soul as she uttered them and Odessa stopped breathing, the visceral fear that she'd said words he might act upon lighting a terrifying blaze in her heart that threatened to annihilate her.

His eyes widened, shock slashing through the bewilderment. And, hell, if that wasn't the saddest, funniest and most heartbreaking thing she'd seen in a while.

For the first time Ares was rendered speechless.

And somehow she found the strength to accept something else her foolish heart needed to know. It was time to guard her heart. Because months...years of this would be untenable.

She took one step back. Then another.

Her eyes narrowed as he jerked forward, as if caught by the strings of her emotions.

As she took her third step he stopped himself, features shuttering.

He remained there, a pillar of ruthless fortitude, watching as she silently begged him not to let her go, but knew he wasn't going to stop her.

Wasn't going to do anything but leave.

A week later, she summoned a smile for Sergios as they sat down to play chess, infusing enough enthusiasm into the smile for his contemplative looks to lessen, but not totally dissipate.

They hadn't discussed his son's absence, but she knew he wasn't pleased about it.

Join the club...

She wanted to blame those hormones Ares had mocked for missing his body next to hers in the dead of night. She'd tried telling herself she'd been through worse, after living under her father's ruthless commands for almost three decades, but her heart taunted her.

You knew early enough that Elio didn't love you. He made no bones about the fact that he'd have preferred a son to a daughter.

With Ares, her heart had refused to believe for a very long time. Now that hope was gone. But she needed to keep her vow front and centre in the heart that was now being pulverised by the realisation that she'd never got over Ares Zanelis. That despite the almost-decade that had passed he'd remained the ideal in her mind and her heart. She feared he always would, but she needed to put that fear aside. For her child's sake.

'I'm old, *mikros*, but not so old that you should pretend to play badly enough to make me feel good about winning,' Sergios griped.

Her gaze snapped to his, guilt riding her about spacing out.

At his droll look, her eyes dropped to the board. In three short moves she was about to forfeit the game.

'Oh, I'm sorry…'

He waved her apology away, but while his customary humour lurked in his eyes his expression was surprisingly solemn. 'Don't be sorry, *mikros*. Do something about it.'

She started at his direct, gritted tone. Surprised that for the first time she was catching glimpses of where his son had inherited his steel from. Sergios might couch his interactions with humour, but at his core he was implacably loyal. Fiercely determined.

'I… I don't know what you mean.'

His mouth twisted, the motion so reminiscent of his son that her breath caught. 'Yes, you do. Only you're wallowing when you should act.' A flash of anguish marred his weathered features. 'If I'd acted sooner, instead of remaining stubborn back when things were unravelling in my own life, perhaps things would've turned out differently for my family.'

She reached over the table and covered his hand with hers, swallowing the lump in her throat. In the context of her own pregnancy and already loving her baby more than life itself, she couldn't fathom going through what he'd endured.

'Sergios, I'm—'

He patted her hand. 'You mean well, I know. But I'd much prefer you direct that sentiment somewhere more proactive.' His gaze dropped to her belly, and there was an expression of fondness and pride in his gaze when he lifted it back to her face. 'My grandson deserves the happiest home you can provide. And, no, I don't mean the one you're contemplating, separated from my bull-headed son should he not pull his act together.'

At her visible shock, he snorted.

'I'm not blind. You two pretend all is well for my sake. I wish you'd save all that effort for fixing things before they're irreparably broken. Or do you not want that?' he challenged, again with that blade of ruthlessness that made her understand once and for all that she'd sorely underestimated Sergios Zanelis.

'I… Yes, I do.'

He squeezed her hand. *'Kalos,'* he grunted, then his smile reappeared. 'Now, give me a better game. Who knows? Strategic thinking might help you devise how to bring my son to heel.'

They played three more better, challenging games. And she went to bed that night with a slightly altered plan than she'd woken with that morning.

She couldn't shake Sergios's urging. Nor the spark it had ignited. As she pulled the covers over herself the urge to win the most important game of her life burned bright.

Brighter.

Ares had accused her of making him hope—something his mother's actions had clearly eroded. What if that hope wasn't misplaced? What if she had the power to make them both happy beyond their wildest dreams?

The strong kick in her belly just then made her gasp, then smile in the dark. At least she had one person in her corner. Well, two. Ultimately, Sergios would support his son in whatever decision he made, but for now she could siphon strength from the only father figure she'd truly known.

She wouldn't just fight for her children.

She would fight for her husband too.

That spark turned into a conflagration less than a minute into the video conference calls with Ares's team after breakfast the next morning.

'We're thrilled to have you on board the design team for Odessa Tower, Mrs Zanelis. Your designs are quite breathtaking,' the team leader gushed.

She sucked in a breath. 'I'm sorry…what did you say?'

Nervous glances met hers. 'Did I say something wrong?' the woman asked.

'No,' Odessa said hurriedly. 'I just didn't catch the name of the property, that's all.'

'Oh…it's called the Odessa Tower. Is that not correct?'

Her fingers tingled, and then the sensation rushed through her until her whole body was engulfed. The memory of Ares's evasive look flashed through her mind. He'd named his latest project after her?

When he didn't care for her.

As a taunt, it felt too cruel to contemplate. But could it be…?

The seductive whisper suggesting that it was something else, something she'd yearned for all her life, was too big, too weighty, to dismiss.

She had people waiting for her, giving her strange looks that prodded her to get her act together fast or risk the very thing she'd questioned Ares about. The last thing she wanted was to leave the impression she had no clue what she was doing. Even if it was somewhat true.

Clearing her throat, she pinned on a smile. 'No, you're right. And I'm glad to be on board too. Shall we get started?'

The white-knuckle determination to succeed in her first ever venture kept Odessa focused on the meeting when every cell in her body wanted to examine every facet of what she'd just learned.

Ares had named his latest project after her.

Because he wanted to perpetuate the ruse that theirs was a genuine marriage? No, she couldn't make that argument stick either. Ares had no need to prove himself beyond the bounds of making his father happy.

And yet…

Odessa sucked in a steadying breath, attempting not to be even more disarmed when they settled on three of her designs for the mega-penthouses along with two more from other designers. She struggled not to gape in wonder at the initial 3D projection of how her work would look when it was completed, in time for the official opening in four short weeks.

'Mrs Zanelis?' the team leader prompted hesitantly, clue-ing Odessa in that she'd been staring, agog.

Cringing, she offered an apologetic smile. 'Forgive me. I was just marvelling at how efficiently you've all worked to produce this.'

Her praise did the trick, drawing pleased murmurs which carried through to the end of the meeting.

The moment she signed off, her hands flew to her mouth.

After a good five minutes of trying to absorb the news, trying not to let her heart soar at the connotations of it, she brought up a search engine on her laptop, her fingers tapping out frantic requests.

With each revelation her breath shortened further.

Every Zanelis project and iconic piece of real estate held a significant meaning to *her*.

Sapphire Island. Her favourite gem.

Gemini Place. Her star sign.

Occhi d'Argento. Silver Eyes.

Odessa Tower.

She stopped after the tenth one, her heart shedding the last of its protective barriers. Perhaps she was wildly over-exag-gerating the importance of all of this. But if she wasn't… If Ares had even a shred of feeling for her over and above her role as his long-term incubator…

Before she could change her mind she reached for her phone, her fingers aiming for the number at the top of her contact list.

'Odessa.'

His voice was deep and resonant, rumbling through her being to settle in a place she was beginning to suspect would always be reserved for this man. The truth of that shook through her, forcing her to grip the phone tighter.

'Is something wrong?' he demanded, his voice sharper.

She started to shake her head, before she remembered he couldn't see her. That the fact threatened to make her giggle took her by alarming surprise.

Grappling her wayward feelings under control, she responded. 'No, there's nothing wrong. But… You named your new tower after me?'

Even from thousands of miles away she sensed his wariness.

'Ne,' he said after an age. The silence stretched out before he added, 'We're trying to create an image, aren't we? It made sense.'

Her heart plummeted, and then a wave of anger took over, thankfully shrouding the swell of hurt. 'Made sense to who? Because if that's the true reason—'

'Why wouldn't it be?' he interjected, with what sounded like a touch of defensiveness.

Which—absurdly—made her feel fractionally better.

'Because firstly, you didn't consult me, and secondly, you're forcing me into more pretence.'

Again, silence reigned. Then he sighed. 'If you must know, it was the first name that entered my head.' His tone had morphed into gruffness and clear reluctance. He hadn't wanted to admit it. 'Nothing else made sense after that.'

Her grip eased, her breathing turning shallow as elation bubbled once more beneath her skin. 'I see.'

He cleared his throat. 'But—'

'It changes nothing. I'm aware,' she slotted in, before he could.

But his protest was useless. He'd admitted the truth. And the vice around her heart was easing.

'Was that all?' he rumbled. 'I have a busy afternoon.'

The urge to put her plan into action bit at her, but Odessa didn't want to do it over the phone. This was too important.

'No, that's all.'

For now.

Expecting him to ring off, she held her breath when he lingered.

'You're well?' he asked.

No. I miss you more than I can express.

'I'm well,' she said instead. 'So is the baby. I'll see you soon.'

She hung up before he could query that. Before he could talk her out of it.

Standing, she left the study, eager to put thought to action immediately.

Sergios stood outside the door. His gaze probed, hard and direct, and again Odessa wondered how she hadn't seen this side of him before. Perhaps she hadn't wanted to see it? Examine what it might mean to her?

She answered the question in his eyes. 'I'm leaving, Sergios. As soon as it can be arranged.'

'And your destination is…?'

'Abu Dhabi is wonderful at this time of year, I hear,' she said.

His smile was immediate and approving, the hands that gripped hers warm and firm. 'Good, *mikros*. Very good.'

CHAPTER TEN

THE DEEP PEACH dress with silver piping did very little to hide her pregnancy.

Not that she was trying to. On the contrary, Odessa loved nothing more than to smooth her hand over the soft chiffon and her swollen belly, her heart kicking when she felt movement beneath her touch.

Her much-enhanced cleavage did draw a blush to her cheeks—especially the way the silver piping moulded and emphasised her breasts, cinching beneath her bust before flaring to the floor. She loved the way the three silver rope spaghetti strap design emphasised her tan. Her hair, left to grow even longer over the past few months, was caught in an elegant chignon, a few sun-streaked highlights gleaming in the dark caramel tresses.

A nervous smile curved her light peach-glossed lips, and no matter how long and deep she inhaled, she couldn't quite catch her breath.

Because of what lay ahead of her.

Odessa wasn't entirely sure it was a good idea to combine the grand opening of Odessa Tower with attempting to put her marriage on the right track, but she'd made the decision and was determined to stick to it. Not least because the past four weeks had been hectic, with Ares cagily resisting her every attempt to find ten minutes to talk.

As if she'd conjured him from thought alone, she sensed him

in the doorway. Nerves held her still and she didn't turn around immediately. Instead, she tried to compose herself, to think through how she would convince him to give them a chance.

If he said no...

Her heart lurched, but she pushed the feeling away.

If he said no, she'd have no choice but to revert to her initial plan to meet with her lawyer and fight for her children.

But, *Dio mio*, with every fibre of her being she hoped he didn't.

Thee mou, she looked glorious.

A delicious peach—pun very much intended—that every atom of his body screamed at him to devour. He hadn't paid much attention to the changes that happened in pregnant women until his own wife had fallen pregnant. He should have. Because over the months he'd been bombarded with surprises. Some unpleasant stomach-churning when her morning sickness had hit full-force and nothing had seemed to alleviate it. Then the very absorbing, carnal and viscerally *primal* impact of watching her body change. Seeing her belly swell with his child.

He understood now how some men were rampant with protectiveness.

A pregnant Odessa was sexy on a level that continued to baffle and flay him—which was why he'd grasped those nights she'd graced his bed with desperate hands. Until he'd ruined even that with his careless words.

Ares wasn't ashamed to admit he was both thrilled with and dreading her making good on her promise not to remain in Africa.

Ne, he knew he had a battle on his hands—he could see her determination to take him on brewing in her eyes. His mistrust had hurt her, and his past pain still had a stranglehold on him that was in danger of shattering his marriage.

But he'd face that battle soon enough.

At almost eight months pregnant she positively *glowed*.

Her stylist had aced her appearance with that shade of peach. And the way the silver set off her beautiful eyes and the bodice hugged her breasts…

She spun from the floor-length mirror to face him, and Ares realised he'd groaned under his breath.

He straightened from leaning against the archway that led to her dressing room, silently watching her putting the finishing touches to her attire.

Shimmery silver earrings dangled from her ears, drawing his hungry gaze to the long, graceful line of her neck. With a savage punch of arousal he remembered that erogenous zone. His shaft hardened and his mouth watered.

Angling his body so his tuxedo hid the evidence, he forced his gaze from her breasts to her face. 'We need to get going. Are you ready?'

His voice was husky and rough, and he watched heat flow up her gorgeous face. Biting back another groan, he locked his knees to stop him from charging across the room and tasting that erogenous zone once more. He feared it would be just the start.

'Yes…' She lowered long, beautiful lashes and swept up her silver clutch. Then she darted another look at him. 'Do I…?' She laughed and shook her head. 'Never mind. I won't have time to do anything about it even if I *don't* look okay.'

A hard bark of laughter left his throat. 'You're joking, right? You'll be the most beautiful woman there tonight.'

Her stunning eyes grew wide. 'Thank you. You don't look so bad yourself.'

The smile that teased her lips snatched the rest of his breath away. For a moment he was thrown back to the girl who'd broken her father's rules and ventured into the forbidden part of the estate. The girl who'd hung around the garage, not afraid to get herself dirty while she washed the cars with him and his father. The girl he'd placed on a pedestal…which he was beginning to suspect was her rightful place after all.

'Ares?'

He realised he was staring and caught himself, smoothly holding out his arm in silent command. She glided towards him, a goddess. And, hell, even the silver points of her heels playing peekaboo with her hem was sexy to him.

Could anyone blame him?

They hadn't made love since she'd uttered those two words that had shaken him to the soul. That had made him turn tail and flee, despite yearning to reach for her.

Have faith.

He deserved every second of this suffering.

'Are you sure you're all right?'

He clenched his teeth, then failed immediately to resist. He pulled her scent into himself once more, tortured himself with the glorious softness of her skin.

'I will survive,' he clipped, then tossed up a prayer that this would prove true.

For some reason that response sent a dart of hurt across her face. A common occurrence, he admitted, his own mood plummeting. Because this too was his fault, wasn't it?

Hell, he seemed to have lost his way along this journey.

Stances he'd taken had left him tossing and turning at night until he was certain he was being driven out of his mind. And for the first time in his life he was avoiding his own father, because the old man didn't fail to let him know by word or look how he was failing. Hell, Sergios had uncharacteristically called him a fool earlier on today!

Silence reigned until they were approaching the lift. Then she looked around, searching for the very man in his thoughts. 'Is Sergios not coming with us?'

'He claimed he didn't want to intrude, so he went ahead an hour ago.'

She sent him a searching glance. 'You don't believe him?'

Despite his inner turmoil, his mouth twitched. 'He's visited the tower twice and the restaurant three times this week alone.'

She smiled, taking his breath away. 'He's excited.'

'*Ne*. He boasts to everyone who will listen that his daughter-in-law decorated the tower.'

Her stunning silver eyes widened. 'Really? But I only designed a fraction of it.'

'An important fraction to him. To me,' he tossed in after a second.

He sensed her gaze on his face, and with a compulsion he couldn't resist he met hers.

'To you or to your team?' she asked, a touch hesitantly.

'I am my team.'

And your husband.

Eyes still clinging to his, she swallowed. He wanted to trace the line of her throat with his fingers so badly he had to clench his fist to kill the temptation.

Because he was becoming painfully aware that he'd taken a wrong turn somewhere along this journey. That he'd clung for far too long to slights that had been out of her control. Her care and affection towards his father these last few months had been eye-opening. And even while they'd been apart she'd thought about them, prayed for him. The way she'd cared for herself and their unborn child during this pregnancy...

If he'd caused her irreparable harm—and he was fearing he had—did he deserve her?

The question shook him to his core, his whole body jerking in reaction to it.

'Ares?'

He shook his head, feeling a rare panic—the kind he'd experienced only once before, when Bartorelli had seized her in Athens—crawling over his skin.

He'd been dealt with once and for all, thankfully. But what now? Would he succeed this time around? Or was he fated to let her slip through his fingers like she had all those years ago?

He glanced down at her, attempting to harden himself against impending pain. Because if he failed...

'Everything is fine,' he reassured her, despite not believing a word of it.

He could fix things. *Couldn't he?*

Those two words plagued him all the way to their destination—his greatest business achievement to date.

Ares stepped out after they'd pulled up to the red carpet leading into the tower he'd spent three years pouring his vision into. He ignored the intense flashes of cameras as he helped Odessa out, and then he simply couldn't pull his gaze away as she stared up at the structure he'd named after her.

He'd wanted something unique, to stand out against the many stunning masterpieces of the Abu Dhabi city landscape. The end result far surpassed his exacting expectations.

Set entirely on a raised concrete platform, surrounded by a shallow lake that jetted plumes of water into the air, the soaring sixty-floor O-shaped design was set in ten concentric silver mirrored rings, each a reflection of her stunning eyes in every mood. Powerful spotlights lit the structure from below, while strategically placed lighting silhouetted it beautifully against the night sky. Reflections from the rippling water made the whole building glimmer, seeming to move in hypnotic beauty.

Not unlike the woman next to him.

Ares hadn't quite known—or perhaps had readily accepted—his subconscious's intentions when he'd selected the colour, but now he did.

Everything he did was influenced by her in one way or another.

It was time to stop fooling himself that she wasn't important. That all he wanted from her was the child she was carrying and the other children she'd agreed to provide him.

It was time to *have faith.*

Every other outcome left a searing hollow in his chest that intensified the panic gripping him.

'I've never seen it at night-time. It's even more breathtaking,' she said, her voice low, husky.

Perhaps it was not meant for his ears alone, but he couldn't help hoping it was.

'*Ne*, it is,' he agreed, not shying away from the throb of emotion in his voice.

The flash from another camera drew her attention from his building and he was both irritated by the distraction and a little jealous of her open admiration for what he'd built.

He wanted her to look at *him* that way. Not to see the layer of wariness in her eyes when she glanced at him.

He wanted to be done with this opening that had attracted some of the most influential people in the Middle East and from around the world, all of whom wanted a piece of architectural history.

A deep sense of urgency gripped him all through the launch, but he throttled it down. Odessa, along with the design team, deserved her due for a magnificent job.

Pride filled him as he listened to gushing accolades about the decor his wife had helped create. As he watched her blushingly accept her due.

His wife.

That thing shifting and settling within him as he thought of her not as the woman carrying his child but as the woman he'd once imagined making a life with felt heavy.

Moving.

Significant.

And right.

Have faith.

Yes.

It was a huge relief when he claimed her four hours later, tugged her arm once more into the crook of his and firmly stated that his pregnant wife needed to rest.

'Thanks for that,' she murmured as he walked them towards the magnificent doors and into the foyer of the tower. 'My feet are killing me and my back feels as if it's made of concrete.'

He led them into the lift and pressed the button marked *'Odessa Penthouse'*.

'Then you won't mind if we spend the night here and go home tomorrow.'

'So we get to break in the tower?' she asked, eyes wide. And then a heated blush swept into her cheeks. 'I mean...'

He laughed, welcoming the brief relief to the churning unease in his gut. 'I know what you mean, *eros mou*. And, yes. We'll be the first to spend the night in Odessa Tower.'

His voice felt thick from the arousal surging through him, and he didn't bother to hide it. She looked infinitely delicious, and the hunger sweeping through him was fast reaching untameable levels.

It was both a relief and a torture to step into the privacy of the penthouse. Relief because he had a little breathing room to think, and torture because for the first time in his life he was terrified of how the next hour would go.

They stepped into the spacious and lavish caramel, silver and gold living room in time to see the night sky explode in bright colour.

'Oh, I forgot about the fireworks!' Odessa exclaimed.

Suppressing a groan, Ares crossed over to the extensive liquor cabinet and poured a glass of alcohol-free champagne. Returning to where she stood at the floor-to-ceiling windows, he handed it to her, and then, simply because he couldn't help himself, he trailed a hand down her jaw and neck, fighting the punch of emotions as she shivered and swallowed.

She wasn't immune to this, he reassured himself. She'd boldly told him she'd prove him wrong in their agreement. That he'd regret it. And he did now. Surely it wasn't too late to make them a real family?

The tightening in his chest didn't ease when she raised her glass, then gasped at a particularly vivid firework, her eyes gleaming...

Ares wanted to experience these significant moments long after tonight.

'Aren't you having a drink?' she asked.

He shook his head. 'I've had enough of toasts tonight.'

Her eyebrows shot up. 'Chomping at the bit to get on to the next project already?'

The slight quiver in her voice told him she sensed the undercurrents between them.

'Something like that,' he answered easily, even while his stomach churned.

Because this would be his most important project yet.

She lowered her glass, her eyes shadowing slightly, and she winced.

'What is it?' he rasped.

She grimaced, one hand reaching behind her to massage her back. 'I know it's technically impossible, but I feel as if our child has gained another pound between dinner and now!' Her eyes widened as he relieved her of the glass, shed his tuxedo jacket, then dropped to his haunches before her. 'What are you doing?'

He lightly grasped her ankle and unbuckled her shoe. 'Relieving some of your stress—as is my right,' he said, and the pounding need for things he'd thought impossible but which now seemed imperative echoed in his voice.

Her lips parted, but she didn't protest at his assistance, instead bracing one hand on the glass wall and the other on his shoulder. 'Thank you.'

He undid the other shoe and set it aside, then his hands trailed up her slim calves, massaging the firm flesh. His body roared at her husky moan.

'I want to do more,' he offered.

And he meant so much more than easing her aches. Now that he'd given himself fuller permission to envisage their future, endless scenarios bombarded him. One in which the heartache of loss and rejection was frantically overcome with greater, deeper emotion.

Like love.

That soul-shaking feeling that had always clung to the edges of his existence and never gone away. No matter how much he'd willed it to. No matter how much he'd convinced himself that this woman wasn't worth it, that her actions were too reminiscent of his pain to ever be set aside.

But now shame stung him for condemning her so roundly. For tainting her and what they might have with the brush of his mother's heartless actions.

She sucked in a shaky breath, then nodded. 'Okay.'

Dropping forward onto his knees, Ares continued his ministrations, digging into her tight muscles, and watched her head fall back.

'Oh, God, that feels so good.'

Her whispered words sent a powerful sensation straight to his chest, then lower to his lately forsaken libido. He let in the sublime sensation, opening himself up to what could be.

Before he could drive himself insane with the promises whispering in his head he drew out his phone. Keeping one hand on her, and absorbing her every reaction, he sent the electronic command he needed to.

A few minutes later a familiar voice flowed through the inbuilt speakers: *'Ares, your bath is ready.'*

His wife's gaze snapped to his, her beautiful eyes wide in surprise. 'Oh…is that my voice?'

He slotted the phone back into his pocket. 'Yes. I programmed the penthouse virtual assistant to have your voice.' He rose and swept her into his arms.

Her eyes widened even more as her arms slid around his neck. 'It's not in the whole tower, is it?'

Ares shook his head as he strode into the breathtakingly luxurious bathroom. 'No. It's for just this penthouse. For my ears only.'

She shifted in his arms and heat intensified in his groin when another flush crept into her face.

'That pleases you, doesn't it?'

Her beautiful lashes swept down, but he noticed her altered breathing. 'There's something...hot about it,' she murmured sultrily.

'Indeed,' he concurred, stopping next to a tub wide enough to hold six easily.

The lights had been set to a seductive ambience, emphasising her perfection as he reached behind her and lowered her zipper. She was braless, and once he'd disposed of her panties she stood before him, a ripe goddess whom he fully accepted had commanded his world since the first moment she'd stepped into it all those years ago.

'*Thee mou*, you're perfection. Aphrodite herself,' he breathed.

Mine. He remembered uttering that possessive on their first night together. That had been a claim from a position of dominance. Now it was more of a plea. A resurgent hope. And it was one he was determined to make a reality, because he was man enough to accept that everything he was, everything he'd achieved, was empty without her.

He glanced at the gently swirling scented water, felt sensation roaring in his ears. 'Alone? Or together?' he asked gruffly.

Breathtaking silver eyes examined him, long and deep. Then she whispered, 'Together.'

The word was barely out of her mouth before he was shucking off his clothes.

He helped her into the tub and washed her body while raining kisses on every inch of exposed skin he could reach. He revelled in her sighs.

Then it was his turn to gasp in wonder as his roved his hands over her swollen belly and felt their child move within.

'He loves that...' She sighed, a captivating smile curving her sensual lips.

'So he should. He's warm and happy.'

Her breath caught, and then she was tilting towards him. Her eyes searched his again, shades of wariness making him stiffen a little. But before he could petition for himself, step on the road to making things right, she cupped his jaw. Inhaled shakily.

'Ares. Take a chance on this. Take a chance on *us*,' she whispered fervently against his lips.

And, sweet heaven, the way his heart leapt should have terrified every last cell in his body. But it was immediately channelled into a far more satisfying outcome. One he'd been starved of for too long.

A new beginning would work for them.

It had to.

He stepped out of the tub and scooped his wife out, his mouth greedily seeking hers as he marched with urgent feet to the bed.

'Ares! I'm wet,' she protested huskily, beautifully, when he set her down next to the emperor-sized bed in the bedroom she'd designed so spectacularly with silver to match her eyes.

His lips curled in a smile he knew reeked of a very masculine satisfaction. 'Yes. And you're about to get wetter, *eros mou.*'

Her deep flush was beautifully predictable. Infinitely arousing.

Ares wanted a lifetime of that.

Tomorrow, he vowed silently to himself, as soon as he was done with slaking this savage hunger, he would embark on making it so.

'Please... Stop torturing me,' she moaned, after he'd spent an age exploring her.

He raised his head from her heated skin, drunk on her beauty. 'But I like watching you come undone for me.'

'Even if the wait torments you too?'

She reached for him, grasped him boldly, and stroked him with enough pressure to siphon the air from his lungs.

'You're a witch.'

'A little while ago I was a goddess,' she tossed back, her half-moon eyes glinting with feminine power.

'Hmm...both are equally enthralling.'

It was the last thing either of them said for a very long time.

* * *

'Wake up, sleepyhead.'

Odessa struggled to prise her eyes open. She moaned in soporific pleasure as firm, warm fingers threaded through her hair and gently massaged her scalp.

'Oh, that feels so good…'

'I'd love to keep going but we've landed. We need to leave the plane.' A soft kiss brushed her temple. 'I'll deliver a full-body massage when we get home if you shift your delicious behind right now,' Ares said, deep amusement in his tone.

'Promise?'

'Ne.'

Opening her eyes, she focused on him. His hair was sexily dishevelled, his eyes sharp as he watched her. 'How long did I sleep?'

'Last night or this morning?' he rasped, with a touch of teasing.

She rolled her eyes. 'It's not my fault you wore me out.'

Odessa tensed slightly when his lids swept down, and she felt the edginess she'd had since that telling plea in the bathroom last night return to shimmer over her skin.

She'd sensed something was brewing with Ares. But she'd fallen into an exhausted stupor soon after they'd made love last night and she'd slept in this morning, her heavily pregnant body demanding rest. She'd struggled to dress herself in time to make their plane, and made a beeline for the jet's bedroom as quickly as her waddle could carry her.

Now, after a little rest, she knew she couldn't put this off any longer. 'Can we talk when we get home?'

His amusement evaporated, to be replaced by narrow-eyed intensity. Then he nodded. 'Yes. There are a few things we need to settle, I believe.'

Her nerves intensified, but since she'd initiated this Odessa took a breath and powered through with a nod.

'Kalos,' he breathed, and then, rising, swept her into his arms.

Surprised by the move, she linked her arms around his neck. 'I thought I was meant to be walking?'

He shrugged his powerful shoulders and sent her a devilish wink as he exited the bedroom. 'This way gets us moving more quickly.'

She couldn't disagree, so she clung on, hiding her face in his neck when she saw the pilot and flight attendants patiently waiting for them to disembark. She would probably never get used to this level of influential luxury. But she prayed that if it meant being given a chance to remain at Ares's side for the next several decades then she'd learn to live with it.

She was repeating that prayer when they swept into the driveway of his...*their* Athens home.

The promise of a massage—hopefully after she'd pleaded her case once and for all—was very much at the forefront of her mind as Ares sauntered into the large marble foyer of the mansion.

She was preparing appropriate words to express how much she wanted to stay married without the shackles of their agreement when she saw Sergios and a vaguely familiar-looking man approaching from the living room.

With a panicked gasp she realised she was staring at her lawyer—the man she'd only communicated with so far via video call. 'Mr Georgiou. What are you doing here?'

Ares stiffened. 'You know this man?'

Her heart leapt into her throat, both at the lawyer's presence and at the pain and disappointment etched on Sergios's face.

She knew the instant Ares deciphered his father's expression too. He went stiff, his movements careful but stilted as he set her down. A quick glance showed his intensified wariness.

'What's going on?' he rumbled, his eyes scouring her face.

'I... Can we talk in private, please?' she pleaded.

He slanted a glance at the short man, who was grasping rather quickly that his presence here was a big mistake. 'Tell me who you are and what you want with my wife,' Ares demanded, his voice a thin, deadly blade.

The man cast her a deeply apologetic look, then introduced himself. 'I'm your wife's lawyer. We had an appointment yesterday, and when she didn't turn up for our meeting, I thought I'd...'

He spread his hands expressively, while Odessa's heart plummeted.

She'd completely forgotten about the meeting she'd scheduled weeks ago.

The transformation in Ares was heart-stopping. Perhaps it was because it appeared as if he'd stopped breathing as he rounded on her.

'Since when?' he seethed.

Odessa swallowed, her hand darting to her belly as her son chose that moment to kick her—hard. Wincing, she answered, 'A while.'

'How long is "a while"?' Ares demanded.

She cast her mind back, her senses reeling. 'A few weeks.'

Sergios's expression grew harder and Ares sucked in a sharp breath. 'Leave my house. Now.'

The bespectacled man mumbled a quick apology before he darted out through the front door. A purse-lipped Demeter was waiting to shut the door firmly behind him.

Ares's eyes blazed with a mixture of censure and...was it pain?

'That talk you wanted. I'm guessing it has something do with this?'

She shook her head vehemently. 'No! Not this. Ares—'

He stopped her with a raised hand. Glancing around them, he issued a swift order to his father and the staff. With another speaking glance that had her lowering her eyes, Sergios walked away, the staff scurrying after him.

CHAPTER ELEVEN

ARES STARED AT HER, and a bitter silence throbbed between them.

Then, without speaking, he strode towards his study.

Odessa followed at a slower pace, her mind reeling at how two minutes could completely change the landscape of her life. But while she had a few things to explain, she wasn't giving up.

A sense of *déjà vu* swept over when she entered, to find Ares pacing in front of the mantelpiece.

'You consulted a lawyer?' he rasped, his voice ice-cold shards, his eyes holding the same disbelief, formidable censure and, perhaps most shocking of all, the same pain she'd seen in his father's eyes. 'I want to ask how you could, but what I really should be asking myself is why I believed you'd be different.'

Righteous anger stiffened her spine. 'Don't you dare play that old nonsense with me. You know deep down that you can trust—'

He waved an imperious hand at the door. 'You just proved conclusively that I was a fool to entertain that notion. "Have faith"?' he scoffed, but the edge of his voice was off, something resembling anguish underscoring his words.

'So I made an appointment with a lawyer to talk through my options? So what? Don't you dare judge me for it when you would've done the same in my shoes.' She stopped, shook her head, because the most important thing between them remained unsaid. 'I promise you I was going to cancel. I'd changed my mind about how I needed to tackle this.'

'When?' he threw at her, his frame still frozen in brutal fury. He shook his head before she could speak. 'Don't bother answering that. You only claim you'd changed your mind because you've been caught,' he snarled.

His wan pallor remained, but she didn't believe he was in any way diminished. Hell, she would bet good money that he was feeling immensely, powerfully vindicated right now.

Purpose such as she'd never seen before bristled from him… from the clenched fists to the taut muscles that bunched when he moved. Ares didn't intend to give an inch.

Despair weighed her down as she shook her head. 'Just when I think we're getting somewhere you shatter my hopes.'

His head reared up, vicious emotions bristling from him. 'You have a nerve, speaking of hopes!'

'Do I? Even though I kept repeatedly hanging on to mine even when you pushed me into a corner? What hope did I have when you kept telling me I wasn't good enough to stay in my child's life? But I fought that. You expected me to sit back and take whatever you dish out? How is that rational?'

His jaw clenched. 'If you were so determined to prove me wrong and stay in this marriage, why did you need to seek out a lawyer?'

She sighed in disbelief. 'You see how that works, Ares? You demand unfailing loyalty. But what right do you have to mine when you wouldn't budge about taking away something so vitally important to me?'

'Even if I wouldn't, you've proved that I was once again blind to trust you.'

Odessa was glad she felt numb, because it meant she didn't crumble over the fact that her heart had shrivelled to nothing. That she was witnessing the end of her marriage—a marriage that had started on extremely shaky ground and only grown shakier.

There would be a time to mourn it—perhaps far too soon and much more devastatingly than she'd feared. Because even in a half-baked marriage she had been the most intensely happy she'd ever been. But for now she raised her chin, refusing to be cowed.

'I won't beg you to believe me. You either do or you don't. But I won't stay here to be vilified for something I haven't done. Feel free to sue me if you wish.'

He laughed, harsh and wicked enough to draw blood. 'And be named a monster just like your father? Or is that what you were counting on? That I would slip up somehow and you could slither your way to the true freedom you want?'

It was her turn to laugh, but she snapped off the sound in under a second before the strong hysteria behind it took hold.

'Look at me, Ares. Do I look like I'm slithering anywhere any time soon?'

When he didn't answer she turned away, viciously swallowing a sob before it could tumble free.

'Where are you going?'

She shrugged. 'I may not have your millions, but I have enough to check in to a hotel for a week or two. Or I'll sleep under a bridge. Who knows? All I know is anywhere you're *not* is good enough for me right now.'

It hurt to say the words. *Badly.* But her heart hurt worse. And she needed a moment or three to lick her wounds.

'Odessa—'

'We have nothing more to say to each other, Ares. Whatever you want to accuse me of next, feel free to tell my lawyer.'

Lies. She would be firing that particular lawyer the first chance she got. He was just a sweet old man, and he'd proved that the great Ares Zanelis could easily scare him off. She needed someone fearless in her corner for the battle ahead.

'This isn't done,' he said, from far too close behind her.

Her fingers tightened on the door handle. The urge to look back, gorge herself on his image one more time, was overwhelming. By the skin of her teeth, she managed to suppress the temptation.

'Put a hand on me and I'll scream the place down. I called a lawyer before. I'm not above calling the police too.'

She heard his sharp intake of breath and an extremely remote part of her almost smiled. She was willing to bet he'd never had a woman say that to him before.

Well, she was also willing to bet he'd never shattered a woman's heart quite as unassailably as he'd demolished hers.

The sense of reprieve she'd wanted withered away when she stepped out of the study, and she only made it halfway down the corridor before true reality struck her. She was walking away from Ares. From her marriage, such as it was. Her heart was ripping itself to pieces and she couldn't breathe.

Her hand shot out, clung to the wall as her legs threatened to give way.

She started when firm hands gripped her arms, but they weren't the hands she craved. Looking up into her father-in-law's eyes was difficult, but she faced him, the knowledge that she'd done nothing wrong burning within her.

'I never... I didn't...' Her voice faltered, tears prickling her eyes.

His lips thinned, but the warmth had returned to his eyes. 'I know.' He looked over his shoulder towards the study. 'I heard some of what happened in there.' He exhaled deeply. 'Putting my son in his place is one thing...opening his eyes to his faults is another. You'll have to try harder, *mikros*,' he urged.

Her shattered heart twisted. 'I don't think I can get through to him.'

His smile was edged in sadness, but the hands holding hers remained strong. Purposeful. He led her to a chair in one of the alcoves dotting the corridor, his gaze unwavering as he said, 'You were brought together once more for a reason. I believe in you.'

Odessa watched him walk away, wishing she could resent him for the burden he'd placed on her.

The burning in her chest remained, unwilling to die. She turned her face up to the sun beating down through the windows across the hallway. She hated it shining so fiercely when her whole world had collapsed into darkness.

Nevertheless, she'd closed her eyes and was praying for strength when the study door opened and slammed, footsteps rushing into the hallway.

Evidently Ares wasn't done with saying his piece either. For better or worse, they needed to settle this once and for all.

When the footsteps skidded to a halt, she opened her eyes. To find a haggard-looking Ares staring at her.

He looked almost…desolate. Frightened. *Pleading.*

'Odessa—'

She held up her hand before she could lose her courage. 'I'm only going to say this once, Ares. Then I'm through. You don't want my love. I get it. But are you so selfish that you'd deprive my children too? What will you tell them when they ask why I'm only around part-time? Because, yes, I will fight you on full custody. Will you be able to look them in the eyes and say it's because I don't want to be with them? Or are you going to admit that you were so terrified to open your heart that you closed theirs to me, too?'

Stark disbelief flashed in his eyes, but hard on its heels came shock, then bewilderment. 'You think I don't want your love?' he rasped, in a bleak, shattered voice.

Her fists bunched in her lap and she cautioned herself to *breathe.*

'Yes. I most certainly do. You've been pushing me away since you turned up at my father's graveside in Alghero. You've used one excuse after another to hold me at arm's length. The moment you could you left Zanzibar, leaving me to chase after you.'

He laughed, a caustic sound that electrified her every nerve-ending.

'You make me sound…' He stopped, took a chest-heaving breath, then shook his head. 'This is far more than just a childish I-pull-your-hair-because-I-like-you playground tactic.'

'You're damn right it is,' she stressed, through teeth gritted so her emotions didn't spill out like a pricked balloon. 'This is my life you're messing with. I know it doesn't mean that much to you, but—'

'No!'

The vehemence of his tone snatched her breath away. Then a red haze wove over her eyes. 'Excuse me? What do you mean, *no*?'

'I mean no, you're not allowed to think for single second that your life doesn't mean that much to me. Not when every damn minute since the moment I set eyes on you you've filled my mind. You've haunted me every single day and night since. I can't make a decision without wondering how you will feel about it. I can't buy a property without wondering whether you would like it, how you would design it if we were together. *Thee mou*… You only need to look at everything I've built and own and you'll find yourself in there somewhere.'

She swallowed, a seismic shift occurring inside her at the knowledge that she'd guessed right all those weeks ago when she saw the name of the tower.

But that didn't mean… Did it?

'In the months after I left Alghero I could barely function without you.'

Her eyes widened, but the acid in his voice killed her rising elation.

'I'm so sorry that was a hardship for you,' she said.

His hand slashed the air. 'You are a living organism that lives within me. The blood that runs in my veins. I can't take a breath without you. And you… You think I don't love you?'

'*Stronzo!* I'm not a damn psychic! I can't read your mind. And your words and actions have left a lot to be desired.'

His eyes widened. 'Did you just call me an A-hole?'

She stumbled to her feet, glared at him when he jerked towards her, his hands shooting out. 'Yes! Because you deserve it. How was I to know you loved me when you threatened to take away one of the very things we dreamed about? Growing a family together?'

Anguish and shame creased his face. 'It was a knee-jerk reaction to the blows I've been dealt before. I thought I needed to safeguard my heart that already belonged to you. When you rejected our agreement so vehemently I welcomed it, because it meant that you'd stay and fight long after the children were born. That I would have you around one way or another.'

'Let me get this straight… You were willing to tear my heart out of my chest just to test my loyalty and devotion and to keep me around?'

He stared at her with stark intensity for several seconds, then turned and strode towards his study.

Curious despite herself, she followed, to find him at his desk, rummaging through the papers before he turned with a document in his hand. Striding back, he thrust it at her.

She took it, but didn't remove her gaze from his face. 'Tell me what it says,' she ordered, and the fight in her tone made his eyes widen. 'Now,' she insisted—then gasped when her baby kicked, as if demanding to be heard too.

Ares's eyes grew wider, his hands shooting out reflexively. 'Odessa…?'

'It's just the baby kicking. He's not happy right now, and I don't blame him. I'm far from happy with you myself.'

He swallowed, a wave of jagged emotion that closely resembled panic sweeping over his face. 'That document changes the terms of our agreement.'

'Changes it how?' she demanded.

'There's no time limit on our marriage. You can either leave now…or never. If that's what you…'

He stopped and sucked in a long, shaky breath, and had it been any other time Odessa might have been stunned by this visible show of vulnerability.

But right now she wanted to get to the bottom of their discussion. Because her heart was straining at the bonds tying it down, and the power of that straining was fired up by hope.

Hope she wasn't going to let take over.

Not yet.

Perhaps never.

'And there's no petition for full custody,' he went on. 'If you decide to leave after our child is born there'll be no constraints on your participation in his life.'

She swallowed the lump that had been forming at his words. 'You said child—not children. You're willing to let me walk away after he's born? What if I decide to take him with me?'

She noticed the way his eyes shone whenever she referred to their child, the pulse of love that gleamed for a single moment. But she didn't let that sway her.

Not yet.

'*Ne,*' he confirmed. 'Whatever you want. As long as you don't stop me from playing a part in his life.' His face tightened with pain. 'I couldn't bear that.'

Neither could she. Her fingers shook as she grasped the document tighter. 'So what you're saying is that you've changed your mind about everything you wanted without bothering to consult me?'

'Odessa—'

'What makes you think I want just one child? You know that I hated growing up alone! That, like you, I wanted to find healing in a big family who love and care for each other. That I want to be the kind of mother we both wanted for our children.'

The hand he speared through his hair visibly shook. 'I was too afraid to hope for it, Odessa. What my father and I went through…' He stopped, and swallowed, then exhaled heavily. 'I wouldn't wish it on my worst enemy. And even the smallest possibility that it could happen again was unthinkable to me. It was easier to build my life around the fact that it would one day manifest in some shape or form and take steps to guard myself against it.'

She tossed the paper away, pain ripping her apart. 'You know what I went through with my own father. What he did to my mother. How could you think that I would ever do something like that to my own child?'

A flash of shame darted over his face. 'I didn't. Not for the most part. But…cruelty isn't the only weapon. When I fell deeper in love with you I felt a different sort of terror. How could you love me back when I had put my own goals in front of your desires?' he said in a barely audible rasp.

He squeezed his eyes shut, both hands gripping his nape in a move of despair so unlike him her shattered heart bled—not for herself this time, but for him.

'I've ruined everything, haven't I?' he asked bleakly.

Her eyes fell to the paper on the floor, then she grasped his hands as he lowered them. 'All you had to do was let me in, Ares. Talk me through what you were feeling. Then I would have told you that I've never stopped loving you. Not when I was sixteen and too shy to talk to the boy with the golden hazel eyes. Nor when I turned seventeen and lay with you beneath the stars, knowing it was the happiest time of my life so far. Not even when you left without saying goodbye and I cried myself to sleep for months. And I love you now because you have fulfilled one of my many dreams by becoming the father of the child I always hoped to have. All that is left now is for you to fulfil my greatest wish. Be the love of my life that I've prayed you'd be from the moment I saw you.'

His jaw had been gaping since she'd started speaking. Now he stared, wide-eyed, as if she was the most entrancing thing he'd ever seen, his fingers tightening around hers.

'*Thee mou*, Odessa…'

'Don't keep me waiting, Ares,' she implored desperately. 'Make my dreams come true. Please.'

He took a single lunge towards her and swept her into his arms, a shudder moving through him as he folded her close. 'Yes. I don't deserve you, but… Please… *Yes*. To every single one of them. My remaining years will be devoted to you and our child…our children. I love you so much, Odessa. I'm so sorry I let the past get in the way of our future.'

She pulled back far enough to cradle his jaw. 'And I'm so sorry about what happened to your sister.'

His eyes glittered with emotion and he swallowed before he nodded. 'I've tortured myself with whether I could've done more…'

'You were a child yourself. And Sergios needs to forgive himself for not reading the signs earlier. It's time for you both to live the life she would've wanted you to. Remember her with love, not with pain, and honour her by being happy.'

He pressed his forehead to hers. 'I almost let my fears get in the way. For that I'm sorry, *eros mou*.'

She indicated the piece of paper. 'You were prepared to sacrifice your own wishes for me. It means the world to me, but I'm so glad we don't have to be apart, Ares.'

Another shudder moved through him. 'Never. For as long as I have breath in my body we will be together. *Always*.'

His firm, gruff vow was sealed with a deep kiss that swept away the last of her fears and misgivings, leaving only hope and ocean-deep love.

They were still kissing, still whispering fervent words of love, when a throat was cleared.

Sergios stood on the threshold, a mile-wide smile on his face. 'Pardon the intrusion, but spare an old man's heart and tell me this little turbulence is behind us?'

Their unborn son kicked hard, happy and content and strong

enough for Ares to feel it. His face was transformed in absolute awe and, laughing at his expression, she answered Sergios.

'It's smooth sailing ahead, Baba.'

His eyes filled at the affectionate term, and he approached, arms outstretched. After a warm, loving hug, he slapped his still-silent son on the back, nodded once, then left them alone.

Ares, his hand still on her belly, dropped another kiss to her lips. 'I love you, *kardia mou*. So very much.'

'*S'agapo,*' she echoed, her heart full to overflowing.

EPILOGUE

Three years later

'YOU HAVE YOUR two babies, Kyrios Zanelis. Now what?' Odessa teased him from her private hospital bed.

Yellow roses, her favourite flowers, covered every spare surface in the room and on her bedside, a large picture of them with Paris, their almost three-year-old son, continually drew his eye, even though the flesh and blood versions were right there in the room with him.

Ares stared at his wife, glowing and exhausted from bringing their second child into the world only four hours ago.

How she still managed to be the most beautiful woman in the world was beyond him. Perhaps one day, decades from now, he would stop wondering how he'd got so lucky.

For now…he stared down at his new daughter, the pull and twinge in his chest building until he couldn't quite catch his breath.

'Two more, at the very least,' he answered. Then, based on pure greed, he added, 'Or three if we can manage it. Please.'

She laughed, flinging back the hair he'd lovingly brushed ten minutes ago, making his heart flip over several risky times. 'You drive a hard bargain, *agapo*.'

Her husky endearment, one of many he'd been privileged to receive from her in the last three years, made his heart somersault a few more times. He never tired of the feelings. And dear God, he hoped he never did.

'It's hard not to when you show me every day what it's like

to be surrounded by so much love. So much happiness. You know I'm a greedy man, *agapita*. This sleeping beauty in my arms and the little rascal making his grandfather laugh hard enough to bring tears to his eyes, makes me want as many such treasures as you can gift me.'

'She's beautiful, isn't she? They both are,' she said with a happy sigh, her gaze lingering on him in a way that made his whole being light up with impossible joy.

Emotion clogged his throat as he looked down at his daughter, the child they'd already decided to name after his late sister, Sofia.

'They have your beautiful eyes,' he murmured, the wonder of it overwhelming him anew. 'I prayed they would, and now I'm two for two.' *Ne*, there was a hint of smugness in his tone, but he could live with it.

'You prayed?' There was teasing. But there was also devotion. Promises given and offered back.

He looked up, met those silver eyes that had stolen his heart the first moment, even though he'd fought it far too long. 'Oh, yes. From the moment I saw you, I wanted babies with you. Babies with eyes exactly like yours.'

'Ares,' she breathed his name and like a magnet compelling him to her side, he approached her bed.

With his free hand, he meshed his fingers with hers, drew them to his lips and dropped kisses on them. 'I love you. *Efkharisto*.'

'Efkharisto,' his father echoed, looking up from kissing his grandson's chubby cheeks with a tell-tale sheen in his eyes.

Ares shook his head and glanced over at his father. 'No, Baba. It is I who should thank you, for making me see that my future was with Odessa and making me take you back to Alghero.'

Sergios nodded. 'We all won in the end, *yios*.'

'Yes, we did,' his beautiful, sleepy wife murmured from within his arms, her fingers finding and lovingly cradling his cheek as she smiled up at him. 'Love brought us home.'

* * * * *

HER IMPOSSIBLE
BOSS'S BABY

MILLIE ADAMS

MILLS & BOON

CHAPTER ONE

HER BOSS REALLY was the *worst* boss in the entire world. Polly knew she couldn't prove that scientifically. But she felt like her two a.m. summons to the lair of His Beastliness was empirical evidence that Luca Salvatore was indeed the worst.

Worst, worst, worst.

She let the word serve as the lyrics for her ragey walk through the lobby of Luca's building. The night doorman didn't even ask.

"*Buongiorno*, Miss Prescott."

"Hello, Antonio," she said as she carried on through the glossy building, because there was no call to be rude to Antonio just because she hated Luca.

She was granted instant access, probably because Luca would be a bear if he was kept waiting for over two seconds. It made her want to walk slower. But then he would just make up the minutes later in the most annoying way possible. She knew it. Because she knew him.

Four years, eight months, three weeks, five days and three hours. That was how long she'd had this job. That was how long she'd been dealing with Luca Salvatore. Dr. Luca Salvatore. Who was in fact a doctor in more than one way, because he was so obsessive and meticulous that in order to work in the innovative field of medical technology he'd gotten an MD as well as a PhD.

He was brilliant. No one could contest that.

He was also a first-class pain in the ass.

But this job had come to her in a stroke of luck so random and fortuitous the idea of walking away from it had—until this week—been completely out of the question.

For her part, she had run away from home as soon as she was able. She had gotten accepted to a university in Italy that allowed American students to study for free, and she had left Indiana faster than you could say Hoosier. She had never intended to go back home.

Not to her father's uncontrolled cruelty, or her mother's manipulations. Between the two of them, her entire life had been a guessing game. Not knowing who they would be at any given time.

They had been a nice enough suburban family by all accounts. Except for the accounts that were coming from inside the house.

She knew just how much a person could hide about who they really were.

She'd never wanted to be vulnerable, because vulnerabilities could be manipulated. She'd built an impenetrable fortress around herself using the knowledge she'd gotten watching her parents play games with each other and with her.

She'd vowed never to hurt anyone with her behavior, but she'd also made sure to take the lessons of her childhood on board and make them work for her instead of against her.

She had made sure when she arrived in Italy that she

didn't look lost or confused. She had done her very best to look as if she had been to all the beautiful places thousands of times before. She knew it didn't benefit her to look open and vulnerable.

But that was how she had met people at school. Made friends. It was how she had maneuvered her way into an internship at Salvatore Medical Technologies. She wasn't specifically interested in technology, but in the inner workings of a company that size. She was studying marketing because she was so interested in how façades work. And what was marketing if not a carefully crafted and directed façade?

She was an expert with those.

She was also an expert at sizing people up instantly. In her household growing up it had been a matter of emotional survival. She could read a change in a person's mood in a moment. She didn't want to give her parents credit for her success, but she definitely felt like her ability to read a person and a moment had gotten her far.

She'd taken the lump of coal she'd been born into and made it a diamond.

She could still remember the first day at Salvatore. But only vaguely. The day she could remember with absolute clarity, was the first time she had seen Luca Salvatore.

When he had walked into the stunning, modern building, he'd had the look of a shark cutting ruthlessly through the water. His black suit was tailored exquisitely. Showing off broad shoulders and his lean waist. He was tall, well over six feet. But it was not only his physique and height that differentiated him from every other human being in his vicinity. His face was that of a fallen angel.

His black hair was pushed off his forehead, not one strand daring to defy him.

His jaw was square, chiseled as if from stone. His cheekbones hollow, his nose angular and proud, befitting of a Roman emperor.

His eyes were nearly black, and even though he didn't look at her, she'd had the sense that if he did, it would slice her neatly in two.

And then there was his mouth.

She had never given much thought to the shape of a man's mouth. But his was mesmerizing. Firm and uncompromising, and her first, immediate thought was what it might take to get him to smile.

She was, after all, expert at managing the moods of others.

She'd always had to be.

She found she wanted to manage his.

It had been an instant crush. Swift and painful.

She had never felt such an immediate attraction to another person in her life. But then, she had never seen another human being as beautiful as Luca Salvatore.

Of course, what she had discovered very quickly after that was that his personality did a lot to balance out those looks.

He was the most difficult man she had ever known.

Not the most frightening. No. Luca wasn't the type to go around hurting people. That would imply intent.

No, the thing about Luca was that he lived in his own sphere. And in that sphere the only thing that mattered was his goal.

He did not believe in pleasantries, he did not believe in compromise.

She had watched him cut a swath of terror through his staff with his willingness to fire people at will, and his near impossible standards.

That was how she had ended up with her job.

She had been standing next to his assistant—the third one he'd gone through in that month—when he had fired the other woman.

Polly had never seen a person look both relieved and devastated at the same time. Until she had come to work at Salvatore. Then it was an expression she saw often.

And when the woman turned to walk quickly out of the building, she had definitely looked both.

Upset because she had lost her job, relieved because it meant she would never have to deal with Luca again.

And then, for the first time, Luca had looked at Polly.

She had been right. It had been like being cleaved in two.

Even knowing what she did about him, what an ogre he was, how difficult he was, she had been immobilized by his beauty. Those dark brows had been locked together, his irritation written in every line of his face. She had been frightened, for a moment, that she was about to be on the receiving end of his philosophical sword. That she was about to be the next casualty of his mood.

She knew, in that moment, that she could easily be… ruined by him. That he could take her life and bend it around his with ease.

And she would always have to be on guard for that.

"What is your name?"

"Polly. Polly Prescott."

He had looked at her. As if he was scanning her. A machine taking a diagnostic of an object.

"Do you have any experience acting as an assistant?"

"Yes. I'm an intern. I assist whoever needs it."

"Brilliant. You're hired."

"I'm what?"

"Polly Prescott, you're now my assistant."

"I have school."

He had laughed.

"I will make whatever arrangements necessary for you to continue with your studies and integrate the hands-on experience that you're getting at the company."

That was her first experience with just how far Luca was willing to go to get his way.

There was no end to how far.

Her employment contract had been—and remained—one of the most ridiculous things she had ever seen. She wasn't simply a full-time employee, she was on call. Twenty-four hours a day, seven days a week. Which was how she found herself storming into Luca's building at midnight. It wasn't even a strange occurrence.

She entered the code in the lift that would take her upstairs to Luca's penthouse.

She was long past being impressed by the beauty of the place.

If only the same could be said of the man.

He made her heart stop beating every time. Made her breath catch in her throat. And she saw him for extended periods of time every single day. It was still like that.

The good news about Luca was that he was so incredibly difficult to deal with that there was no romanticizing her feelings for him.

The truth was, she was in lust with him. An inconvenience, but hardly fatal.

Sure, it consumed her every waking hour, as did he, but she was aware of it. So that made it…fine.

And possibly not even her problem soon enough.

On a whim she had applied for a job in marketing at a major Milan fashion house two weeks prior. She had been shocked when they'd called her. But they had found out that she had been an assistant to Luca for the past five years and had been intrigued. From there she'd had three phone interviews, and that morning, she had gotten the call that the job was hers if she wanted it.

She was an intriguing prospect, but more than that, she had been Luca Salvatore's personal assistant for longer than any other person had ever managed to keep the position. Luca was famous.

The breakthroughs his company had made in nanotechnology for medical use were extraordinary. And it wasn't just a team that Luca had hired to make these breakthroughs. Many of them had come from him personally.

He was a genius. There was no question.

He was also renowned the world over for being one of the most difficult bastards on the planet.

That was the cost of brilliance, she supposed. When she was being charitable.

Tonight she didn't feel all that charitable.

Tonight, she had a new job offer. Doing something she actually wanted to do, instead of just being Luca Salvatore's girl Friday. Or whatever she was.

She was practically his nanny. That was the truth of it. She was in charge of running interference between him and all of the people who needed to deal with him on a daily basis. There were some days when he just simply couldn't raise his head and be bothered to spare a civil word for people he was supposed to have meetings with, and often, it was her job to go in his stead and do the communicating.

She was in charge of procuring his food, his clothing, making sure that his hotel room was exactly as he would require it. She often went ahead of him to major events and made preparations for his lodging. She managed a massive team of people, and Luca only ever had to deal with her.

It was, he had explained many times, the only way that he could concentrate on his important work.

To minimize and streamline the unimportant details.

Her job was fashioned entirely of unimportant details.

And yet she also knew that those so-called unimportant details had to be managed with precision, or her mad genius of a boss would fly into the kind of rage that nobody wanted to deal with.

She let out a long breath, steeling herself, when the elevator reached the top floor.

And the doors opened, and she stepped into Luca's pristine antechamber before using her key card to unlock the door.

She stepped inside. "I'm here, Luca."

She had called him Dr. Salvatore initially. He was quite anal about that. But she had been given permission to call him Luca three weeks into the job.

It had been strange.

It still was.

Because it humanized him.

And nothing about him was human.

"I'm in my room."

She could tell by his voice that he was in a mood. But then, if he called at midnight, he was always in a mood. He kept the strangest hours of anyone she had ever known. Sometimes she wondered if he slept at all. The truth was, he probably plugged himself into the wall for a couple of hours at the end of every day.

Maybe took off his head for a few minutes and stuck it on a charger.

She strode through his massive living area, her shoes clicking on the black marble tile. And went straight into his bedroom.

He emerged from his walk-in closet just as she did. Wearing nothing but a pair of black pants, resting low on his hips.

He was the robot, but when she saw him her brain short-circuited.

Those broad shoulders, equally broad chest. His well-defined pectoral muscles, his abs...

If she touched him, she would probably find that he was made of steel, rather than flesh and bone. But she had never touched him, so the temptation to do so remained.

After all this time, being in his bedroom shouldn't signify. Seeing him shirtless shouldn't signify, and yet it did.

There was something obscenely sexual about his chest hair. She couldn't get over it.

He was ten years older than her. And her boss.

If she ever confessed her fixation with him to a medical professional she would be clinically diagnosed with daddy issues. But no matter how many times she told herself that she couldn't stop the fixation.

Regrettably, she had learned that for her a sexual fixation was a near impossible thing to exorcise when the object of said fixation was in her path continually.

"What are you doing?" she asked.

"I need to pick a suit. For tomorrow night's speech."

"You have to do it now?"

"Yes," he said, as if she was the foolish one. "I need to practice the speech. And everything needs to be as it will be tomorrow."

"You can't practice in the venue right at this very moment."

"Everything needs to be the same with me," he said.

She felt the last straw descend upon her, and crack her patience completely in half. It had been a monstrous workload in the lead-up to the Singapore conference and Luca had been worse than usual. She'd been toying with taking another job as things got more and more hectic. But she'd been…torn.

Because Luca was…she'd been right. When he'd looked at her the first time she'd known he could destroy her and in many ways she'd let him. Her life revolved around him. Her every move, her every breath.

She'd thought about leaving but she had also felt paralyzed by the thought of a life without him.

Now though…

She could see herself far too clearly.

She'd told herself it was lust. She'd told herself she was armed against all things thanks to her dysfunctional childhood, and in reality she'd…

She'd been holding herself back because of him. Not taking new jobs, not realizing her own potential because she'd let herself get obsessed with him.

Or worse.

Her chest hurt when she looked at him and what was *that* emotion exactly?

She didn't want to know.

She could see he was exasperated, he didn't like having to explain himself. He also didn't care if she was tired. He didn't care if she was upset.

He cared about himself.

She'd put herself in the exact position she'd promised she never would.

Luca wasn't manipulative, not in the slightest. In that way he was nothing like her parents. But the core issue was the same. She cared for someone who didn't care for her. She bent and twisted her life to suit someone else's needs when she'd sworn never to do that.

And if she took a step back and tried to be somewhat sympathetic to the gorgeous billionaire who always got his way, she could appreciate that it must be frustrating to him to try and explain the way that his brain functioned to mere mortals who couldn't even understand what nanotechnology was, much less how it functioned in a medical setting.

She found she had difficulty drumming up sympathy for him, though.

And the truth was, she didn't need to. Because she had another job offer. What was she doing standing in her boss's bedroom in the middle of the night while he stood there shirtless, demanding an opinion on which black suit he was going to wear to speak to a room full of people?

She wasn't afraid of him. She never had been. He had said many times it was one of the things that he appreciated about her.

She met his complete, uncompromising, blunt nature

with relentless cheer. Sometimes with sharpness, but always with efficiency. She had learned that half the problem he had with his past assistants was that they simply crumpled beneath the pressure of working for him. He had appreciated her backbone.

She doubted he would appreciate it now.

"Luca, I cannot believe that you called me out here in the middle of the night to help you choose a suit so that you could rehearse the speech."

"Why? It is entirely consistent with everything you know about me."

The problem was, she couldn't even argue with him.

She was going to anyway, though. "But surely you must understand that it's unreasonable."

"It is part of your employment contract. You're on call."

"Be that as it may, no normal employer would ever subject an employee to this."

"At what point have I ever pretended as if I was a normal employer? No one else is like me. You know this."

"No one else is like you," she said, looking up at the gilded ceiling in his bedroom. "I sure as hell hope so, Luca, because I don't think the world could withstand having another human being on its surface that behaved the way that you do."

"Honesty is appreciated, attitude is unnecessary."

"Oh, I'm sorry. I am running on two hours of sleep because you got me up at two in the morning after staying at the office with you until midnight. I was finally about to go to sleep and then you call me to come down to your personal residence, where you are half-naked, asking for help with something that is simply not pressing by the standards of any other human being. You are a robot, Luca. And I have tirelessly put up with you for the last five years. And I'm not doing it anymore."

"What are you talking about?"

It was all abundantly clear now. She was at a crossroads. She'd been tempted to just stay on the beaten path. To just keep on going. To just stay with Luca and stay stagnant. His favorite piece of office equipment, rather than pursuing her own dreams.

Her own life.

She had to put a stop to it.

She had to be her own best advocate because what was the point of anything that had happened in her whole life up to this point if she failed herself now?

"I quit."

"You must be joking. Nobody quits."

"No. You fire them. Because you find fault with everything they do, and I'm the one person you couldn't find fault with. But I find fault with you. I quit. I'm done. I'm going home and I'm going to bed."

"You cannot quit," he said.

"It's too bad. I am quitting. I have another job, and I don't need yours. I'm getting into marketing. I'm not going to be your sprightly little gofer, running to and fro doing whatever you want."

He looked incensed. Outraged. She had never seen precisely that look on his face before. She had seen him inconvenienced. She had definitely seen him angry. But this was something else. "We have a massive exhibition happening in Singapore next week."

"I am aware. I have planned nearly every detail of the exhibition because I'm the one that's had contact with every presenter, every person involved at the venue, everyone managing food, lodging—"

"You cannot quit before the exhibition."

"I can. And I will."

"You will not. You will give me two weeks' notice as your contract dictates."

The exhibition was all he cared about. Not her upset. Not what he'd done. And she found it sparked a fury she couldn't quell.

"You and your contract can go to hell."

She turned around. And she was just about to walk triumphantly out of the room. Finally. She ignored the tugging in her chest, she ignored the feeling of being bound to him. She ignored the pang of regret that she was never going to see Luca in person ever again, and she was just about to crow her victory, her freedom, when he spoke again.

"If you do not give your proper two weeks' notice, I will ensure that you never work anywhere else ever again."

She turned around. "I already have a job."

"*Cara*, if you think that I do not have the power to remove you from that position before you even begin, then these last five years have been for nothing. Because you have never truly known me. Two weeks. Or your professional life is over before it even begins."

CHAPTER TWO

RAGE WAS A red haze over his vision. A sliver of ice in his gut. Worse, because it was Polly that had made him angry. And that was not Polly's purpose.

She was his assistant. Efficient, perfect in every way. Polly Prescott fascinated him, as no woman ever had.

She had been nineteen when he had first given her the job. And her innocence and inexperience in all things had been visible in those wide blue eyes every time she had looked at him.

He could never understand why other people treated her like she was older. Perhaps more experienced. It was apparent to him that she was fresh off of whatever plane she had arrived on, likely from a small town, having never been in a major city in her life.

But she was hungry. And it was that hunger that had made her such a valuable assistant. She also lacked fear.

He wanted things done exactly as he wanted them done. More than that, he needed it. He did not allow for mistakes. He did not coddle the emotions of others. She seemed to understand that instinctively.

She managed everything in his personal life that required managing. And she did so with ease. At this point, she did so without him even having to ask. The idea of having to train somebody else to do what Polly did on instinct was unthinkable. Particularly this close to the Medical Technology Summit, and to the unveiling of all of his upcoming research that was entering clinical trial stage.

His mother had been the only person in his life who understood him. Who loved him as he was. When she was gone, he'd lost everything. He'd nearly lost himself.

Where his mother had accepted him, his father had sought to change him. To fix him.

He'd always been a person who had obsessions and hyperfocus. His mother had fostered that. She'd helped him learn everything about a topic he found interesting, had added toy cars to his collection whenever possible, along with facts about different engines, makes and models.

His father had hated it. He'd thought it a sign of a weak mind to be so tunnel-visioned when it came to interests. He'd thought it embarrassing that Luca had no friends at school. His mother had told him that people who did not fit in were destined to change the shape of the world, to make it better fit more people.

He'd liked that. When he felt himself not fit, he'd imagined the shape of everything changing around him and he had felt better.

He had been a source of tension between his parents, and he knew it.

When he was nine his mother got sick. Diagnosed with a late-stage cancer that had no hope of being cured. She'd been ignored by her doctors when she'd brought her symptoms to them, and when the illness was discovered it had been too late.

It had destroyed his life. Until he'd found a new focus.

A new purpose.

Medicine.

When it came to illness, particularly the illnesses of women, the medical community had been complacent for too long in his opinion. He had set out to learn everything he could. About technology and about the human body. About how they could both help each other.

There had been so many breakthroughs over the years. But still not the one that he had been hoping for.

But now he was on the verge of finding exactly what he needed for early detection of ovarian cancer with simple, accurate technology that would provide much more information than a blood test followed by a scan. With this, it was possible that the disease could be detected at stage one, and be screened for as part of yearly physicals.

It was the kind of technology that would have kept his own mother alive.

And while all of these things would sell themselves, and backers and researchers would be drawn to the mere rumor of its existence, he knew that making new medical technology ubiquitous was more complicated than that.

Hence the summit.

But for the summit, he needed Polly.

Whatever happened after that, he could focus on it then.

But he would do everything in his power to keep her with him now.

That was all that mattered.

"That is an incredibly horrendous thing to say to someone who has worked for you faithfully for five years."

"Quitting on the verge of something this important to someone you have worked for for five years is an incredibly irresponsible thing to do. And frankly, I thought you were better than that."

"I'm past the point of being able to be guilted into doing your bidding, Luca. I have done nothing less than everything you have asked these past years."

"And why was this the straw that broke the camel's back?"

"Because the camel had somewhere else to go. You have been unreasonable, inflexible, ogreish, some might say, every day these past five years. But I knew that it was the best place for me to be in order to gain experience for what I wanted to do later."

"And I will be an invaluable reference for the rest of your working life if you simply do what I ask now."

Yes. He was inflexible. He was in his very nature, down to his core. A person could not do the level of research that he did and also be the kind of person who bent with the breeze.

His work required focus. It required single-mindedness. It required a certain amount of selfishness around each and every endeavor.

Lucky for him, he had always been accomplished at those things.

His own father had found him confounding. Frustrating. He could admit that he had been a difficult child. Never content. Always obsessed, and there was a point where his father had been forced to contend with him on his own, and it had not gone well.

Luca could be philosophical about that.

Even if he did enjoy that his success was something his father benefited from, and therefore could not ignore. Especially as his father had told him once that he would never amount to anything, because no one as truly strange as his son was could ever make his way in the world.

So Luca had made his way in the world. And then some. Not only that, he was working to change the world. And it was precisely the characteristics his father had told him would preclude him from success that had brought him success.

Luca had found that he could pay people to handle what did not serve him or his work, and that was sufficient.

He didn't need to change. He simply needed to be powerful enough to change the world around him.

He had done so.

He did not accept critiques regarding his personality. Because his personality was irrelevant.

"Have I asked you to do anything that was not explicitly outlined as a possibility in your contract?"

"Your contract did not say that I might be called to your home to consult with you when you were bare-chested, no."

"You seem perturbed by that."

She looked at him, and he saw her cheeks turn a slight shade of rose. She was affected by his nudity, and that was a terrible thing for him to observe. She was his assistant. She was out of bounds in that way. He had placed her there the moment he had first noticed that she was beautiful. He had not noticed immediately.

When he had hired her his immediate thought had been simply replacing one incompetent person with the next, as he knew the churn would continue.

But Polly had broken the cycle. She had become a

one-woman management team. The Swiss Army knife of personal assistants.

And then one night, May twenty-fourth, four years prior, he could recall it clearly, the light in his office had caught strands of gold in her hair, as she had leaned in to hand him his espresso. It was three in the morning, and they were at the office late, with her assisting with whatever he needed.

He had been gripped then, with a hunger that had surpassed anything he had ever known before.

Sex was an appetite, like any other. He could forget about it sometimes, the same as he forgot to eat when he was deeply involved in a project. But eventually, it had to be satisfied. That was how he had always seen it.

A practicality. A necessity.

And because he saw it that way, it made it simple for him to observe the rules around it. And one very clear rule was that one did not make sexual advances to those who were subordinate.

Polly was his subordinate, and an extremely important one. Which meant that that momentary, violent hunger had to be locked away. Which he had done.

Very few things had the will to defy him. But Polly did. And in that, he supposed it shouldn't be such a surprise that on occasion the strength of his need for her defied his rules as well.

But it was nothing he would ever act on.

This was the first time he had looked at her and realized she felt the same.

She always seemed bright-eyed, efficient and practical. He had acknowledged his attraction to her, but he had never thought about her own attractions, desires. He had never taken the step to thinking of her as a set being.

She was a tool. A lovely one. But had never been a whole person to him. Why should she be? It was not reasonable or practical.

And there she was, blushing prettily and demanding that he consider her feelings around the work that he asked her to do. The schedule he asked her to keep.

"You will continue to do your job. There will be no argument about it."

"Two weeks," she said, her blue eyes flashing. The color in her face intensified, and this, he thought, was anger. "I will give you two weeks, Luca. And not a day more. That means the day after the summit ends, I'm coming back to Italy, and I will not see you again."

"I assume that means you'll be flying commercial, then. How nice for you."

She laughed. "I've survived it before. I can surely survive it again."

"I'm not certain that you can. I think that you have forgotten everything that I've given to you, because you're so dedicated to your own fiction. We both know that you are not a sophisticate. Not the one that you pretend to be. When I met you, you had absolutely no job experience."

"I was getting an education."

"And a fine one you got. But don't forget that *many* people have degrees, and the thing that sets you apart is your very particular job experience."

She looked outraged by that. Because he was right. He knew that. "Currently, what sets me apart is that my boss is unreasonable."

"What boss would allow an employee to simply walk away from something this major?"

As far as his personal story went, he was not inclined to share it with the world. That his mother had died of cancer was a basic truth, anyone could discover it for themselves if they wished. But he didn't speak of it.

It would be apparent to that person that the work he did came from personal experience. He did not know if Polly knew that. And he had no inclination to tell her.

It shouldn't make a difference.

"That's the thing. Mostly, it's not about being allowed to do anything. Because it is generally understood that a boss does not own his employee. But you treat me like you do."

"I remind you again of the contract—"

"That's all I am to you, isn't it? I'm a contract. And what you ask doesn't have to be reasonable or human. It simply has to be in the contract. You don't care at all why I might want to leave."

"You said yourself. You have no desire to be an assistant forever."

"I don't. But most especially, Luca, I have no desire to be *your* assistant forever."

He smiled. He couldn't help himself. "Is that supposed to wound me, Polly? Do you think you're the first person to remark that I'm difficult? That I am unpleasant? I know that. I don't care. What I care about is that I accomplish the work that I have set out to accomplish. I don't want friends. I don't want a wife. I don't want children. I want none of the things that would require I managed to find the sort of personality that makes other people comfortable. What I want is to save lives. That is what

I do. If within that realm you find me unfeeling, then I must accept it."

She looked conflicted. But she did not argue. "You have your two weeks. But don't expect me to be cheerful about it."

"I don't require your cheer, *cara*. I simply require your compliance."

CHAPTER THREE

THE NEXT WEEK at work was a study in willpower. Luckily, Polly was in ample possession of willpower. But it was almost like Luca was going out of his way to be difficult. She would have thought that if it was anybody else. That he was doing his level best to make everything as unpleasant as possible to punish her for daring to leave him.

But Luca didn't do things simply for the sake of them, and she could say that she'd never once witnessed him being *petty*. It just wasn't him. He was a man who did things as and only when they were strictly necessary. At least, they had to be necessary in *his* mind.

The trouble for Luca was that what seemed necessary to him did not always seem necessary to other people.

Her included.

Hence the blowup over his midnight suit selection.

But where another person might have gone out of his way to be tirelessly accommodating to make her think that she had made a mistake, or would have gone out of their way to make the last week miserable, Luca was simply Luca. But in the lead-up to the summit, he was more of himself than he often was, which was a particular sort of difficult that really should almost be categorized as its own thing.

The Luca Salvatore Effect.

Perhaps she could get medical studies done on her brain after she finished with the job. Maybe it would become an officially recognized condition.

What happened to a person when they were subject to Luca over long periods of time.

If it became a recognized medical condition Luca might actually care about it, and learn about it. Perhaps that was the path to personal growth for him.

That made her smile. She suppressed it.

She was run ragged. She was absolutely resolved in her decision to leave.

She was fantasizing about the new job. About the freedom she would have there. The freedom to work normal hours. Or maybe just slightly extended hours rather than being on call twenty-four hours a day.

The freedom to leave her job and not think about her boss.

Constantly. Continually. Every moment of every day.

Even now, she wasn't in the office, she was at her own apartment making phone calls and working on the details with the hotel in Singapore, and she was thinking about Luca.

About getting his room ready when they arrived in Singapore, about exactly what he would need. About how his mood would turn even more rigid upon arrival because he would be anticipating giving a speech, being out of his element, the necessary evil of stepping away from his research.

Of course, it was to talk about his research. So there was every chance he would glory in that.

Then, her thoughts turned to how he had looked the night she had quit. His bare chest. And the anger in his eyes.

It was a confusing combination of things, things that continued to occupy her brain space in spite of herself.

But that was the problem. This wasn't just a job. There were too many things tied up in it. It had been a matter of survival. Realizing her dreams, and then eventually it had been…her attachment to Luca.

That was the problem. He was the *worst*. She acknowledged that. She knew it. She felt it. He was unreasonable. He did things that no normal person would ever do, and he expected her to do things that no sane human being would expect their employees to do. And yet, she found herself anticipating him. She found herself in some ways feeling even strangely protective of him and his eccentricities.

Then there was the fact that he was really effing hot. Which kept her from imprinting on any other man. So here she was, suspended between a raft of uncomfortable feelings, none of which she wanted.

He had been her whole life for these last five years.

Perhaps that was the problem. There was nothing and no one else. She had been far too focused on changing her life. On making something better for herself. And that had encouraged her to make her job all-encompassing. Really, the issue was her desperation. To escape what she had been. To never have to go back to the life that she had lived with her parents.

To maintain control.

In the strangest way, even though Luca was a tyrant, she *was* in control in this life. She managed all the particulars of his daily life. While she was often creating an environment that suited him, she knew everything about it.

She was the cruise director.

Perhaps that was her problem now. She was on the cusp of a change. Nobody wanted change. Change, even when it was change that you wanted, even when it was change that felt inevitable, was frightening.

She was going to move away from Rome. It had been her home these last five years.

Her first time out of the United States, and she simply didn't miss it. She hadn't gone back. She had spent these past years traveling, but she'd had this as her home base.

She had lived in the same apartment now for three years.

That was the problem.

She was leaving everything that she knew now. That was why it all felt unsettled.

It wasn't Luca.

Because she didn't want to believe that she had *softer* feelings for Luca.

When he was just the most unreasonable human being on the planet.

And yet.

He didn't care about her. The fact that his activities hadn't in any way changed in the past week indicated that. He was nothing in response to her leaving. He had been perturbed when he had first heard about it because it was a change he wasn't in control of. And when it came to not liking change Luca was a champion.

But it had nothing to do with her. Nothing to do with

actually wanting her around, or caring about her in any regard.

And the same went for her.

She didn't care about him. She just felt attached to her life.

Understandable.

That was all.

When it was finally time for them to leave for the summit, she felt like there was a guillotine about to fall.

Because this was it. The end of the road.

Maybe she should have arranged to stay over in Singapore for a while after. A little bit of time between the end of one job and the beginning of another. Time to explore a part of the world she hadn't seen before, and perhaps embrace new experiences.

For one fleeting moment she imagined what it would be like if she cut loose entirely. If she forgot herself. If she found a man—a man that wasn't Luca—and had a wild fling.

Her whole being rejected that instantly.

That just wasn't her.

She wasn't a virgin out of any sense of principle.

It was only that...

You are preoccupied by him.

Was that really the only reason?

Because yes, he was sexy. Gorgeous in a way that no other man had ever been to her, but she didn't have feelings for him. Surely impossible attraction wasn't so strong that it could be the sole reason she had never taken a lover.

She pushed that out of her mind deliberately, because she knew that Luca was going to arrive any moment.

She was bustling around on the private plane making sure that everything was in order.

Making sure his favorite food and drink were available, and that everything was the exact right temperature.

"I don't see three notebooks," she said, digging around the space.

The stewardess frowned. "Aren't there two?"

"Dr. Salvatore has requested there be *three*. That is standard for any flight exceeding three hours."

"Can't he bring his own?"

She felt her hackles rising. "Dr. Salvatore does not pay a staff to ready things for him so that he can spend precious thinking time pondering the quantity of his own notebooks."

And there it was. As easy to find as ever. The umbrage that she felt on his behalf when things were not exactly as he had dictated they be.

The issue was…she hadn't done this job all these years without undergoing a certain level of indoctrination where Luca was concerned.

The man was curing cancer. It sort of balanced out the whole being an asshole thing.

That didn't mean she could or should work for him forever, but it wasn't as if she could prove his eccentricities weren't merited.

The woman looked askance at Polly and Polly felt… *peeled*. Like the flight attendant was seeing something other than Polly's professionalism at work and Polly did not like it.

"You must be new," Polly said, pinning the other woman beneath her most pointed gaze and clinging to her haughty PA front because it was better than being *seen*.

At that exact moment she heard heavy footsteps behind her, and she turned to see Luca standing there. She couldn't explain the physical reaction she had to the sight of him.

She had seen him yesterday, after all. He ought to be commonplace in every way.

But then, hadn't she just spent the past week trying to untangle why her feelings for him, her feelings about leaving, didn't seem as straightforward as they should.

"There is an issue with the notebooks," Polly said slowly. "But it will be remedied."

His gaze never left her.

"Good," he said.

Polly dialed the private airline concierge at the airport. "I need a notebook brought to Dr. Salvatore's plane within the next fifteen minutes. Yes." She gave the specifications, and then got off the phone. Because there were measurements, materials and page space requirements.

"Everything will be in place," she said.

He nodded once, and then disappeared into the bedroom at the back of the plane, closing the door behind him.

She let out a breath, and the stewardess looked at her. "Are you afraid of him? Is that why you're so concerned about his notebooks?"

Afraid? This woman thought… Polly was afraid?

She frowned. "I'm not *afraid* of him. But Dr. Salvatore is a genius. And there are certain things that he requires so that his brain is free to think about medical mysteries. I might be leaving my job but—"

"So, you don't like it. *Or* him."

This was now some weird battle of wills between her

and this other woman. Like she was bound and determined to make Polly admit that Luca was unreasonable. And Polly thought he *was* in many respects, but she had context for him. And dammit she would not say it to this other woman.

"If you take issue with Dr. Salvatore and how he works, then perhaps this should be your first and last flight for him," she bit out.

Luca chose that moment to come out of the bedroom. "There is no need to be defensive of me, Polly. Though it is appreciated. I didn't realize you were so concerned with my image. Having said that, I don't care if the attendant finds me unreasonable or not." His focus was turned to the other woman. "All it requires is that she do her job. Is that possible?"

The flight attendant nodded, looking the kind of intimidated that Polly simply didn't feel around him anymore.

After all that, the notebook finally arrived, and they were able to settle in to take off.

She tried to live that experience through the eyes of a woman who had never encountered Luca before.

She tried to dissect her own response to it.

It was unreasonable to feel like Luca needed three notebooks. Luca felt like he needed three notebooks, but she knew that it was… It was one of his particular habits.

One of his ways.

She wondered when she had become so understanding to those ways.

She would like to think that she *wasn't*. She would like to think that this was just her, doing her job as well as she'd always done to the end. After all, she had just gotten angry with him about calling her to his apartment at midnight. But was that the ridiculousness of the request, the hour, or the way it had made her feel to look at him half-naked?

You don't have to know. Because you're getting a new job.

She felt relief. For the first time in a week. Maybe for the first time in five years. She didn't have to know the answer to the question about Luca. Because she simply wasn't going to be part of his life anymore.

You were never part of his life. You might as well be a paperweight.

A paperweight he really liked, but a paperweight all the same.

She had gotten very used to flying by private jet. She liked it. It was going to be hard to give up.

But she didn't need luxury.

She wanted to be important. A main character in her own life. She had never been that growing up. She had been the supporting character to her parents, and she was simply tired of it. She'd been a prop. Used when convenient, ignored when not. They were the main cast, they were all that mattered.

It was the same with Luca.

Because he could see one perspective, one way of being, and it was his own. Everything else was one of those insignificant extras.

They didn't speak, as was customary on a long flight. She had brought a book, and Luca filled each notebook. She wondered sometimes if he did it because he had asked for them, and he was trying to prove to himself and others that his eccentricities were a necessity. Or perhaps he simply knew that a long flight produced three note-books' worth of thoughts.

"You could digitize your notes," she pointed out.

She didn't know why she said it. She was only baiting him. And after hours of sitting across from him, having food, having a nap, it was like commentary was just begging to be made. Even though she knew better.

"I do not see the point in changing something that works," he responded, without looking up at her.

"You have endless stacks of notebooks," she said.

"Yes. I do. I also have the space to organize them."

"If they were digitized they would be searchable."

He looked up at her like she had sprouted a second head. "I remember what is in every notebook."

There was something earnest in the way that he responded to that, and it reminded her why it was sometimes easy to defend him, to feel confusion about him. He wasn't actually being difficult, or obstinate for the sake of it. He genuinely *couldn't* understand why she would suggest such a thing because he couldn't imagine having a hard time remembering where he'd written what.

She had to wonder what a childhood with a brain like that must've been like. Were people in awe of him even then?

"Have you always been like this?" she asked, saying it out loud in spite of herself.

But why not? She was leaving.

"Like what?"

"You're so particular. About *everything*. And certain. Though, your certainty is usually founded."

"You've worked with me for five years, you only now wonder?"

"I'm leaving. Maybe that's what made me wonder."

There was a clock ticking on this, she realized. She would never understand herself or what her life had been for the past five years if she couldn't understand him. It suddenly felt imperative.

"I don't know how to answer the question. I have always been myself. Have you always had your average capacity for memory?"

"Yes," she said. "I have always been this way."

"So have I. Though not always interested in medicine. My mother died when I was ten. That changed the course of my life."

He said it matter-of-factly, but there was something underlying his tone. An intensity that she recognized. It came up with certain medical discoveries. Certain things.

"I'm sorry," she said. She had never really thought about Luca's parents. She had always thought he had sprung fully formed from the ground a full-grown man.

It was impossible to imagine him as a child.

And now she was imagining him as a child in pain.

"I decided that I wanted to find out what could be done. To prevent other people dying in the way that she did. I wanted to fix it. Of course, you cannot fix something like that. Not with all the medical discoveries in the world. I might be able to prevent other people from dying, but I cannot bring her back. It is an obvious thing. But one I did not fully think of as a child. I was driven, I think to try and restore what I'd lost." He lifted a shoulder. "Now I'm simply driven."

She knew many of his other employees thought of him as emotionless. But she'd always known that wasn't true. He had a great many emotions surrounding what he wanted and needed in his environment. He could be exacting, short-tempered and ill-humored. All of which were emotions.

What she hadn't witnessed were…softer emotions.

But now she was forced to imagine him as a small boy. Missing his mother. Believing, on some level, that he could use his incredible brain to bring her back.

"What did you…think about before then?" she asked.

"Toy cars," he said.

"Toy cars?"

"*All* cars. But I had a large collection of toys."

"Did your parents buy them for you?"

"My mother did. My father thought it was strange. To collect something so obsessively and know all of the details about it." His lips curved upward. Almost a smile and yet somehow not. "It is strange. He was correct."

She felt bound up by the sympathy blooming inside of her. Looking at his stark, handsome face as he recounted loss, pain.

The feeling of being different. An outsider.

She knew that all too well. She'd always felt outside. She hadn't been able to invite friends to her house because her parents had been so volatile and unpredictable. She'd made a mask of ease that she wore with the outside world. She'd learned to fashion herself into a very nice facsimile of someone who was having a normal experience of life and growing up. She'd learned to close herself off, to protect herself from her mother's fractious insults and her father's explosions of verbal rage where he'd been willing to say anything, no matter how cruel, to get a response.

Like reducing the people around him to tears was the ultimate source of power.

She'd become a placid shell. Watching, always taking in information from the scene around her, never ever giving the deep, real parts of herself away because that would mean exposing herself to pain.

She'd thought it would arm her against Luca, she supposed. But the problem was, he wasn't manipulative.

Luca could only ever be Luca.

It was…him. And perhaps it was that lack of veneer that had finally gotten beneath her protections.

"I don't think it's so strange," she said softly. "And anyway, why would you make your child feel like they were strange?"

"He didn't want me to be. He was quite a successful man, my father. Relatively, I mean. He wanted me to be like him. But in order to do that, he felt that I would need to behave differently. He was a salesman. Everything he did was about connections. I was bad at them. But, I found success my own way. I don't need to learn the things that he thought were so important. I simply need to lean into my own strengths." He looked down at his notebooks, and then back at her. "That does mean filling in three physical notebooks on a long-haul flight."

She sighed. "I suppose I can't argue with you."

"You could," he pointed out.

She could, but it would be like flailing at a brick wall. "I don't need to," she said.

She decided to take another nap. And by the time they landed, she was well-rested.

A car met them at the jet and whisked them away, and she did her best not to marinate on the conversation they'd had earlier. Did her best to not sink into sentimentality.

Why had she ever asked him these things about his

life before? She could imagine him, a small boy, left with the one parent that didn't understand him, and it made her chest get tight.

Of course, now Luca was a genius billionaire, so when people didn't understand him they mostly said nothing.

But it was still a function of his life. A feature of who he was.

It was still a thing he had to cope with.

He was a terrible boss. He was inflexible, and completely one-track-minded. And yet, he was nothing like her parents. And perhaps that was why, in spite of herself, she felt affection for him. Or something adjacent to affection.

The realization made her heart jump, and she began to catalog the details around them. The beautiful buildings, the pristine cleanliness that was normally absent in major cities.

It was genuinely one of the most spectacular places she had ever seen in her life, natural splendor colliding with man-made innovations.

She could see why he had chosen this place as the site where they would learn about new advancements in medicine.

This place felt like the future. Luca was brilliant when it came to anything that had to do with his work.

And something else entirely when it came to other details about life.

But he was honest. And there were no guessing games with him.

Maybe that was why she wasn't afraid of him. Maybe it was why she didn't find him intimidating in the way that many people did.

Because she would rather know where she stood. Even if the ground was precarious.

When they arrived at the hotel she was momentarily distracted by the glory of it. Traveling with Luca meant she had been exposed to a heavy amount of luxury over the past few years, but this was beyond her expectations.

The hotel was a square column with great open sections that spanned several floors, held up by lit pillars covered in twining vines. A resplendent representation of nature in the middle of the city.

The lobby was modern and sleek, with a great glass pillar at the center, almost like a greenhouse, containing a veritable jungle while all around them were modern amenities and clean lines.

Luca barely gave their surroundings a second glance. Instead he went directly to his room and left Polly to see to the details. Both of the summit itself and their star.

She didn't mind. This would help her get out of her own head.

Because there was no time to think. Everything was moving at a rapid pace. She had to ensure that all of the details were in order.

These sorts of events were the part of her job she loved the most.

There was a certain amount of smoothing over his interpersonal relations that she did, and she enjoyed that.

She realized that she was Luca's marketer in many ways.

She sold the man, because he refused to do it.

His work sold itself, but he... He was another matter.

When she checked the clock she realized it was nearly time for the opening speech of the summit.

Of course, Luca would be giving it.

He was a very compelling public speaker. For all that he lacked when he was trying to make connections around the room, he compensated for it beautifully when he was on the stage. He was such a magnetic man. So brilliantly handsome. So absolutely enthralling.

Maybe she was biased.

She didn't think she was.

Until this past week she had been convinced she didn't much care for him at all, but faced with the prospect of leaving him, her thoughts were turning in an entirely different direction.

She used her key card—because she always had a key to his room—and let herself in.

And was stunned when he walked out of the bathroom wearing nothing but a towel slung low around his hips. Water droplets were sliding down his broad, well-muscled chest, and she felt desire strike her like an arrow straight between her thighs.

Why was she doomed to encounter him half-dressed so many times in a row? It wasn't like it had never happened before, but it hadn't happened quite so frequently.

"I'm sorry," she said.

She felt her face betraying her. It was so hot she knew it had to be bright red. Surely he wouldn't miss that.

"It is no matter," he said, as if he'd missed it entirely.

For all he seemed obsessed wholly with his work, she knew he had lovers. His lovers were part of what she dealt with on occasion when he was too busy to manage them. Once he was done with them, he was done.

And yet, he always seemed so dispassionate to her.

It was impossible to imagine what it would be like when he was with a woman. When he…

Perhaps, virgins should not attempt to fantasize about how their bosses made love.

Made love.

There was no question that Luca did not make love.

He would probably be the first to say it. In wholly blunt terms.

She couldn't even hate him for that.

He was honest. And maybe that deserved some level of appreciation.

It wasn't his honesty she was appreciative of at the moment, however.

"It isn't professional," she said.

"Right," he said.

For a moment he looked apologetic. And she realized he had thought that she meant him, and not her.

"I meant *me*," she said. "I should have knocked."

"You have a key to my room for a reason. You are supposed to assist without interruption."

"Still. It would have perhaps been a good idea for me to make sure that you were not in a state of undress."

"I am not a maiden," he said.

She looked at him. "Was that a joke, Luca?"

"Yes and no. It's true. But also, I was being funny."

She laughed, in spite of herself. Because every moment of the last five years hadn't been terrible. And this one certainly wasn't.

"Well. It was amusing."

She felt a sudden tension rise between them, and she turned away from him. "I am going to get ready. And I will meet you in the ballroom."

"As you wish."

CHAPTER FOUR

LUCA COULDN'T GET Polly's expression out of his head. She had been looking at his body. It wasn't the first time. She had done so at his apartment last week the night she had quit.

She was aware of him physically. And she was nearly not his assistant anymore, which was pushing the bonds of his control.

He could not want her.

And yet.

He liked clear rules, and he liked to follow them. He spent so much of his time pondering the mysteries of humanity. Of science. The human body, and what men could accomplish when they studied that body.

There was no room for gray areas in his life.

Polly had been his first window into understanding the lure of reaching for something you should not touch.

Obsession, he'd called it. Because he was familiar enough with obsession and that didn't have to be sexual. It wasn't forbidden for him to catalog her outfits, her mannerisms, the way her hair moved when she tossed her head. And how it changed depending on whether she was amused, annoyed, or upset.

Obsession, because it could be nothing more.

Or rather, it had never been able to be more because she was his assistant and he would never, ever violate his position of power by seducing his assistant.

He thought about how she was leaving him, and he was beset by rage again.

But there was something about the rage that stoked the fire of that forbidden desire even higher.

This was not attraction as he knew it.

He was attracted to women. Their round bodies, their softness. He was not particular about the particular shape or features of a woman. He simply enjoyed the all-encompassing air of femininity. Soft skin, floral scents. When he indulged himself, he appreciated every aspect of that indulgence.

But it was never *this*. This aching pull that he had felt ever since that night last week.

Her defense of him on the plane had added a strange sort of sensation to the mix.

He was also not a man who enjoyed novelty.

He liked to be assured of things. To be certain in them.

In his work, he dealt in the miraculous and mysterious. He did not need any more of it. That was what he told himself. And yet, he found himself being fascinated by her in new and distracting ways.

And he was not a man given to distraction.

"Go and ready yourself," he said.

She nodded, and scurried from the room, as efficient as ever.

And he was left to get ready. Everything he was meant to wear was chosen, and ordered, so that it would be easy for him to put together, easy for him to find which suits went with which speech.

It was no matter to him whether anyone understood that or not, but for him, each detail flowed into one another. And it was an exceptionally important thing. Disrupt one link in the chain and the whole of it was compromised.

He would have to find someone else who could handle his details.

He thought of that as he put on his black shirt, black tie and black suit. He did not have to run through his speech again, he had it memorized. Each and every word. Every pause.

He was very good with this sort of thing. He had ample time to rehearse. If he could rehearse everything, he wouldn't need an assistant. But unfortunately, life moved at a pace, and interaction was often random.

None of that mattered tonight, though. Because tonight, he was going to be giving the most defining speech of his career, introducing the early detection processes and technologies that had been so long missing from the world of medicine.

Everyone wanted a cure for cancer. He among them.

But in the absence of a cure for advanced cancers, early detection was almost as good.

He would be saying just that tonight.

There was a knock on the door. He knew that it was her. She did not normally knock, but she had indicated that she thought she should have after walking in on him in a state of undress. Also, it was just how she would knock. Brisk, efficient. Not timid, even though what had occurred earlier had clearly embarrassed her.

He was fascinated by his assistant. He had made a study of her.

How could he not?

He had never known anyone like her.

She was expert with all people. Soft when she needed to be, hard when it was required. She seemed to possess the ability to make anyone feel at ease. And the truth was, if he could see that it must be profound.

She also seemed to take people exactly as they were, with no questions. She evaluated them and the situation, clearly and cleanly, and then moved on.

She accepted him in a way no one else ever had.

Not since his mother.

"Come in," he said.

The door opened. And there was Polly, wearing a fuchsia-colored dress that conformed to her curves, hugging her body tightly, flaring out down past her knees. The neckline was plunging, revealing the plump curve of her breasts.

Damn, but she was beautiful. He was not a man who wanted what he couldn't have, as a general rule.

That had been a choice.

It had nothing to do with compartmentalizing or appetites or anything of the like.

No. It had to do with being a small boy who looked at groups of kids playing together and couldn't figure out how to approach them. It had to do with loving a mother who had gone, never to return.

Having a father he could never please no matter how hard he tried.

He had given up on desiring what he could not have.

He was a billionaire. There was never a reason—not one—for him to ever be desirous of that which could not be his.

And yet, he wanted her.

In that moment, more than he could remember wanting anything.

It was a craving.

What would it look like, peeling that dress away from her body, exposing more of her skin?

He nearly growled, but he held it back, because he knew well enough to know she would find that disturbing.

"It suits you," he said, keeping his tone brisk.

She blinked. "Thank you."

"Everyone in attendance will be very impressed."

"With your assistant?"

Polly was occasionally miscaptioned as his date. It never bothered them.

He didn't bring dates to things like this. There was no reason. He didn't need to date, he needed somebody who understood him. Somebody who understood the business.

Someone who could take what he was trying to say and spin it into something interesting.

She was very good at that.

He did not take her arm, he never did, though he had known a momentary temptation to do so.

They walked out of the hotel room together, and to the elevator.

She was beautiful at his side, as ever. And he found himself fighting the urge to touch her.

He was on the cusp of the most important thing he had yet discovered and launched to the public, and he was drowning in novelty. He didn't like novelty.

He could not afford the distraction. This was not the launch of a product designed to simply generate income.

This was something that could very well change the world. His libido had no space in the equation.

He was a man of infinite control. In fact, it had never even been difficult for him.

One fuchsia dress and a pleasing collection of rounded curves would not derail him now.

They moved into the ballroom, all the glittering opulence. He felt the tension sometimes, the necessary generation of massive funds when it came to working with this sort of technology. He wanted everything to be freely accessible to those who needed it. And yet, the actual work itself required massive amounts of money to keep it moving. And so, it required playing a game. It required the generation of wealth.

His own personal fortune had been amassed with investments elsewhere. Property portfolios, and other work. While his medical corporation generated billions, it was all put back into research, and medical funding.

For him, the act of making money was a simple thing. It all related to that focus.

Focus that would not be splintered now.

He moved away from Polly and made his way to the front of the room. His very presence signaled that it was time for everyone to take their seats.

And then, he took his place on the stage. Every word, every inflection was planned. And every portion of the speech was articulated exactly as he had intended.

He knew exactly what he was about.

The excitement in the room was palpable. This discovery changed so many things.

And while the room was full of a great many investors, people who cared primarily about the monetary value of something like this, there were also people who took it for what it was.

A chance to save lives.

And the truth was, while the medical-industrial complex certainly had its issues, issues that Luca himself fought against, it was also made up of people. And even investors loved people who got cancer. Even they felt an investment in this change.

Because the truth was, they lived in a world where money could only help with your treatments to a point. If the ability to discover and detect an illness didn't exist, then you were not insulated. Not even by your billions.

Everyone benefited from this.

"As part of the research phase, we will be looking specifically at monitoring those with family history who cannot pay for conventional medical care."

A ripple went through the crowd. "We will be sourcing participants from around the world. That way we can see the effectiveness on people who come from a variety of backgrounds. It is important to our research that we spread the information as broadly as we possibly can. We must collect all the data that we can. This is the beginning to what we truly all hope for. A cure. And this proves that we are not defeated by answers that have eluded us for all this time. There are still discoveries to make. And we will make them. This is the beginning of a very exciting summit. We will pool knowledge, and together we will find the answers to the most pressing medical concerns we face in society."

The applause when he got off the stage was deafening.

He ignored it. He didn't do this for accolades.

They were immaterial.

He did not do this for glory.

He felt Polly's gaze on him, he knew it was her without having to look.

But he did look, and he saw that her eyes were glistening.

She was emotional. He wondered why.

It was not, after all, a personal thing to her, at least not as far as he knew. He had done a background check on her when he had made her his assistant, and nothing in her files suggested she had experience with losing a family member to disease.

He went to his table, one occupied by the chief investors, and sat by Polly. He ignored the investors and leaned toward her. "Are you upset?"

She shook her head. "I'm not upset. I'm simply moved. I understand more now why this matters to you."

She cared about that? She was angry with him. If she wasn't, she wouldn't have quit.

It made no sense that she would be moved to tears by his experience in that case.

She changed the conversation, shifted it, included the investors. She was good at that. She maneuvered it so that he had only to answer questions about the research. And peppered things with delightful, humorous anecdotes and personal remarks. The kind of conversation that left everyone feeling as if they had had a good interaction with him, even though Polly had done most of the conversing.

He did not know what he would do without her.

Anger began to build inside of him, and it only got worse in the following days. As she continued to prove utterly indispensable, and ravishingly beautiful every night for the formal events.

What had been contained by the rules of society, of professionalism, now felt less clear. He'd banked his need for her all this time because it was the right thing to do. But she was leaving now, which meant every word, every interaction, felt like it had a different meaning to it. Different rules.

Or worse: no rules at all.

He was a man who often relied on rules.

And now she was Polly, without the fence of appropriate boss/employee relations surrounding her.

So when she did something for him, he couldn't simply dismiss it as her doing her job.

When he earned a smile it no longer felt like it was strictly her duty.

When her fingertips brushed his he wasn't obliged to pretend he didn't feel sparks of electricity winding through him, that his gut wasn't tight with need. That his body wasn't on high alert.

It built, over the course of all these days. It was nearly physical pain.

The hotel itself was one of the most storied venues in all of Singapore, and yet Polly made it look pale in comparison.

It was such an odd thing. Her beauty had always been undeniable. And yet, she had never been the type to actively court attention. Her beauty had never been *sensual*.

It was as if it was a costume that she put on, and yet once he had seen the inherent sensuality in her he could not unsee it.

He felt utterly entranced by it. By her.

On the last night, she wore gold. She was utterly resplendent, and he was meant to focus on the conclusions of the week. All upcoming research projects from universities and smaller medical tech companies. He was choosing investments himself, that he might help further broader medical research.

That should be his focus.

And yet, he found himself captured by Polly. He noticed that many men were. Her long hair fell in waves over her shoulders. Her body was on tempting display, barely covered by the liquid gold gown she wore.

And after this, she would be leaving his life forever. It was the thing he had been avoiding thinking about. Suddenly, it was all he could think of. It filled his mind, filled his vision.

She had been everything these past few years. She had been compelling, constant, consistent.

She was the content of the inner workings of his life. And he could not remember a time when he did not have her.

At the same time, he wanted to bury his fingers in her hair and claim that sweet mouth for himself.

He thought that, standing right in the glittering ballroom where everyone was celebrating a successful summit.

He thought only of kissing Polly.

What if he did? What if he claimed the one thing he should not have? What if he claimed the one thing he should not want? How different would it feel?

Perhaps he could do something with this gnawing ache. This craving, by making it real.

Suddenly, sex became something different. Something beyond the usual appetite, something beyond even a general craving.

He would die if he did not have her. He was not a man given to excess. And so this first experience of wanting something excessively was like a drug.

He had never taken those either. Only because he knew himself to be a man of obsession. A man who would likely lose himself entirely if addiction were to ever meet obsession.

And yet, that was what she felt like.

Addiction. Obsession.

Something he could not control.

People were dancing. He never partook in such things. These were nothing more than business events to him, and he did not participate in the more festive aspects. But as he saw her standing there on the edge of the dance floor looking on, he realized that either she would stand there alone—which was a crime all on its own—or another man would ask her to dance. Another man would take her in his arms.

He could not allow that. He crossed the room to her. "Luca—"

"Dance with me," he commanded.

"What?"

"You do not need me to repeat myself. You heard me. Dance with me." He realized then that he had repeated himself anyway.

"Oh."

That was neither an affirmation nor a rejection. So, he took her hand without waiting for either one. He brought her out to the dance floor and pulled her against his chest. The contact was electric. Her breasts brushed against him, and he wanted nothing more than to clear the room and strip her body of that offending dress. It was beautiful, and yet it was an obstacle. And he supported the removal of obstacles.

"Luca," she said, her eyes round. Was she afraid of him? Or was it something else? He could not read it. He did best when emotions were simple. Like science. When there were definitive answers. When things became open-ended he found he could not know them, and when he could not know something, he was only ever angry at it. And yet, he was not angry at her.

"Do I scare you?"

"Yes," she whispered.

"I'm sorry."

He stepped away from her, regret filling him.

But she took a step toward him, and put her hand on his forearm. "No, Luca. You scare me because I want you too."

CHAPTER FIVE

HER HEART WAS thundering in her ears. Had she really just told her boss that she wanted him?

Had she really just *assumed* that he wanted her?

But the way that he had touched her…

Luca was a great many things, but subtle was not one of them. And the last week had felt like an assault. Like suddenly all that was sensual in him had been turned on to her, with the full force of a tractor beam.

It had been the most exciting, delicious, terrifying week of her life.

She had done her best to ignore it. But every moment of every day had only ramped up her arousal. Had only made her desire more insistent.

She was leaving him.

He was the only man that she had ever wanted like this.

She was sure every therapist in the world would say that that was not how you dealt with your daddy issues. She didn't care. She didn't want healthy. She wanted something that felt good. She wanted something for herself.

Because her feelings for Luca were a complicated tangle and she was never going to be able to work through them.

She was taking another job. She was moving across

the country. She wanted him in a way that blotted out any potential need for other men.

She wanted him.

It was a terrible thing. A great and terrible thing.

"Be explicitly clear in what you mean," he said, closing the distance between them. They were surrounded by people.

Everyone would know.

But then, the fire that had burned in Luca's dark eyes these past few days had been bright enough, hot enough for anyone to see it.

In fact, one of the female scientists had said something to her just last night.

"I thought he was your boss. I didn't realize the two of you..."

"We aren't."

"He certainly wants to."

"It would be inappropriate," she had replied.

"Sometimes inappropriate is the most fun."

She didn't think she wanted Luca because it was *inappropriate*. Rather she wanted him because...

Because she had never known anyone else like him. Because she had never seen a man so beautiful and remote. He was like a lost gem, and he would hate to be compared to a gem but it was true. He was hard, all angles and brilliant light.

He was painful to look at. Painful to care about.

She did care about him. That was the worst part.

How could you not care about a man this brilliant? This singular?

And it had never been easy. It had never been anything half so simple as having a crush on her boss.

She knew every inch of Luca's life. Every brick that comprised who he was. And she knew that there was not a single space for another person. Not as a partner. Not as anything other than a useful tool.

But she knew also that this was the only way that she could ever purge that need for him.

Now that she actually would be leaving him.

The very idea of trying to love Luca made her want to die. A woman could dash herself upon those rocks over and over again, and she would never find any satisfaction.

She had seen women leave his home.

Looking high on the experience of having been with him. He never called them again.

She knew because eventually she had to block or reroute their calls. Luca wasn't a playboy, but he wasn't celibate either.

He had told her once, very bluntly, that for him sexual release was a necessary function. But that he felt nothing emotional about it. Any more than he would eating a meal.

That lived inside of her.

And the same likely couldn't be said for her. It was very possible that if she slept with him she would experience emotional ramifications. And he wouldn't.

But she was strong. She could withstand it.

And tonight, she was finally going to get something that she wanted out of this relationship. Maybe for a few minutes, he would even see her as a human being, and not simply a more complex than average paperweight.

What would happen if she was honest with him? If she told him this thing was destroying her from the inside? That it was growing so unbearable it was part of why she was finally leaving, this sensation that she cared for him while she was nothing at all but furniture to him? That it felt too big to be contained anymore?

That she didn't understand it. Because how could she when she'd never even touched another man?

She wasn't going to admit that.

"Luca," she said slowly. "I'm not afraid of you. I'm afraid of how powerful this feeling is between us. I want you."

The sound he made was like a growl. It made her feel electrified. "I want you," he whispered, so close to her now that she was dizzy with the scent of him. "Naked."

"Yes," she said.

"What is the protocol? Do we have to stay? Will we be seen as rude?"

He was genuinely asking. This was part of her job. Guiding him when the social situation didn't make sense to him. Though he didn't often ask so bluntly.

The truth was they would be seen as two people sneaking off to have sex. Which was exactly what they were.

"Everyone will know," she said. "They won't find it rude. Though we might end up being the subject of gossip."

"I don't care about that," he said.

"Neither do I."

She was leaving. She wouldn't be part of this world anymore. She didn't care.

They had never even kissed. But she didn't need to test her need for him that way. She already knew.

He took her hand, and she was stunned by how rough it was. How strong. Hot. "Then if they already know, there is no reason to be subtle about it."

He sounded relieved by that. He would be. He wasn't subtle. Thank God. Because another man might not have answered her so honestly regarding their shared desire. There were no games here, and for a woman without experience, that was ideal.

He pulled her away from the dance floor, straight through the ballroom. Her heart was racing, her whole body on high alert.

She wasn't going to regret this.

This felt like her compensation. Her severance. Her parting gift.

To finally have something from him.

To finally have some of his control.

Oh, she'd dreamed of it. As much as she'd tried to pretend she didn't. As much as she'd told herself she wasn't unendingly curious about how he was in bed, she had wondered.

Did he ever let himself off leash entirely?

And what was that like?

All that focus, force and obsession, zeroed in on another person.

The idea was dizzying.

They were silent in the elevator, and then, his hand over hers, he led her back down the hall toward his suite.

He opened the door, and closed it. And as soon as it closed behind them, he wrapped his arm around her waist and pulled her heart up against him. Her breath exited her body in a gust.

Right then she wanted to cry. Right then it was too much, and so was he.

She was leaving him. He was infuriating. Why wasn't it simpler?

"Do you know how much I wish I could hate you?" she whispered, their mouths a mere whisper from each other.

"Why is that, *cara*?"

"Because you're the worst boss. Because you don't see me as a human being. Because you have treated me like an incidental these past five years."

"I treat you the same way I do everybody else."

The words were a knife's blade, turning inside her.

"Exactly," she said. "And you shouldn't. You should treat me like I'm special. Because I do things for you that nobody else does. And now I know for sure, you feel things for me that you don't feel for anyone else who works for you."

"It is attraction, Polly."

He said it so blandly. As if it could never be that simple.

"Nonetheless, Luca, the way you treat me leaves me feeling so hungry for something more. You make me so angry, you make me feel small sometimes. And yet I can't hate you. Because you are the most complex, interesting man I have ever known, and do you have any idea how much it pains me to say that? A man shouldn't be interesting and complex simply because he displays baffling behaviors."

"I am baffling even to you?"

"Yes."

"I thought you understood."

He almost sounded hurt. If he had been anyone else she would've imagined that he was. Perhaps that should make her feel bad. But it didn't. "I baffle you and yet you want me anyway?" he asked.

"Yes," she said. "And I feel like I deserve this."

"You are so confident you will enjoy it?"

"Aren't you?"

He moved closer, and she felt like she might faint. Being this close to all that beauty had left her feeling nearly drunk.

"No more talking." The words were hard. Blunt. Arousing.

That was when she found herself crushed roughly against him. His mouth crashed down upon hers, and there was nothing left to say. There were no more words left in her entire being. She was made entirely of need.

His mouth was hot and hard, his tongue insistent as a requested entry. She granted it. She wanted him to devour her. She wanted...

This was such an explosive fantasy. Seeing him like this. When he pulled away from her, he was breathing hard, his eyes wild.

She had done that to him.

It was different than his frustration over his exacting standards not being met.

This was him at the edge of control. This was him pushed to his limit, by her.

She had power.

And she felt electric with it.

She had never been kissed before. And yet she was confident that no kiss could ever match what his did.

Because he was the man who had changed her life with a glance. She had been so certain she had seen him, and evaluated him as she did everyone. That she had seen everything. But nothing could have really prepared her for him. It was why he was dangerous and wonderful all at the same time.

And now that she was leaving, now that this was it...

She could finally have him. Just for tonight.

This explosive, wonderful, terrible, dangerous, sharp thing.

She was confident that no one could ever fully understand what this was. It wouldn't be like anything else that had ever existed before or since.

Luca Salvatore was a singular man.

She knew sex with him would be singular as well.

As if determined to prove her point he wrapped his arm around her waist and lifted her up off the ground as if she weighed nothing. He carried her through the sitting room, propelled her back into his bedroom.

"I want to see you naked," he said. "Do you have any idea how much?"

There was something burning in his eyes that was completely unfamiliar to her. She had thought that she had known Luca and all of his moods. But here it was. The hidden depths. The thing that she had never seen. She had imagined that he might be during sex as he was with everything else. There was an intensity to him, yes. But it was always entirely within his control.

He seemed to be pushing at the bonds of it now.

There was…desperation in his eyes. She had never imagined that. It took her breath away.

"No," she said. "Tell me how much."

She needed it. After all these years of feeling like nothing more than a particularly useful paperweight to him, she needed to hear that it was different. Now, at the end of this. At the end of them, she needed to hear it.

"I know everything about you," he said. "About the way that you move, about the way that you complete tasks. There is a very particular way that you hold your wrist when you are annoyed with me. A way that you move your head when something interests you. You smile a particular way when you are pleased, and a different way when you're upset. I don't normally notice those sorts of things about people, but you have been an object of my fascination from the moment I first hired you. You are a study in contradictions. I think most people don't notice them, but I do."

She wanted to hide. She had never imagined that Luca looked at her that way. She had never imagined that he looked at her like much of anything.

She'd never thought, for one moment, that he had *seen* her quite so clearly.

"But…"

"You don't think I notice details like that. But I only know details that matter."

There was nothing he could've said that could've possibly aroused her more than making it clear that she mattered.

But this was somehow more than sex.

He kissed her again, hard and insistent. "I do not know how your body looks without clothes on," he said. "I'm studying your face now. Your eyes are filled with… I don't have a word for it. But you like this."

"I do," she said, not feeling embarrassed, not at all, because this was just so honest. He was honest. That she had always appreciated about him, whatever else was going on.

"I've never seen you aroused."

"You have. It's only I do a good job of hiding it, I think."

"Not always. Though I would consider you interested,

not aroused in those moments. I noticed the way that you looked at my body when we were at my house."

"*Anyone* would want to look at your body."

She found it easy to return his honesty with honesty. "Anyone would want to see yours."

"I can assure you that is not the case," she said. "But I'm glad that you do. For my purposes at the moment."

He reached behind her and grabbed the zipper of her dress, releasing it, letting the dress fall around her waist.

Need arced through her, and she found herself more aroused as her breasts were exposed to him, as the dress slipped down over her hips, revealing that she was wearing nothing more than a pair of very brief underwear.

She wasn't embarrassed. Because of his honesty. Because he made his appreciation for her form so apparent as he gazed at her.

"Beautiful," he said.

He kissed her neck, and then he bit her. She gasped. She wrapped her arms around his neck and he consumed her. She began to tear his clothes away from him. She didn't have the patience to go slow in deference to her inexperience.

She didn't have patience at all. She needed him. Like air.

This was five years in the making. Whatever she had told herself about how she felt working for him, this was undeniable.

She wanted him.

Every night she had spent in his bedroom watching him dress, every time she had been pinned beneath his stern gaze. Every time she had watched his intense anticipation when he had been working on a project, it had all coalesced into this moment. It had been foreplay.

Even if she hadn't quite appreciated the extent of it. She did now. She was slick with need for him.

She was also innocent. She didn't know what was happening to her body.

She knew all about sex.

She knew about climax.

She had brought herself to it more than once.

She was human, after all.

She was just a very guarded, protected human, which meant that always, these things had been better for her to experience on her own. Without anyone else.

She let out a shuddering breath as he kissed her again. As he moved them both to the bed, as he removed all the layers of clothing between them.

"Please," she said. "I have to see you."

He moved away from her, and she looked at his masculine form in awe. She had seen his bare chest many times. But never so that she could openly stare at it. So that she could touch him. She reached her hand out and placed it flat on his chest. "You're beautiful," she whispered.

He made a rough sound of male satisfaction. Then she let her eyes move down lower. To that thick, aggressively male part of him.

She had never seen a naked man. She was not one for sexual images, even though she didn't have an issue with people who did enjoy them.

She had just never been interested.

She had on occasion brought herself to climax at night

when she couldn't control her riotous thoughts. Her fantasies about her boss.

But she didn't go out of her way to seek out sexual arousal. There had never been a point to it.

He was the first. And he was… He was beautiful.

Just as she had known he would have to be. Because he had called to her, always, in a way that no one else and nothing ever had.

If there was one thing she trusted about herself, it was her instincts. When it came to people and what they were concealing. And she had sensed that what he was concealing was something that she wanted. She had been correct.

"Have you looked your fill?" he asked.

"No," she said. Because she knew, somehow without a doubt, that this would never be enough.

"Touch me," he said, his voice hard.

She reached out and pressed her fingertips against his chest, dragged them down his stomach, all the way down to that hard, masculine place between his thighs. She wrapped her hand around his shaft, biting her lip as she did so. Experimentally, she stroked him. She thought about telling him that she was inexperienced, but ultimately changed her mind. She didn't want anything to alter the experience between them. She wanted to have him. All of him, as he would have any other woman.

He closed his eyes, his breath hissing through his teeth. And then, it was like he couldn't bear it any longer. Then, he was kissing her. Then he had her pinned to the mattress. She wrapped her arms around his neck, parted her legs for him, and he pressed that hot, hard length against her slick flesh. She groaned, arching against him. He kissed her neck, down to her breast, sucking her nipple in deep. She couldn't breathe for how glorious it was. He moved down, so that his face was between her legs. He cupped her rear and lifted her up off the mattress, devouring her most intimate heat as if it were a delicacy he couldn't get enough of.

She didn't even think to be ashamed. She didn't think to hold back. She moved her hips in time with every stroke of his tongue, every scrape of his teeth. She was lost in it. She felt like she might die. He called yet more and more desperate sounds from her body, and met them with sounds of masculine hunger.

He pushed two fingers inside her slick channel, filling her. She cried out in pain and pleasure, her internal muscles pulsing around him as an orgasm was extracted from her with the most intense precision.

It was Luca Salvatore to his core.

Even in this he was unmatched.

Even in this he was everything.

When he looked up at her, his eyes were nearly black, his pupils expanded so much he was pure predator. And she could see that he had lost all control. He moved his body up the bed, gripped her thigh and hooked it over his hip as he kissed her, as he thrust himself inside of her with one brutal stroke.

It hurt. She cried out into his mouth, but he swallowed her pain. And turned it into pleasure. He began to move, hard and unyielding, taking no quarter, taking no prisoners.

He was so deep inside of her she could scarcely breathe. She could feel him, each dominating inch as he claimed her over and over again.

Whatever she had been before this, she couldn't re-member. For now, she was simply Luca. And he was hers.

He was not her boss, and she was not his assistant.

She was not leaving.

And he was not cold.

They were together. They were a conflagration. An expression of need burning so hot, so bright, that nothing would ever be able to dampen it.

With each stroke, her pleasure built. Until she was at the end of herself. At the end of everything. She came again, a hoarse cry of need escaping her. And his own release came on a roar as he poured himself within her.

She was left storm-tossed, sweat-slicked and ex-hausted.

He did something entirely unexpected. He pulled her into his arms and held her fast as their breathing calmed. And then she found herself drifting off to sleep. When she woke, it was with a start. She was still lying next to Luca. They were both naked.

And she knew she had to leave. She had no other op-tion. Because if she stayed, she would never be able to go.

She felt like she had been slashed with broken glass.

She felt like she was destroyed. And she couldn't be destroyed. She had to remake herself. That was the whole point of taking this other job. It was the whole point of leaving him in the first place. It was the whole point of tak-ing this chance and having one passionate night with him.

She had to leave. She sneaked out of the hotel room, and he never once stirred. She went back to her room and gathered her things.

Then she went straight to the airport, and got the first flight back to Italy.

And as she sat in her economy seat and stared out the window, she tried to come to a place of acceptance with the fact that she was never going to see Luca Salvatore ever again.

CHAPTER SIX

OBSESSION WAS LUCA'S strength and weakness. It was what enabled him to put his head down and work tirelessly to find a solution to whatever problem was pressing against him in the world of medicine. It was what had delivered his success to him—both financial, and in terms of scientific discovery.

It was also what crippled him now.

He could think of nothing but her. After launching the greatest medical discovery of his career, he could not think of medicine. He could think only of Polly.

It was unacceptable. Never in his life had a woman bewitched him so. Never had a woman commanded his mind and his body in such a fashion. It should not be so. And yet it was.

He could not account for why he was so obsessed with her. It had been sex. Nothing more. It was extremely common for him to not be able to remember the physical details of his lovers after the fact. He could remember the rush of release, but not the specifics. His brain simply released them, because they were not important.

The details of Polly's body, of the way she had cried out his name, the way that she had clung to him, haunted him.

He could not forget.

He had never wanted to forget quite so much.

He cursed his brain, and the way that it was put together, which was not something he had done since he was a very small child.

He had taken all of his weaknesses and turned them into strengths. He had dominion over them. Except in this. Except with her.

It was good that she was gone. It was good that she had gone to Milan, to marketing. And he had done as he had promised. He had written the most sterling recommendation letter for any person that had ever existed. Because he was a man of his word.

He was. In spite of what she thought about him. In spite of what she had said about him seeing her only as a thing.

He fought the urge to sweep everything off of his desk. His brain was cluttered, and his surroundings were not, and yet, he found that *everything* bothered him right now. Even his notebooks.

Because of her. This was all because of her. Her breasts, her lips. Everything. The way that she cried out his name, the way that she had clung to him after.

Then she had run away.

Her audacity. She could have stayed.

Yes, he had told her that she would have to make her own way home, but clearly in the aftermath of their sexual encounter, he wouldn't have held her to that.

Clearly.

Clearly.

But then, she didn't want to feel anything for him. She thought the absolute worst of him. And perhaps he had no right to feel unhappy about that. He found that he did. He swept his notebooks onto the floor, picked up his coffee cup and threw it at the wall. It broke. The mess was not satisfying. The broken mug was not satisfying.

Nothing was Polly.

Nothing did anything to ease the ache inside of him, not even his research. If he saw her again he would…

Why leave it to chance? He should offer her her job back. Offer her twice the amount of money. He couldn't function without her. It had been eight weeks. And he was no closer to feeling like he could manage himself than he had been when she left.

Yes.

He would go to Milan and offer her her job back. He would not call. He would show up in person. And then he would be able to work out his obsession with her easily. Because she would not be a fantasy living like a ghost all around him at all times.

She would be back in her physical form. And she would be his assistant again. Which would put up a barrier.

That was the problem. The lack of rules surrounding Polly anymore meant that his mind was free to dwell on the sex. He would simply restore her as his assistant and all would be well. Yes. That's what he would do.

He had chartered his private plane for Milan only moments later.

It would take no time at all to get there.

Luca didn't even fill one notebook on the flight. Granted, it was a short flight, but the behavior was out of character. When he had attempted to write, he had only managed one word: Polly.

It was unbearable.

Unendurable.

She had taken his brain and she had done something to it. Hijacked it.

And then she had left him.

He was a mass of teeming energy by the time he disembarked from the plane. By the time he got into the waiting car to wing his way down to the fashion house.

It was across a large, crowded square, a massive historic building that stood proud and tall, and inconsequential as far as he was concerned. It was nothing compared to the work that he did. And nothing compared to the work that she could do with him. If she needed to feel more appreciated, if she needed him to learn a new way of speaking with her, then he could do so. He could learn.

He had made efforts to do so before, and he could do it with her.

He was determined in this.

He walked across the square, and he saw a door open at the top of the massive stone steps. His gaze was drawn there, to the flurry of movement, a red scarf, blond hair.

It was her.

His body recognized her on a cellular level. It was not visual. It was visceral. He felt her. To the depths of himself.

It had always been so. It wasn't just her movements that fascinated him, he realized now. It was the movement that she created within him, different than any other human being.

Different than anything.

His.

It was so clear then.

She belonged with him. Together, they would make massive advancements in medicine, and if she needed a new title, promotion, if she needed to be second-in-command of the company then she could be so.

Because she was what made him work.

He strode up the steps, without pausing, without thought.

She saw him.

She felt him. He knew it. Because he could see it there in her eyes. That recognition. The shifting of the tides within her soul, he knew it, because he felt it.

He felt what another person felt. He was confident of it.

It was a novelty.

Something he had been told he was incapable of. Something many people had said he did not possess the ability to do, and he had done it. Without even trying. Hell, he didn't even want it. But there he was, standing there, making eye contact with Polly, absolutely certain that what was happening inside of him was the same reckoning inside of her.

She shook her head. And he nodded as he approached her.

"Yes," he said. "I've come for you."

"No," she said. "You shouldn't be here."

"There is nowhere else that I ought to be. I think you know that."

"I don't know that." There was something fearful in her expression now, though in the past he knew that she had said she was afraid of him only because of the degree to which she wanted him. Maybe it was the same now, and yet he didn't think so.

He did not like that.

"I'm not here to hurt you. I'm here to offer you a job."

She blinked. "A job?"

"This past month has been hell. I cannot function without you. I need you."

"You... You need me?"

"Yes. I have tried. I have been through one assistant every week since you left. Nothing works as it should. My life is disordered, and I cannot afford to have a disordered life. I need you."

"You need me to do things for you," she said.

Yes. He did. And yet, she made it sound as if it was inconsequential. It was not. It was everything to him. His work, his life, the way that it functioned. He felt as if he was crawling out of his skin without her there. As if he was going to have to unzip the essence of what he was so that he could find release by expanding to fill the room, escaping his human form.

It was terribly uncomfortable, and something he had not experienced since...her.

"I need you to come back and work for me."

"I don't want to come back and work for you. I have a job."

"I will give you a promotion. I will double your pay."

"Double?" She looked stunned.

"Yes."

"That's outrageous and astronomical."

"It is not. I will make you second-in-command of the company if that's what you wish. I will give you shares. Whatever it is you want, but I need you back." He was on the verge of debasing himself, did she not see that?

"Luca," she said, her gaze sparkling with fractured light. "We slept together. And you have come to my place of work to tell me that you need me...to come back and do a job for you."

"Yes. I have thought of nothing else since you left."

"You have to be kidding me. I'd… I gave my virginity to you, and *you* have been thinking of nothing but how I…used to bring you coffee?"

He didn't know what to do with the first part of what she had said, so he let it filter past, and dealt with the comment about the coffee. "It is not only coffee. My notebooks are in disarray, no one has been able to anticipate—"

She howled. Like an enraged beast. "You have got to be kidding me!" She stepped away from him.

"Wait," he said. He returned back to what she had said. About her being a virgin. "I didn't know," he said. "That you had not been with anyone before."

"Well now you do."

"Why?"

"Because my boss was such a demanding, controlling pain in the ass that I never had time to go on a date, never had time to get a kiss, much less get penetrated. The hilarity is, it had to be you." She shook her head. "It had to be you because you're the only man that I know, because you…" She stared at him, her breasts rising and falling as she seemed to be grappling with what to say next. And then she simply turned away from him. "I can't do this, Luca. You're you. And I have always respected that. You are a man who is infinitely complicated. A man who is meant for bigger things than getting his own coffee. I understand that. You're trying to save the world. But I'm not. I'm just trying to save myself. I have to live. And I can't do it with you. I cannot be your assistant." She started to walk away, and he gripped her arm, stopping her, turning her to face him.

"Don't leave me," he said.

He saw all the color drain from her face, and then he noticed the circles under her eyes. That her lips were the wrong color. That her body had changed. Yes, her body had changed. She was wearing a sweater, different than the stark skirt suits that she had worn when she worked for him, but he could still see that her breasts were larger. There was a hollowed-out look to her, and yet her waist was not smaller. He frowned. "You don't look well." Terror overtook him. She looked exhausted. She looked… She could very well be a woman with the disease that he feared most. The disease that he…that he had spent his life fighting against. "You must go to a doctor."

"I'm not unwell," she said.

"Yes, you are," he said. "You look remarkably unwell, and in fact you look like…" He found himself struggling to say it, and he was a man who was nothing if not matter-of-fact.

"You don't need to worry about me," she said.

"You look as if you might have cancer," he said.

She covered her face with her hands, and he could see that she was pressing hard against her eyes. "I don't have cancer, Luca. I don't… I'm pregnant."

CHAPTER SEVEN

SHE FELT DEVASTATED. Standing there looking up at the horror on his face. She hadn't been able to let him think that she was sick. She just couldn't do it. Even after...

When she had seen him charging up the steps she had been certain that he had known somehow. How could he? She wasn't certain, but he was well-connected with the medical world, and she wouldn't put it past him to put some kind of alert on her name, privacy laws or not.

They hadn't used a condom the night that they were together, and surely he must realize that.

She hadn't thought about it until it was far too late to do anything about it. But he must have... Luca Salvatore did not forget anything. And yet, he had forgotten a condom. And she was living with the consequences of it.

Though, she had decided that she was not... She wasn't sad about those consequences.

She had been shell-shocked at first, of course. But the more she had sat with that, the more she had realized she wanted this baby. That she wanted a chance to build a real, healthy connection with her child, to love someone wholly and utterly without the need for protection. Not only that, she was more than able to take care of a child physically. She had an extremely supportive employer, she made enough money.

She knew enough not to repeat the mistakes of her parents.

And perhaps it wasn't ideal for her baby to not know its father, but she had thought that maybe someday in the future...

Except she couldn't imagine Luca as a father.

Staring at him now, at the abject horror on his face, she still couldn't.

He hadn't come for her. He had come for her excellent personal assistant skills. He had not come for the baby, he had come for his own convenience.

She hated that moment where she'd hoped it was for her. She hated herself for feeling it, for being so weak with him. Always.

She had decided that she would not be telling him about the child. Except... Except then that horrible, stricken look on his face when he had thought that she might be genuinely ill.

"You cannot be," he said.

"I assure you, I am. Medically confirmed and everything."

"No," he said. "That isn't possible. I have taken my share of lovers, and I have always exercised precautions."

"Luca," she said, outraged on so many levels right at that moment. "You didn't use a condom."

Yes, they were in fact standing on the steps of the Milan fashion house yelling about condoms, but at least they were speaking English. So probably only three quarters of the people around them knew what they were talking about.

"Yes, I did," he said. "I never forget such things."

"You did," she said. "You did with me. You forgot, because you had a…a human moment. That's what people do, Luca. They throw away all of their good sense so that they can have an orgasm. And that's what we did. We didn't think of anything. Not the repercussions, not the consequences to each other, not the devastation that it might create. We decided that nothing else mattered except being together, and look at what it's gotten us."

He looked undone. And the thing was, she was pretty sure that he was more upset about forgetting to use a condom than he was about her being pregnant. More upset that he had been called out on overlooking something, which she was entirely certain he had never done before.

"You must come with me," he said.

"I must do no such thing. I am on my lunch break, and I intend to go eat."

"Then I will go with you."

"No," she said, beginning to walk away from him.

"You cannot stop me from walking on a public street," he said.

"I could call the police and tell them that you're harassing me."

"People know who we are," he said. "They know that we have an association."

"You're a genius, Luca. You cannot be unaware that women are often harassed by men they know. Particularly men they had slept with."

"It is not harassing you to want to know more about the situation that you find yourself in." He paused for a moment. "The situation we find ourselves in."

She let out a heavy sigh. "Oh, Luca. You don't have to do anything in response to this. I had already decided."

"Are you not keeping the baby?"

"I am," she said. "I had a difficult relationship with my parents, and I am never going to have a family if I don't make one myself. This is an opportunity for me to do that. I'm financially able. And therefore it just seems... like a reasonable time for me to have a baby. But I don't need you to be involved."

He frowned. "But I am the baby's father."

"Yes. You are. But many fathers are not involved in the day-to-day lives of their children."

"But those men are bad fathers."

"Maybe not. Not if it benefits everybody for the man to stay away."

"You think the child would be better off without me?"

He said that with so much genuine wonder that it made her feel like she had been stabbed clean through. It was easy to think that Luca couldn't be wounded. Yet it was clear she had hurt him.

It was so difficult, because the truth was, she suspected that he wouldn't be a good father because of the way that he was. Because of everything about him. Because of the way that he had to live his life. And yet she didn't want to hurt him.

She hated the revelation that she was able to *hurt* him.

Luca had always seemed invulnerable and untouchable, and today he seemed undone in a way that she didn't care for.

She especially didn't want to be the cause of it.

"Think about it," she said. "You don't want a child. You can't even handle having to get a new personal assistant. If you think your life is disordered now, think of how disordered it will be when there's a baby. You won't be able to do things whenever you want, you will be subject to the schedule of another human being. You've never even had a relationship, have you?"

He shook his head. "No. I haven't."

"And why is that?"

"It doesn't fit into my life."

"Exactly. And I knew that about you. I knew that about you when I slept with you, and I know it about you now. I never expected more from you than one night."

"You did not ask me what I wanted."

"You just said it doesn't fit into your life."

He met her gaze, his eyes like steel. "Then my life will have to change. Because it already has. Because you are pregnant with my baby, and I will not be a bad father."

"I don't know what you think—"

"You will marry me. And return to Rome with me today."

Luca's brain was working as fast as it ever had. He had to react appropriately. It had never been more important. He was a genius. He knew that. He understood the inner workings of the human body in ways that most did not. His brain was filled with an enormous amount of education, but while he understood the inner workings of the human body he often did not understand the workings of the human mind. The human soul.

It hadn't bothered him, not in general. Because he had fashioned a life that catered to his strengths and not his weaknesses. Because what he was accomplishing with the human body mattered much more than him connecting with a few other people.

He had assumed, when he had bothered to think about it at all, that this was simply the balance of things. If you could understand one, you would not be graced with understanding of the other.

But he needed both now. He needed all of it now.

Because he knew one thing for certain, he would not be shut out of his child's life. He would not have his child thinking that its father didn't want them.

That was impossible.

He knew what that felt like. He had been a motherless boy, because his mother had died. She had not chosen to be away from him, and it had been an unbearable pain.

But in many ways he had been fatherless. With the man living in the same house that he did. In many ways, he had not had a father, and that was the other man's choice.

If any one thing had devastated him in a way he could not find purpose for, it was that.

He had lost his mother, but at least in that he had found the aim of his life.

He found nothing in the rejection of his father except pain.

He could not bear the idea of being *that* for his child.

Could not bear the thought of a child walking out in the world with a wound because he had not been able to…change.

"I have a job here," she said.

"Can you do it remotely?"

"I don't know. I don't know if I want to."

He wanted to offer to move his own work, and yet he did not think that he could manage that. He was on the verge of changing many things in his life, but that felt a bridge too far.

"We can sort that out later. It does not have to be all the time. But while you are pregnant I want you near me. I want to be able to see for myself that you are okay."

"I'm going to be fine. Many, many women carry babies and give birth every year."

"And some of them die."

He had meant that to be an expression of concern. She looked at him in horror. "Luca," she said. "No pregnant woman wants to hear that."

"I've never spoken to a pregnant woman before, not as far as I know, so how would I know that?"

"Clearly. Clearly you never have."

"Marry me," he said.

"No," she said. "You ran me down in the streets of Milan to demand that I come back and work for you after we had a night together. I don't want to marry that man. I don't want to marry a man who can't even acknowledge that he forgot to use a condom with me, because he needs so desperately to maintain his control."

"I admit it then," he said. "I lost control with you. I didn't even realize that I did. Do you have any idea how terrifying that is? I have never once in my entire life done something that I wasn't fully aware of."

It galled him to admit it to her. It was something he hadn't even fully been able to admit to himself.

"I think that isn't true. I think that you have done a great many things in your life you're unaware of, it's just that you don't realize you've done them because they affect other people's feelings. And you don't care about that. You never have. Everything in your life is about you. And I… I accept that on some level, I understand it. I even… I understand why it needs to be that way. But that doesn't mean they are the kind of man I want to marry. Caring about you would be a terrible mistake. It would end only in pain."

He felt like he had been slashed about the chest. Felt like he had been physically wounded. What she had said about him was so…so desperately unflattering. So outright, plainly…true. He was everything that she said. His life was centered wholly on himself.

Hearing her say it made it seem like less a necessity of his work, of himself, and more of a flaw.

And he would have to change it, but in order to do that he would need her to come back to Rome with him. In order to do that, he would need her to come with him. He would need his child. So he had to stay uncompromising, he had to continue to see things his way in this moment so that he could do the things that she was suggesting he try to do. At least, that's what he thought she was doing.

"You must let me," he said. "You must let me try."

"You can try by inches. You can try by coming to see me. By fostering a relationship with me that has nothing to do with the company. By…coming to visit your child after they're born."

"No," he said. "You must marry me because that is the right thing to do. Because statistically children do better when they have two parents in the home."

"Statistically, maybe, but when one of the parents is a genius billionaire, and the other one is financially solvent herself, I'm pretty sure that they might be able to defy generalized statistics."

"If you care about this baby then you must want what's best."

"Of course I want what's best. Don't forget that you found out about this baby fifteen minutes ago and I have known for a while now."

"You weren't going to tell me."

He might have gone his whole life never knowing. She had thought it would be best.

It was like a stab wound. He did not indulge his feelings. He never had. If he did…he would never get anything done. He practiced perfect control in all areas of his life because if he did not, the world would control *him*.

His father had despised him. Everything he was. Everything he thought and did. To live in that sort of environment and feel the weight of his every disapproving breath would have killed Luca. And so he had learned to close off his own sensitivities and focus on his mind, not his body or his heart.

But she had gotten to him.

Deep.

She shook her head. "I really wasn't. Because I knew that it would end… I knew that it would be this. Proclamations and demands, and forcing me to meet your expectations."

"You knew that I would want the baby, and you were going to withhold them from me?" Any guilt that he might've felt at forcing her hand now was completely mitigated by that.

"That isn't exactly…"

"You will marry me. Or I will fight you for full custody of the child."

"How dare you?" She took a step toward him, and he

was almost certain she was going to strike him. "How dare you threaten me."

"It isn't a threat, it is a fact. One of us has to have primary custody of the child, you think it should be you simply because you're a woman, simply because you're the mother. I do not. I think that it should be me because I possess greater resources than you do."

"Financially, maybe, but when we are talking about the thimble where you keep your emotions, believe me when I tell you your resources are not greater than mine."

"Do you think I'm this way because I feel nothing?" He leaned closer to her, the rage inside of him building, growing, expanding, claiming every part of him, taking control of him. "I am this way because I feel everything. And if I paused every moment of every day to ponder those feelings I would never get anything done. I would never do anything. If I felt all the things within myself, there would be no new screenings. There would be no new discoveries. I would be lying on a floor somewhere probably addled out of my mind on some substance or another trying to figure out a way to stem the tide of pain that lived within me. Do not ever tell me that I don't feel as much as other people. The air around me offends me. Why do you think I need everything managed the way that I do? I feel *everything*."

She looked shocked by that. Good. He did not speak about himself. It wasn't an interesting topic of conversation, and he wasn't friends with anybody. So there was never a reason to try and explain to another person how the world worked for him.

It had never been a reason. But there was one now.

"And if you have a child who was like me, if you have

a child who cares only about toy cars, and doesn't know how to speak to other children, then what? Because I know... I know what it's like."

"It doesn't give you the right to force me into things," she said.

"The way I am doesn't give you the right to exclude me from them either. And because we are both immovable, we are at an impasse. And the one with the most power is the one that can force the bend. I have the power, *cara*. You can decide what you wish to do in response. Bend or break."

Any guilt he might've felt was stemmed by his resolve.

Her eyes filled with tears. And he did not let himself care.

"Fine. I'll marry you. Legally. I'll give you what you're asking for, but on paper only. You will... You will make me second-in-command at your company. But I will not work directly beneath you. I will work in the public relations portion."

"That is acceptable."

"I want my own wing of your house. I will not encounter you in a hallway unless I choose to."

"Done."

"That means we will not be living in your penthouse."

"I don't care. Consider it vacated."

"If you wish, you could stay there."

"I will live under the same roof as my child."

"As you wish." She looked at him, her gaze hard. "If you make this miserable, believe me when I tell you I know how to make it hard for you too. Because I grew up with parents who were extremely accomplished making each other's lives hell."

"And how will that be for the child?"

She looked as if he had struck her. "I know enough to know how to keep it away from the child, because that is something my parents declined to do."

"Do you think they also thought they were not including you in their games?"

"Don't speak to me of games. Not when you're playing them just the same."

He shook his head. "This is not a game to me. You will be my wife. There will be no argument."

"I'm not sleeping with you."

"I didn't ask you to."

They never made it to lunch. Instead, she was bundled back on his plane, she quit her job over the phone, and they were back in Rome before dinner.

"I'm sorry, I don't have this imaginary house you imagine we will be sharing different wings of," he said. "We'll have to make do with another room in the penthouse tonight."

He gestured to the door, and then went off to his own room.

He closed himself inside, and let the silence bear down on him. Everything in his life had changed in a single day. He preferred change to take place over a very long period of time, slowly and surely, if it had to occur at all.

But he would marry Polly as soon as he could obtain a license. He would change.

For his child, he would change everything.

Because everything he was, everything he had done until this point had been a tribute to his mother. And what would any of it matter if he could not pay tribute to the flesh and blood he had created?

It would not matter at all.

And neither would he.

Polly didn't think that he would be a good father. But it didn't matter what she thought.

What mattered was what he would do.

CHAPTER EIGHT

POLLY SAT ON the edge of the bed, shell-shocked.

She had said things to Luca that she deeply regretted. Because they had been unnecessarily hurtful. She had been lashing out because she was upset. Because she was afraid. But then he had reacted... He had reacted the way that she had been certain he would. Inflexible, cruel in kind, when he didn't even mean to be.

She hadn't told him the honest truth. She hadn't thought that caring about him would be hell.

But that loving him would be.

She cared about him already. That was the problem. She had cared about him for quite some time, in spite of herself.

And now she had let him drag her back here, had quit her job...

If she had loved her job then perhaps she would have fought harder on that point.

The truth was, it was difficult to care as much about marketing for the fashion house when...she really did believe that Luca was changing the world. And she really had felt in some small part that when she was working with him, she was working in tandem to do so as well.

She believed so strongly in what he was doing.

Part of her was happy to be back working for the company, particularly in a position that suited her better.

None of her was happy about the surrounding circumstances.

She hated herself for the threat that she had issued. Was it so easy for her to decide to be like her parents when it suited her?

They had been so cruel. It had been up to her to manage their feelings, and it had been such a painful existence.

And when backed into a corner, she had been the same. Manipulative, taking things she knew to be weaknesses and exploiting that to hurt the other person.

She was deeply unhappy with herself. And yet, she was so tender regarding the whole situation that she didn't know what she could've done differently.

How could she accuse Luca of not knowing how to deal with people when she had just proven that in a difficult situation she was no better?

The question he'd asked haunted her. Would she know what to do with a child like him?

She wanted to think so. After all, she had been very good with Luca. And not in a sacrificial way. She… She had come to appreciate him. The way that he was. Except then she had been cruel. She had used that as an excuse to allow herself to not deal with the complexities of their situation. Because that was the truth of it.

She had chosen what she had thought to be the path of least resistance.

It had been cowardly.

Maybe that was why she had given in to the marriage demand. Of course, she didn't want to find herself in a situation where she didn't have custody of her child, but she had to wonder if in part she had given in as penance. Because when she had heard herself throwing her own reasoning back in his face she had been appalled.

She was appalled by him as well.

Neither of them had been the best versions of themselves.

But they had both been true to type. And even more difficult truths to stomach. He had been inflexible, and she had bent round his inflexibility to whisper poison in his ear.

She had hurt him, and so he had lashed out. She didn't want to be hurt so she had done the same.

And now she was marrying him.

If she didn't marry him, she might lose custody of her child. He was a billionaire after all.

More to the point the idea of sharing anything with Luca—especially a human being—seemed exhausting and impossible.

Maybe what you're really afraid of is living in the in between.

Maybe.

Maybe what really felt impossible was being with him without being with him.

In her ideal scenario, she didn't have to be with him at all. It made it easier, to just ignore that he'd ever been the biggest part of her life. If she could make him disappear.

But she couldn't have that so in many ways marrying him seemed easier than…

Than living near him, seeing him, dealing with him, without actually having him.

That made her feel like she was weak but…

She might be weak right now. Just a little. She certainly wasn't cool, collected Polly who knew how to work a room, but didn't let it work her.

She felt thoroughly *worked*.

She stood up from the bed, and wiped at her eyes. She should go and apologize to him. Maybe. Except she was afraid. Afraid of what would happen if she went to his room. Afraid of what would happen if they were alone. Not because of what he would do, but because of what she would do.

He had haunted her dreams this past month.

The terrible truth was, she had missed him. Even the infuriating things about him.

It would be such a terrible thing to love him.

I feel everything...

His words scraped against a raw part of her soul. She didn't want to consider that. Didn't want to think about the possibility that he felt more than everyone else. And that was why he was the way that he was. It was easier to dismiss him when she had convinced herself he wouldn't care.

But she had been confronted with how very much he did care.

With her own callousness, and her own inability to look at another person and really see them.

How could she accuse him of that when she had done the same? How could she act like he was somehow less able to consider other people when it was clear every person did it all the time.

Everyone made themselves the main character.

She had done the same.

She lay down on her bed, and tried not to weep.

But she did anyway.

She could remember crying piteously the first time she

was aware of her parents forgetting her birthday. They'd been on a high with each other and had planned a weekend trip away. She'd been left alone at nine to make her own dinner and put herself to bed.

She'd cried, and no one had been there to care.

She had never wanted to be sad and small and crying because she couldn't get what she wanted from another person, never again.

But here she was, weeping over a man as impossible as the situation she found herself in.

And she couldn't escape to Rome, because that's where he was.

She had been running for a very long time, and she had finally reached the end.

The next morning, when Polly got up, it was late, and Luca was nowhere to be found.

But it was past time for him to be at the office, so it stood to reason that he was there. He was a creature of habit.

She maneuvered around the kitchen, which was relatively familiar to her. It was perhaps childish to demand that he buy a whole new house so that they could avoid each other. She had been angry. Furious.

They were going to have to have a talk, and she was going to have to find a way to be fair. Because she hadn't been.

She had beaten herself up about that until she had fallen asleep. She knew that she was going to have to bite back a few of the more regrettable things that had come out of her mouth.

She went to his very fancy espresso machine and made

herself a coffee. Then she stood at the window, looking out at the city below. It was difficult to fully figure out how she had gotten here.

And yet, it was five years in the making.

Of ignoring feelings for him that had been building, of declining to take care of her sex drive. Yeah. That was the problem. Her latent sex drive. And not the fact that she had been wholly obsessed with Luca.

She gritted her teeth. She had heard of pregnancy hormones making women emotional, but she had never heard of pregnancy hormones forcing women to be brazenly honest with themselves. She didn't like it.

She sat down on the wide, ridiculously large couch that took up most of his living area. And when the door opened behind her, she nearly jumped out of her skin.

"Luca," she said.

"Yes," he said.

"I didn't expect you."

"Why is that?"

"I assumed that you were at work."

"Why?"

"Because that is your routine," she said.

How absurd, to sit here with him and speak to him about work. How absurd the last few days had been. They had been naked. She had tasted this man. He had been inside of her. And yet… He had come after her about the job. And then he had claimed her because she was having his baby.

And still, they weren't acknowledging the passion.

Truly, her internal honesty was getting to be a little bit much. "I was not at work," he said. "I was seeing to the business of getting our marriage license."

"What?"

"Yes. We're getting married. Now."

"Now?"

"Yes. Should you like us to wait?"

"I... I assumed that we would be having a wedding."

"It will be a wedding. Though not one that is traditional or shrouded in ceremony. Simply something legal to ensure that everything is as it ought to be."

"Oh."

She had never really given any thought to getting married. She had never thought she would get married.

She scanned herself, trying to see if she felt any sadness over not getting a fancy wedding with a wedding dress and people looking on.

No. She didn't want that anyway. Would his father come? Her parents? All of that seemed silly. And anyway, a lot like inviting pain and trauma that neither of them especially needed especially in the middle of all of this.

"It will... It will be in the news," she pointed out.

"I'm known for being practical. I don't think anyone will think anything of it. Anyway, this is not pretense. You're having my baby, we are getting married."

"People already know we... There were some items about us sneaking away during the summit. After your triumphant speech."

"Were there?"

"Do you really not read any press about yourself?"

"You know that I don't. I find myself steadfastly uninterested in anyone else's opinion of me. It does not benefit me to read, therefore I don't."

"Very admirable, Luca, but a great many people wouldn't be able to keep that up."

"I'm not other people."

She let out a hard breath. "No. You aren't. To that end, I have to tell you that I'm sorry about some of the things that I said yesterday."

"That's nice," he said.

That rankled. Was *he* not sorry?

"We both said things we didn't mean."

"I didn't."

"You… You didn't?"

"No. Not at all. I only say things that I mean, Polly, you should know this about me."

"You mean, you weren't being a less evolved version of yourself to get your way?"

"Of course I said things in order to get my way, but that doesn't mean that I didn't mean them."

"I… Never mind. I'm not sorry."

"You were quite hurtful."

"I don't care."

He shrugged. "That's fine. You're not the first person to say such things to me."

That, she found, was more bothersome than it had a right to be. That he found her basic, and like everyone else. What a horror.

"I… Let's go. Let's just get this over with."

"You are angry with me," he said.

"Well spotted."

She stood up, and just stood there for a moment. "I should change."

"You don't have to."

She was wearing a soft pair of black pants and a matching shirt. "I should."

"Because it's a wedding?"

He was wearing a suit.

"No. Because I don't want to look shabby next to you."

It was a silly thing to say, because anyone or anything would look shabby standing next to him. Luca Salvatore was nothing if not spectacular at all times.

With that in mind, she disappeared into the bedroom, and procured one of the items of clothing that he had set there. It was a soft blue dress, knitwear, and forgiving. But it was nice, and it flattered her figure, even as it changed. She put on some makeup. A bit of nude lipstick and some shiny eyeshadow. Some blush, because otherwise she was going to look like the corpse bride.

She was marrying him.

And as she walked back out to the living room and saw him standing there in that dark suit, it was like a truth rang inside her, clear and bright as a gong. It wasn't even that weird that she was marrying him. Because if she was going to marry somebody it almost had to be him.

Because Luca was the single most defining relationship of her life. He had been, even before she had slept with him. He was a man that she was singularly preoccupied with. A man unlike any other. She shouldn't want to touch him again.

It would be the worst thing in the world to love him.

She reminded herself of that. She didn't feel quite as much conviction as she had before.

"Now we can go," she said, eager to move past the moment.

She noticed that Luca's tie was crooked. Out of habit and impulse she moved forward to straighten it. But when her hands made contact with the fabric, she was far too aware of the heat emanating from his body. The scent of him. The sound of his breathing. She saw about her task, and moved away from him quickly. "There. Everything is right."

"Yes," he said, his dark eyes fathomless. "It is."

They did not touch one another as they departed from the penthouse, and made their way down to the lobby. He opened the waiting car door for her once they got outside, but she managed to avoid his touch even then.

They were driven to a small building, historic in spite of the fact that it was nothing more than a registrar's office.

"I thought it was slightly complicated to get a marriage license in Italy."

He laughed. "Nothing is complicated when you are a billionaire. And of course we'll draw up a document to protect both of our assets."

"A prenup?"

He nodded. "Of course. It is sensible. It will hold both of us to the terms we'd agreed to."

"I suspect you already have that all handled?"

"Obviously."

She wondered right then if that was the real reason he pursued wealth. Another way to eliminate complications. He certainly didn't seem to revel in luxury.

She was marrying a billionaire.

That thought made her feel slightly off-kilter.

They were taken before the officiant, and the ceremony was done in Italian, with no fanfare whatsoever, and no kiss. It was simply a legal matter. They both signed paperwork, and she had to sign an extra paper making it clear there were no impediments to the legality or morality of her marriage.

All in all, it took no time. And she felt foolish for

changing. Felt foolish for believing it would even be half so momentous as a ceremony in front of a justice of the peace. It wasn't that. It wasn't anything.

It was quintessentially Luca, she supposed. All business, nothing else. When they found themselves back in the car, though, his gaze met hers.

"You are my wife," he said.

He said it matter-of-factly, as he did many things, and yet it made her burn.

There was an answering heat in his eyes that made it difficult for her to breathe.

"And you are my husband," she said. But the moment she did, she had to purse her lips together, as if to bite off the rest of that statement.

She looked out the window, her heart beating in her chest like a trapped bird in a cage. They had agreed that this wouldn't be...physical.

She was supposed to have a job at the company. They were going to raise the baby together.

She looked at his profile, taking a chance at pinning her gaze to him again. What would it look like? Raising a baby with him? She hadn't even wrapped her head around what it would look like for her to raise a baby with herself.

She was caught up in a sweeping tide of change. One that had begun with her deciding to leave him. And had ended with her back here, married to him.

She was utterly stunned by the whole thing.

Suddenly, she felt dizzy. She had been unwell off and on the past few weeks. Not morning sickness so much as sickness whenever it felt like showing up. And it was definitely happening now.

He studied her. "You don't look well."

"I'm…fine."

What good would it do to let him know that she felt like collapsing? What good would it do to show weakness?

Her parents had only ever used it against her. He had tried to use the baby against her.

She turned over that harsh, sharp thought. What he'd done amounted to using their child as leverage, it was true. But the subtle difference was he had laid it all out on the table in front of her, rather than trying to manipulate her.

She shoved that to the side.

She wasn't angry with him, not like she had been before, but she couldn't trust him either.

She couldn't trust anybody. She never had, she was hardly going to start now not when she needed to keep her guard up the most.

She was vulnerable. More than she had ever been. She was growing a life, thank you very much.

And then she was going to have to figure out how to raise that life.

That made her falter internally. Because there were things about herself she wasn't sure she had dealt with. Things that gave her pause when it came to the idea of raising a child. Because her child would depend on her. Her child was going to be learning about life from her, and…

She suddenly felt utterly, desperately unqualified.

"What is the matter?" he asked.

"I'm overwhelmed. By the idea of raising a baby. By the fact that we're married. You can understand that, surely."

"Perhaps that's true, but I also think you're physically unwell."

The car pulled up to the front of their building, and she began to unbuckle, but he got out of the other side of the car and rounded it, opening her door before she managed to free herself. Then he bent at the waist, and reached down to pluck her up from the car like she weighed nothing.

She wasn't used to that. He had never touched her before that night in Singapore. And then, his touch had been decisive, and bracingly, unapologetically sexual.

But this was...

He was holding her like she was a fragile thing. Like she was precious. He had her head pressed against his chest, and she could hear his heart beating.

A reminder that he was a human man. Whatever she had said to him. However he sometimes behaved.

And she felt awash in guilt all over again. She had apologized to him once. But she wasn't sure if she had meant it. Or if it had been about soothing her own guilt, rather than truly acknowledging that she had potentially caused him pain.

She knew him well enough to know that he was...so in control of everything around him that of course his biggest vulnerability was that which he wasn't proficient at. She had stabbed him right there. Between the ribs. Right where she knew she could get to him.

And as he held her close, she felt...him.

His warmth. His strength.

She didn't care that people were staring at them.

It didn't really feel like there were any other people there at all.

She was dizzy, lightheaded. Maybe her illness was the cause of all of these feelings. Fizzing up inside of her.

Maybe it was them.

He held her, even in the elevator. They said nothing, and she was painfully aware of the sound of their breathing.

Of them.

Then they reached the top floor, and he whisked her out of the elevator, and into the penthouse.

He laid her down on the couch, and went into the kitchen, where he turned the tap which had instant hot water in it, and began to make her tea.

"Something herbal," he said. "It will settle your stomach. You like cinnamon, don't you?"

She did. Quite a bit. She usually got a sprinkle of cinnamon on top of her coffee. She often got a spice cake, or a pumpkin spice cake, or similar treat. She enjoyed a chai latte occasionally. What shocked her was that he knew that.

"I do," she said. "How do you know that?"

"I have watched you eat these many years now, have I not?"

"Yes," she said. "But I didn't think…"

"You did not think I would notice."

She winced. "No. I didn't. But that says more about me and what I think about myself than it does about what I think about you."

He arched a brow. "Does it?"

She let out a long, pained breath. "Yes. It does." She sat for a moment and stared down at the floor. "I'm sorry."

CHAPTER NINE

LUCA LOOKED AT her as if she was delusional. "You apologized already."

She swallowed. "No. I'm not sorry because I feel bad. I'm sorry now because I know that I hurt you. Worse, I tried to hurt you while telling you that you were unfeeling. I knew that you weren't, or why would I have even bothered to insult you?"

He looked stunned by that. He paused his movements, his hand still around the mug of tea. "I suppose that's true."

"I am really sorry. You didn't deserve that. I was angry and upset, and I knew that I was in a fight with you I couldn't win. I lashed out. I'm not making excuses."

He frowned. "I wanted you and the baby here with me. I don't know how to be sorry for accomplishing that."

That felt different than what he had said earlier too, even if she couldn't articulate it. But in all things, it was honest.

It wasn't that destructive, hideous catastrophe that she had lived through with her parents.

When they did nice things for her it was usually to get at the other one. Often making her feel special simply so she could be used as a pawn later. And then, when they didn't need her she didn't signify. When they were angry, she was in the way.

And they loved to deflect anger onto her.

No emotion was ever what it was presented as. But that wasn't true with him.

What he had done had been heavy-handed. But he had been clear on his goals.

He had achieved them. That was who he was.

She swallowed hard. "At least you're honest."

He frowned. "I am sorry, though, if I hurt you."

His eyes met hers, and there was honesty there. As bracing and clear as it ever was.

"Thank you." She didn't know how to articulate the ways in which he had hurt her.

She was a silly girl, that was the problem. She knew that he...that he was never going to be a man to fall madly, passionately in love with a woman.

I feel things...

No. Not because she didn't believe he had feelings, but because she believed he had one true love. And it was medicine. It was healing the world. He was a single-minded man, and she was having difficulty figuring out how he was going to slip that focus. But when he had approached her on the steps in Milan, she had been convinced that he was there for her. When really he had been there to offer her a job. She had been terrified of course, because she had been certain that he must know about the pregnancy. But...

She just didn't want to get into that, because she didn't know how to explain it. Not to him, and not to herself.

He brought her a hot mug, and placed it in her hands.

Her fingertips brushed his. He had been her boss for five years.

And now he was her husband.

More than that, he was the father of the baby that was inside of her. She had been the one who was cold and clinical. She had been the one who had decided to cut him out of her life, like this was a photograph, and she could simply take scissors to it and excise him from the frame. In one brutal snip.

Just the same as she had chosen to run from him that morning after they had first made love. She was treating him like he might turn into her parents. Like he might become a monster she didn't recognize all of a sudden. He was difficult. But she understood the ways in which he was difficult. Luca had always been himself. Every inch himself. He had always been honest and up-front.

She was the one hiding.

She always had been.

Not just from him, but from everyone. Perhaps even herself.

He moved to a chair opposite her. And kept close watch on her as she took a slow sip of her tea. "This is the first time you've ever brought anything to me," she said, looking down at her cup.

"You don't work for me."

"Technically I do."

"I'm not your boss, just as you requested. It is a space to the left of me, rather than beneath me."

She snorted.

"What?"

"I *was* beneath you. That is how we ended up in this situation."

She did not know why she had brought that up. Just the mention of it made her stomach get tight. She knew his body. She could never not know it. She knew how it felt to touch him, taste him.

She might not be able to read his mind but she knew how he felt moving inside her.

That gripped her now. Held her in thrall.

"Yes," he said.

He looked thoughtful for a moment. "It is interesting. I do not often see the women that I sleep with again."

She winced. "That's sort of a bracing truth."

"Does it bother you because I was your only lover?"

She should've known that he would bring that up, and that he would be very blunt when he did. "I don't know about that, but maybe it makes it feel like we are on an equal footing."

"I would love to offer you the chance to make things equal. Because I know it isn't considered appropriate for two people who had a sexual relationship to have a power differential."

"It isn't considered appropriate," she said, trying to keep the reluctant amusement out of her voice. "But when it comes to sex people often behave inappropriately."

"I haven't. Before you. Technically, though, that night you were not my assistant."

"Oh, come now, you kissed me before midnight."

"Well, what time was it in Rome?"

She couldn't tell if he was being serious or funny. "It doesn't matter."

"It does to me. I wanted you before that night. You don't think that I was suddenly aroused for the very first time when I saw you in that dress?"

His earnestness caught her off guard, and she didn't know why it did. Because that was normal for him.

And she had to stop being shocked by it. She had to stop judging him through the lens of her parents.

He made her want to be honest in ways she never was. "Well… Tell me then. When did it start?"

"May twenty-fourth. Four years ago. It was three thirty in the afternoon. You were standing in my office. By the window. And at that time of day the light just clears the building across the way, and allows for a shaft of it to pool on the floor right by my desk. It caught your hair as you bent down, placing a cup of coffee on the desk. I saw you, and I could not look away. I realized that what I really wanted was to touch you. To rise up from my seat and kiss you. I also knew that I couldn't."

"You couldn't?"

Her breath was held fast in the center of her chest, everything in her suspended. "I thought you were a billionaire and you could do whatever you wanted."

"No, that is clearly forbidden by human resources."

"And you care about that?"

"Yes. It's there because people can get hurt if the rule is not there, and I never try to cause harm. I do it enough on accident as it is."

Her stomach twisted. "I see."

"Rules are very important."

"You know, there are a great many men who disregard those rules. Men who…don't struggle with the things that you do. They don't care."

"I do. I wouldn't have devoted my life to healing people if I didn't care about those around me. I would never have wanted to hurt you. I'm sorry that I did. But I am not sorry that you're here. I'm not even sorry that you're having my baby."

"Did you want children?"

"No. I didn't. But now that this child is growing between us, I find myself thinking about it in an entirely different way."

"How did you think of it before?"

"I didn't. I used condoms with all of my lovers, and I did not plan to ever have a relationship to progress past that point. It is a cliché, but my work has long been my mistress and I never believed it left room for there to be a significant relationship in my life."

In some ways, it was very similar to her. She hadn't thought outright that she would never have children, but of course, she didn't have a lover. So the odds of accidentally landing herself with the child were zero. "But now you want one?"

"I want this child. Perhaps that doesn't make sense. I know that the baby is the size of a raspberry."

"Of course you do."

"Anything medical, I am expert on. I also know that there is a chance that the child won't make it to term."

"I'd rather not think about that."

"Really? I would've thought that in some ways it would be easier for you to miscarry."

He wasn't trying to be cruel, but still, it hit her like a brutal blow. "Well, maybe you're right. But I don't feel that way. I haven't felt that way. Not even for a moment in the beginning. In fact…" She had cried. She had wept like she was dying, and then she had felt afraid. Afraid that her initial sorrow would mean that she was robbed of the life growing inside of her. It had been the single most contradictory, frightening thing she had ever been through. But in the end, she had been clear on the fact that she wanted the baby. That wasn't ambiguous. Not in the least.

"I don't want you to lose the baby either."

"I have terrible parents," she said.

She had never spoken of her parents. Not to anyone. "I mean, really terrible. They were so toxic, with each other and with me. What they did was tantamount to emotional abuse. It's why I'm so good at putting a mask on every day of my life. It's why I don't like being vulnerable. Or caught unawares. It's why I always pretend like I know exactly what's going on, even when I don't, because what I know is that when certain people think they can get to you, then they will. And if you show them what you really feel, they'll manipulate it. I learned that from them. I didn't think that I was like them. Until I lashed out at you yesterday. So now I know that when things get difficult, I'm not necessarily at my best."

"I didn't know that," he said. "About your parents."

"Of course you didn't. I didn't tell anyone. I tried to leave that life, that version of myself in Indiana."

"I knew you were from Indiana because it's in your file. But you have never spoken of it."

"Because there's nothing to say. I didn't want to be that girl anymore so I moved to a new country and became a different one."

"An extraordinary feat," he said. "Truly. I only know how to be the man that I am and that comes with its own set of issues."

"I know."

They were silent for a moment. "I would like to let you

go and even things out between us. In regard to lovers. But I can't. I cannot be fair or impartial when it comes to the subject of you allowing other men to touch you. I cannot be…the way I usually am. So perhaps in that regard I have become new. Or maybe something has become new inside of me. Probably in the time since May twenty-fourth four years ago."

There was something so earnest and lovely in those words. Maybe not everyone would see it, but she did.

She took a sip of the cinnamon-flavored tea and leaned back on the couch. She began to feel sleepy and set the cup on the table beside her.

He picked it up, and put a coaster beneath it, but didn't scold her. "Rest," he said. "I will be here when you wake."

When she did wake an hour or so later, it occurred to her that it was a singular thing for him to promise. He should be at work today. He didn't go.

The next morning when she woke unwell, he didn't go to work either. Or the next day, or the next. It was a complete and total rearranging of his routine and no one had ever, not once, disrupted their life on her behalf. She didn't know what to make of it. Only that it made her sore right at the center of her chest.

She crept into the kitchen to find Luca cooking. As if he didn't have a full staff for such a thing. As if he couldn't magic something up with the snap of his fingers.

"What are you making?" she asked, hearing how small her voice sounded even in her own ears.

"An omelet. Protein. Vegetables."

She thought she probably shouldn't tell him she had no interest in protein or vegetables, and instead wanted cookies all the time. Given that Luca was so very Luca he would probably frown on that.

Processed sugar for his baby? Never.

Except the baby was also hers. So there would be sugar.

The idea of trying to live with this man, compromise with him, raise a child with him, was suddenly daunting.

She sat down at the kitchen island and leaned forward. "I will eat the omelet. And thank you for it. But right now I usually crave sweets in the morning."

"Unhealthy," he said.

He was so predictable.

"Be that as it may," she said. "It's what I want. And while I'm all for health, happiness is part of health."

"Not in a practical sense."

"Actually, yes, Luca. In a practical sense. We aren't just bodies rattling around the physical world. We're more than that." She cleared her throat. "I'd have thought that you'd know that more than anyone. Considering how the order of the world affects your mind. That's not physical. Not having three notebooks on a plane isn't necessary for physical health, but you don't *feel* right if you don't have them."

"And you are trying to make the case that you don't feel right if you don't have cakes?"

"Indeed."

"Hmm."

"I'll have the omelet," she conceded.

"You are welcome."

"I did thank you," she pointed out. "But I had the thought we're probably going to have to discuss the ways we're different from each other, and the ways that might

express itself in our lives and in our...parenting styles."
She cleared her throat, wanting to be careful now. "I am
actually not trying to say anything unkind, but you're a
very particular man."

"That isn't unkind. It's true."

"Yes, but I used the truth to be hurtful the other day
and I'm sorry for it. So I'm trying to prove I'm not out
here using elements of what's honest as a sword. I'm just
trying to look ahead."

"All right, tell me what you're thinking."

He put the omelet in front of her and her stomach
growled. "I don't always eat healthy. I like sweets."

"I like sweets," he said.

She narrowed her eyes. "I have never seen you eat
sweets."

"Everything in moderation."

"Well, I'm going to eat them. And I don't want to over-
whelm a child with data on what every medical journal
the world over says about diet."

"Fair," he said. "But I will require that it is taken into
account. I'm not opposed to treats but we must consult the
World Pediatrics Journal regarding diet as a baseline."

"Most parents won't be doing that."

"I am not most parents."

She couldn't argue that point. She didn't even want to
because then he set a mug of herbal tea next to her and
it made her feel like she was glowing inside. It made her
feel cared for.

No one had ever cared for her before. She had done a
lot of caring for other people. And maybe it was a really
small thing. Breakfast and a cup of tea. A couple of days
of missed work. And yet, for him it wasn't. She knew that.

"If it's that important to you," she said. "It's very important to me that whatever is going on between the two of us, we never let it spill over onto our baby. Our child. Luca, there are going to be times when you frustrate me. But I never want our child to be aware of that. I never want for your mood or my mood to become their problem."

He nodded slowly. "Agreed."

"And it's important that our child comes first. That is going to mean that sometimes you have to make sacrifices with work. But I don't want a father for my baby that's going to be half there and half gone."

"You were more than willing to have me be all gone."

"Sometimes I think that's easier."

He looked away. "No," he said. "It isn't. Because when my mother was all gone, then there was nothing soft left. There was no one left who looked at me and everything I was and smiled. I lost every ounce of support I had once had. I would have rather had her one day a month. One day a year. I'm glad I had her for the time that I did. Had I not had her at all, what would I be?"

She hated thinking of him like that. Alone. Vulnerable. She did feel protective of him, in spite of everything. She felt...

You care about him.

She tried to swallow past the lump in her throat.

"Right," she said, her throat scratchy. "But your mother didn't choose to leave you. You remember your mother so fondly because of all the good things that she did for you. Because of the good she saw in you. And I assume because you were the most important thing in her life. You and I do important things. Having a baby doesn't erase that, or negate it. Neither of us should give up what we love. But if we were to make a list of the things that we loved…"

"The child should be the first thing."

"Yes. And at the very least they should feel that they are."

"Are you suggesting again that I'm going to have difficulty loving a child?"

She snorted. "I'm leaving space for both of us to have to spend time adjusting to this. We both love work."

"You love work?" he asked.

"I spent five years giving you and this company the entirety of myself. Why would you think I didn't love work?"

"You did quit."

"Because I didn't love being nothing more than an assistant."

"You say that as if you were inconsequential, and indeed I believe that you think you were to me. You weren't. You are…insulted that I came after you to offer you your job back, as if it was a small thing." He shook his head. "I chased you down. I put my pride away. I cared absolutely nothing for it, because I needed to have you back. It was essential. Important. I cannot think that you do not know that."

She hadn't. Well, she hadn't thought of it that way. But of course, there was actually no real separation between Luca the man and his job. What she had taken as a weak showing in the face of their passion had likely been altogether powerful for him. He had gone to her because he was admitting that he couldn't handle life without her.

"Well. I do care. And I'm sorry that I didn't see the

gesture for what it was. I can now. So let me try and explain to you... I left because I could have actually stayed your assistant forever. But it wasn't what I set out to do. It wasn't the schooling that I got, it wasn't... That job was my everything, and so were you. I needed it to change. But now things have changed again. We have to be willing to change with them."

"Even if it means eating omelets?"

She turned her fork sideways and cut a bite off with a fearsome motion. "This isn't a permanent change. I'm simply indulging you for the day."

"I consider myself extremely fortunate."

He was teasing her again. So unlike him, and yet, more frequent now than it had been before.

"And thank you," she said. "For taking care of me."

"Of course."

CHAPTER TEN

LUCA DID RETURN to work the next day. There were things to see to, and they were of utmost importance. But then, everything in this job was. Still, he'd had to put everything aside out of concern for Polly's health and well-being for the past few days. At first it had given him no small measure of discomfort. To discard his routine. To be away from his work for an extended period of time—not that he hadn't checked in, or completed tasks in his home office—but eventually, he had realized that it was a good thing.

He wanted things to be as Polly had said.

He wanted to rearrange his life.

He felt a powerful connection to this child. This child who wasn't yet born. He could already feel the desperate pull to rearrange everything so that he could be a good father.

Not the sort of father who would reject and shame his child. A father who would care for them no matter what.

He found himself thinking about Polly, back at the penthouse. He found his mind more there than in the office, and given that he had not been into the office for some days prior to this, it surprised him. More than that, he found he wanted to hold on to this.

It was a rare thing, this sort of moment when he could hold multiple thoughts in his mind. Multiple concerns.

Yes, single-minded focus got a fair amount of things accomplished. But he wanted to be single-minded in his parenting as well. He wanted to hold his child with him, even as he went about his day.

In many ways, he did that with his mother.

She was his motivation. His reason.

But practically, she required nothing of him.

She was a memory, and nothing more. Living for a memory of a person was much simpler than figuring out how to foster a relationship with a person who was here.

She had a doctor appointment scheduled for later that same day, and he made a call down to the office. He let them know that he would be attending, and that he wished to help conduct the tests and exams. No one argued, even though it was unorthodox, because he was Dr. Luca Salvatore, and his reputation in medicine preceded him.

He was eager for Polly to return to the office, because he did not like her absence. Even though she would be taking another job, she would be here, and things would feel better. They would feel right. He did decide to call her and let her know that he would be at her appointment.

"I should've thought to include you," she said.

She had been extraordinarily different with him these past days. When she had apologized to him, because she had hurt his feelings, and not to make herself feel better, it had shifted something inside of him.

No other person had ever treated him that way. Not since his mother.

His mother had known and understood that he had so many feelings, and that they were complicated. That he didn't know how people expected him to express them, nor did he care.

But she had seen him. And he didn't think that Polly had this entire time, but she certainly did now.

He hadn't thought he cared about that.

It hadn't occurred to him that it might be a nice thing to have someone understand him.

He had decided that he by and large didn't need emotional connections with people, but he was going to be a father, and that meant he was going to have to forge an emotional connection with his child. So perhaps it was only a good thing to practice by forging emotional connections with other people.

And trying to get a sense for what it felt like when they had them with him.

"I was happy to include myself," he said.

"Yes. Well. I suppose that's not surprising."

"I will see you in an hour."

"See you then."

They rode in the same car over to the private doctor's office. They were taken into a room where the doctor did an initial Doppler check to establish that the fetal heart rate was normal. All was well, and he felt the tension in his chest ease that he hadn't been aware was there.

"And an ultrasound," he said.

"We typically don't—"

He looked at the doctor. "I am aware. But I would like to have one done. I called ahead."

"Of course, Dr. Salvatore."

They were ushered into the sonogram room, and he introduced himself to the technician. "I would like to perform the sonogram," he said.

Polly looked at him, her eyes wide. "What?"

"I'm a doctor."

"You aren't an ultrasound technician," Polly said.

"No. But I have the necessary qualifications and knowledge."

"I don't want you to do it," she said.

"I told you that I—"

"Yes," she said. "You are a doctor. But you're not *my* doctor. You're the father of my baby, and that's it."

"Is that all?"

He felt...scalded by that.

"Yes, Luca," she said. "That is all."

"You're acting like I don't have feelings again," he said.

She shook her head. "I'm really not. I'm asking you to be reasonable. To consider if it's a typical thing for a father to be in charge of running the ultrasound, or if you should trust the people who make this their expertise to do their jobs."

He scowled. Mostly because he could see that she was potentially right. He still wanted to be the one to do this. He wanted to be the one to make sure that everything was okay. It was important to him.

"You can stand there," she said. "And look. And if you see something of concern, why don't you ask the woman to linger there."

The ultrasound tech was looking between them and Luca didn't bother to try and read her expression. He didn't care. He only knew that he was irritated, in part because she might even be right. And even if she wasn't, he could see that it was going to benefit him to bend here. He didn't want to bend. Medicine was the way he cared. It was all he was.

And yet again, Polly didn't understand that. She didn't understand that for him this was caring.

How else was he supposed to show it?

He wanted to be in control of everything happening. He understood that. He didn't see what was wrong with it, though. That was the problem. She was being stubborn right now.

The ultrasound tech readied the equipment, and Polly looked at him. "What?"

"I'm going to have to put the gown on."

"Yes," the tech said. "It's going to be an internal ultrasound."

"In that case, Polly must be certain that she wants one. I directed this, but didn't think the implications through."

"It's okay," she said. "I would like to see the baby."

"You're certain?"

He had been controlling this, from the beginning. And he logically knew the way that ultrasounds work, but he hadn't fully considered what that might mean to Polly, or that she might find it invasive. He did sometimes shut off the full implications of things. He knew that to be true.

And he felt regretful that he had perhaps inadvertently caused the situation when what he had been trying to do was make himself feel better.

"I do want to see," she said. "But I need you to turn around right now."

He did, though he didn't understand why she was being shy now when he had seen her naked.

He was struck then by a completely unexpected arrow of lust. He had done a very good job not thinking of her that way. She had been poorly. And he had been obsessed with the idea of having her back at his side. Of sorting out all of these things pertaining to the baby. Pertaining to them.

He hadn't thought of that night. Deliberately. Because he had been intent on hiring her back. But suddenly, it was replaying itself in his mind. Vivid. Intense.

He curled his fingers into fists, and waited. Listening for the sounds of her disrobing.

This feeling, of course, was exactly why they were in this situation.

This feeling and May twenty-fourth.

And that night.

He really hadn't used a condom.

He still couldn't... He couldn't quite believe it. He couldn't remember it. Couldn't even remember thinking about it. And that was completely outside of his experience. Contraception, protecting both himself and his lover had always been paramount rules.

But he hadn't thought of rules when he was with her. Not even a little bit.

"You can turn around now," she said.

He did. She was lying on the table with a sheet draped over her knees, and the angle he was at prevented him from seeing anything.

"Sorry," the tech said. "This part is always cold. And a little bit uncomfortable."

He couldn't see what was going on beneath the sheet, but he knew. Because he knew the procedure well.

He found that he could not entirely find the doctor in the scenario though, and that was odd.

He felt a knot of worry, concern about her potential discomfort.

These were things he had never felt when he had done

residency. And while he didn't practice medicine in the traditional sense, he had learned to do it.

He had always felt disconnected from the experience the patient was having, but not now.

The black-and-white screen flickered, and then, he could not tear his eyes away. It took a moment, but then he was able to see a fluttering. The amniotic sac. The embryo itself. "There he is," he said, unable to hold back a smile. Unable to be rational. Because this was such an early stage of development. Anything could happen. And yet he didn't feel detached. He didn't feel as if he knew he should. He felt something broad, expansive growing inside of him.

Love.

Deep and intense, along with it the desire to protect. Fiercely.

This was beyond the scope of anything he had ever known before. It was beyond him.

"Incredible," he said.

Even though it wasn't. It was run-of-the-mill. It was average. People did this every day.

But he could not find a single thing that felt commonplace about it.

Because Polly was carrying his baby in her womb. This was the result of their night of passion, his loss of control. The culmination of a hundred things that felt unlikely and yet right at the same time.

He felt…gratitude that transcended logic. He felt something that he could not easily name. He felt everything. All at once. Like the cover had been lifted on something bright and intense inside of him, and now that it was revealed it couldn't be hidden.

He looked at Polly, because suddenly it was very important that he see her face. That he see what she was feeling.

Her eyes glittered, but he couldn't figure out what exactly the tears were for. Tears, he found, were a constellation. They could contain many truths. They were never half so simple as sadness, or happiness. They spoke of intensity. Overwhelmed. Sometimes he thought it wasn't that he couldn't understand what other people were feeling, but that people were very quick to simplify feelings. Tried to put one name to them when they had a depth, and all-encompassing nature that was different than simply happy or sad.

Often he was angry because he was afraid. Often he was happy, but tired, because that happiness had come at a cost. From many sleepless nights. Right now he was grateful, but with it came a measure of awe. Of uncertainty.

He moved closer to the screen then, and began to examine the black-and-white image. Because emotions might be something that he found difficult and complex, but there was nothing complex about the physical.

To his eye, everything on the scan looked normal. "Go back," he said.

The ultrasound tech looked at him. "To where?"

"I would like to get a look at the heart chambers."

"It is very early."

"I would still like it. Along with a full panel of blood work."

"I don't order blood work. The doctor will, if she sees a need."

"I see the need."

"Luca," said Polly. "Let's discuss this later."

She was speaking to him like he was a naughty child. And that irritated him as much as he had been awestruck the moment before.

The ultrasound tech moved back to the heart, and he watched. Watched it move. Flutter.

"Thank you."

When they were finished, Polly demanded he turn around again so that she could get dressed. At that point, the tech left the room.

"You didn't have to be that difficult," she said.

"I'm not being difficult."

"I didn't know that you were coming here and you were going to try and act as a doctor. I thought that you were here as the father."

"I was," he said. "But for me the two things are not different. Because nothing inside of me is different."

"You cannot be this obtuse. Surely you understand why it's frustrating for a professional to have somebody looming over them like that."

"It was not looming."

"You were," she said.

They exited the exam room, and went out into the front of the office. She made a new appointment.

"That is during my workday."

"I don't care."

They walked out, and a car was waiting for them. She got into the back, not waiting for him to let her in.

He slid in beside her. "Did you need to be told that I was going to want to have involvement in the medical side of this?"

"No. I didn't need to be told. We needed to talk about it. Because what you are wanting to do, is it normal?"

"I'm not normal," he said, feeling at the end of this. At the end of himself. "You know that. You have worked with me for five years. What about me has ever said normal human being."

"I don't think of you that way," she said. "I don't think of you as being weird. Or abnormal. But this isn't normal. And when something is going to be abnormal, then surely it must occur to you on some level that you have to actually speak to the other person involved in the situation before you go...being that."

"If I knew, if I had that level of clarity, then maybe I would. But it seems perfectly logical to me, and I don't understand how it doesn't to you. I am a medical doctor. I did a residency. I have done all the schooling, and all the training. I also have a doctorate in medical research, and have been responsible for many advancements in the field of medicine over the past decade. You know this. Why would you think that I would...not want my eyes, my expertise, my opinion involved in the single most important medical event that has ever occurred in my life."

She said nothing for a moment. "You're afraid, aren't you?"

"I'm not afraid."

"Yes, you are. You thought that I was sick when you came to Milan. You're afraid of things going wrong for people that you... I don't know, do you care about me, Luca?"

"How can you say that? My life would not function without you in it, and you are well aware of this."

"All right. It's all about how functional your life is

or isn't because I am in it. I forgot. That's not caring."
She was silent for a moment. "You care about the baby,
don't you?"

"I do care," he said. "I want you to allow me to care
in the way that I know how to show it."

She looked at him, something in her expression softening. "That's admirable. But you also have to care in a
way that the other person can receive it. It feels stressful
for me. To have you be… There in an official capacity.
There is a doctor. I want you there as…"

"Your husband? Because you don't want me to be your
husband in any other capacity. It is you who are inconsistent."

Just then, the car pulled up to his building. He got out,
and this time, he was the one who didn't pay her any
mind. He was the one who didn't pause.

He walked into the building, a tangle of anger growling around his chest. Yet again, a whole layer of emotions he couldn't quite so neatly define. But anger was
certainly the hottest part. It made him burn.

She caught up to him by the time the elevator doors
opened, and she got inside with him.

"Are you suggesting that you want to be my husband?"
she asked when the doors closed.

"I asked you to marry me. You were the one who issued edicts about our physical relationship. And about
what we would and would not be."

"Can't you see why?"

"Yes," he said. "Because it is impossible to approach
any of this fully logically. And I would prefer it if we
could."

"We're human. Not Vulcan."

"I've been accused of being a Vulcan more than once."

"I know. By me. But you told me that isn't how you are. You have to find a way to let that part of you come forward. The part that feels."

"It's uncomfortable."

"Incubating your baby is pretty uncomfortable. I don't know if you've noticed. But I've been rather unwell."

The elevator reached its destination and she swept out.

And it was like everything in him went blank. It was like everything was calm. Clear. He saw her.

Just as he had May twenty-fourth at three thirty in the afternoon. When she walked into his apartment the sunlight tangled with her hair. Illuminating it. Casting it in gold.

Feeling.

Yes. He could open himself up to feeling. To all of it. To be a better husband, to be a better father.

But she had said that she didn't want what he felt.

Now she *wanted* his feelings.

She was entirely and utterly inconsistent. But more than that, she was radiant. More than that, he wanted her.

So she wanted feeling. She was going to get his feeling.

He crossed the space, and wrapped his arm around her waist. And before she could say anything, before she could beg him or protest, he lowered his head and claimed her mouth with his.

CHAPTER ELEVEN

HE REMEMBERED THIS. From that night. This passion. A conflagration, that was far beyond anything he had ever experienced before. Kissing had never been this. Desire had never been this. Need had never been an all-consuming driving urge that swamped his thoughts and made them go blank.

It was like sanctuary.

All day, every day, he was bombarded. The world around him was too loud. The feelings inside of him were too big. The thoughts inside his head so fast it was difficult to grab hold of one of them. And they never stopped. Never.

Except now. It was like everything whittled itself down into one singular point.

All that mattered was the sound of their breathing. The feel of her mouth beneath his. The way that her body felt beneath his hands, warm and supple, and all that he truly desired.

There were no thoughts. Because they were unnecessary.

And the feeling was only good.

And yet, nothing half so simple as good.

Sharp and poignant. Decadent and punishing. A revelation and a condemnation.

A baptism and hellfire.

He paused for a moment, for a breath. He pulled away and he looked at her. He waited. For her to say no. For her to pull away.

She didn't. Instead she stretched up on her toes, wrapped her hand around the back of his head and pulled him down for a kiss.

Another one. This one more intense than the last.

Her hands were demanding, her mouth even more so. He tasted her deeply, his tongue sliding against hers, his arousal hot.

Overwhelming.

But in a good way, rather than in the way the world could feel all too often.

In this moment, there was no fear. No medicine. No discoveries yet uncharted that went anywhere beyond them.

And she… She was a discovery yet to be made. Yes, he had been with her once before. He had seen her naked. Answered the questions that he'd had about his assistant. But he was a curious man. And he could never be satisfied with just one panel of evidence. With just one moment of discovery. He needed to go deeper. He needed to find it all.

He needed to examine every angle. Every line. Every possibility.

And so slowly, he began to take her clothes off of her body. He gave thanks for the fact that it was three thirty in the afternoon. But the sun was shining down through the window.

That he would finally see her skin and all this golden light.

Because it was what he had wanted all these years. It was what he had denied himself because of propriety and rules.

But he would not deny himself now. Not anymore.

He realized then that he was entirely comprised of self-denial. Because he was so careful to never make a misstep. So careful to steer clear of doing the inappropriate. Of being wrong. Of showing that he cared more, of showing that he hurt more.

Of drawing attention to the real ways that he was abnormal.

But not here. Not now. He would allow himself this. To want more. To need more.

To need her.

So he unwrapped her like she was a sacred, precious gift, and he let himself get drunk on the glory of her every curve. The glorious softness of her skin. Her breasts were larger, rounder than they had been that first night they were together.

Her nipples were tight, a delicious berry pink that called to his appetites. And he decided to indulge them. He lowered his head and slid his tongue over that tightened bud, growling as he did. She gasped, holding his head to her, and arching against him. He sucked her deep, trying to assuage the roaring need drowning out the sound of everything but his heartbeat. Feeling. He was all feeling now.

This was what she wanted. Him. Like this.

She could have it.

And so would he.

In all of its splendor. In all of its glory.

Because he could feel the air, skimming over his skin,

a heightened sense of need and desire and being alive that he wasn't sure anyone else felt. But he did.

And right now, it was a good thing. Because her touch coupled with that sensitivity was all the drug he would ever need.

And someday, if he was ever found lying on the floor, addled by addiction, it would be her.

That addiction would be her.

He had been obsessed with her from the beginning.

And he had blinded himself to what that meant.

Because it was this. Always. From moment one.

She pushed at his shoulders, and he allowed her to do so, moving away from her. "It's my turn," she said, beginning to tug at the buttons on his shirt.

She undressed him, her fingers clumsy, and he found that endearing, because Polly was so rarely clumsy. She was always in charge. The master of everything, everything around him, all the details, his whole life.

But she was trembling now.

"Are you afraid?" he asked.

She shook her head. "I'm shaking because I want you."

And this was why emotions were so difficult.

Because sometimes shaking was fear. And sometimes it was this.

He gripped her chin between his thumb and forefinger and leaned in, kissing her again.

She pushed the shirt from his shoulders and let it fall to the floor. She looked at him with the same sort of greed he knew had been on his face when he had examined her.

A triumph.

Physically, he had always been attractive to women.

It was everything else about him that created difficulties.

It was one reason he was very obsessive in his workout routines. Health being a primary goal and focus, of course. But, anything that made things easier was of course a boon. And he had found his physique absolutely made things easier.

She clearly appreciated his work.

She put her hand on his chest, let her fingertips drift down his abdomen. He closed his eyes, growled.

This was what it was like to feel. To only feel. To not think. To not worry about what he did next. To not worry how he would be received.

Some people felt this way all the time.

He was all right if he only felt that here. With her. It was a gift.

And one he would never take lightly.

He stripped the rest of her clothes away, and she did the same for him. And both of them were brilliantly, gloriously naked in that afternoon sun. He kissed her. Her neck, her collarbone, down the valley of her breasts. Her stomach. He lifted her up from the ground and set her gently on the edge of the couch, where he draped her legs over his shoulders and began to lick into her. Deeply, ravenously.

Her taste haunted his dreams.

He had wanted no one since her.

And while it was not entirely unheard of for him to close off his libido when it was convenient, it had never gone and done so on its own without his permission.

And yet with her...

She was what he wanted. Not sex. No other woman would do. He wanted her.

He licked her until she cried out his name. Until he felt her give up her control. Until he felt her release wash over them both.

And then he moved over her on the couch, lifting her thigh over his hip and claiming her in one smooth stroke.

Her fingernails dug into his shoulders.

Pain. Pleasure.

All the layers of humanity.

He began to move, his need utterly blotting out everything else. Her breath in his ear, the press of her breasts against his chest. The tight, wet heat of her body as she enveloped him.

"Polly," he said. He said her name over and over again like an incantation, a prayer.

And then he felt his release begin to rise inside of him. He held it back as long as he could.

He didn't want this to end.

He wanted her.

This moment.

Forever.

But then she cried out his name, arching against him, her internal muscles pulsing around him, and he was lost.

He gritted his teeth, buried his face in her neck, and came hard.

"Don't run from me," he said, eyes blazing into hers after the storm subsided.

"I won't," she said softly.

He moved away from her slowly, and then went into the bathroom to get a damp cloth.

He brought it back, and kept his eyes on hers as he pressed it between her legs.

"Thank you," she said. "But it was…fine without."

"I just want to take care of you," he said. "And I can acknowledge that the way I tried to do that earlier didn't look like care to you."

She closed her eyes. "It did. But it made me uncomfortable. I could see where you were coming from. But…"

"I'm not allowed to always have my way."

"No," she said. "That's part of sharing your life with somebody."

"That's probably why I have never done it before."

"I haven't really either, Luca."

"You said that you were a virgin," he said.

"Yes," she said. "I was." She moved the cloth away, and sat up, wrapping her hand around his bicep. "Because I had made a life for myself where I had all the control, and I liked it. I didn't see the point of inviting another person in."

She sighed heavily. "But that's only part of the story. I also had a job and a boss that were completely all-consuming. And I couldn't imagine being with another man while I was so enmeshed in your life."

"Because I took up all your personal time?"

"That was part of it. Because of course nobody wants to be in the middle of an intimate moment and have their boss call and demand they tell him which tie he ought to wear for his next speech. But it was only part of it. I wanted you, Luca. And I couldn't want somebody else while I wanted you."

"Oh," he said.

"Did you really not know?"

"I really didn't. But then, you were my assistant, and that made you off-limits. And even though I had moments of failure in that area, I did my best to close off my thoughts of you. Now I'm glad that I don't have to."

She sighed heavily. "What are we going to do? Because if we introduce sex, then we are really in a marriage. And the potential to hurt each other…"

"We are really in a marriage. We got legally married."

"I get that. I mean, I get that you see it that way. But I wanted to protect myself. Keep something that was mine. What am I going to do if things sour between us? You have all the power, and you already threatened to take our child away."

"I will never threaten something like that again. I'm sorry."

"Are you sorry because it scares me?"

"Yes. I am. I'm sorry that I used my position to terrorize you. That was the whole point of not having sex with you when you were my assistant. And then I did it anyway. It was the only way that I knew how to try and convince you to come with me."

"Last time I asked you said you weren't sorry."

"As I got my way. But now I can see how I ought to be sorry about how I did it. About not giving you time. Not trusting you to come to the best conclusion."

"Neither of us knows how to be in a relationship."

He shook his head. "No. But we have a great many things to learn. And you are having my child. Also, I want you. I never wanted anyone the way that I want you. I've never forgotten myself. I've never forgotten to think. But when you touch me it's like everything fades away. It's like I understand…what it's like to be somebody else for a while. I suddenly don't feel consumed in an obsessive sort of way. Everything feels simple. And good. Like the only thing in my life is your hands on me. When normally I feel pulled in a hundred different directions all the time. I want that. I want more of it."

"But you're not in love with me," she said.

"No."

One of the many emotions he had no experience with, and no burning desire to try and explore. It would be far too much.

But he wanted her. And logically it made sense. It made a perfect kind of sense. They were already having a child. This connection between them existed. Why take all the energy it would require to suppress it? That would be madness. And he was not a man given to madness.

On purpose. Because he'd always had the feeling it could take him if it tried.

If he let it.

"I can't promise you the same thing that another man might. But then, from what you told me about your parents you know that what starts as love can end as something entirely horrific."

"I do."

"So I am not offering you that. But I am telling you that I will try to learn to care in a way that you can receive. And that I will always be honest with you."

"I know that," she said. "Because for all that you frustrate me sometimes, you have always been honest with me. Always. You never tried to manipulate me. You strong-armed me so that you could have your way, but it was entirely obvious what you were doing. You never promised me one thing and delivered another."

"I won't do it now. But I cannot see a future where we continue to live together, work together, raise a child together, and we ignore this thing between us."

She sighed heavily. "But sexual attraction doesn't last forever."

"No. But decisions can. Especially decisions that you make every day. I want our child to have the best life possible. And even when my father was himself, having my mother in the house made it better. You need that other parent. For when the one is unable to do their best. You need both. Just in case one needs to be lifted up. And I fear very much that I might need that."

"Just decide that you're going to be as single-minded when it comes to being a good father as you are with anything else. If you do that, I'm confident that you're going to succeed."

"Yes," he said, looking out the window. "I can do that."

"You don't have to be afraid."

"But I still want you there. I have always wanted you there. Since you were my assistant. You made everything better. You always have. And you will make this better too."

"Okay. Okay, Luca. Let's give this a try. Real marriage. Raising our child."

"Thank you." He leaned in and he kissed her. And when their lips touched, there was nothing but feeling. "That's all I want."

"Me too."

CHAPTER TWELVE

LUCA HAD GONE back to work after their afternoon love-making session. She wasn't even really mad about it. Really, she wasn't mad about it at all. Because if he didn't do something that felt quintessentially Luca she might start to get concerned about him. But she didn't want to sit at home, and she hadn't started her job at Salvatore yet. Really, she wasn't entirely clear on what she was going to do. But for the first time in her memory that wasn't the most all-consuming thing on her mind.

They were committing to... Well, in his mind it was real marriage. Love and romance and the like didn't seem to signify for him. And she wondered why it should matter to her at all. Because he was right. Her parents' marriage had started real enough. She didn't know anything about the relationship between his parents but he made it sound like his father was useless. At least, when it came to Luca. So what did it matter if people got married for conventional reasons? It didn't guarantee happiness. Why should love mean anything to her?

It never had before. But maybe that was part of the problem. She had avoided the concept of marriage and childbearing because she hadn't wanted anything that looked like her parents. But now that she was married, now that she had a child on the way, she couldn't help but wonder if…

It really would be a terrible thing to love him.

Except, she couldn't look at him anymore and see the remote man that she had once imagined existed behind that armor he wore all day every day. That man of steel who was so committed to work that everything else was an inconvenience.

No.

He was passionate. He was hot. A fire blazing inside the shape of a man.

How had she ever imagined that he was anything less?

He was… He was a study in contradictions. Because he could be so uncompromising, and then when she called him on it he often apologized. Unless he didn't. Unless he stood firm because he simply couldn't see what she was saying.

But for all that he often did that first, then he would normally try. Try to understand where she was coming from, try to see where she was coming from. And now he was saying he was committed to trying to care for her in the way that she could receive it.

Change, for him, was harder than it was for most and she knew that. She'd felt like he hadn't cared for her, and now here he was rearranging his carefully curated life for her.

She had known few people who listened quite that well. Who cared so much about doing the right thing.

She decided that she needed to get some fresh air. She got dressed, and left the scene of her indignity, going down to the Roman streets and letting herself blend into the crowd.

She had immediately loved that about Rome. The anonymity of it.

The way that she felt like she could blend, and more than that, the way that she felt like she could be anything she wanted to be.

She had been so trapped in Indiana. On that same street, in that same house.

Her life hadn't been small because she lived in a small town, her life had been small because she had been crushed in her parents' fists.

She knew a shiver of fear as she tried to imagine living life with Luca. Yes. There was a scenario wherein she could see herself being crushed.

But she didn't have to be. She could keep talking to him. Especially if he kept listening.

She walked into a couple of clothing stores and looked at the offerings. She loved all the beautiful clothes in the city. But unfortunately, considering that she was about to change and expand in several different ways, there really was no point in buying fashion.

She thought wistfully for a moment about what could've been. That life in Milan. At the fashion house, where she would undoubtedly be getting free clothing as part of her job.

All she could muster up was wistfulness. There was no sadness. There was no regret.

She hadn't been as happy doing that as she had thought she might be. And really, the day she had taken the pregnancy test, everything changed.

She hadn't realized all the ways it had changed yet, but it had.

She was different.

Her future looked different.

Maybe, if she was going to be living in Milan a single unencumbered girl without a baby on the way, that job would've been perfect.

You would've had to have never met Luca.

She sighed heavily.

Yes. She would've had to have not met Luca. Because meeting him had changed her life. Forget sleeping with him.

There was something about him. Something that had grabbed hold of her and refused to let go the first moment they had met.

He was just so singularly him.

And on paper, all the things he was should be mainly annoying.

She walked out of the boutique, and continued down the street. And then, through one of the reflective windows, she spotted a little red car.

It was a toy store. There were teddy bears and a large, magical-looking tree positioned in the window. A little village. And that red car.

It called to her. Because it spoke of Luca.

Yes. He could be infuriating. Yes, on paper, he was a disaster of a boss, and not much better as a man.

But he was also a boy once. A boy who had loved cars. Until his mother had died and all he had been able to care about was how to keep someone else from experiencing that kind of pain.

His whole life had been consumed in that pain. And he had let go of that thing that he loved most. In order to give himself over to his mission.

She found herself walking into the toy store without

thinking. Because she wanted to see to him. The way that she had as his assistant, but something else, something deeper.

She asked to see the car, and turned it over in her hands. Yes. She needed to get this for him. Her chest felt tight as she paid, and had the car put in a little box, and gift wrapped.

It occurred to her then, as she walked out of the store with the car in a jaunty yellow bag, that she did know how to care for him.

She had been doing it for five years. All those things that people were so quick to call ridiculous, she recognized were integral to him.

Like when she had gotten angry at the flight attendant for not understanding why he needed his notebooks.

They mattered to her. As they mattered to him.

They weren't inconveniences. And they weren't him being particular. Not really. It was what he needed. Nobody else was him. So why did other people get to make proclamations about what he should change, what was important, and what was an incidental?

Yes, there was a place for them to compromise. Of course there was. Because she didn't need to be cared for in a way that worked for her. She had lived with parents who didn't care for her at all. But that wasn't Luca. And so asking him to meet her in the middle didn't seem outrageous. But it also meant seeing him as he was.

But she had never had any trouble with that.

He could be frustrating, certainly. And she felt then, as she walked down the lovely, sunny street, that it was fair to be frustrated even by things he couldn't easily change. Because when you lived with somebody that was the state of things.

But she didn't feel anymore like there was Luca, a typical man, and all of the little quirks that made him into something more of a project.

They were all him. They didn't separate.

And so caring about those things was caring about him.

And she wanted him to have the car.

Because she mourned for the lighter things that he had cared about once, that he couldn't afford to care about when his life became something heavy. When she got back to the penthouse, he wasn't there. She decided that she was going to cook for him since he had done so much of that for her over the past week.

He liked to cook. It was something that she had always found interesting about him. Because most single men didn't seem to enjoy that quite so much. And a man of his status could certainly afford somebody to do it for him.

But of course he didn't really like a surplus of strangers in his home. Because everything needed to be where he wanted it. And that seemed quintessentially him.

She decided to make pasta with olive oil, tomatoes and some Parmesan. Simple, but she had found since moving to Rome that simple was her preference. When the ingredients were so spectacular, there was nothing not to like about simple.

She hummed as she put the food together, as she made a salad.

And by the time he walked through the door, she had everything ready, with her gift for him at the center of the table.

His eyes met hers, and he smiled. It was brilliant.

She could count on one hand how many times she had seen him smile in an unguarded fashion, and every single one of those times prior to this it had been in connection to a medical discovery.

This was the first time that smile had ever been directed at her.

Oh, dear.

She really liked him. A lot.

But imagine loving him.

Only a foolish idiot would love him.

Really.

She swallowed hard. "I made dinner."

"I can see that."

"I got you a present. But we should eat first."

"I want to open my present," he said, looking suddenly like a petulant child, and her heart squeezed. Because she wondered if he had ever been able to afford to be a petulant child.

"No," she said in her best stern matron voice. "You have to eat first."

He growled. But sat down. He dished his plate, and she was walking by him to go do the same, when he grabbed her around the waist and set her down on his knee. "I'd like to share with you."

"Share with me?"

He pressed his fingertips to her jaw and turned her head. Then he kissed her. Long and deep. "Yes. I would like to share with you."

He swirled his fork around the pasta, and brought it up to her mouth. She opened without thinking, and took a bite.

Then he did the same, taking a bite for himself. It thrilled her. And she wasn't even quite sure why. Perhaps because this meticulous man with such a routine was being playful with her. Was giving her things that she was entirely certain he had never given to anybody else before.

It felt… It felt like a revelation.

And it made her tremble.

Because it felt dangerous.

Oh, so dangerous.

"I should get my own plate," she said, wiggling away from him.

"I don't like it when you're demanding."

"Well, that's too bad. Because on Wednesdays, I feel I might be very demanding."

"Wednesdays?"

He looked like he was considering whether or not he should make a note in his calendar. *Polly will be demanding. Recurring event.*

"Or Thursdays. I'm unknowable."

"You are not."

"I'm not?" She sat down at the table, her heart pounding a little bit harder than it needed to be.

"No. You are very knowable, Polly. You like summer and sunsets, and cake. You keep chocolate in your purse. Half the movies you watch make you cry."

"Those first few things are not unique, and also how do you know that about the movies?"

"I've overheard you telling a great many of your co-workers about a movie you have seen over the weekend, and about half the time you say that it made you cry. You are very soft, but at the same time you are very strong. I do know you."

"Oh."

"Tell me. About your parents."

"I did."

"You gave me a general idea for why they were a problem. And I want to know. Specifically. My father did not want me to be the person that I was. He wanted me to be the person he wanted me to be. And that I think is a terrible thing for a father. My mother loved me exactly as I was, and even then losing her, she helped me find myself. That is what a good parent does. Even when they aren't there, the love that they gave you does its good work. And so I want to know. What did your parents do that is so terrible that you left Indiana—"

"A lot of people leave Indiana."

"What did they do that was so terrible that it makes you not want to return home? I assume you don't wish them to even know you're having a child."

"I can try to explain it to you," she said. "But I'm afraid you'll just…" Suddenly, awfully, she found herself getting weepy. It was the pregnancy hormones. And him. Maybe just somebody else asking about her life. About her. "You can't just put me on the spot like this, Luca. I have perfected my mask."

"You haven't. I had the right of you from the moment you first walked in here. I knew that you were not half so sophisticated as you pretended to be. I knew that you were overawed to be in a company that size. I knew that it wasn't the blasé thing that you were trying to pretend that it was."

"Well. You are insightful."

Her chest felt tight.

"Tell me," he said.

"I have told people. I told the guidance counselor at my school when I was in high school, and he just said it was normal to have conflict with your parents." She blinked back tears. "It's so hard to explain. Because it's like I was responsible. For being an emotional barometer. I had to read the situation around me and react accordingly. And if I didn't, then I was going to have to deal with the consequences. Because it wasn't so straightforward as my father walking around acting angry. He would seem fine. And in fact, he would bait me into conversations that would end with him screaming at me. Because he wanted a fight. And so he would manipulate me until he got one. And my mother... She wanted me to be obedient. Biddable. And the way you accomplish that is by making sure that someone doesn't have a sense of themselves. Of their worth. She was an expert at making me question myself. If I would tell her about something that happened at school she would ask me if I was sure that that's what happened. Somebody hurt my feelings she would say... Maybe that isn't how it went. Maybe you were the one in the wrong. Before I would leave for school she would say, did you think that looked good?" She shook her head. "It was just such a perfect storm. But they didn't beat me. They didn't starve me. They just made me feel like everything around me was unstable. Like I had to walk on my tiptoes to avoid causing an avalanche. That was all."

But it had been so heavy. And carrying it all this time had been a weight she hadn't known was still resting on her shoulders.

"That would have been my undoing. I already question everything that I do, and often have to question my interactions with people. If somebody sought to undermine me in that way, it would've broken me."

"You're the smartest man in the world."

"That wouldn't have made me immune to the sort of gaslighting you're talking about experiencing." She loved how he didn't protest the label. "It is incredibly damaging. When you feel as if you cannot trust your own perception."

Her heart twisted. "You feel like that a lot, don't you?"

"Yes. And so I take refuge in the things that I can know. The things that I can learn and memorize. Because when it comes to those things, I am vastly superior to the people around me."

He was gently teasing. Except he also meant it.

"You are. You definitely are."

"I'm sorry. Do you… Do you feel as if I'm unpredictable? I know that sometimes the things that I want don't make sense to the people around me, and that must feel unpredictable."

"It did at first. But eventually I learned exactly what you wanted. You're actually very good at saying what you want. Nobody has to guess. It isn't a game that you're playing. I find that extraordinarily comforting. Given the way that I grew up. Given the way that my parents excelled at making their moods into a guessing game that I was forced to participate in. And… I'm trying to figure out how to say this. But the things that you need, the details. The details that you had me in charge of that you say you don't want to be bothered with, when in fact they are so important because if they aren't dealt with…"

"Nothing works for me."

"Exactly. They are not separate to you. They are part of you. And they are not a burden."

"Thank you. Though I will be working at changing how I regulate those things."

"Alternatively, you're a billionaire, and you could hire about six people to see to those things."

"Yes. I can. But the problem is… I became very dependent on you. And when you left, I thought that everything felt wrong because I needed you there to manage me. To manage all of the…the peculiarities. But it was more than that, and I couldn't see it. Also I… I suppose I cannot depend quite so much on one person for that sort of thing."

"There's nothing wrong with that." She moved toward him. "Nothing wrong with wanting to be more self-sufficient. But as far as I'm aware, that is part of having a partner. You figure out how to do things for each other. How to help each other. How to serve each other." She went to the center of the table and took hold of her gift bag. "Here. Open this."

He looked at the bag, and then up at her. "All right."

He took hold of the bag, and she watched, her breath frozen in her lungs as he began to pull the paper away, as he reached inside and took out the little red car.

His face was blank. She couldn't read it. She had no idea if he was happy, or if he was upset. If she had crossed some kind of line.

"Do you… Do you like it?"

He looked up at her, something fearsome in the depths of his gaze. "You know, I have never liked opening presents in front of people."

"Why not?"

"Because I know my reaction is not what people are looking for."

"I'm not upset by your reaction. I just want to know if you like it."

He smiled then. Slowly.

"Of course I do. It is…incredibly thoughtful. I don't think anyone has known me since my mother. But you do. You listened to me. You… You're right. That is what our partnership can be."

It still somehow felt like not quite what she was reaching for, but she didn't want to define the ache inside of herself.

She didn't want to have anything to do with it.

Because it was too much. All of this.

The intensity of the feelings that had held her in their grip since…

Since she had first met him.

It really would be a terrible thing to love him.

But she wasn't sure if she had the resources left to fight against it. Not anymore.

She stood, her heart thundering hard. Then she walked over to where he sat, and put her hand on his chest. "Luca."

He reached up, and pulled her head down, kissing her. Consuming her. And when they pulled away, there was something like wonder in his eyes. "I really love this gift that you gave me. But I don't lose everything when I look at it. Only when I look at you."

It meant something to him to say that. To feel that. She might not know entirely what, but she could hold close that it did.

She kissed him, holding his face in her hands as she did. Cradling him. Because he was precious.

Oh, no.

She was familiar with lust, protectiveness.

But this was something different.

This was something more.

He was such a brilliant man. Such a beautiful, brilliant man. And really, what other man on the face of the earth would she rather have as the father of her baby?

He was strong and determined. He… He loved. With so much of himself. His mother's death had taken that love and turned it into something he was trying to give the world. Everything he did was care.

Of course he would be the most wonderful father.

"You are amazing," she whispered against his mouth. "And I'm so sorry that I doubted what manner of father you would be. There is no other man I would rather have as the father of my child."

He growled then. And he lifted her up onto his lap, onto the dining chair. Her thighs were on either side of his waist, and she could feel his growing arousal there between her legs.

They kissed, and he held her close. Tight. Like she was the one who was precious.

No one had ever treated her that way. But he did. Imperfectly, perhaps, but she wasn't perfect with him either.

She was sometimes petty, and often selfish. She possessed far too great an ability to take the things he did and make herself feel persecuted because of them when there were moments she just had to accept his behavior wasn't about her, and she didn't *need* to make it about her.

It was easy for her to think that because some of the

things he did were different than ways other men behaved, that he was somehow the project, but the truth was, she didn't know how to blend her life with another person's. She didn't know how to see grandly beyond her own perspective.

She was no less work. And perhaps she was more, because he had spent his life taking fearless inventory of himself, because he had been forced to. Because the people around him had always been harsh and uncompromising in their appraisal of him. Because people had treated him as if he didn't have feelings, which meant the way that their approach to him was often bracing.

Yes, she had been badly treated. By people who had wanted to treat her badly. Her parents had been difficult. They had been undeniably cruel in many ways. They had done nothing under the guise of care, and it seemed to her that often throughout Luca's life people had said horrendous things to him under the guise of helping him. Under the guise of forcing him to behave in a way that made them more comfortable. Not in a way that might make him more comfortable.

She committed herself then and there to being different. To handling him with greater care.

She kissed him to show him that.

And he kissed her back, physically demonstrating to her that she mattered too.

They could do this. They could make this partnership. They could have this life.

She felt a renewed sense of purpose. A sense of joy.

Luca wasn't her job.

He was her choice.

And she wanted to show him that.

She moved from his lap, and took his hand. "Come," she said, smiling.

"I'm not a dog," he said. "You can't give me commands."

"I think you'll find I can if you want to follow them," she said.

And he did, because he went with her into his bedroom.

She moved to him, beginning to unbutton his shirt, revealing the hard planes of his chest. The glorious acres of muscle that his clothes spent all day hiding—a real tragedy in her opinion.

She divested him of his shirt, kissing the hollow of his throat, his chest.

"I think you'll find yourself much happier if you take orders from me."

And that was how she found herself lifted up off the ground and deposited to the center of his bed. She watched with hungry eyes as he took off the rest of his clothes, and then moved to the bed, a glorious predator in his natural habitat.

There was nothing uncertain about him here.

Of course, there was nothing uncertain about him in most areas of his life. It was only that the last bit of time had thrown him into something he had never dealt with before.

And she was witnessing firsthand how difficult that could be for him.

But this… Oh, no, in this he was a master. And that was clear.

He moved his hands over her clothed body, slowly. Achingly so. She felt like she was going to jump out of her skin.

She was alive with need. And it went somewhere beyond simple desire. Not that desire had ever been simple with him.

It had been bound up in restraint. The restraint of knowing she couldn't act on it because she was his assistant. And knowing that even once she had she had to keep parts of herself back to avoid getting hurt.

What if she didn't.

What if, for the first time in her whole life, she was honest with another person.

She was honest with herself.

What if she gave everything?

Absolutely everything.

What would happen then?

And she felt all the resistance inside herself beginning to fall away.

She felt as if a light shone down upon her.

Radiant. Honest.

She felt as if she was seeing herself for the very first time.

And she wanted him to see her too.

He kissed her neck, and undid the buttons on her dress, slowly peeling the thin fabric away from her body.

He took off her bra, kissed his way down her stomach to the center of her thighs. He fastened his mouth to her over the lace panties that she wore, and she gripped him tightly.

He seemed to delight in the act of pleasuring her. Tasting her.

And she surrendered to it. He stripped her naked, his tongue sending her over the edge, his clever finger driving her mad.

And with each stroke there between her thighs, she felt her resistance fall away yet more.

Not a physical resistance. There had never been any physical resistance to him at all. But the emotional resistance.

It would be such a terrible thing to love him.

She did love him. She had. She had told herself that as a warning that came far too late.

Alarm bells that went off after the disaster had already occurred. But why was it a disaster?

She had learned to arm herself, protect herself, because caring about people who didn't care for you had been the hallmark of her life, and she had hated it. She had run from it.

But she couldn't let her parents define what she was capable of feeling forever.

She couldn't allow that to define her. To decide how happy she got to be.

Because it was all just fear. Fear that held her captive. Fear that manipulated her.

It was all it was.

She was allowing herself to be manipulated yet still. She didn't want it. Not anymore. She wanted to be herself.

She wanted to feel herself.

She wanted to feel him.

And when he traveled back up her body to claim her mouth in a searing kiss, it was everything. The taste of her own desire on his lips, the evidence of how much he cared about that. Of how much she was able to surrender when she was in his arms.

This was honest. It was raw, it was real. It was everything. That she wanted so badly for the two of them to be everything.

She wanted to find out everything she could be. Everything she could have.

And she felt closer to that than she ever had in her life.

When he thrust inside of her, it was like the sun had come out from behind the clouds. Blinding, brilliant and clear. And when he began to move, building a symphony of pleasure from deep within her, she surrendered.

It was so beautiful it was almost painful. It was so brilliant, she could barely look directly at it.

It was everything. So was he. So was she.

They were everything. And it didn't scare her.

Because Luca had never taken her feelings and used them against her. Because he had never sought to twist or manipulate what she felt.

He probably didn't even know he could. Because he probably didn't realize how much she cared.

They both suffered from the same thing. They had both been in a desert when it came to love.

She didn't want to be. Not anymore.

She kissed him, and he growled, lowering his head and biting her neck, making her gasp with pleasure.

She exulted in him. In his power, in his strength.

In the fact that there was safety in it.

Because he would never use it against her. He never had.

She could trust him. It was like a wave broke over her, warm and excruciating all at once. She could trust him not to manipulate her. He was safe.

When had another person ever felt safe?

Not ever.

He would never use his power against her.

Not the power of his mind, not his heart, not his body. He was exacting, and he was demanding, but there was always him right at the center of it.

And he was a very good man. That was what it came down to. Everything else they could learn to navigate. But he was good.

She had never known what it was like to love somebody who was good.

That realization broke her open, and when her orgasm struck her like a wave, it broke something inside of her. Then she began to weep. She clung to his shoulders, as she cried out his name.

Because she was all in on this. All in on him.

It was everything. So was he.

They were everything.

She clung to him. And then she whispered in his ear. "I love you."

CHAPTER THIRTEEN

HE PULLED AWAY from her, his dark gaze fierce. "I don't know that I can say that to you."

She wanted to weep. Not because she was heartbroken. Because he was everything she had believed him to be. "You don't need to. A dishonest man would say it to keep me happy. To keep me doing what he wanted. But you're not a dishonest man. That's why I know that I can love you. It's why… It's why it doesn't scare me. Well, that's a lie. And I want to be honest. It scares me, Luca. But I have been falling in love with you by inches all these years. When I left as your assistant, it wasn't because I found it difficult to keep up with your demands, even though I said that it was. Even though I wanted to believe that it was.

"I wanted to be singular to you. Not just an employee. And the fact that I might never be broke my heart in a deep and difficult way.

"I didn't want to admit it. So I made up stories. Because I'm very good at that. Because what I learned from my parents was how to twist reality when it didn't suit me. And even though it was used against me, I figured out a way to take that and make feelings and truths for myself that made me more comfortable. I want to be more like you. I want to see things as black and white. I want to see the heart of the matter. I feel like you do. I feel like the way that you deal with me and all the people around you is so… It's honest."

"You say that like it is a good thing. To have nothing nuanced to say about a situation, but I don't know that that's the case. I also have nowhere to hide. And sometimes I wish…"

"You have managed to hide though, haven't you? Because people don't get close."

"It is the only way for me to hide myself. Because as you can see, when you get close enough, you can see everything. Thank you for the car. I feel grateful for it. And deeply uncomfortable to have that part of myself so exposed."

"Why?"

"Because it is a vulnerability. And when people can hit you at your most vulnerable then…"

"I won't use it against you. I promise. I know that I did."

"It's all right. Because that moment was possibly the closest I came to trying to manipulate you. It might've been a clumsy manipulation, as you pointed out. I did not pretend to be doing something I wasn't. But I did use fear against you."

"And we both regret it. We can move on from it."

"Thank you."

"Are you terribly uncomfortable?"

"I'm not uncomfortable. But I find that I… I find this challenging."

"Why?"

"I can't put into words."

"And perhaps I find that most difficult of all. I am used to knowing everything. Everything in my sphere. I have built a life for myself that doesn't challenge these deficiencies in me. And here you are. Forcing me to work on every single thing I decided I didn't have to work on. I don't find it especially fun."

"Maybe it's not supposed to be fun. Changing. But sometimes it's necessary."

"Yes."

He looked at her. And there was something like wonder in his eyes. "Why do you love me?" The hunger there was something she couldn't deny, even as she felt a small wave of sadness wash over her. She wasn't going to demand that he suddenly feel the way that she did. She wasn't going to demand that he suddenly feel differently than he did.

But she wanted him to. Still, loving him had to mean loving all of him. And he was not going to turn on a dime. Not when there was clearly a block inside of him where the idea of love was concerned. Not with her child, it didn't seem, because he was able to see clearly the ways in which his father failed him, and he wanted to combat that.

But in every other way, it seemed to be very difficult.

"You are somebody who took great tragedy and turned it into purpose. Anyone would admire that." She cleared her throat. "But it's more than that. You are every inch yourself, and that makes me want to be the same. When I've spent my whole life hiding. Being with you has changed me. It's allowing me to get down to the truth of myself in a way that nothing else ever has. I don't feel afraid to be myself because you're yourself. I love your

passion. Both from my body, and for medicine. For figuring out how to be the best father you can be. The way
that you see yourself is so…unkind sometimes, Luca.
And that makes me sad. But I'm also in awe of what it
has allowed you to do. I can appreciate that, even while
wishing you could be a little bit kinder to yourself. I love
how you listened when I said you had to give care in a
way that people could receive it. Even though I made
you mad. Mostly, I love that I could trust you with all of
this. I know that you won't take it and realize that you
could crush me with it. Because that's not who you are.
You're a brilliant man, and you could've taken all that
brilliance and used it to exploit those weaker than yourself. You could've made money at the expense of other
people, and instead you dedicated yourself to try and save
others. That's incredible. It is something that most men
with that capacity simply don't choose to do."

"Those don't seem like extraordinary things to me.
They simply seem like the right thing to do."

"And it is your clarity on that which I also love."

She looked him in the eyes. "Don't devalue the things
that you do simply because they seem clear to you. They
don't seem clear to the rest of the world. And if they did,
it would be a much better place. You are part of making
it better. I love you for that also."

"I'm sorry. But this is much like opening a present,
and not knowing quite how to react."

"You don't have to. You don't. Just be you. And that's
enough. I promise you."

They were silent for a long time after that, and she felt
her heart rate return to normal. Some of the adrenaline
of the previous moment wearing off.

But it didn't feel finished.

It didn't feel over.

She was in love with him. And she wanted more. But she knew she had to let him get there in his own time.

And as she lay beside him with her hand on his chest, over his heart, she did her best to believe that it was all possible.

But Polly had never seen a future that contained love like this.

So she had a difficult time planning for it. A difficult time seeing how she might triumph.

But she had to trust. Because she had put her faith in this love rising up inside of her, and she needed to believe in it.

She needed to believe in them.

And as she listened to his breathing slow and his heart rate return to normal she held fast to that.

She had to believe in him.

She had to.

CHAPTER FOURTEEN

LUCA'S LIFE WAS entirely different than it had been three months ago, and he was…happy about it in many ways.

Polly had begun work at the company, dealing in marketing, and she seemed to thrive in that role. He liked watching her achieve things, accomplish her aims.

He liked her.

He loved having her living with him. He loved having her in his bed.

He enjoyed watching the changes that the pregnancy was making on her body.

This commonplace thing made miraculous because it was theirs.

Because she was his.

But she told him that she loved him nearly every day, and it was creating a dissonance inside him he was having difficulty ignoring.

It was beginning to build, like a low-level frequency that began to drive you mad.

How could it not. This… This declaration of love.

It was beginning to ring so loud in his ears that he couldn't hear anything else.

They went to another doctor appointment, and it was

like something with claws had reached into his chest and speared his heart. Like it was being pulled asunder.

He couldn't seem to find any protection for it. And it was a monstrosity the likes of which he had never experienced before.

Nor did he want to.

And it was a terrible thing, because he wanted her in his life, he wanted to claim this thing that he was certain he could have, and yet, he was undone by the feeling that he was doing it wrong.

He was different. He could think he was doing the same things as other people and discover he wasn't, actually. He could think he knew what someone else needed and be wrong.

Wrong. Wrong. Wrong.

His father had always told him he was wrong.

His mother had told him he was right as he was, but she had died and he had no way of knowing if she would have always thought he was okay, or if she would have seen him struggle later and...

What if he was broken?

What if he would never be able to be there for her in the way that she needed?

He wanted to be.

She had told him that he needed to show care in the way that another person could receive it. The truth was, she had said she loved him. And that must mean on some level it was the sort of care she wanted shown back to her.

What did he know about that?

But even if so, it was like having somebody watch him open presents.

He wasn't sure if his response was acceptable. He wasn't sure if it could ever be.

He was sure of nothing.

Nothing at all.

What he wanted to do was engage in an exploration of his own soul. Come to some kind of medical conclusion, and yet that was the problem with humans.

Nothing was half so simple. Even when he wanted it to be.

He understood that for most people, medicine and medical science was the mystery. But to him…it was this.

And he had no way of knowing if this was just him, or if it was something that could be changed. Learned. If his mother had lived, would everything be different? Would he be…not a top medical scientist, not leading the field in research and development, not a billionaire, but a man. Who understood how to have a wife, who understood how to be a father.

Was it a lack of what he had been able to see and learn and experience that created these problems now?

All he knew was that he felt inadequate. Down to his very soul.

And for her part, she seemed happy. But what if she wasn't? And what if he could never know? What if she was simply putting on a brave face? Or what if she was blinded? Blinded by the love that she claimed to feel for him. Hadn't her parents kept her with them, kept her unhappy, likely because she was a child who had loved them?

He hated the idea of that. Truly.

And yet, she was…

She was the greatest thing in his life.

And also caused him the most unrest. The most pain.

She came into his office that day at three thirty in the afternoon. And he was stunned by her beauty. All over again.

Because everything was May twenty-fourth, over and over again. Because everything was her, trapped in the golden light of the sun. Because everything was them.

And he supposed it would always be that way. But he wondered if he had the capacity to make it something more than what it was now. To make it all the things that needed to be.

"Do you miss Milan?"

"No." She didn't look confused, and she did not ask follow-up questions. She just went about her business in his office as if it was hers. He supposed she knew where everything was in it. Knew it just as well as she knew him. Which was well.

"If you could go back, would you, though?"

She shook her head. "No. I had actually somewhat decided that I wasn't entirely happy with the job. It's difficult to go to any other job after you've been doing the work that we've been doing. Especially when I see the strides that you're making. It isn't that there isn't validity in something like fashion. Of course there is. I really do believe that beauty and art make life worth living. But you make living possible. For so many people. And that work just feels so essential. It's difficult to leave it behind."

He nodded slowly. "Yes."

This office was sacred. Their working relationship was sacred. It was a rule. And yet, suddenly things did not feel neat inside of him. They felt like too much. Too big. And the gall of her saying she loved him sounded inside him over and over again.

He was overcome by it. Overwhelmed by it. He could hear nothing else.

And this was the thing he would always have a hard time explaining to other people.

Sometimes the noise inside of him was so great that the noise on the outside added to it was unbearable. That what was soft to them was overwhelming to him. That what felt like a breeze to them could become daggers beneath his skin, because the world within him was so overwhelming, so insistent, and he did not know how to share it with another person. Didn't know how to let anyone else know.

And he had tried with her. He was still trying.

But the way that he could most effectively communicate was through touch.

Not in the office. It was against the rules.

And then he found he could not hold himself back. She lived with him. Shared his bed with him. He had upended his routines for her. His life. And it somehow still didn't feel like enough. The unfairness of it all weighed down on him. Heavy and insistent and intense.

He wrapped his hand around the back of her neck, and he pulled her in for a kiss.

She gasped. Shock, but not displeasure. He knew her well enough to know that. He could trust that.

That, somewhere deep within him became a rallying cry.

He kissed her, and suddenly, it didn't seem to matter quite so much that everything was everything. That everything was overwhelmed. That everything was foreign.

Because she wasn't.

She was just the right amount. Just the perfect thing to take him out of his own head, and ground him in his body in a way that felt real. In a way that felt right.

So he kissed her, because it was the only thing that could quiet this noise inside of him.

She wrapped her arms around his neck, and kissed him back, and even though he hadn't said anything she seemed to understand. That he needed her. That he needed to demolish this last wall.

The sacred space of work.

Rules. What were any of his rules?

What did they mean? He didn't even know anymore.

He had lived his life by them, and they had only gotten him so far.

Yes, he had made all of these advancements in medicine. He had been part of so many wonderful things, but as a human being, as a man, he did not feel as if he understood anything new. Anything real.

Anything deeper.

But there was her.

And she made the life he'd built for himself feel inadequate. He had been certain that he'd built up a kingdom, he had accomplished great things. He had made all he did well so big that his inadequacies would seem like nothing, and yet.

There was her.

She made him feel like he had to find a different way to be. A different way to feel, to breathe. She made him feel like he needed to be new, so that he could have her.

Her.

He had her now. She was his wife.

Dammit all, she was his wife. Not his assistant. She couldn't simply quit. She was having his baby.

And he needed her.

And so he kissed her. Lifted her up and set her down on the edge of his desk.

And then, in a wild fury, he stepped away from her, went to his door and locked it securely. Her eyes widened.

"I need you," he said.

"Okay," she said.

He wanted her to say that she needed him too, but hadn't she already said the most?

Hadn't she already said that she loved him?

"Tell me," he said. "Tell me that you need me too." It wasn't fair. He needed it all the same.

"Of course I need you," she said.

He was... He could see through her eyes. How little he made sense. Asking her if she wished that she could leave, and then locking the door, putting her up on the edge of the desk. Demanding that she tell him how much she needed him. Of course. He made no sense at all.

Not even to himself.

But he couldn't stop himself now.

So he claimed her mouth again, and again. Stood between her thighs and pushed her skirt further and further up her legs. He pressed his hand to her slick flesh, teased her until she was gasping with pleasure. Until she cried out for more. More of his touch, more of him.

And he gave it to her.

He undid his belt, the closure on his pants, and claimed her in one decisive thrust.

He hadn't believed her the first time she had told him that he had forgotten a condom.

Such foolishness now. He couldn't even imagine the man that he had been then. The one who had been so convinced he could never lose control.

A loss of control was life with Polly.

It was just life.

And so he took her. Over and over again. Letting himself feel everything.

The tight, hot clasp of her body. Her hot breath in his ear as her pleasure grew. As she began to whimper with need.

Yes. He needed her.

What if he always did? Like this.

What would be left of him?

He blotted that out. He gave himself over to his body.

To this radical feeling of being entirely in the moment. Of being entirely in himself.

He clung to her hips and held her fast as he thrust, hard and wild.

She clung to his shoulders, and cried out his name.

And he found himself falling. Tumbling over the edge into the abyss. His pleasure was all-consuming. But then suddenly, it was just Polly. A bright and brilliant sunrise that overtook his soul.

Her name was a prayer on his lips, and he shouted it into that sacred space of his office. Which was now no longer given to work. But given to her.

There were no longer any barriers left within him. And when he pulled away from her, to look into her eyes, the intensity of the pain that he felt was so absolutely overwhelming that he couldn't breathe.

"Polly," he said, his voice rough.

"Oh, Luca," she said, touching his face.

He pulled away from her. "I'm sorry."

"Don't be."

"But I lost control."

"Luca, you live every day of your life with such control I find that I enjoy being the thing that makes you lose it."

But he didn't. Yes, it felt good in the moment, but he found himself less and less able to claw back some of his agency. He found himself given entirely to the feelings that she created in him, and he couldn't simply come back to himself.

And if he couldn't do that, then he could maintain control. And if he couldn't maintain control...

He didn't even know who he was.

He pushed the dark thought away, and looked at her. At her wide eyes.

"I love you," she said.

It was like a knife blade wedged beneath his skin.

"No," he said. "I don't want you to love me."

"Why not?"

"Because it's impossible... It was impossible for me to give you what you want. It is impossible for me to care for you in the way that you need to be cared for."

The words were like flame, migrating up his throat, making him feel useless. Worthless.

He hated himself in that moment. More than anything. He hated himself.

But it was true. It wasn't fair, if he could never love her in the way that she needed to be loved in order to feel it.

If he could never care in the way that it would matter to her. He had strong-armed her into marriage. And she felt things for him that...no one else had ever claimed to feel.

She felt things for him that he hadn't imagined anyone could.

And what fool was he but he could not return it in equal measure.

He ignored the burning pain at the center of his chest. He ignored everything. Everything but this one clear truth. He would take her. He would use her, as he had done when she was his assistant, and in the end it would be no different. She would leave him. She would be wise to do so.

When he was not able to give what she needed him to give, when he could not make her feel what she wanted to feel.

When every moment of their lives was her giving him the most wonderful, thoughtful present imaginable, but she couldn't look at him and understand the way that he felt. And he couldn't find the words to tell her.

He would fail her.

As he had failed to be the son that his father wanted.

He had perhaps lied to himself. That he could become the father his own child would need.

He had a purpose. That purpose was medicine.

It was clear. It was clear. He knew exactly what to do with the human body, but the mysteries of the human soul were beyond him. His own most of all.

How could he have thought to bring her into this mess?

It was wrong.

He had to let her go.

He had to.

"Polly, we cannot continue on like this."

"What are you saying?"

"I will never be able to feel the things that you want me

to. I will never be able to show you the sort of care that you want, and I fear that it will be the same with our child."

"Have I expressed disappointment in what you have given me?"

"No. Sometimes."

"And when I have, I have asked for clear change, haven't I?"

"Yes, you have. But... With this revelation of love and my inability to return it..."

"Have I asked you to? Have I told you that it is unbearable for me? Have I told you that I need you to say the words back to me right now?"

"No. But you will. You will, and there will come a time when I have to figure out how to be this thing for you, and I don't know how. I don't want to spend half a lifetime failing you until you get to the point where you have no choice but to leave."

"Luca, what have I ever done to give you the idea that would happen."

"You quit the job. And whatever you say, you quit it because of me. Because of how I made you feel. Someday that will be true in our marriage. Someday... Someday you will do with me what you had to do with your parents. You had to walk away because they did not love you in the way that you needed to be loved."

"You don't trust me."

"I do trust you. That is the problem. That choice, it would be the right choice. It would be the correct decision. And I would not be a good man—I would not be the good man that you have said you know me to be if I didn't...if I didn't take the first step in letting you go. Rather than wasting your time."

"You promised me," she said. "You promised me that you wouldn't manipulate me. You promised me that you would be there for me."

"I'm trying. With all of the limitations of my soul, I am trying. But I do not want to be the villain in this story."

"It seems to me you don't want to try to be the hero either."

"You don't understand."

"I do understand. I understand how difficult it is to open yourself up, to try to…clear away all the debris that gets stocked up inside of us because of life. Because of the ways that other people have hurt us, because of the way they make us feel about ourselves. I understand. I understand that this is you, being trapped in the pain that you've experienced, and maybe even pain you feel you've caused. But if you care about me at all, then listen to me. Believe me. When I tell you that I am willing to be in this marriage as long as it takes for you—"

"As long as it takes for me to learn how to love you," he said. "Come now, Polly. Do not play these games. You have no intention of being in a marriage where you're not loved. You want me to change. You need me to change."

"You need you to change," she exploded. "Because you want this. I know you do. You want to be a good husband, and a good father."

"I can't do it," he roared. "Because… Because it never stops echoing in my head, because I can't make it stop. Because I'm trying to do my job, and it's you. It's only you. And the things that you said to me, and the way that it makes me feel when I look at you, and I cannot turn it off. It's with me all the time. All the damned time, Polly. And I cannot… I don't know how to be this way. I don't want to be this way. I want to be myself, however incomplete that is."

"Who told you that you were incomplete."

"You know who did. Do you want to know what happened to my cars after my mother died?" He suddenly felt charred. Hollow. He was going to give her this memory. But she wouldn't understand why it was so terrible. Except... She had told him. About the things her parents had done to her, and how nobody had listened.

"He packed them all up in big black garbage bags. And he took them away. He said that my preoccupations, my obsessions were not healthy. My mother was gone, and then my cars were gone. And I had nothing. Nothing to hang on to. I knew everything about them. And they were... They were like a point on a map to me. A way for me to see my place in the world, and I understand that they were toys. I understand that it shouldn't have eroded something inside of me, not the way that my mother's death did. But it was like my world wasn't safe. It was like I could trust nothing. And all I could do was cover my ears and cover my head, and lay on the floor and scream. And I didn't know how to come back from it. I hate...that feeling. I hate caring like that. And I can't ever do that again. I can never be that boy who lost everything. Ever."

She reached out and put her hand on his arm. "You aren't afraid for me. You're afraid for yourself. And that is why I want different for you. It's why I want better. Because you remember the loss so severely. But what about the love?"

She righted her clothes, and moved away from him.

"What are you doing?"

"I'm leaving. For however long you need me to. You are right. It is a good idea for us to exist in the middle. It would be best if we…figure this out all the way. I'm so sorry that those things happened to you."

"Aren't you going to tell me they don't matter?"

"No. They do. But I'm asking you to try and care anyway. I'm asking you to try to love anyway. Not because I don't think those things wounded you. But because I know they did. Because I think we both deserve more. And better."

She didn't shed a tear. She didn't cry or beg. He knew that she wanted to. Because he had always seen beneath her mask. But instead she smiled, a sad smile. A constellation of happy and sad. Layers. Complexity.

And then she walked out of his office and closed the door behind her.

And something threatened to break apart inside of him. Something threatened to put him right back on the ground where he had just said he never wanted to go. So he took a breath, but he thought of his purpose.

He thought about medicine. And how his life had been complete before Polly Prescott had walked into his life and shown him he might be missing something.

He would think about what was next. He wouldn't think about her. His life had been just fine before.

And it would be just fine again.

He would see to that.

CHAPTER FIFTEEN

POLLY WENT TO a hotel, because she had to believe that he
would come to his senses. He would find her, she wasn't
worried about that. He was resourceful. She wasn't exactly trying to cover her tracks.

But as the days passed, she genuinely began to worry.

That she had perhaps overplayed her hand strongly.

That she had perhaps overestimated the connection
between them.

Though she hadn't.

She knew that he cared about her. More than that, he
loved her, or he had the potential to.

But it scared him.

Her heart broke for the boy that he had been. And it
broke for herself.

Because she was still being strong. She didn't know
how to be anything else. She had tried. She had put herself out there. She hadn't managed his feelings. And look
where it had gotten her.

She had thought that it was growth, and that growth
would bring happiness. But she wasn't happy now.

She lay in bed, a king. She ordered room service.

She went to work virtually. Because she did still have
a job. A job that she loved.

Anyway, he was still her husband, so it wasn't like they were broken up entirely.

She wanted to ask him what he thought was going to happen. Because they were still having a baby whether he wanted to be with her or not, and the way it had all dissolved...

Surely he wasn't thinking that he wouldn't be part of their child's life?

Poor Luca.

He wasn't a liar. Or a manipulator. All the things he had said he really believed. That he might not be enough for her. That he might hurt her.

But she also knew he was genuinely mostly afraid of being hurt himself. How could she blame him?

His father had been cruel. Outrageously so.

She couldn't be wholly angry at him for his inability to let that go instantaneously.

But he was right. She believed on some level that he would love her. Someday. And he had tried to tell her that wasn't the case.

Like it was a kindness.

"I still don't believe you," she said, mostly for her own benefit. Mostly for her own heart.

"I still love you."

And that, she did believe. Even though it made her cry so hard she could barely breathe.

He was trying to work. And he couldn't. And it infuriated him. He needed to keep everything separate.

This was what he was good at. This was his purpose. His mission. This was what mattered.

And yet... She was in everything.

She was even in his motivation to do work. Because medical discoveries made the world a safer place for her too. And he could so easily recall the terror he had felt when he thought that she was sick.

Lately, his research brain had been thinking about maternal mortality rates around the world.

He had been thinking about complications and pregnancy, childbirth. Ways that they might be mitigated. Tests that could be implemented.

His focus was split.

His heart was…

He gritted his teeth. He couldn't compartmentalize. That he needed to. He felt like…like he imagined other people must feel, except he was certain it was stronger. More powerful. Nobody could truly understand the way that he felt.

Not even Polly, for all that she showed him sympathy. What did she know. What did she know about him. Even if she gave him sympathy, she didn't really understand.

And when did that become a good thing to you? This idea that you can't be understood.

Protection. The word whispered across his mind. The landscape of all that he was.

For all the good it had done him.

He could feel her. Even now. She occupied him. She obsessed him.

He…

Suddenly, that temporary sealant he had managed to get over the crack inside of him began to burst.

He loved her.

The realization was harsh. Swift. And that was the gong. Not her love for him resonating inside of her, but his own. But he was afraid to speak, afraid to acknowledge. Afraid to know.

He loved her.

He loved her, and he wanted her. He wanted her to love him. But if he failed her and she left then he...he would be reduced to nothing yet again.

And it would be worse, so much worse than anything else he had ever endured.

Why did people want this? Why did they write endless songs about it? Why did they...luxuriate in the glory of this feeling that felt like dying?

He loved her.

He loved her, and he wanted her to stay with him forever, she wanted to have this baby, and more besides.

He wanted a life where he could love more than one thing.

He wanted everything.

He wanted to be there for his child, no matter who that child was. No matter how they thought and felt. He wanted to change himself in his own perceptions to meet them where they were.

And he wanted to do the same for Polly. What he had been trying to do was control everything. Yes, he had done a great many things to try and give her what she wanted, but only within the bonds of control. When that control began to slip, when she was more consuming than the day-to-day work, or the rules that he had set out for himself, he had run.

He had run. Because what he felt for her was bigger than anything else that had ever existed inside of him.

And he had to go to her. He had no choice.

He had to.

Because what was the alternative?

He knew this life. It had sustained him for a very long time.

But something she had said had hooked into him. Into the truth of it all.

She wouldn't accept half because she wanted him to have everything.

And he wanted to know.

He wanted to know what that was like. And he wanted her.

There was no pain on this earth that was so strong it was worth hiding away from her.

All he had to do was surrender.

And there was nothing on earth more difficult than that.

But Polly was worth it.

Polly was waiting for room service. So when there was a knock on her hotel room door she got out of bed and opened it without checking.

And froze. It was Luca.

With the wild look that he had in his eyes in Milan. And somehow right then she saw the truth of it all. From the beginning.

"Luca," she whispered.

"Don't speak," he said. "I need to. I love you. I love you, and I am very sorry that I couldn't admit that before. I'm sorry that when I began to feel it, really feel it, what I did was run away. I made excuses. And I was right. I was. Because I could not have loved you in the way that you loved me if I hadn't stared down the fear inside of myself. And fear is all it is. I have been afraid. Afraid of what it would be like to lose you. Of what it would be like if I loved you with everything I was, and lost you anyway."

"Luca," she said, her heart twisting. "I can't believe that I ever thought you didn't have feelings. Because I began to realize that you love everything. Everything that you have done since losing your mother is you putting love out into the world. Rather than keeping it to yourself, rather than hiding it. You are one of the most generous, good men to ever exist. And certainly the best one I've ever known. And I'm okay with this not being perfect. I'm okay with it taking work. For both of us. Because I have never been more free in my life than I am when I'm with you. I have never been happier. I've never been more myself."

"It's the same for me," he said. "I have always been made to feel ashamed about…"

"Right. Even I've said things. Things I shouldn't have."

"I deserved it."

"No. Nobody should ever be made to feel like who they are is a detriment. Who you are is a gift. And it's why I love you. Not in spite of. Because of."

"I feel the same. You… You bring a balance to my life I didn't know I needed. What I didn't think was especially possible."

"You don't really like it that much."

He chuckled. "I love you. That's enough."

She looked up at him, and she felt her heart swell.

She had been wrong. All this time. Being in love with him was the key to everything.

He was a wonderful man to love.

"You are amazing, Dr. Luca Salvatore."

"As are you, Polly Prescott."

Luca could definitely be a difficult boss. But he was the best husband. And over the years he proved that he was also the very best father.

To all six children that they had.

And when he was finally able to announce a definitive cure for the cancer that had killed his mother, all of the children were present to pay tribute to the grandmother they had never known, but the grandmother whose love had shaped their lives every day.

Because she had been Luca's reason. And that reason had led him not only to change the world, but to the most glorious, joy-filled life anyone had ever known.

And when each of the children presented him with a small car in front of a crowd of thousands, nobody understood why.

But Luca and Polly looked at each other and smiled.

Everything he had ever lost had been given back in greater multitudes than he could've ever imagined.

And the love between them was more powerful than anything else ever could be.

* * * * *

COMING SOON!

We really hope you enjoyed reading this book.
If you're looking for more romance
be sure to head to the shops when
new books are available on

Thursday 26th September

To see which titles are coming soon, please visit
millsandboon.co.uk/nextmonth

MILLS & BOON

MILLS & BOON ®

Coming next month

ITALIAN BABY SHOCK
Jackie Ashenden

'I'm so sorry,' Lark said quickly as the phone vibrated again. 'But I really need to get this. It's my daughter's nanny.' She bent to pick the phone up off the table, turning as she looked down at it.

He could see the screen over her shoulder. On it was a photo of a baby, a little girl dressed in pink. She had a cloud of soft, rose-gold curls and blue, blue eyes.

It was a singular colour that rose-gold, as was the intense blue of her eyes. He'd never met anyone else who'd had hair that hue apart from his mother. And as for that blue…

That was Donati blue. Two hundred years ago the Donatis had been patrons of a painter who'd created a paint colour in their honor. And that's what he'd called it.

Cesare went very still as everything in him slowed down. Everything except his brain, which was now working overtime. Going back over that night. Going over everything.

Because if there was one thing he knew, it was that the baby in that photo was his daughter.

Continue reading
ITALIAN BABY SHOCK
Jackie Ashenden

Available next month
millsandboon.co.uk

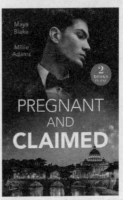

LET'S TALK

Romance

For exclusive extracts, competitions
and special offers, find us online:

f MillsandBoon

X @MillsandBoon

📷 @MillsandBoonUK

♪ @MillsandBoonUK

Get in touch on 01413 063 232

afterglow BOOKS

Afterglow Books is a trend-led, trope-filled list of books with diverse, authentic and relatable characters, a wide array of voices and representations, plus real world trials and tribulations. Featuring all the tropes you could possibly want (think small-town settings, fake relationships, grumpy vs sunshine, enemies to lovers) and all with a generous dose of spice in every story.

♪ @millsandboonuk
⊙ @millsandboonuk
afterglowbooks.co.uk
#AfterglowBooks

For all the latest book news, exclusive content and giveaways scan the QR code below to sign up to the Afterglow newsletter:

SCAN ME

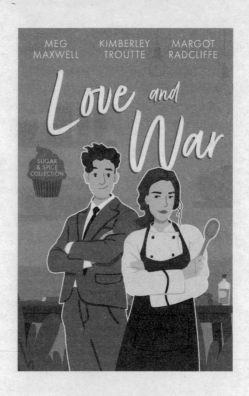